THE
ACADEMY

Patrick Bet-David

PERMUTED
PRESS

A PERMUTED PRESS BOOK
ISBN: 979-8-88845-559-3
ISBN (eBook): 979-8-88845-560-9

The Academy
© 2024 by Patrick Bet-David
All Rights Reserved

Cover art by Danny Munoz
Interior design and composition by Alana Mills

Permuted Press
New York • Nashville
permutedpress.com

Published in the United States of America
3 4 5 6 7 8 9 10

PROLOGUE

"**H**ow did this happen?" said the man by the window. He was holding back the curtain to get a better view of the street below. A million people thronging the streets of Tehran tonight, maybe more. Tearing down all visible images of the Shah, smashing department store windows, setting fire to a nation that had once held so much promise. And the security forces had been cowed into silence, doing nothing about any of it.

"Two ways," said Sargon. "Gradually...and then all at once."

The gradual part, Sargon thought, happened so slowly that it was possible for a time to pretend it wasn't happening at all. How many years had he discussed with his colleagues the resentment building against the Shah, or talk of the Ayatollah returning from exile? So many whispers passed around like canapés at cocktail parties and decisions made in meetings that officially never happened. And then, suddenly, everything was different. The terrorist attack at Cinema Rex and his sister dead. Scrambling to contain things when it was clear that it was too late. A shift so swift and profound that it would have seemed impossible if he hadn't watched it happen himself. 1978 had

1

been a very bad year. Sargon didn't have much hope for 1979, either.

"What are you talking about?" said the man by the window. He was tall and angular, with a face that seemed to be perpetually in shadow. Sargon thought he must have worked hard to make sure that no one ever got a good look at him.

"Something I read once."

"You think this is a time for joking?"

"No," Sargon said. "I think this is a time for crying. But there is work to be done."

The man by the window closed the curtain.

"The rumors are true, then?"

Sargon nodded.

"The Shah will be in Cairo by morning. The new prime minister will motion to dissolve the SAVAK."

"And the country that you and I worked to build all these long years will cease to exist."

A very small smile came over Sargon's lips.

"It will exist still. Persia existed long before you or me, Namirha, and will continue long after we're gone, no matter what the masses out there have to say about it. But we are entering a dark the likes of which we have not seen in a long time, and I fear it will be some time before we emerge again."

"You say that like all of this was inevitable," Namirha said. "If you had only listened to me…"

Sargon rubbed a hand over his face. How long had it been now since he'd had a good night's sleep? Years. His hair was going gray now; he had started cropping it close against his scalp. His once handsome face was now lined, with deep bags beneath his eyes. His body was still strong, but some days, when he woke up in the morning, an old man was staring back at him in the mirror.

And that entire time, Namirha arguing with him about how to approach the protests, sure that his was the right path.

"Tell me, how many do you think it would have taken to stop this?" Sargon said. "How many would you have needed to disappear in the middle of the night to stem this tide? A hundred? A thousand? More than that, I'm sure."

"We could have been strong," Namirha said. "Made it clear from the earliest protests that we were not going to tolerate things. Taken care of the sympathizers before they could spread their lies. Made someone think twice about the consequences before they ran out shouting into the street. But instead, we shrank from them, like we were the ones who were meant to be ashamed."

"Maybe so," Sargon said.

Namirha frowned.

"I don't like it when you agree with me so quickly. Put up a fight, at least."

"We tried my way. It failed. I don't know for sure if your way would have changed anything. But I would be a fool to say I don't have any regrets."

The noise from outside the window was growing louder, the sounds of glass smashing and feet stomping and a steady rhythmic chanting that rose and fell in waves as new protesters joined in. Sargon thought he heard a scream.

"You know what I'm going to say now," Namirha said. "What I'm going to ask you."

Sargon took a long inhale and held the breath in his lungs. He had been waiting for this moment, ever since he brought Namirha into the Academy all those years ago. Namirha had grasped the possibilities immediately, the ways in which they could use its knowledge and power to reshape the world around them. Sargon knew exactly what Namirha was capable of—the loyalty, the clarity of vision, and the brutality. This was a dangerous moment, but men like Namirha thrived in times of chaos.

"The List is secure," Sargon said.

"Where?"

"A safe house across town."

"What neighborhood? The situation on the ground is changing quickly. We'll want to be able to move it."

"And you think you're the best man to keep it safe."

The edges of Namirha's lips curled upward.

"Don't you trust me, old friend?"

"Namirha," Sargon said, "I barely trust myself right now."

"What is the point of having power if you don't use it?" Namirha said. "We could end all this madness now. Or at least buy time for saner heads to prevail. Instead, you insist on doing nothing."

"Do you think this is easy for me? To sit back and watch Iran burn? But to risk exposing ourselves when there is no guarantee it will be enough…I can't do that."

"Then you're a coward."

Sargon said nothing. The difficult thing was how much cowardice and wisdom sometimes looked alike—and how long it took to determine which it really was.

A loud crash came from the other side of the room. Namirha and Sargon both fell to their knees, the pistol that each man wore habitually at his hip raised and ready to fire. The office was eerily still, save for a slight breeze coming in through the broken window. The noise from the street was getting louder.

Namirha went over and picked up the chunk of concrete that had been hurled through the window. Sargon half expected the man to stick his gun out the window and start firing down into the crowd. But Namirha holstered his pistol and let the concrete drop back onto the carpeting with a thud.

"Where will you go?" Sargon said.

"That's no concern of yours anymore," Namirha said.

"I hate that things turned out this way."

"Almost enough to do something about it."

Sargon bit his tongue. There was no use arguing with Namirha when he got like this—not that it had stopped him before. Namirha cracked his neck and made his way over to the door.

"I've learned my lesson," Namirha said, his hand on the doorknob. "The next time, I will do what's necessary. No matter the consequences. And no matter the counsel of my so-called friends."

Sargon felt a slight chill run down his spine. There was ice behind Namirha's eyes.

"Take care of yourself, Sargon," he said in a voice too cold to be friendly. "And that family of yours."

Sargon gave a whispered goodbye, and then the man was gone.

He waited a full minute before he rose from his chair and locked the door to his office. He pulled the curtains closed tight and found the corner of the thick rug. With a grunt he pulled it back and began tapping patiently at the floorboards until he heard the hollow thump. Sargon worked his long fingers along the wood, feeling for the familiar knot. He pressed down, and the board shifted just enough for him to reach beneath it and retrieve what was there.

It was a ceramic scroll, a foot in length, with thick knobs at either end. The sort of object that wouldn't look out of place at the National Museum exhibits among the other artifacts of ancient cultures, but that would hardly attract particular notice among the jewels and riches. Sargon ran a finger along the scroll, feeling the places where the ceramic had been carved into impossibly tiny grooves. It made his head spin sometimes to think of how much information was encoded into such a small item…and how dangerous that information could be if it fell into the wrong hands.

He would miss Namirha. But their time together had come to an end. Sargon couldn't trust anyone but himself with something so precious.

A new noise from outside the window, this one the percussive blast of an explosion. Boys hurling Molotov cocktails, or something even more dangerous? Either way: time to go.

He bundled up the List. His wife had her instructions—already his family was making their way through the convoys he had arranged for them, last favors called in to men he had served next to for all these years now. He had told her that he would join her in a few weeks, when things were safe for him. His wife was a smart woman; he suspected that she had known he was lying. He wondered if he would ever see his son again, and if the boy would understand what had happened. He felt his heart aching for a different, easier time. But that was behind him now, and it would do him no good to dwell on it.

Sargon took a last look around the office and decided that he needed nothing else. It was remarkable how much he was ready to leave behind. He took a deep breath and went out into the chaos of the city.

CHAPTER ONE

On a highway just outside of Burbank, Ashur Yonan raced through the afternoon sunlight. His red motorcycle swerved from lane to lane as he pushed the bike faster, the 600 cc engine growling as the speedometer flirted with a hundred miles per hour. This had been his father's bike, a 1994 Kawasaki Ninja. The only other thing Ashur had left of his father's was his gun, tucked away in the drop space above his bedroom door. His mother didn't know about either.

He narrowly avoided colliding with a gray minivan as he passed a speeding Miata. He slid into the middle lane alongside an Oldsmobile, and for a brief moment he could see its swinging air freshener. Then he was beyond it, squeezing through a little sliver of daylight between two SUVs. One of them laid on the horn, but soon the honking was faint against the roar of the wind against his helmet. Ashur laughed, but it sounded strange to him.

The helmet hid his olive-skinned face, a scruffy beard, and dark shadows under his large brown eyes. He was eighteen years old, tall and fit, all his muscles taut now as he strained against the motorcycle. A few years back he'd joined a boxing gym, marveled at the way his young body turned shredded from consistent work at the weights and in the ring. He loved the feel of his fists against the heavy bag—and even more against the headgear of his sparring partners. They told him not to come back until he could control his anger. So he'd never gone back.

Blue and red lights suddenly flashed in Ashur's mirrors as he flew past another exit. He hadn't even seen the cop merge from the on-ramp. With a mutter he slowed his bike and pulled off to the side of the road. He got out his wallet and took off his helmet, running a hand through his curly black hair. The officer got out of his car, a strong jaw beneath a pair of aviator sunglasses.

"The hell are you running from? You know how fast you were going, son?"

Ashur handed over his license and registration, his back stiff. "Yes." The syllable was almost a snarl.

The cop's eyebrows shot up. He pulled his sunglasses off and looked at Ashur for a moment. Ashur felt the sweat running down his back. How many times now had he found himself like this, one authority figure or another waiting for him to apologize for something? He had learned that there was power in not pretending to be sorry for the things he did. It meant that things were harder for him sometimes, maybe. But Ashur Yonan did not grovel.

He braced for the cop to say something smart, puff out his chest, and assert his authority in front of this punk kid he'd caught going ninety on the Five. Maybe he'd even cuff him, try to scare him a little. It wouldn't be the first time Ashur had felt steel against his wrists—the rent-a-cop at his high school had put a pair of handcuffs on him after his last fight, the one that finally got him kicked out for good. Mostly Ashur thought the man had just liked playing at being a real cop for a moment, but he thought he had seen a little bit of real fear in the man's eyes, too, like he wasn't quite sure what Ashur was really capable of.

"Must be pretty bad, whatever you're running from," the cop said. "Your girlfriend break up with you?"

Ashur searched the cop for a sign that he was belittling him, but all he saw was genuine concern. He resisted the urge to tell him it was none of his business and instead let out a sigh, feeling his anger deflate a little. "No, sir. Just thinking about my dad."

"You two don't get along?"

Ashur's throat tightened.

"He's dead." He hesitated for a moment, wondering if the cop would believe him, but then he admitted, "I'm on my way to visit his grave."

The cop exhaled. He looked down at the license, then handed it back to Ashur.

"I'm sorry. You're too young to not have a father. I'm going to let you off this time, okay? But if you don't slow down, you'll be dead, too."

Surprised by the man's kindness, Ashur slipped his wallet back into his pocket. The cop turned to walk back to his car, but then he stopped and put a hand on Ashur's arm. Ashur tensed—maybe the guy was having second thoughts about going so easy on him.

"I'm sure things look pretty bad right now, son. But you can't outrun your problems—no matter how hard you push that engine. You've got to face them head-on."

Ashur stared at him. For a moment he had the uncanny feeling that he had heard this before. Was his father speaking to him through this man, from beyond the grave?

"Yes, sir."

The cop gave him a quick slap on the shoulder, then put his sunglasses back on and walked toward his car. Ashur waited until he couldn't see the cruiser before he put his helmet back on and revved up the bike once more. Next time, he knew, he might not get so lucky.

By the time Ashur arrived at Forest Lawn Cemetery, he had almost managed to forget the cop's words. He parked his bike against the curb on the street closest to his father's plot. The only other vehicle around was a sedan, inky with dark custom paint, half a block down, its engine idling.

There was a man standing over his father's grave. His was older—late sixties, perhaps, but tall and broad-shouldered, his complexion a shade darker than Ashur's. There were a few wrinkles near his eyes, but his hair was still jet black, as was the goatee surrounding his stern mouth.

Ashur frowned and started toward the man. He looked at Ashur with dark eyes and held his stare. Something about the man stopped Ashur briefly—a sense of coiled fury that Ashur felt like he recognized.

"What are you doing at my dad's grave?" he said. He wished his voice sounded more sure of itself.

"This must be a difficult day for you," the man said. He spoke unexpectedly softly. "I'll give you your privacy."

The man turned to leave, heading back toward the waiting town car.

"Hey!" Ashur called after him. "I asked you a question!"

The man did not turn, but he stopped for a moment.

"Did you know my father?" Ashur said.

He had never seen anyone else at his father's grave since the day they had buried him. Each year he and his mother had some version of the same fight—Ashur asking her again to come with him to pay her respects to the man who had been her husband for nearly fifteen years, and Rose insisting, as she poured herself another drink, that the man wasn't worth her time, or anyone else's. Ashur knew it had been a long time since his parents had been happy together, but something in his mother had hardened since his father's death. So now Ashur and his mother just repeated the same fights they had been having for the last six years, neither of them willing to change or give an inch. He stayed in the house only because he knew his father would not have wanted him to abandon Rose, no matter how difficult it was to be with her.

The man turned, slowly now, as though he had been waiting for Ashur to ask exactly this question.

"I knew your father," he said. "A long time ago. Before you were born, even."

"Why did you come here today?"

"To pay my respects," the man said, nodding to the gravestone. But then a little smile came over his lips. "Though I suspect a part of me was hoping I might see you, as well."

"Me?" Ashur said.

The man nodded, and then turned his attention to the Kawasaki.

"A beautiful motorcycle," he said. "Your father's, yes?"

Ashur looked at the bike. It had been his father's pride, one of the few indulgences the man had permitted himself. His mother hated it—it was too loud, too dangerous, and far too fast, which, of course, were the very reasons that Ashur loved it so much. He had been surprised when she hadn't tried to sell it after the accident—but then, Rose hadn't done much of anything in the wake of her husband's death, retreating into herself more and more. Ashur had told her it was stolen after he got his first ticket racing out in Palm Springs, and she hadn't asked any questions after that.

"There is power in the things we leave behind," the man said, his eyes still on the motorcycle. "The way we imbue them with little bits of ourselves. Our legacy, in a way. I'm sure he would be happy to see you enjoying it."

"How did you know him?" Ashur said. It had been so long since he had met someone who knew his father—he felt an almost physical craving to hear more about him, to learn more. There was so much he didn't know, stories that he could imagine his father would have shared with him as he got older, experiences that could have helped him as he tried to navigate the world. But instead he was here, all but alone, angry at everything and unsure of where to turn.

"Let's say I was an old family friend," the man said.

Ashur frowned.

"Then why have I never met you before?"

The man smiled again, this one smaller and sadder than before.

"Your mother and I didn't always see eye to eye," he said. "I kept my distance, out of respect. But you're a man now, Ashur. Capable of making your own decisions."

Ashur's eyes grew wide in surprise—the man knew his name! And then he realized, with a bit of shame, that he still hadn't asked the man who he was.

"What is your name?" Ashur asked.

"Call me Dobiel," the man said. He extended his hand, and Ashur hesitated for a moment before taking it. The man had big hands, hardened and calloused, and Ashur wondered what it was this man had done in his years of work to earn himself hands like that.

"Tell me," Dobiel said, releasing his strong grip on Ashur's hand. "Beyond the motorcycle—was there anything else your father left you to remember him by? Odishoo always was a thoughtful man, and I know he wanted the world for you."

Ashur stiffened at the question. He thought of the gun, an old semiautomatic Beretta 9 mm, that his father had kept on a high shelf in his closet. The day after the accident, Ashur had taken it down, wrapped it in two old T-shirts, and kept it hidden in a shoebox in the crawl space under his bedroom. He had taken it out to the desert a few times, set up the beer cans that campers left scattered by the rest stop, held his breath, and listened as the loud crack reverberated in the echoing emptiness. He had half a box of ammunition left, and the ability to hold something that had once been his father's had brought him more comfort than he would have thought possible for two pounds of cold metal.

Did Dobiel know about the gun? Ashur had never told anyone about it. And for all this man's knowledge about him, and his family, he didn't think now was the right time to start.

"No," he said, hanging his head. "Nothing."

"Really..." Dobiel said. "Nothing at all?"

"No," Ashur said, looking up now with a familiar fierceness—who was this man to question him like this?

The man seemed to consider this for a moment, and then he shrugged.

"Just as well, I suppose," he said. "Sometimes, legacies are more trouble than they're worth."

Ashur frowned.

"What are you talking about?"

The man shook his head.

"Old things," he said. Then he reached into a back pocket and produced a business card. Ashur took it.

"Your father expected great things for you," Dobiel said. "As do I. And I suspect you will have the chance to show who you really are, sooner than not. If you ever need anything…"

With that, the man turned to leave, heading back to the dark, waiting car. Ashur fought down the urge to chase after him—there were so many things he wanted to ask, stories about his father he was sure he had never heard before, little things that others might dismiss as trivial but that Ashur was hungry to hear. Talking with this man made his father seem, however briefly, just a bit more alive. But he resisted the impulse and watched as the man climbed into the town car, the red of the taillights receding until they disappeared around a corner.

Ashur looked down at the card in his hand. It contained only the name Dobiel—no last name—and a phone number with a California area code. As mysterious as the man who had given it to him. Had he really waited eighteen years to introduce himself to Ashur? And what had he and Rose disagreed about? There were so many questions Ashur had, but no way to get any answers now.

So instead, he walked across the soft grass of the cemetery until he reached the familiar plot, kneeling beside the flat gravestone marker. He ran his fingers over the words etched into the marble:

Odishoo Yonan
1967–2002
Loving Husband, Loving Father

Ashur had insisted that his mother put those words on the marker. Beside the epitaph was an angel blowing a trumpet; that, too, had been Ashur's choice. The man at the funeral home had seemed surprised that it was Ashur making these decisions, but he had told him he was proud of him for doing so, now that he was the man in the family. Ashur had hated him for that, talking down to him and doubting what he was capable of.

The cool marble brought back memories of an Independence Day years ago. He had been five or six; it had been hot, almost too hot to eat the hamburgers his dad had grilled. Someone was visiting them, but he couldn't remember the visitor's face. The man had seemed out of place among all the sunshine and the smell of fresh cut grass. Ashur remembered, once the sun had gone down, dropping a burning sparkler onto his foot, and his father pushing the visitor aside as he screamed in pain. His mother was crying, berating him for being so careless. Odishoo had rushed him back inside, setting him on the kitchen counter and running cool water over the burn. He had whispered words of comfort and told Ashur how proud he was of him after Ashur told him he was ready to walk on his own.

Tears burned now in Ashur's eyes, but he wiped them away before they could fall to the grass. He knelt in silence for several long moments, the way he always did when he visited his father's grave. Then, with another sigh, he stood and trudged back to his bike.

It was twilight by the time Ashur made it to the tree-lined neighborhood. He wasn't ready to go home just yet, wasn't ready for the fight he knew was coming with his mother. So instead, he parked his motorcycle on a quiet side street, the way he always did, and walked the two blocks until he was looking into the backyard of Kiki Johnson.

The light was on in her bedroom window—she was home from gymnastics practice. Probably studying, with the cute little frown she got on her face when she was concentrating. Kiki was heading to Brown in the fall, a testament to the long hours she had spent frowning down at AP chemistry textbooks and calculus problem sets and practice SAT tests. Ashur still couldn't believe that she was leaving.

Girls had never been a problem for Ashur. But he had never been in love before. Maybe that was why girls came so easily. He was always honest and up-front about what he wanted, frank in a way that seemed to surprise the women and then make them want to be with him even more. He enjoyed sex—it was fun, a good escape, the physical release and the little moments of quiet, playful intimacy. But he was careful to keep things casual, always. You can't lose what you don't have, so he made sure never to have anything too precious.

But Kiki Johnson was different. He had met her in history class his sophomore year. She always sat in the front row, raised her hand to answer questions faster than anyone else, and seemed to know more about certain topics than their teacher, who sometimes seemed like he didn't quite know what to do with her. But she wasn't a know-it-all either—or if she was, she was the first one Ashur had ever liked. It didn't hurt that she was gorgeous, exactly the kind of look Ashur went for. Her father was Black and her mother was Puerto Rican, and Ashur thought she had the perfect warm skin tone. No one in her family knew where her piercing blue eyes came from, and both sides claimed credit for the perfect bubble butt that made Ashur's pulse quicken when he watched her doing one of her floor routines.

He made his way as quietly as he could through the bushes at the edge of her yard, then snuck his way across the lawn until his body was pressed up close against the siding of her house. There was a television on somewhere, the faint blare of a studio audience laughing and the flickering lights filtering out through the sliding glass door. He shimmied along the house until he was under Kiki's bedroom, prayed none of the neighbors had called the cops yet, and then rattled the long drainage pipe that hung down from the gutter three times. He held his breath and waited.

The window to Kiki's bedroom slid open, and Kiki poked her head out and squinted down at Ashur.

"What are you doing?" she said, speaking in a low hiss. "My dad is home."

"Say you're taking out the trash," Ashur said, smiling up at the sight of her.

"Do you know what he'll do if he catches you here?"

"What, kick me out of school again?"

Kiki sighed and rolled her eyes and closed the window, and Ashur went around to the side of the house where the trash cans sat behind a fence. Kiki's father was Mr. Johnson, the assistant principal and defensive line coach for the football team, who had made it his personal mission to see that Ashur never set foot in the high school again. It didn't help that Ashur's last fight had dislocated the shoulder of the star defensive end before the game against their rival high school—though in fairness, it had been three against one, and Ashur had earned himself a pair of broken ribs and a chipped tooth and something in his knee that still made a funny clicking noise when he moved it the wrong way. No matter: he had a history of "aggressive behavior," and no coaches watching his back, and he had had just about enough of high school by that point, anyway.

A few minutes later he heard the front door creak open, and then Kiki was wandering around the side of the house, carrying a half-full garbage bag. She shook her head when she saw Ashur, but she was smiling too, and she dropped the bag and came over to him and kissed him hard, giving his butt a little squeeze. She tasted a little bit like peppermint, and he never got tired of the feel of her lips against his.

"He's going to get suspicious if I keep being so helpful," Kiki said, dropping the bag into the garbage can.

"He will not," Ashur said. "You're Daddy's Little Princess. Cleaning up the castle is part of your job."

"You can't keep coming around here like this," she said. "He's going to catch you, and then he's going to kill you, and then he's going to call the cops to come pick up your body."

"You never seem to mind," Ashur said, pressing her body up against the house and kissing her again.

"I'm serious," Kiki said after another kiss.

"So then come out with me," Ashur said. "Somewhere safe, where your scary dad will never find us."

"I can't," Kiki said. "You know that."

"See? This is why I keep coming around. It's the only time I get with you."

Kiki smirked, and then reached a hand to run through Ashur's dark and curly hair. As she studied him, something different came across her face—concern, maybe, or sympathy.

Ashur didn't like it when other folks felt sorry for him, but there was something about Kiki that made it feel all right, like he didn't have to worry so much about being tough.

"How was it today?" she said. "Going to see your dad."

Ashur took a deep breath and leaned up against the house, one foot up and his hands behind his head. He thought about telling her about the strange man he had met, but something kept him from it. It wasn't that he didn't trust Kiki—the whole thing just seemed too strange, and he didn't feel like trying to explain something that he didn't fully understand himself.

"Hard. Like always."

Kiki reached down and took his hand, and Ashur let her. Her hand felt small in his but strong, her grip tight from years spent navigating the uneven bars and the rings.

From somewhere inside the house, a particularly loud laugh sounded, more like a bark than anything else. It was so hard for Ashur to imagine Mr. Johnson laughing, watching dumb TV like anyone else. The only time he had ever seen the man smile was when the superintendent approved the motion to have Ashur expelled. Kiki had told him that her father was complicated, and that the man he saw at school and on the football field wasn't the same person she saw at home. Even if she was right, it didn't make him hate the man any less.

"I have to get back in," she said. "Or he's going to think a coyote ate me."

"What coyote would be dumb enough to try and mess with you?" Ashur said.

"A desperate one," she said. "Something hungry enough to try."

They kissed again, slower and a little sadder, and Ashur found the small of her back and drew her in close to him.

"We're still on for the trip, though?"

In all the months they had been seeing one another, Kiki had been careful to make sure there was no way her father could find out about Ashur. That meant not being together anywhere one of his football goons could see them and report back to their coach the kind of boy his precious daughter was hanging around with. At first, Ashur had thought she was embarrassed by him. He hadn't minded much, back when he thought he still wanted to keep things casual. But in time he had come to realize that she was trying to look out for him, keep him safe.

He had been planning this trip for weeks, an overnight to a little town up north on the coast. In the last year, since he'd left school, he'd had plenty of time to explore Southern California on his Kawasaki—when he had the gas money to do it. Kiki had been hesitant at first—she didn't like lying to her parents—but Ashur had been persistent, and eventually she had relented, concocting some elaborate story that Ashur himself couldn't always follow.

"I wouldn't miss it," Kiki said, her eyes shining.

From inside the house, they heard her father calling her name. She gave him another quick kiss, and then she was gone, disappeared around the corner and back inside.

Ashur lingered along the side of the house for another moment, looking up at the sky. It was still early, and with all the light pollution you couldn't see any stars, anyway. He let out a long, slow breath, and then crouched down and started working his way along the edge of the lawn, back toward his bike and the home he knew he'd have to go back to, sooner or later.

He rode home, thinking about his father.

THE ACADEMY

NOVEMBER 28, 2002

Ashur walked into the fall sunlight with a smile on his face that had nothing—or at least very little—to do with the fact that he had just gotten out of math class. Today was the day he had been waiting for all his life: his twelfth birthday, the day boys became men in the Yonan family. The tradition had been passed down from generation to generation, and now, finally, it was his turn.

Ashur couldn't wait for his dad to pick him up so they could talk, man to man. His parents had been arguing for weeks about this, loud conversations that went late into the night. Ashur knew that his mother didn't want his father to tell him about something—a family secret, maybe, but beyond that he couldn't tell. But Rose hated it when Odishoo told him tales of Assyria and Persia, of great emperors and the lands they ruled.

As he walked by the football field, Ashur's head was full of visions of powerful warriors and beautiful princesses. But then something caught his eye and made his stomach drop: a group of kids gathered around a new student, just arrived from Iran. He could hear them laughing, and it didn't sound friendly. He walked faster.

One of the kids gave the new boy a shove—light for now, but Ashur knew it was only the start.

"Look at this loser!" the kid jeered. "Fresh off the boat. And wearing a Michael Jackson shirt?" Another shove. "No one wears Michael Jackson shirts, you little FOB!"

The new kid was smiling, but his eyes were wide with fear. "Tank you," he said in a heavy Persian accent.

"No one likes your shirt, idiot," another punk said. Another shove came, this one hard enough to make the boy stumble backward, tripping over his shoes. The boy's smile was gone now as a big kid leered over him. "We don't want your kind here."

Ashur could feel his face getting hot. With his hands balled up at his sides he walked into the middle of the group. The boy cowered away from him, assuming he was another bully. But Ashur smiled at him, extended a hand to help him up.

"What's your name?" he asked. His Farsi wasn't great, but he knew enough to ask this. The boy lit up at the sound of a language he understood.

"My name is Nima," the boy said.

"Look at these two love birds, speaking terrorist." It was Larry, the biggest middle schooler by two inches and thirty pounds, big and mean. "I didn't know there even were gay terrorists."

Ashur looked at him. He had been called names before, but he hated being called a terrorist.

"Leave him alone," he said through gritted teeth. "He didn't do anything to you."

A mean grin came across Larry's face.

"Aren't you that idiot who got up in front of the whole class in fifth grade and said you'll be king of Iran or some dumb shit?"

Ashur didn't reply—he knew that was exactly what he had said, too naïve to know how it would sound to the others. He put an arm around Nima and tried to steer him away from the football field.

"Where do you think you're going?" Larry said, following the two boys. "Off to plan the next 9/11 with your family?"

That hit a nerve. Ashur hated being called a terrorist, but he hated people saying things about his family—people they had never met before—even more.

"What did you just say?"

"You heard me. I called your family terrorists. What are you going to do about it?"

The other kids surrounded the pair, shouting, "Fight! Fight! Fight!"

Ashur could feel his muscles tensing, and there was a bitter taste in his mouth. But he reminded himself that he was only two periods away from seeing his dad. He held on to that thought as he turned away.

"Pussy," Larry called after him. And for a moment, Ashur thought it might be over.

Then he felt something hit his back, hard. *Larry's foot. He fell to the ground and spat out a mouthful of dirt as someone yelled, "Did you see that?! Ooooh! Larry kicked his ass!"*

Ashur jumped to his feet and ran at Larry, tackling him to the ground. He started swinging at Larry's face. A few of Larry's friends jumped in to pry him off, but Ashur kept punching, pummeling the bully's face as he screamed with rage.

But then someone bigger than him—much bigger—grabbed him from behind and picked him up. For a moment Ashur thrashed, still intent on hurting Larry as badly as he could.

"Knock it off!" said the deep voice of the assistant principal. "You're all coming with me."

Ashur had been sitting outside the principal's office for almost an hour. He had already told his side of the story twice—first to the assistant principal, and then again to Principal Lamas. He knew he shouldn't have taken the bait from Larry, knew that he had hurt the boy—Larry had a black eye, and had gone straight to the nurse's office to get bandaged up. But he also knew that he hadn't started the fight and had only stepped in to protect another boy from the bully. Surely Principal Lamas would understand that.

The door opened, and Odishoo walked in. Ashur cringed—he had spent the whole morning looking forward to seeing his father, and now that was ruined. But the anger he expected to see on his father's face was instead the kind of concern that hurt Ashur even worse somehow than if he had been mad.

"Hey, son," he said quietly. "You okay?"

Ashur nodded. He hadn't been hurt too badly. But he still felt terrible, in trouble for the first time at school, and on this of all days.

Principal Lamas opened the door to his office and asked them both to come in. He and Odishoo shook hands, and Ashur could see the two men regarding one another, sizing the other up.

"I wish we were meeting under better circumstances, Mr. Yonan," Principal Lamas said.

Odishoo sat down.

"As do I," he said. "Please, tell me what happened."

The principal took a deep breath, looked briefly at Ashur, and then turned back to Odishoo.

"Your son nearly put a boy in the hospital today," Principal Lamas said. "If Assistant Principal Jackson hadn't stopped them, I fear we would be having a much worse conversation."

"Is this true?" Odishoo said, looking at Ashur.

"He called me and the new boy a terrorist," Ashur said. "He said our family was the reason for 9/11. He got what he deserved."

"That is Ashur's version of the story," Principal Lamas said. "We heard a very different version from the others who were there. They say Ashur instigated the fight. This kind of violent behavior is not acceptable in this school."

"They're lying!" Ashur said, unable to contain himself. "Ask Nima!"

"Nima didn't seem to understand what was happening," the principal said. "Even when we found a teacher to speak with him in Farsi, he would only apologize for the entire incident."

Ashur could see the frustration on Odishoo's face—the same frustration he felt himself. But then his father's face turned smooth again as he spoke with the principal.

"Can I speak with you privately, Mr. Lamas?"

The principal nodded.

"Wait outside, Ashur," his father said. "I'll be out in a minute."

Ashur wanted to argue, but he didn't. Instead, he put his head down and went out into the little area outside the principal's office. He knew he had let his father down. But as much as he wanted to, he didn't let himself cry.

He spent the next few minutes feeling his insides churn. He couldn't believe how unfair it was, the principal believing the other boys instead of him. He knew Larry was popular, the star of the football team the high school coach was already salivating over. But shouldn't Ashur's word count just as much as theirs? But the worst thing—the thing that nearly made him want to throw up—was the thought that his father might not believe him, either. That, he thought, would be horrible.

When his father stepped out of the office and signaled for him to follow, Ashur jumped up. They walked to the car in complete silence, Ashur's heart thudding in his chest.

"Dad, do you believe me?" he said.

Odishoo paused for a moment, then turned to look at Ashur with hard eyes.

"I do believe you. You have your faults, like anyone else, but I have never known you to lie."

Ashur felt tremendous relief at hearing these words. But he was confused, too—his father seemed more angry with him now than he had been before. He went to ask a question, but before he could, his father continued.

"But that still doesn't make it right, you taking things as far as you did," Odishoo said.

"I don't understand—are you telling me I shouldn't have defended myself?"

"There are times that you need to defend yourself physically. But you have to learn to control yourself, too, even when you're angry. Especially *when you're angry.*"

Odishoo shook his head.

"You will be offended many, many times in your life. If you react the way you did today every time, there will be too many people for you to fight. You need to learn to control your emotions. You will be called worse things than just a terrorist, and people will do worse things than kick you in the back."

Ashur frowned.

"But do you think what happened today was fair? Do you think it's fair that Larry got away with a lie? And that Principal Lamas didn't believe me?"

Odishoo gave him a sad smile.

"Welcome to the real world. Life isn't fair all the time. And as a man, you need to understand that."

Ashur pushed himself back into the passenger's seat. He had spent all day—weeks, months, years even—waiting for his father to call him a man. But now that he was here, it suddenly seemed a lot less fun than he had imagined.

"But how do you keep people from treating you unfairly?"

Odishoo smiled again, bigger this time.

"You can't prevent it completely, but you can learn to be a better judge of character. That skill only comes with time and experience, dealing with many people."

"I don't like that."

"Doesn't matter. It's a law of life—just like there's a law of gravity, there's a law of unfairness. Can you change gravity, even if you don't like it?"

"Of course not."

"So then why waste your time worrying about it? Unfairness is the same way. You need to learn how to deal with unfair people in your life. Because they're not going away."

Ashur looked down at his hands.

"I guess I understand what you're saying."

"Good." Odishoo reached over and ruffled his hair. Usually Ashur tried to dodge out of the way, but this time the feel of his father's hand on his head was comforting.

"Now, I have good news and bad news. Which do you want first?"

Ashur frowned.

"What's the bad news?"

"You're suspended for the rest of the week."

"Are you kidding me!" Ashur said. "But I didn't do anything! Larry is the person who should be suspended, not me."

"Didn't we just talk about the law of unfairness?"

"But it's stupid, Dad. I don't deserve to be suspended."

"And what can you do about it?"

Ashur started to say again how unfair it was, but then he thought about everything his father had just said. "Nothing, I guess. Just live with it."

"Okay then. Now, do you want the good news?"

Ashur nodded. Odishoo took his chin in his hand and turned his face to him, smiling one of the biggest smiles Ashur had ever seen.

"Today you are a man. And today you learn our family's secret history."

All the unfairness of the day suddenly evaporated. It was not ruined, after all. He was still going to become a Yonan man.

"Finally!" Ashur said. *"That's what I've been waiting for!"*

"I know," his father said, turning over the car's ignition.

As they drove away from the school, Ashur turned to Odishoo.

"Can you please not tell Mom about me being suspended until tomorrow morning? Please? I don't want anything else to ruin my birthday."

Odishoo was quiet for a moment, navigating the car out of the parking lot.

"Let me think about that one."

CHAPTER TWO

When he made it back to Burbank it was full dark, and Ashur parked his bike in the little alleyway two blocks down from his apartment. He had moved here with his mother six years ago, after his father's death, and Ashur had never gotten used to it. He couldn't think about their old house without thinking about the life he had left behind: his father in the big backyard, listening to his favorite Iranian music while he smoked his pipe, his eyes closed with pleasure as he sat after a long day at work.

As Ashur turned the corner, he could see that the apartment was still lit up. He hoped his mother had left the lights on by mistake or had fallen asleep watching TV. She was drinking more than ever now, buying cheap handles of vodka that she mixed with thin orange juice, and most days he managed to leave before she woke from wherever she'd fallen asleep the night before. He lingered outside the door for another moment, trying to keep the feeling of calm that had come to him as he wrapped his arms around Kiki. For how long, now, had coming home been the worst part of his day? He took a deep breath, turned his key in the lock as quietly as he could manage, and eased the front door open.

The sound of the TV assaulted him as he walked in, some slick salesman telling viewers to *act now!* or else risk missing this special offer. He tiptoed across the kitchen, praying he would make it into the bedroom without another fight. He was exhausted, his mind still whirling from the meeting with the mysterious stranger at his father's grave. All he wanted to do was put his head down and go to sleep.

"Where were you?"

His mother's voice was only a little slurred. Ashur thought about pressing forward as if he hadn't heard her, locking his bedroom door and ignoring the pounding and the insults that he knew she'd hurl through the thin particleboard. He had done that plenty of nights before, his headphones up as high as they would go to drown out the sound of her yelling. But instead he sighed and turned to face Rose.

His mother had once been a beautiful woman—even after everything, it was possible to see that, in the set of her cheekbones and the rich olive tone of her skin. But there were dark bags under her eyes now, and her unwashed hair was stringy and lank. Ashur kept a photograph of his parents' wedding day in the shoebox in his closet where he had all his most precious items, the ones he didn't want his mother to find: his father proud and handsome in his wedding suit, his mother all done up, young and beautiful and smiling. Rose had destroyed most of the other family photos, one of the many things that Ashur thought he would never be able to forgive her for.

The glass in her hand was empty, but Ashur knew it wouldn't stay that way for long. She stood from her chair, groaning a bit with the effort.

"I went to visit Dad," Ashur said, trying to keep calm. "I told you that."

"You went to go visit a pile of bones," his mother said, coming toward the kitchen. "Dust."

"I was paying my respects," Ashur said, his eyes narrowing. "Like you should have been."

"You were playing make-believe. Pretending it mattered. Pretending that man was worth anything."

Rose shook her head, tottered over to the freezer, and removed a tray of ice cubes. Ashur had heard it all before, but it still made him shake with rage, hearing his mother talk about his father like that. Rose continued to fix herself a drink, the glass tinkling as she filled it, not even bothering to look at her son as she spoke to him. As though his presence there in the kitchen barely registered with her.

"When are you going to grow up, Ashur?"

Every muscle in Ashur's body tensed. The notion that Rose could lecture him about responsibility—about what it meant to be a man—was absurd. His mother hadn't held a job in the six years since Odishoo's death. There had been a bit of money from selling the old house, a few dollars in savings, but that had quickly run out. Since then they had scraped by on government assistance and whatever Ashur could scrounge together from his after-school jobs. Ashur would have laughed if he weren't so angry.

"Is this what being an adult looks like?" he said. "Sitting around all day, drinking? Wasting our money on vodka and cheap cigarettes?"

A nasty smile came over Rose's mouth then, as she brought the fresh drink up to her lips for a sip.

"You must really think you're someone, to talk to me like that. In my house. Under my roof."

"Your house? Who pays the rent? With what money? Who pays for the food I eat? Is it you, or the food stamps?"

Rose looked at him for a moment, and then blinked.

"Tell me, Ashur, how are your classes going?"

Ashur seethed in silence. His mother hadn't seemed to care, one way or another, when he didn't look for another school after he was expelled from high school. A real mother would have been angry with him, maybe, told him to stop wasting his life. But Rose had just sneered at him, as though she had been waiting for him to fail.

"And those college admissions essays?" she said. "You must be a shoo-in, with your sad story. The poor little boy who went around punching people until they kicked him out of school. You must be so proud of yourself."

Ashur locked eyes with his mother. He hated her when she got like this, mean and cruel. Worst of all, she knew him well enough to know how to hurt him.

"I'm not in the mood for this tonight, Rose," he said. "I'm going to bed."

"Don't call me Rose," his mother said. "I am your mother. However much you wish that wasn't true."

"Just…leave me alone, okay?" Ashur said. There was no use in arguing with his mother when she got like this, but it hadn't stopped him before, and he knew that if he didn't get out soon, things would start to spiral. He started walking toward his bedroom, but Rose followed him.

"You think you can just wander in here whenever you want, insult me, and then tell me you're not in the mood? You don't get to decide that. You still live under my roof. I'm not through with you!"

Her voice was starting to rise.

"Just go to sleep, Rose," Ashur said. "You're going to wake the whole neighborhood."

"You Yonan men are all the same," she said. "Worthless. That's what's wrong with you. Too much Yonan blood. I should have never married your father. I can only pray to God that no woman is dumb enough to make the same mistake with you."

Ashur was nearly to his bedroom door, but this last insult was too much. He turned around quickly, looming over his mother.

"What makes you think I would ever want to get married, and risk going through what Dad had to go through with you?"

"That's right," his mother said. "Blame me for everything. Let me be the reason poor Ashur never even tried. It's my fault you quit school. It's my fault you got in all those fights. It's my fault you'll never make anything of your life. Nothing could ever be your fault. That's the difference between you and your father. At least he tried—for a little while. You gave up before you even started."

The edges of Ashur's vision were starting to blur a little. He could feel the way his muscles were tensing, taste something bitter in his mouth. Instinctively he brought his hand up to the scar at the corner of his eye, feeling the place where the wound had closed but still left the skin jagged. His mother watched him, and for a moment something seemed to soften in her: the memory of her son in pain, and what she had done. But then she hardened up again, fast.

"That stupid man," she said.

"Why do you hate him so much?" Ashur said.

"Because I knew him," she said. "Better than you. Better than anyone. Don't you ever wonder why you're the only one who still cares about him?"

Ashur hesitated for a moment. He hadn't wanted to tell her about the mysterious man at the cemetery that afternoon—Dobiel had even told him that he and Ashur's mother hadn't gotten along, and that that was the reason he hadn't come around much. But when his mother talked to him like this, it made him feel completely alone in the world. Sometimes, he even started to believe the hateful things she said. Seeing someone else at the grave—knowing that he wasn't crazy to care about Odishoo's memory the way he did—was powerful enough to push back against all that. He needed Rose to know that not everyone in the world agreed with her.

"I'm not the only one who still cares about Dad!" Ashur spat.

The comment caught his mother off guard. She tilted her head to the side, swaying a little now, as though the news had staggered her. Probably just the drink catching up with her, Ashur thought, but there was still something satisfying about shutting her up for the moment.

"What are you talking about?" she said.

"There was a man today," he said. "At the cemetery."

"He must have been lost," Rose said. "Trying to find someone else. Someone who mattered."

"He knew Dad," Ashur said. "He knew me."

"Impossible," Rose said. But there was something new sneaking around the edge of her expression now, eating away at the hardness and the cruelty. Was it doubt? Or something darker, a temporary flicker of fear? Whatever it was, Ashur was satisfied, seeing it there.

"It's true," Ashur said. "He said he even knew you. And that you hated him. It felt good, to know I had company for once."

For a long moment, Rose said nothing, working over something in her mind.

"Impossible," she said quietly, more to herself than anything.

"He even told me his name," Ashur said, feeling a bit bolder now. "Dobiel."

Whatever fear had been in his mother before was quickly replaced by something new: anger, white-hot this time, more powerful than the cruel mocking with which she usually tormented Ashur. She let her head loll back until she was looking at the ceiling and let out a jagged scream, the sound filling the space of the little kitchen. Ashur staggered backward a few steps, shocked to hear so much noise coming from his mother—how long, he wondered, until one of the neighbors called the cops?

She reared back and hurled her glass, the drink splashing out as it hurtled across the room. The glass shattered against the wall behind Ashur, missing him by only a foot. Shards were lying all around him, and he stared at his mother, his mouth agape.

"Are you crazy?!" he said. "What are you doing?"

There was something almost inhuman about his mother now, her body coursing with fear and rage. Rose extended a long finger toward him, the rest of her body strangely limp.

"Do not lie to me!" she said.

"I'm telling the truth!" Ashur said, confused. He *always* told the truth—even his mother, in the depths of her drunken sorrow and meanness, knew this. So then why would she even suggest it? The only reason Ashur could come up with chilled him: because she was scared that what he was telling her was true.

"You fool!" Rose said, shouting the words across the kitchen. "You naïve, worthless fool! You have no idea what you're doing."

Ashur was seething, his body coursing with adrenaline. By now he knew how all the arguments with his mother would unfold, could feel their essence and contours as they slipped into another round of fighting: arguing about money, arguing about living together, arguing about his father. But this was different, raw and ragged in a way their fights usually weren't. A part of him was almost excited, seeing that it was still possible to make his mother feel like this. But there was something dangerous about it, too. Still, he pressed on.

"You know him, don't you? Tell me who he was!"

"Never!" his mother said, her hands balled into tight fists, crossing the space until she was standing right before him, shaking with anger.

"What are you going to do, hit me again?" Ashur said. He thought she looked like she wanted to. When she didn't say anything, he grabbed her hands. She shrieked and tried to pull away.

"Let go of me!" his mother said.

But instead, Ashur took her hands, still clenched in fists, and started to hit himself across his face.

"Hit me!" he said. "Go on, hit me! Hit me harder! Does that feel good? Isn't that what you want?!"

"What are you doing?" Rose said. "What's wrong with you?"

"Tell me who he is!" he said, still hitting himself. By now his mother's hands had gone limp as he held them. She was sobbing, bitter tears and a choked sound coming from her. He let go of her, turned, and punched a hole in the drywall of the kitchen.

"You're going crazy!" she said, crumpling to the floor. "Just like your grandfather. You crazy fool. I cannot have you like this. Leave this house!"

"You think I want to be here?" Ashur said. "Living with you? I stayed because you would die without me."

Rose lay crumpled on the floor, still racked with sobs, looking now like the dried and shriveled husk of a mother Ashur had once had.

"God, why did you give me a son like this?" she wailed. "What did I do to deserve it?"

"You don't have to worry about that anymore," Ashur said. He turned around, walked into his room, and slammed the door so hard the whole house shook.

He had thought about leaving before. Sometimes it felt like that was all he thought about. But each time, his father's voice would come to him. Reminding him that he was the man of the house, and that it was his job to take care of his mother, no matter how difficult it was to live with her. But now, as he moved around his room, collecting the few precious things he owned, all that he could hear was the sound of his own heart beating in his ear, and the faint noise of his mother's crying through the thin door.

There was something about that man at the cemetery. Something that had scared his mother—and moved her to a new anger that he had never seen in Rose before. He needed to find out what it was, and it was clear that Rose would not be the one to tell him.

Ashur stuffed a few sets of clothes into his backpack. Took the few snapshots he had left from the shoebox in the closet.

Then, after checking that the door to his bedroom was locked, he stood on his bed and opened the ceiling panel. Carefully he brought down the Beretta, wrapped in an old T-shirt. He kept the clip separate—and the box of 9 mm ammunition, still half full. Other than the motorcycle, the gun was the last physical thing he had to connect him with his father. He unwrapped the pistol and held it for a moment, the familiar feel of the metal, the roughness of the crosshatched grip. Feeling it now made Ashur feel comforted and sad all at once. He waited again for his father's voice to come to him, telling him what to do. But again there was silence.

"Where are you, Dad?" he whispered quietly. But no answer came. So he wrapped the gun in the T-shirt and stuffed it as far down into his backpack as he could.

He waited by the door of his room until he couldn't hear any more sound coming from outside, his ear pressed up against the wood. The adrenaline from earlier had mostly burned off now; he was more exhausted than ever. But he knew that if he went to sleep, by the morning his resolve would be gone. He needed to leave—tonight.

He opened the door quietly. His mother was still on the floor of the kitchen, propped up against the wall. For a horrible moment he thought she might be dead. But then he saw her breathing, ragged and awkward. She looked pitiful, crumpled up like some broken thing. Ashur had tried to look after her, to protect her from herself—his teenage years had been spent fighting against her, trying as best he could. He felt like he had failed. But there was no way to change that now. And after to-night, he swore to himself he wouldn't look back, though he knew that would be an impossible promise to keep.

THE ACADEMY

As Ashur walked the lonely dark blocks to his bike, he realized he was leaving behind his first love—his mother—who had just broken his heart for good. The engine roared when he started it, drowning out the sound of her cries still echoing in his ears.

When they arrived home, Odishoo called out for Rose. But the house was silent—she was out, running errands or visiting a friend. Odishoo smiled at Ashur as he sliced lemons for their tea—no need to tell her about the fight, or the suspension, just yet.

"You already know some of our family history," his father said. "Our family grew up in Iran, but we are not Persian—we are Assyrian. The Yonans are descended from kings and emperors, great warriors—your grandfather was named for the fierce Sargon, an Assyrian king. But we loved our adopted country, especially after the reforms and modernizations of Mohammad Reza Shah Pahlavi."

Ashur nodded along—he knew most of this already, but he didn't dare interrupt his father, for fear that he might miss something new. Odishoo sighed, the memory clearly painful.

"That is why the day I learned we would have to leave was so upsetting. I remember it so clearly, even though I was young.

"It was 1975. We were watching television, your grandparents on the sofa and me on the floor, when Mohammad Reza Shah Pahlavi—Reza Shah's son—said to the interviewer, Mike Wallace,

"'The brown-eyed people are teaching the blue-eyed people something. The blue-eyed people have to wake up from their complacency, from this torpor in which they put themselves by taking too many sleeping pills.'

"I was so excited to see our king say those words about the Westerners! So proud that he took such pride in Iran. But when I turned back to my parents, my father had a look on his face that I had never seen before. He looked like the Shah had just said the worst thing he could say about anyone. I was upset at my dad—why wasn't he as enthusiastic as I was about the Shah's boldness and courage? His reaction confused me."

Ashur had heard this much before, but usually the story stopped there. Today, though, Ashur knew he would learn more—he was officially a man now, and so he would get to hear the parts his father had kept from him before. This was his family history, all of it.

As they walked through the house to the backyard, Ashur asked, "What did Grandpa think about what the Shah said?"

A sad smile came across Odishoo's face.

"My father's first words were, 'It's over.' I didn't understand what he meant. But he looked past me, to my mother. He told her they had to get me out of Iran even faster than they had planned. 'This thing is going to get very ugly, very quickly,' he said. 'The empire is about to fall.'

"I had often overheard his concern about the Shah's vision for Iran, talking with other government agents at our home. But this was different, a new kind of worry I hadn't seen before."

"What was wrong with the Shah's vision?" Ashur asked. "Isn't having a visionary leader a good thing?"

"Visionary leaders tend to attract enemies," Odishoo said. "Even if the vision is a good one. And when that vision is fulfilled, envious enemies dislike that leader even more."

"But all the great leaders we learn about in school were bold visionaries," Ashur pressed. "Abraham Lincoln. Julius Caesar!"

Odishoo arched his brows.

"And how do those stories tend to end?"

Ashur thought for a moment.

"With the leader being killed."

"Or someone on the inside turning on them," Odishoo said, nodding. "Even if they make things better for others, things don't end well for them. Or for their families and loved ones. It's a difficult thing to explain."

Odishoo smiled at his son, but there was a sadness mixed in that Ashur didn't understand.

"You know, I have always felt it is my true calling to teach you everything I can, Ashur—to prepare you for something big in your future. You are destined for greatness, but it's a greatness you must discover yourself."

Ashur blushed at his father's words.

"You really think so?"

"I know so. But not everyone can understand that." Odishoo frowned. "Not even your mother, although she loves you very much.

"Your mother doesn't like when I tell you about our people's history. Her experience in Iran was very different than mine. She grew up in a small city in Azarbaijan, in a family who believed that communism would make their lives better. She still believes that the wars in the world are the fault of capitalism and big business."

Odishoo's frown deepened.

"And she hated Mohammad Reza Shah Pahlavi."

"But why?" Ashur wondered how many nights this disagreement had been the cause of his parents' arguments.

"She sees him as an egotistical man whose competitive drive caused the empire to fall. She hates everything he stood for, truly hates it." Odishoo's frown lifted a bit as he pushed open the back door and ushered Ashur ahead of him. "This is why, when we talk

about Iran or Assyria, we do so outside, son—out of respect for your mother."

"I don't understand," Ashur said, frowning. "How can you be married to someone you disagree with on something so big?"

The sad smile returned to Odishoo's face.

"Love is a funny thing, Ashur. Hopefully there will be time to teach you all about that, too."

CHAPTER THREE

He rode his bike through the night, the feel of the wind against his body on the empty highways nearly enough to keep him from thinking about the fight with his mother. He didn't worry too much about where he was going—he knew these roads so well by now, speed the only thing that mattered. Ashur didn't even need to look at the speedometer—he knew what 100 mph felt like, knew the way the bike started to rattle and whine when he pushed it faster, like some animal driven nearly to exhaustion. He gritted his teeth and kept riding.

He grabbed a few hours of sleep on the beach near Malibu, the sky purple in the pre-dawn and his body worn out from the long day. Eventually, Ashur knew, he would need to make some kind of a plan. His part-time job at the Big Boy wasn't enough for him to live on, never mind afford a place of his own. He thought vaguely about Las Vegas, mostly for the excuse to drive another long stretch of highway. Before he was expelled, he had talked with an Army recruiter who came by the high school. He liked that idea, going somewhere no one knew him, using his physical skills for good, dedicating himself to something greater than himself. Would they still take him now, after everything? He wasn't sure, and he was a little afraid to find out.

But all of that was in the future. For now, only one thing mattered to him: his trip with Kiki. He'd been looking forward to it for months now, savoring the idea even as she shooed him away from her house or pressed a finger to his lips when he tried to kiss her in public, terrified of her father finding out about them. He wasn't going to let his mother, or anyone else, ruin their time together.

Kiki had told her father that she was spending the night at a girlfriend's house, so they would have the whole evening together. Ashur hadn't told her anything about where they were going; he wanted the day to be a surprise. His only instructions to her had been to get herself a proper motorcycle helmet.

The plan was to meet up in the early afternoon. He made his way over to Glendale, weaving his way through the slow midday traffic. Kiki had said to wait for her by the library—so like her to pick the library, he thought with a smile, even with the Galleria next door.

As he cruised the streets crowded with people shopping and chatting, a billboard rising high above the road caught his eye. He came to a stop at a red light and squinted through his visor into the sun—it looked like there was a man standing up in front of the billboard, waving down to the cars as they passed. The figure looked oddly familiar—families below on the street were pointing up at him and laughing, and Ashur wondered how he had gotten up there. Then he recognized the man: stovepipe hat, elongated face framed by a beard, a body that looked almost stretched out. It was Abraham Lincoln, the words on the billboard behind him filled with the scrolling text of a famous speech, espousing the ideals of decency and freedom.

"The holograms just keep getting better," said a guy in wraparound shades on the sidewalk, grinning as he snapped a picture with his phone. "Cleopatra blew me a kiss over on the One-Oh-One last week. I nearly crashed!"

Ashur kept looking up. The thing was so lifelike—not even a flicker. And Lincoln hadn't repeated any of his movements while Ashur watched, so it wasn't just a projection playing on a loop. Once the speech was over, the billboard behind the figure morphed into a single word—WORLDCORP—and then their slogan, Powering Peace and Prosperity Around the Globe. Ashur frowned—that seemed like a lot for a global conglomerate to be promising. Still, the hologram was impressive.

Someone behind him leaned on their horn—the light had turned. Ashur revved his bike and pushed forward, forgetting about Abe Lincoln and pressing on.

He parked behind the library and took off his helmet. He wished he had taken a shower before leaving the house, but Kiki told him she liked it when his hair was messy. The day was starting to get warm, so he took off his purple jacket and hung it across the handlebars. Both the helmet and the jacket were emblazoned with a black lion, matching the tattoo on Ashur's left forearm. It was the same tattoo his father had, Ashur's done in clean, bold black lines—but this was no ordinary lion. It was as though someone had crossed a lion with an eagle, its wings spread out behind it. He had gotten it at thirteen—he had always looked old for his age, and the man at the tattoo parlor had barely glanced at the fake ID that Ashur handed him, along with the sketch of exactly what he wanted on his skin.

He had paired the jacket with vintage jeans and brown boots, his favorite outfit for riding. The sign on the bank as he'd rode through Glendale said the temperature was pressing up against ninety, but the forecast for the coast was in the seventies. *Perfect weather*, Ashur thought, though the bike's speed would whip the wind enough to chill him and Kiki.

As he waited, his mind drifted back to the fight the night before. It felt so strange, to finally be leaving for good after thinking about it for so long. He thought about how terrified his mother had looked when he told her about the man at the cemetery. He still had the man's card, tucked deep inside his wallet. Maybe, once the trip was over, he would give the man a call, see what else he could do. Being out of options meant that he was willing to try just about anything—if it didn't work out, then he figured he was right back to where he was now. And it felt almost good, knowing Rose hated someone more than him. He shook his head—it would do no good to think about these things once he was with Kiki.

Just as he was starting to get antsy, the back door to the library flew open, and Ms. Kiki Johnson stepped into the bright midday sunshine. Ashur's jaw nearly dropped when he saw her. She was wearing tight black jeans, a black jacket, and black boots—a perfect biker chick outfit, so unlike what he had seen her wearing before. He could see her magenta sports bra through her shirt, and there was a sleek gray helmet tucked under her arm. She broke into a grin when she saw Ashur, hurried down the steps toward him.

"What do you think?" she said. Ashur tried to play it as cool as he could, but he could feel the smile spreading over his face.

"I think you probably caused some heart attacks in the periodicals room," he said. "The poor old guys reading their newspapers didn't even know what hit them."

Kiki laughed and slapped him playfully on the arm. He pulled her in close for a kiss, her nose twitching as his stubble tickled her face.

"You look amazing," he said, pulling away for a moment to get a better look. She did a nifty little twirl, and he could see where the purple thong was riding up her back.

"So what's this secret plan of yours?" she asked. "Remember, nowhere people will recognize us."

"I don't think anyone is going to know it's you, wearing that," he said. "Unless they recognize your bubble butt."

"That's not funny!" she said, but she was still grinning.

"You're right, it's not funny," Ashur said with a bit of a smirk. "Just perfectly round, and the sort of thing you can't forget once you've set your eyes on it."

"Is this your idea of cute?"

Ashur shrugged.

"Is it working?"

Kiki stuck out her tongue and pulled her helmet on.

"Seriously, though. Where are you taking me?"

"Do you trust me?"

There was a moment of hesitation while Kiki thought about this.

"Yes. I do."

"Then climb on. I'll tell you when we get there."

Kiki started to make a little noise of protest, but Ashur already had his own helmet on and was revving up the engine. He loved the feeling of Kiki on the seat behind him, her legs against him and her arms wrapped tight around his torso. She let out a happy little shriek as he pulled out of the parking lot and into traffic, weaving his bike around the cars.

He went straight on the 134, heading towards the 101. He ignored the cars turning off the 405—the typical way to get to the Pacific Coast Highway—and instead kept going on the 101. He exited Las Virgenes Road, took the canyon route to the beach. It was the perfect stretch of road for any biker who enjoyed taking sharp turns at 60 mph along steep cliffside drops. Kiki's grip on him got tighter, but the girl loved the feeling of speed almost as much as he did and clung to him while screaming with excitement.

By the time they got to the PCH the weather was perfect: clear skies and warm enough for the chill of the wind to feel good against their bodies. Ashur sped between the cars, pushing the bike faster to pass. There was something majestic about riding a motorcycle right by the ocean—and the feeling of Kiki behind him on the bike made the experience that much more thrilling.

After an hour and a half they approached Santa Barbara. Kiki signaled for Ashur to pull over. He exited onto State Street and pulled up to The French Press, a local coffee shop he'd visited before.

Kiki pulled off her helmet and shook out her hair.

"Were you ever planning on stopping?

Ashur grinned.

"Isn't it better to have to tell me to stop instead of telling me to keep going?"

"What do you…" she began, but then she made a face at him. "You have the dirty mind of a thirteen-year-old boy."

Ashur shrugged. "You're the one who made it dirty. I didn't mean anything like that."

Kiki rolled her eyes. "So where *are* we going?"

"You seem to like that question a lot," he said. "Leave that up to me. I promise you'll like it."

"At least tell me how much longer we have left."

"Maybe another hour."

They got themselves some drinks—a coffee for her and a carrot juice for Ashur, Kiki making fun of him for the order. Ashur smiled as she ribbed him—he had long since given up caring what other people, even Kiki, thought about him for liking the things he liked.

A perfect day, just like Ashur had hoped as he planned the trip. But as he sipped his bottle of juice, he found himself staring off, still turning over the events of the last twenty-four hours. Something was changing, that much was clear, and he felt as though the ground was shifting beneath his feet. Leaving wasn't the hard part—it wasn't easy, either, but he had known he would have to leave sooner or later. But the tricky thing was not knowing where he was going—or why.

"Ashur?"

He looked back across the table, hastily slapped a smile on his face that he could tell wasn't convincing anyone.

"Where did you go just then?" Kiki said. Ashur looked down and shook his head.

"It's nothing."

"You sure? Because if there's anything you want to talk about, you know…"

"I'm good," he said, reaching across the table to grab her hand. "Promise."

Kiki cocked her head to the side and looked at him for another moment, like she was trying to read his mind.

"Come on," Ashur said, finishing his drink. "You're going to love this next part."

It wasn't until they took a strong curve an hour later that Kiki finally saw why Ashur was so excited. A gigantic rock loomed up from the beach a few hundred yards before the shoreline, the remains of an ancient volcano. She hugged Ashur even tighter, tapping him on his chest with her hands. He was happy that she liked it; it was one of his hiding spots when he needed to be away from everything, a little beach town nobody seemed to know about.

He exited the freeway and rode until they were right next to the beach. As soon as he killed the engine, Kiki jumped up and pulled off her helmet.

"Oh, wow!" She did a full turn, taking in the quaint old town with its shops and seaside restaurants. "Morro Bay...how come I've lived in Southern California my whole life, and I've never heard of or seen this place before?"

Ashur smiled and took her hand.

"Sometimes the best things we have are so close that we tend not to really see them."

Kiki laughed and rolled her eyes a little, but then she thought about it for a moment.

"You know what? I actually think you're right."

Ashur adopted a look of mock indignation.

"You make it sound like it's never happened before!"

"Well," Kiki said, strolling down toward the beach and giving Ashur a spectacular view as she went. "There's a first time for everything."

It was late afternoon, the light golden in the little oceanside town. Ashur and Kiki walked along the beach for a time, then wandered the streets, peeking through windows. It felt good to be walking together, hand in hand, not worried if anyone would see them and report back to the vice principal. Almost enough to make Ashur forget about everything else. Almost.

At twilight, Ashur led Kiki to the little seafood restaurant a block off the water. It was a quiet spot, not as fancy as some of the other places in town, but the food was great and Ashur had always appreciated the low-key atmosphere. Kiki seemed delighted, sitting by the big plate-glass windows with a great view of the coast. Ashur looked out to where the volcanic rock cast a giant shadow.

After they had ordered, it was Kiki who took his hand, a small smile on her face.

"We don't have to talk about it for long," she said. "But something's up with you."

He shook his head and was about to speak when Kiki held up her other hand.

"And don't tell me it's nothing. I know you too well for that."

Ashur let out a little laugh, but he could feel a pit growing in his stomach.

"I just didn't want to ruin today."

"And you won't," Kiki said. "But if you keep this stuff bottled up, sooner or later it's going to explode. And trust me, when that happens, it's a mess. For everyone."

"Yeah," Ashur said, turning to look once more out the window. Then he sighed and turned back to Kiki. "Rose and I had a fight."

Kiki nodded.

"Not the first time," she said.

"This was different," Ashur said. "She said some stuff. Vicious things. She threw a glass at my head. She crossed a line, Kiki."

"Oh, Ash," Kiki said.

"So I left," Ashur said. Kiki frowned.

"What do you mean, left?"

"I mean I packed a bag. And I'm not going back. That's why I've been a little quiet, I guess. It all happened really fast. But

I don't think it's a good idea, me being around her anymore. I don't want to see where else this goes with her."

Kiki nodded slowly, thinking.

"Maybe a break might not be a bad idea for the two of you. But where will you go?"

Ashur held up his palms toward the ceiling.

"I'll figure something out," he said. "Maybe I'll ride my motorcycle across the country, hang out in Providence. You know, teach trust-fund babies at Brown how to fight or something."

He had said this mostly as a joke, an idle thought to make Kiki laugh. But now that he had said it, he was starting to consider the notion. Ashur had lived in California his whole life—maybe what he really needed was a fresh start on a different coast, a whole continent between him and Rose and Vice Principal Johnson and the ghosts of a life that he wasn't sure he wanted any part of anymore. He could find work out there—he was good with his hands, a hard worker, especially if he found something he liked. And best of all, it meant he wouldn't have to say goodbye to Kiki, or content himself to only see her at holidays or when he could scrounge together enough money for a plane ticket. The more he thought about it, the more it seemed like the perfect plan.

But then he looked back across the table and saw the way Kiki's face had fallen. Clearly that was not the life she saw for herself when she went out east to the Ivy League college she'd worked so hard to get into—some underemployed loser boyfriend hanging around, waiting for her to get out of class, asking her where she'd been as she was making the new friends that she hoped she'd keep for the rest of her life. In that moment, Ashur could see so clearly the ways in which he didn't fit into her plans for the future, even if she hadn't said anything about it yet. But after everything else, the thought of losing Kiki—of losing someone else he loved—was almost too much to bear.

"Forget it," he said. "It was a stupid idea."

Kiki was quiet, thinking about something, the same intense look of concentration on her face she got when she was studying for an AP chemistry test. She was staring at his face, and Ashur looked back, resisting the urge to turn away.

"Do you know that I've never met anyone like you, Ashur?" Kiki said. "Not ever, in my whole life. You're not a normal kid."

Ashur frowned.

"You mean I'm a weirdo?"

Kiki stuck her tongue out the side of her mouth and shook her head.

"No. I mean, you're definitely a little weird. But it's just...I don't really know how to say it. I have this feeling about you, Ashur. I always have, from the moment I met you at school."

"Yeah?" Ashur said, a little skeptical. "What kind of a feeling?"

"I feel like life can only go one of two ways for you. You're not the kind of person who just settles down for a quiet, normal life. That's not you. You might do something reckless and end up in jail, or worse. But I've always felt like you're going to do something great with your life. I mean, really great. Like the sort of person people are going to learn about one day. And nothing that's happened—not even you getting kicked out of school—has changed the way I feel about that. If anything, the feeling has only gotten stronger."

"You sure that's water in your glass?" Ashur said, picking up the cup before her and taking a tentative sniff.

"I'm serious," Kiki said. "I think you can really do something great. But at some point, you have to start to do something about it. You're too good—too special—to just be somebody's boyfriend, hanging around campus and working in some coffee shop in Providence."

Ashur nodded, thinking about this for a minute.

"It's funny," he said. His fists were clenched, and it seemed as though the wings behind the lion inked on his arm were beating as his muscles tensed. "There used to be a time when I thought that I was called to do something great with my life. My dad made me believe that. But then God—or fate, or chance, or whatever it was—took him away from me. And I guess I sort of stopped believing that anymore."

"Ash, can I be straight with you?"

He looked back at her. "Go right ahead."

She hesitated. "It might sting."

"Trust me. It won't be worse than anything I've heard before. Or already thought myself."

"Okay." Kiki took a breath. "I think you need to stop feeling sorry for yourself."

That did surprise him. For a moment, Ashur felt a flush of anger. Who was Kiki, who had never had to deal with the sort of things he had, to tell him to stop feeling sorry for himself? What did she know about the pain of losing a parent, or having a mother who told him he was worthless? For a moment he wanted to push back from the table and leave, get out of the restaurant before she could say anything else. But then the moment passed, and he looked across the table and saw the beautiful woman who had driven up the coast with him, and who cared enough about him to risk saying something she thought he needed to hear. He took a deep breath and nodded for her to continue.

"I don't know what it feels like to go through what you have," Kiki said. "And I know it can't be easy. But you have your entire life ahead of you! And I worry sometimes you're too busy thinking about the past, and all the bad things that have happened, that you'll miss out on all that's still to come." She shrugged and offered him a small smile. "I know it sounds corny, but sometimes the only thing you can do is have faith in what the future holds for you. I really believe that, Ashur."

Ashur waited another moment, thinking about this, but then he smiled, too.

"I really like that about you, Kiki. You're always looking forward. And you don't hold back when you're thinking something. You tell it like it is. I know you're coming from a good place." His smile faded for a second. "But it's just tough sometimes to believe the future will be any better than things are right now."

"I know," Kiki said.

Ashur reached under the table and touched her knee.

"Thanks, Kiki. I mean it. And you don't have to worry about me following you to Providence."

She shook her head and laughed.

"Enough talk—why don't we just enjoy our dinner, and this magic town that you've discovered?"

That sounded pretty good to Ashur, and so he smiled and nodded. Their food came soon, and before long they were back to talking easily, bantering back and forth and teasing another. It felt good, to know Kiki cared enough about him to tell him what she really thought. Good, too, knowing that at least someone out there thought he might be going places with his life, no matter how much he had started to question that himself.

They finished dinner and Ashur let Kiki pick up the tab. It wasn't just that money was tight for him—it was, but Ashur's pride never would have allowed anyone else to pay. But Kiki was the one person in the world he felt comfortable being vulnerable with. Neither of them said anything as they strolled back down to the beach, the rhythm of the waves lapping at the shore the only sound in the darkness. Ashur slipped his hand into the tight back pocket of Kiki's jeans as they walked, and she pressed her body close to his, laying her head against his chest. They didn't talk much, enjoying the quiet and the simple comfort of being close to one another.

Farther down the beach they found a spot where the sand gave way to fescue, the tall grass rising all around them and the sound of night insects filling the air. Ashur spread out his jacket and lay down on his back, looking up at the night sky, as Kiki curled herself around him. He leaned over to kiss her, his hand finding the back of her head and bringing her mouth to his.

"I want to tell you something," he said quietly. "You know I don't say stuff like this lightly, but…" he paused to kiss her forehead. "I get a sense of peace when I'm around you. All the noises in my head get a little quieter. I do believe you were put into my life for a reason."

Kiki smiled at him.

"Come here, you."

Ashur caressed her hair as they kissed passionately under the stars.

The backyard was shady and cool, the perfect place for a story. Odishoo lit his pipe as the two settled into comfortable patio chairs. A CD player was set up on the small table between them, and once they were seated Odishoo pressed play. Googoosh—queen of Iranian music—began singing "Pol," one of Odishoo's favorite songs.

Ashur had never seen his father more content than when he was smoking his pipe and listening to music. It seemed as though the man got lost in a world invisible to all but Odishoo himself. He was the sort of person who could listen to the same song over and over. Ashur knew it grated on his mother's nerves; he'd heard her complain that she was bored out of her mind when his father turned on the music.

Odishoo had other favorite singers—Sattar, Ebi, Dariush, Vigen—but more than anyone else he loved Googoosh. He told Ashur that she had a rare combination of beauty and a sense of graceful seduction that could only be a gift from God. In Iran, she was every man's fantasy; she looked like a Middle Eastern Michelle Pfeiffer and made any dress she wore look like it was part of her skin. Ashur appreciated her, too.

"This is what music is," Odishoo said, closing his eyes as though hypnotized by the song. "It's supposed to grab you by the heart…and take your imagination to faraway places."

Odishoo put down the pipe and put his hands on his head, slowly brushing his hair with his hands while swaying to the beat of the song. Ashur watched him intently, curious about what was on his father's mind, ready for him to continue the story.

When the song ended and the next one came on, Odishoo opened his eyes and looked at Ashur. "What I'm about to share with you isn't for anyone else; this is private family information."

Ashur nodded solemnly.

"I won't talk about this with anyone, Dad. I promise."

Odishoo patted his son's shoulder, then leaned back in his chair.

"When I was a boy, Iran was strong and growing stronger. Not just its military—its economy and reputation were shining. You

know how some of your classmates go to Hawaii for vacation? Well, in the 1970s, wealthy people went to Iran. You were lucky if you could book a hotel room during the summer, things were so busy! Celebrities like Frank Sinatra and Elizabeth Taylor visited Iran for the lavish parties that Ambassador Ardeshir Zahedi was known for hosting. I remember my mother fluttering around the house like a butterfly when he came for dinner once."

Odishoo picked up his pipe and relit it, a dreamy smile on his face as he took a long drag of tobacco smoke.

"When we went to the beach, music was playing all around us, and the sand was packed with the most beautiful women—women who made you believe God had handcrafted each and every one of them. We used to fall in love over and over. And the food! We visited Bandar Pahlavi, by the Caspian Sea. The greatest caviar in the world! It was like something out of heaven, and your spirit would beg for more.

"This is the Iran I remember. A place of elegance and beauty. Great culture. A place people were drawn to. That was the vision of Mohammad Reza Shah Pahlavi."

Odishoo stopped for a moment, with the same faraway look on his face that Ashur had noticed in the car. He took another puff of his pipe.

"The other part of his vision concerned the military. Now, his father, Reza Shah Pahlavi, was one of the most feared men to ever rule Iran. He was a very strong military leader who was not afraid of using force if necessary to lead the country in the direction he felt it should move. He was eventually exiled, and in time his son took over, with a vision of building Iran into a country that could compete with the West.

"That is why the new Shah wanted to build Iran's military into one of the strongest in the world, with the best equipment and *training. He was so proud of Iran. And my father was proud to work for him. Though he worried for him, too. The new Shah was a brilliant man who spoke several languages—in many cases, he spoke English better than the famous TV personalities who interviewed him! He was handsome, confident, and very rich, which made him a media sensation. There had never been so much attention paid to our country.*

"Even now, I run into people who share memories of their time in Iran. They usually end up crying because of how much they miss the good old times."

Tears began to run down Odishoo's face. Ashur had heard his father talk about the heyday of Iran before, but he had never seen him so moved. It troubled him, but Ashur didn't know what he could say that might comfort him.

"It sounds like everything was going so well," Ashur said tentatively. "So then why was Grandpa so worried about what the Shah said in the interview?"

Odishoo wiped his face dry without a trace of self-consciousness.

"What my father was trying to explain to me that day was that history repeats itself. The moment anyone in charge—a king, an emperor, or a president—starts believing that he's untouchable, bad things happen. That's when you start attracting new enemies—and even worse, waking up old enemies.

"The same thing happened to the Assyrian Empire. Assyria was God's country, with some of the greatest inventions in the world! The first written language, the first iron weapons, the first telescope—all Assyrian. We built libraries at a time when reading was only for the elite, established the world's first university. The first place with paved roads and canal systems, locks with keys, calendars!"

Odishoo must have seen the pride in Ashur's face, because he held up a cautionary finger.

"But what happened to the Assyrian people?" he said to Ashur. "What happens when people start believing they no longer need God's favor? Internal turmoil...power struggles...and, eventually, the fall of the empire. The Assyrian people started to believe that they were stronger than God, so they built a tower extending into the sky. They wanted to reach up and fight him—imagine, fighting God! They thought they were invincible. And where are these proud people now? Assyria is no longer a country."

Ashur thought about all of this as his father fell silent, though he could not fully dispel the pride he still felt to belong to such an ancient and impressive people. After a minute Odishoo began to speak again.

"My father believed that three nations will combine to create one powerful empire at the end of days," Odishoo said. "Egypt, Assyria, and Israel. It never made sense to me. Those are the central places of the three main religions in the world—Islam, Christianity, and Judaism. And their followers have a history of trouble living together in peace. But who knows what will happen?

"Our people, the Assyrians, are spread out all over the world now. Punishment for our ancient hubris. Maybe one day, though, Assyria will have a country again. But we will need a great leader to rise up and bring the people together."

Ashur nodded, trying to keep up, though truthfully, he was more interested in his father's history than in prophecies of the future that seemed pretty unlikely.

"Dad, what happened after the interview?" he said. "Why did you have to leave Iran?"

CHAPTER FOUR

They drove south early the next morning, the sky a purple bruise and the freeways blissfully empty. It might just have been the cold of the wind rushing past them, but Ashur thought he could feel Kiki hugging him a bit tighter as he pushed the motorcycle faster.

The trip had been everything he had hoped it would be in the weeks he'd spent planning it. Away from the prying eyes of Glendale, away from her father and his football lackeys, Kiki had finally been able to relax and enjoy being with him, unhindered by the creeping anxiety that someone might discover them. It felt so good to be in public with her, the only sideways glances the envious looks of the other men as Ashur walked with Kiki through the little streets of Morro Bay. Then lying together on the dunes, his leather jacket wrapped tightly around both of them in the cool of the evening, with the stars twinkling above the massive rock jutting out from the water. A perfect night.

But already, winding his way back down the 101, Ashur could feel something pressing against the lingering happiness from the trip. It wouldn't be long before Kiki would head east to Providence for college. He had known that was coming and had ignored it, telling himself vaguely that they would find a way through. But now the trip felt more like the ending of something than a new beginning. Ashur revved the engine, hoping that more speed might push the unwelcome thought from his mind. That was one reason he spent so much time on his bike—for the sort of peace that could only come on the road, his mind too occupied with the long stretches of pavement before him to focus on anything else.

They stopped for breakfast near the beach south of Pismo Beach. As they sat at a table outside, Kiki cradled her coffee with both hands, a small smile on her face as the steam rose off her cup. Ashur picked at his muffin and looked out over the water.

"You're quiet this morning," she said. Ashur tried a smile.

"Just tired." Then his smile deepened, remembering the night before. "Worth it, though."

"It better be," she said, reaching out and slapping him lightly on the arm. But the look on her face changed, somewhere between thoughtful and concerned. "Have you thought any more about what you're going to do?"

Ashur shrugged and spread his arms out wide. Technically he was free now—no longer shackled to Rose and the house he had been waiting to leave for the last six years. But it was funny, the way limitless options could feel an awful lot like no possibilities at all.

"I'll figure something out."

"You could go back to school," Kiki said.

"Yeah? You think your dad's ready to give me a second chance?"

He meant for it to sound playful, but it came out halfway mean, like he was somehow blaming Kiki for what her father had done. But to her credit, she shook it off—he liked that about Kiki, the way she never assumed the worst about him, even if he deserved it sometimes.

"Somewhere else, then," Kiki said. "Or…I don't know. Get your GED. Figure out college somewhere. You're smart, Ashur. Too smart to spend more time at that burger joint."

Ashur winced. That much, at least, they could agree on. The job at Bob's Big Boy had been meant as a temporary thing, an after-school gig to bring in some badly needed cash. But it had been a few years now; he'd taken on more hours once he had nothing better to do, but whatever paltry raises he'd gotten weren't enough to make up for the growing feeling that he was slowly wasting his potential.

"Don't worry about that. Once I pick up my paycheck, I'm done with that place."

"Good," Kiki said, the smile coming back to her face. She had a beautiful smile; Ashur was going to miss that once she was gone. He reached out and took her hand, her fingers a bit cold in the morning chill. Then he noticed that she was looking over his shoulder.

"What is it?" he said, turning around.

"Nothing," she said.

"Come on."

She hesitated for a moment.

"Did you notice anything weird when we were on the road?"

"Weird like what?"

Kiki shrugged.

"I'm probably just imagining things. But I kept seeing this one car on the road."

"It must have been going pretty fast, to keep up with us."

"That's what was weird about it. We'd speed ahead, it would fall behind, and then a few minutes later it would be there again."

Ashur frowned. He was usually the one who noticed things like that, people and patterns that didn't match. But this morning he hadn't seen anything. Then again, his mind had been on other things.

"What did it look like?"

Kiki jutted her chin forward.

"Like the car that just disappeared around that corner. Dark sedan. Not black, exactly... I don't know how to describe it."

Ashur thought for a moment. Who could possibly want to follow him? No one he knew cared enough to do anything like that, and even if Rose was having second thoughts about him leaving, she wasn't capable of hiring someone to tail him. Still, something in Kiki's description was stirring something in him, but he couldn't quite pin down what.

"Think your dad is on to us?" he said to Kiki, grinning.

"Oh, shut up! See, this is why I didn't want to say anything."

"I'm glad you did," Ashur said, bending over and giving her a kiss. "And I'll keep my eyes out for it."

Kiki nodded and kissed him back.

"Yes, you will."

They hugged the coast all the way back to Glendale, Ashur weaving in and out of the growing morning traffic. Every time he saw a dark sedan, he scanned it quickly for some flicker of recognition, but the sea of black Camrys and dark-blue BMWs blended in seamlessly with the rest of the California commuters. Every once in a while he would tilt his head back toward Kiki, as though to ask if she'd seen anything. But each time she just hugged him tighter—nothing yet. Maybe she had been imagining things, anxious now that their dream date was over and she was returning to her normal life. It wasn't typical of her, sneaking out and lying to her parents, and no matter how good it felt, Ashur thought that maybe she was feeling a little guilty. She told him sometimes that she envied his freedom, and what he didn't say was how much he wished sometimes that his father was still there to dissuade him from his worst impulses.

It was midmorning by the time they made it back to Glendale, the streets beginning to grow crowded with weekend shoppers. He knew that Kiki was nervous, being back in town on the back of his bike, but in her motorcycle helmet no one could recognize her. As they crawled down the main drag, he looked up to where Abraham Lincoln had been waving from his billboard the day before. Today there was a man in a toga, scratching intently on a slate tablet that he carried in his hand, every once in a while looking distractedly at the pedestrians below and offering a cursory wave before returning to his work. It made Ashur chuckle to see it—they really were lifelike, those holograms, all the more so when they swapped out a politician for a man who looked as though he didn't have the time to be engaged in public relations, so busy was he exploring the truths of the universe. He tapped Kiki's leg and pointed up at the billboard.

"That's a new one!" she shouted over the sound of the traffic around them. "Who is it? Archimedes?"

"Plato," Ashur said, the man's name suddenly illuminated on the sign behind him. He wondered how the real Plato, who had spent so much time pondering the nature of reality, would feel about being reproduced as a hologram, hawking some massive corporation's image to shoppers on their way to buy a new pair of sneakers. Then again, maybe the man would be fascinated by all of it, seeing how far humanity had come in the thousands of years since he had been alive.

Ashur pulled up behind the library, and Kiki gave his torso one final squeeze before swinging down off the bike. She looked over both shoulders before removing her helmet and shaking out her hair.

"I'm going to be feeling that ride in my legs for days," she said.

"Now look who has the dirty mind," Ashur said, as Kiki stuck out her tongue at him. "No sign of that weird car?"

"Nope," she said. "Not once I said something to you. I was probably just imagining things—it was still pretty dark out."

Ashur put his helmet on the bike and slipped out of his leather jacket—it was hotter inland, now that the sun was full up, and he could feel the heat of the day beating down on him.

"Thanks, Ashur," Kiki said. "For everything."

Ashur hesitated, trying to find the right words to say. He wanted to tell Kiki how much she meant to him, and how much he was going to miss her when she was gone. He wanted to tell her that he was tired of losing the people in his life who mattered most to him, and that he was scared he would soon have to add her to that list. It wasn't that he minded being alone—most people, he had found, were more trouble than they were worth. But knowing that only made him want to be with Kiki more. And he couldn't think of a way to say all that without scaring her off, so instead he nodded and gave her a kiss.

"Where are you going to go?" Kiki asked, pulling back but keeping her arms around him.

"I don't know," Ashur said. "But I'll figure something out."

"I can help you, if you need it. I have some money saved up…"

"Keep it," Ashur said with a sad smile. "I'll be okay, really."

Kiki smiled.

"You know what? I think you will be. I've had this weird feeling the whole trip that something good is going to happen to you for a change. I don't know what it is, but I think it's going to help you, with whatever comes next."

"Yeah?" Ashur said. "I hope you're right."

"Don't worry. I usually am," Kiki said, grinning and coming in for another kiss. And then she turned around and danced up the back steps, throwing one last look over her shoulder at Ashur before disappearing into the library. He kept his eyes on the door for a few seconds after it closed behind her, trying to shake the thought that he didn't know when he would see her again.

Then he sat back on the bike and started to formulate a plan.

He had his father's motorcycle and half a tank of gas. He had a backpack full of clothes and his father's gun stuffed into an old T-shirt. He needed a shower, and a better job, and a new life. He didn't know where any of those things would come from. But first he needed cash. And that, at least, he knew where to find. So he fired up the engine and started heading west, toward Burbank, to pick up what he hoped would be the last paycheck of his food service career.

Somewhere around Griffith Park, Ashur thought he saw a dark sedan in one of his rearview mirrors. He slowed a bit, trying to get a better look, hoping the car might overtake him. But the car—a sleek import, from the quick glance he stole, painted a shade of almost midnight purple—turned off at the next exit. Ashur shook his head—he was glad Kiki had said something to him, as it clearly had been bothering her, but he hoped he wouldn't be spending the next few days on the road scanning for ghosts.

The classic neon sign rose high above the road, unilluminated in the bright morning sun. The statue of the mascot in his checkerboard overalls and shellacked pompadour stood vigil outside the entrance, burger held aloft in his right hand. Ashur typically worked behind the scenes, too surly and honest to be much good with the customers, but when things got busy or another server called in sick, his boss sometimes sent him out front, confident that Ashur was at least competent enough to remember people's orders and bring them their food on time. He had caught his reflection in the window, carrying a burger just like the mascot, and it made him shudder each time.

Ashur parked in the back—the lot was mostly empty at this time in the morning, still too early for the lunch rush. He couldn't tell if that would make it easier or harder to tell his boss that he was through—and only here to collect his paycheck. His mind was already on the road, heading east to somewhere he could start over.

The kitchen was hot and loud, line cooks frying eggs and griddling hamburger patties. Lauren, his favorite waitress, had a plate in her hand and was glowering at one of the cooks for overdoing a burger. She brightened when she saw Ashur, sweeping a strand of blonde hair that had fallen into her face behind her ear.

"My favorite runner!" she said. "You pick up an extra shift or something?"

"Just grabbing my paycheck," he said with a little smile.

"You sure you don't want to stick around and work the griddle for a bit? Would be nice to have someone who can actually read a ticket."

The cook rolled his eyes and pulled out a fresh patty as Lauren winked and headed back into the dining room.

Ashur weaved his way through the familiar sounds and smells until he came to the manager's office, its door cracked open. He knocked and waited for the gruff voice to tell him to come in.

"Yonan!" Joey barked, swiveling around in his chair. The manager was a big man, forehead shiny with sweat and shirt-sleeves rolled up his meaty forearms. Most of the guys in the kitchen were scared of him, but he had never seemed all that tough to Ashur. Joey looked over at the time sheet up on the wall. "I don't have you scheduled for a shift today. And if you're trying to pick one up, you're shit out of luck. Fully staffed."

"I just came for my paycheck," Ashur said. Joey nodded and started leafing through a big stack of papers piled precariously on his desk.

Ashur wondered if he really needed to tell Joey that he was quitting, or if the man would even notice when he stopped showing up for work. But lying by omission still felt like lying, and Ashur Yonan did not lie. "I'm actually leaving town. I figured I should let you know."

The manager stopped what he was doing, his finger frozen where it had been flipping through the papers in search of Ashur's paycheck.

"So that's the thanks I get, huh?" Joey said. "No two weeks, no nothing? Some kind of drive-by see-ya-later, after all I've done for you?"

Ashur gritted his teeth and adjusted the backpack slung over his shoulder. People like Joey took the tiny modicum of power that their position gave them and milked it for everything it was worth. As far as Ashur could remember, all Joey had ever done for him was jerk around his hours, stiff him on overtime, and then act like he'd done him some big favor when he gave him the paycheck he'd earned every two weeks. He wasn't sure what kind of thank-you, exactly, Joey thought he deserved.

"You know, kid, not every boss is going to be as good as me," Joey continued. "Some real assholes out there. But I guess you're gonna have to find that out the hard way, huh?"

"Just give me my paycheck, okay?"

"Ohhh, a tough guy now? Big tough Ashur Yonan, with his fancy lion tattoo and a fresh scowl for every customer. Well, let me tell you something, kid…"

But whatever words of wisdom Joey intended to impart to him were interrupted by the sound of a scream coming from the dining room, and then Joey was pushing past Ashur and out the door to discover what had broken the morning tranquility in his restaurant.

Ashur closed the door behind him—he didn't need anyone else coming by to tell him what sort of mistake he was making. He went over to the desk where Joey had been and started rifling through the stack of papers to see if he could find his paycheck. The more he thought about it, the more he became convinced it was time to leave the Big Boy before Joey said something that would make the idea of punching his boss too irresistible to pass up. Whatever new life Ashur was starting for himself, he didn't need an assault charge making things that much harder for him.

But after a few minutes, another scream came, this one more urgent and terrified than before. Ashur abandoned the papers and made his way out of the office.

The kitchen was eerily empty, the sounds of the cooks gone silent and burgers still sizzling on the griddle making their way past well done and into burnt territory. Something was clearly wrong. Moving more cautiously now, Ashur went to the swinging door between the kitchen and the dining room, peering carefully through the little porthole into the restaurant.

There were two gunmen: one standing by the front door, the ski mask a little haphazard on his face and a pistol in his hand, the other standing on a table in the middle of the restaurant with his back to the kitchen. Ashur could see that the kitchen staff had been rounded up and were standing on one side of the restaurant, the handful of patrons on the other. Joey was in the middle of the room with his hands in the air, the circles of sweat under his armpits even bigger now than they typically were, and a look of absolute terror on his face. But Ashur took no pleasure from his former boss's fear and felt something in his stomach drop as the gunman on the table started waving around a big revolver.

"The register, dumbass!" the man on the table was saying to Joey. "Are you stupid or something? Move, lardo!"

Joey's eyes went wide, and then the manager hastily made his way over to the cash register, fumbling with the keys.

"The hell is taking so long?" said the guy by the front door.

"Maybe he just needs a little motivation…" the man on the table said. He lowered his revolver in Joey's direction and fired off a round, the noise deafening in the restaurant as the bullet lodged itself in the wall a few feet above Joey's head. A new set of screams issued from the far side of the restaurant as Joey dived under the counter.

"Stand up, dammit!" the man on the table said. By the way he said it, Ashur couldn't help but think that the man was enjoying himself. There was nothing panicked or rushed, and even his frenzied shouts sounded more like a fan yelling insults at an opposing team at a basketball game than a robber eager to be done with the job and away before the cops showed up. What

Ashur couldn't tell was whether that made the man more or less dangerous.

Joey got unsteadily to his feet and started punching away at the register again. The manager's shoulders were shaking—he was crying.

"What is it, broken?" the robber on the table said.

"You…you…need to make a purchase to open the register," Joey blubbered.

The robber on the table laughed out loud. It was not a pretty sound. And Ashur remembered that he had his father's gun in his backpack.

While the gunman hurled insults at the manager and made an idiotic joke about ordering a strawberry milkshake, Ashur made his way as quietly as he could back into the office. Frantically he unzipped the backpack and dug down through the layers of clothing until his hand found the familiar shape of the Baretta through the old T-shirt. He pulled it out and unwrapped it, stuck it into the back of his jeans, and made his way quietly back to the swinging door.

Joey had finally succeeded in getting the register open and was now fumbling through the bills. The man on the table was waving the revolver around, demanding a doggie bag, and sounding to Ashur like he was having way too much fun with all of this. The man by the door seemed tense, looking between the kitchen staff on one side of the room and the patrons on the other.

"Come on, man," he said to his partner. "Let's get the money and blow!"

Ashur held his breath. There were two of them and only one of him. If all they wanted was the cash, then he should just let them leave, despite every instinct in his body telling him to burst through the door. He had seen the movies: the way the robbers say that all they need is the money, and how things go sideways when someone decides to be a hero. He didn't want anyone getting hurt just because it made him feel like a coward to hide in waiting. So he stayed where he was, teeth gritted, watching the scene in the restaurant unfold.

Joey brought the cash in a to-go bag over to the man on the table, his arm shaking as he held it aloft, not capable of looking the man in the eye. The robber took the bag from him and threw it across the room to his partner.

"Wait a minute," the man on the table said. "I ordered a strawberry milkshake. Where the hell is my milkshake?"

Joey got a panicked look on his face and instinctively turned back to look at the door to the kitchen. For a moment he locked eyes with Ashur, his face full of fear and pleading. Ashur held his breath—the last thing he needed was for the manager to blow his cover. He said a brief, silent prayer that Joey wasn't dumb or scared enough to do something like that.

"Nah, I'm just messing with you," the robber said, jumping down from the table. The sound of his feet hitting the floor made everyone jump. "Dairy gives me the shits. Ha!"

"Can we go now?" said his partner, a hand already resting on the door. The gunman held up a finger.

"Calm down. I see a few other things I might like to have before we leave."

Something about the way the man said this made Ashur's blood run cold. If they were just after the money, they should be leaving now, hightailing it out of the restaurant—and the state, if they were smart—before someone outside noticed something was wrong. Clearly that's what the robber by the door wanted, too. But the gunman who had been on the table was now pointing his revolver in a casual, almost lazy way, over toward the far side of the restaurant. From his perch behind the door, Ashur couldn't see what exactly the man was looking at. But what he could see was the way the look in the eyes of all the kitchen staff across the far wall was changing. Some of them showed a new fear, sharper and more terrified than before. Others had a hardness coming over them, a set to their jaw that Ashur recognized. Each of them seemed to be performing a private calculation, of their odds of surviving if things went to shit. And whether anything they did might change those chances.

"Come here," the gunman said. "That's right. You. The blonde. Right over here. Don't be scared. Come on."

He was speaking in a softer voice, one that Ashur did not trust at all. It was the way he could imagine the man speaking to a frightened dog before kicking it again.

Lauren came forward, her stride much steadier than Joey's had been. She was glowering at the gunman, apparently unconcerned about the revolver currently pointed lazily in her direction. Her arms were folded across her chest, and she looked furious.

"Get a load of you," the gunman said. Ashur ground his teeth harder and pulled the Beretta from his waistband. He looked around the restaurant, saw the unease rising. The man by the door was looking around, waving his gun back and forth, but he had already asked to leave. He had the feel of a lackey to Ashur, but he couldn't tell whether the man would be loyal enough to stick around to help his friend.

"What do you say you and me get out of here, huh?" the gunman said to Lauren. "I take you on a date. A real nice one. Not in a dump like this. Trust me, I've got the money for it."

He laughed, apparently impressed with himself. The man by the door was practically hopping from one foot to another. The gunman was getting closer to Lauren now, the barrel of his gun nearly touching her as he walked around her. Ashur closed his eyes and thought about Kiki telling him an hour ago that something good was going to happen to him. He really hoped she wasn't wrong.

He pressed his fingertips to the door, opening it as quietly as he could, his gun drawn. He stayed in a crouch as he stepped slowly out into the dining room. His finger reached for the safety, clicking the little lever off. The pistol felt so light in his hands—adrenaline, he guessed; he had heard about things like that, all the senses heightened in a moment of danger. He wondered if he could risk chambering a round, or if the sound would be too much. He had a plan—a loose one, full of things that could go wrong. But he wasn't going to sit back and watch any more.

And then he realized, with a sinking sensation in the pit of his stomach, that the clip was still sitting at the bottom of his backpack, wrapped in a separate T-shirt with the box of ammunition. He was holding an unloaded gun.

Ashur allowed himself a brief moment of panic. Decided there was no time to go back, now that he was already in the dining room. And then he pressed on.

Still in a crouch, he trained his pistol on the man by the door, waiting for him to notice him. He was praying that the guy wouldn't just start shooting, that the sight of a gun pointed at him would be enough to convince him that it wasn't worth it. The man was scanning the room, starting to look a bit desperate, the uncertain posture of lookouts and accomplices suddenly wondering what they had gotten themselves into—and who they had chosen for partners.

Finally, he turned and saw Ashur. He froze, the gun still in his hand but not pointed at Ashur yet.

Ashur tried not to exhale too hard. "Go," he mouthed to the man, nodding at the door behind him.

For a terrible moment, all there was on the man's face was a look of profound confusion, the sort that could turn deadly at any moment. A few of the kitchen staff had noticed Ashur, too, and he wondered how many of them would jump in to help if it came to that.

And then the robber, realizing all at once that he had been given an unexpected out, pushed his way through the door and took off running, the doggie bag of money still in his hand.

At the sound of the door jangling open, the remaining gunman whirled around, training his revolver on the door. It was just long enough for Ashur to get behind him, his own gun raised, and yell, "*Freeze!*"

The gunman paused for a moment but did not drop the revolver.

"Stay right where you are," Ashur said. "I've got you covered."

"Who the hell are you?" the man said. He almost sounded amused.

"I'm the guy pointing a gun at you."

"You're not a cop," the man said. "I speak cop. You're talking in a different dialect."

"Drop your gun!" Ashur said. He could sense the confusion in the room around him, the heightened awareness of a new gun, the possibility of imminent violence.

"Yeah, that's not happening. Tell me who the hell you are."

"I'm serious!" Ashur said.

"Well, that's adorable," the gunman said. "But seriously, who are you? Some kind of vigilante? What, did someone illuminate the secret asshole signal above the city and you came running?"

"No one needs to get hurt," Ashur said. "Just leave, all right?"

The man turned around, entirely unconcerned about the gun pointed at him, and for a horrible moment Ashur was sure the man knew the Beretta wasn't loaded. His eyes were gray and sparkling behind the ski mask as he aimed his revolver at Ashur's chest.

"Tell me your name, kid."

Ashur tasted something bitter in his mouth, felt the rapid beating of his heart. He was staring down the barrel of a loaded revolver held by an unstable psychopath, his only protection the two pounds of steel in his hand and the balls to pretend that it could do anything. He swallowed a mouthful of spit and wondered why the guy cared so much who he was. Maybe he just liked knowing the names of the people he killed.

"Ashur Yonan."

"See?" the gunman said. "That wasn't so hard, was it?"

The man turned and blew a kiss to Lauren, who glowered at him. Then he swept his arms around the room, as though coming back onstage for a final curtain call, and ran out of the restaurant.

For a moment, everyone in the restaurant was silent. And then Joey started weeping.

Ashur realized he was still pointing the unloaded gun at the front door. He let it sag down by his side, his body still thrumming with adrenaline. In the distance he could hear the sound of police sirens approaching.

A sort of happy pandemonium broke out in the restaurant. Everyone was hugging and crying, the shift from victim to survivor so sudden. Lauren ran across the room and threw her arms around Ashur. Her body was shaking as she held him, all the steel in her gone. He held her with one arm, his other hand still holding his father's gun.

"Where the hell did you come from?" she said.

"I just got lucky," he said. "You were the one who stared him down."

"I was terrified!"

"I couldn't tell."

She laughed a little at this, the sound coming out choked through her sobs. Ashur felt strangely calm and wondered if he was in shock.

The sound of the sirens was getting louder, red and blue lights beginning to shine through the front windows. Ashur looked down at the gun still in his hand and wondered briefly if he should hide it somewhere. But the whole restaurant had seen him—there was no use pretending otherwise. So he bent down and put it on the floor, kicked it toward the door, and waited.

Three cops burst through the door, their service weapons drawn, yelling for everyone to get on the ground. The kitchen staff all dove down, hands above their heads, praying no one started shooting. The customers stood indignantly on the other side of the room, half of them sort of kneeling, the others talking over one another, each trying to tell their story. Joey was on the floor, sobbing into his hands, apparently unaware that the police had arrived. Ashur slowly lowered himself and

Lauren to the ground, being gentle with her as she held on to him desperately.

After a minute of chaos, it became clear to the cops that the threat had passed. Soon the restaurant was swarming with police, all going around and taking statements. Someone put on a fresh pot of coffee. One of the kitchen guys went into the back and brought out pies, and people began eating with their hands, ravenously happy to be alive. Ashur stayed where he was, sitting on the floor next to Lauren, watching as person after person pointed toward him.

"He saved us," he heard one woman say. The people around her were nodding in agreement, talking over one another to explain what had happened. Nearly everyone was looking at him now. Ashur felt exhausted, totally drained, but managed a weak smile and to hold up a hand. Mostly he just wanted to get his paycheck and leave. But he was pretty sure that wasn't going to happen.

A police sergeant came over to him after a few minutes, a small smile on his face. He looked down at Lauren.

"Do you mind giving us a couple of minutes to talk, miss?" he said. Lauren nodded, gave Ashur's hand a squeeze, and went back behind the counter to pour herself a cup of coffee.

Ashur got up—he had a few inches on the sergeant once he was standing. The cop nodded over to one of the booths on the far side of the restaurant, and then two of them walked over. Ashur could feel most of the eyes in the dining room on him. He had never particularly liked attention; usually it meant something bad had happened.

The cop sat on one side of the booth, motioned for Ashur to sit down.

"Hell of a thing you did today," the cop said.

Ashur shrugged. "I just got lucky."

"Lucky. Yeah, right. Most people? They stay in the back. Find an office, lock the door. Or else hightail it out the back door. It sounds to me like you put your neck on the line to try and save these people. Whatever luck you got? I'd say you deserved it."

Ashur nodded, trying to take all this in.

"Now here's the tricky part," the cop said, shifting a little on the vinyl seat. "I'm really, really hoping you can tell me you've got your concealed carry permit."

Ashur frowned across the table. There was a pleading look in the cop's eye, and Ashur wondered whether, if he told the man he did, he would let the whole thing drop.

"No, sir," Ashur said. The sergeant winced.

"Yeah. I was afraid of that. The gun yours, at least?"

"My father's."

The cop was nodding, working through some kind of calculation in his mind.

"Look, kid. This thing you did today? I've been working this job for twenty years, and I've never seen anything like it. You're a hero in my book, no matter what."

He sucked in some air through his teeth.

"But we've got a restaurant full of witnesses who saw you waving around an unlicensed gun. A story like that? Only a matter of time before it gets out. And when it does, people start asking questions. So let's just skip all that and start figuring out how we can make this thing work, all right?"

Ashur stiffened in his seat. He could tell the cop was in a tight spot. But something about all this seemed unfair—that after risking his life to save these people, he would end up in trouble. He felt an old, familiar anger rising up in him—he was back in middle school, waiting outside the principal's office, getting sent home for protecting a poor kid being bullied. He closed his eyes for a moment, tried to hear his father's voice telling him all over again that fair didn't account for too much in life.

"Am I under arrest, officer?"

The sergeant inhaled sharply.

"I'd rather not. We have you come down to the station, answer a couple questions." He paused for a moment, looked Ashur in the eyes across the table. "But I can't just let you walk out of here, kid. Do you understand me?"

"Yeah," Ashur said, a new coolness coming over him. "I understand."

The cop nodded, looked around the room.

"Okay. Let's go."

They stood up from the booth. Ashur held his head up, tried not to make eye contact with anyone. But Lauren saw him, and hurried across the room.

"Where are you going?" she asked.

"It's all right," Ashur said. Lauren frowned, and the people nearby stopped what they were doing and turned to watch.

"Officer, he saved us," she said. "You understand that, right?"

"I do," the sergeant said. "Believe me."

"So he's not going to get in trouble?"

There was a growing unease around the room, people murmuring to one another now as they saw Ashur being led out. He was grateful that they hadn't cuffed him, had allowed him the dignity to at least leave under his own power. But the others in the room didn't seem to see it that way.

"It's all right," he said again, louder this time, looking around the room. "Everything is going to be fine."

He almost believed it.

Lauren stepped back, still frowning, as Ashur and the sergeant walked across the restaurant. In the corner, someone started clapping. Soon the whole restaurant was applauding, people whistling and shouting out encouragement. People Ashur had worked with for years; strangers he had never seen before in his life, and likely would never see again. All of them understood what he had done for them, and he got a tiny bit of satisfaction from that before he remembered the raft of shit still before him.

The sergeant led him out of the restaurant and into the waiting squad car.

Ashur had been sitting in the windowless room for hours. He had said no the first two times they offered him something to drink; he had finished the can of Coke half an hour ago. The men who interviewed him had been polite. They cycled through, asked the same questions in different ways, looked back at the two-way mirror with their eyebrows raised from time to time. And Ashur, who did not lie, had told them the truth.

The gun was his father's. No, he didn't have a license for concealed carry. The gun hadn't been loaded when he came into the dining room. And he had no idea why the gunman had been so intent on knowing his name.

For such a simple story, the cops seemed to be having a hard time understanding.

What was he doing at the restaurant on a day he wasn't working?

He was picking up his paycheck.

Why did he have the gun with him?

Because it was the only thing his father had left him, other than the motorcycle, and he didn't want to start a new life without it.

Why was he leaving town, the state, his mother, his girlfriend?

Because there was nothing left for him anymore in California.

Where was he going?

He honestly hadn't gotten that far.

At first, Ashur had only been worried about the charges for having a gun that wasn't his. This was California; he knew they were trying to crack down on unlicensed guns. Still, he had hoped they might go a little easy on him, given that he had saved a restaurant full of people.

But now he was starting to think there might be a whole different kind of trouble. Could the cops really think he had anything to do with the armed robbery? It was such a crazy notion, but once the thought had come into his head, he had a hard time dismissing it. They still hadn't charged him with a crime; he still hadn't asked to speak with a lawyer. But the more time went on, the more he was wondering whether that had been a mistake. He had believed the sergeant when he told him, in the squad car on the way to the precinct, that they were on his side. Maybe he had been too naïve.

He was grateful, at least, to have seen his eighteenth birthday come and go. He couldn't imagine them calling Rose, the way she would hold this over him, another sign of all the ways he was wasting his life.

The door to the interrogation room opened again. In walked a new man, and immediately Ashur could tell there was something different about him. His clothing, for one: a black suit, beautifully tailored and expensive looking, way beyond the pay grade of the average detective, with a dark shirt and a deep purple tie. He was older, in his early sixties maybe, with salt-and-pepper hair and lightly tanned skin. But more than his physical appearance, there was something about this man that didn't remind Ashur of any cop he'd ever interacted with before. A *warmth*—there was no other word for it—radiated from him. Warmth that Ashur could practically feel. Ashur straightened up in his chair.

"Ashur Yonan," the man said. Ashur nodded. "You've had quite a day."

"You're not a detective," Ashur said.

The man smiled a little. "No. I assume you've had your fill of detectives for one day?"

"I already told them everything. But they keep asking me the same questions."

"You're honest. A good quality. And not a common one for most people sitting where you are now."

"They think I'm lying?" Ashur said. Through the exhaustion he could feel himself growing angry again—what more did he need to say for them to believe him?

But the man across from him shook his head. "Not quite. But the men who interviewed you have done this work for many years. They know patterns. Most of the things they see fit neatly with something they've seen before. Your case is…unique."

Ashur frowned. "What do you mean?"

"Tell me," the man said, taking a seat and clasping his hands together on the table. "Is there anything about today that strikes you as strange?"

"I've already told them everything that happened."

"Indulge me," the man said. "Please."

Ashur sighed. He wanted to be done with this, to go home. But as soon as he had this thought, he realized he didn't even know where home was anymore. He would not be going back to Rose; he had made up his mind about that. But where else was there?

He shook his head to clear it, and then thought hard about the day. "One of the men who robbed the restaurant," he said.

"What about him?"

"He was acting oddly. Erratically."

The man nodded, waiting for him to continue.

"He wanted to know my name," Ashur said. "It seemed like he was waiting for that."

The man smiled. "Yes. Several of the witnesses reported the same thing. Does that strike you as unusual?"

"I don't know. I've never stared down an armed robber at gunpoint before."

The man laughed. "No. I suppose not."

"Why did he want to know who I am?"

The man held up a finger. "That is why you've been here for hours. The men on the other side of that mirror," and here he turned and waved back at his own reflection, "have been trying to figure it out. They will eventually decide it was random—a bad batch of meth taken before a robbery, a schizophrenic episode, something like that. The people who perform armed robberies of restaurants aren't typically the most stable population."

"But you don't think it was random."

The man shrugged. "Who can say?" he said. But the look in his eye made Ashur certain that he knew more than he was admitting to.

"Who are you?" Ashur said.

"My name is Zaya," the man said. "I represent an organization committed to the enrichment of a select few highly promising students. But all you need to know for now is that I am your best chance of walking out of this room without a felony weapons charge."

Ashur's eyes grew wide. The other men who had interviewed him had been so focused on getting his story straight that they hadn't even discussed charges, or likely punishments. It had been the unspoken threat, lingering in the background of every conversation. The man saw his expression and continued.

"I don't mean to scare you, Ashur, but it's important to me that you understand your options. You can get yourself a lawyer. They will recommend a plea bargain. You're an adult, so you will serve jail time in a medium-security state penitentiary. You will have a felony record that will follow you wherever you go afterwards, no matter how sympathetic your future employers will be when they hear your story.

"But you're young. You will be released early for good behavior. You will rebuild your life. It will take time, but with persistence and hard work, you can still make something of yourself. You can even become the poster child for Second Amendment activists, if you like—the case that proves that good guys with guns are the only antidote to bad guys with guns. Appear on the news every time another gunman shoots up a Walmart, retelling your story. If you want that."

Ashur closed his eyes. None of that sounded appealing to him, but he couldn't see what other choice he had. He had made his decision in the restaurant—he would do the same thing again, if he had the chance, rather than sit back and let the gunman do God knows what to Lauren. If this was the consequence, then he could live with that.

"Or…?" he said.

"Or you come with me, right now. We walk out of this room together. No charges will ever be filed. Your record will be clean. And, more importantly, you will be given an opportunity to discover your true potential."

Ashur opened his eyes and looked across the table. "What's the catch?"

Zaya smiled. "No catch. What you did today was remarkable, Ashur. You had the courage to act, the quick wits to come up with a plan. And in the aftermath, you were steadfast and honest, not shying away from your decisions. You showed true character. We would like to help you develop that character even further. That is…if you agree to come with me."

Ashur stared across the table. The offer that Zaya was making seemed too good to be true. Surely this had to be some kind of trick.

"The members of my organization feel you have a calling to do something great with your life, Ashur. We want to help you find out what it is." Zaya reached across the table and squeezed Ashur's shoulder, and he couldn't help but hear the echo of what Kiki had told him the night before, and everything his father had said before he died. "But it'll be up to you to have the courage to figure out your calling."

Ashur sighed. "I'm getting a little tired of hearing how great I'm supposed to be."

Zaya laughed. "I consider that an excellent trait. Most people I know can't get enough of hearing just that." Now a serious look came across the man's face. "You find yourself at a breaking point, Ashur. What you do next will dictate the rest of your life. I can give you an opportunity, but what you do with it will be up to you."

Ashur took a deep breath. He looked around the windowless room, at his own reflection in the two-way mirror.

"I don't have much of a choice, do I?" he said.

"You always have a choice," Zaya said. "This one is simply much easier than the others you've had to make today."

Ashur looked at the man sitting across from him. He didn't like the feeling of being trapped—or forced into a decision with no good alternatives.

"Can I have a minute to think about it?"

"You can," Zaya said. "But will it change anything?"

Ashur closed his eyes. Could he call Kiki, talk it through with her? He tried to imagine what she would say when he laid it all out for her. Wasn't she the one who had said he would end up one of two ways: in jail, or doing something great? He was already headed to jail before this man had arrived. Maybe this was his chance for something different.

"All right. I'll come with you."

Zaya smiled broadly. He turned to the mirror, flashed a quick thumbs-up. Ashur could hear the door to the room unlocking with a dull metallic *thunk*. *Who is this man?* he wondered. *And what have I gotten myself into?*

"Excellent. Welcome, Ashur Yonan, to the Academy."

"We didn't leave Iran right away," said Odishoo. "It took years before we came to America. My mother didn't want us to leave without my father, and he had important work to do. He thought it was his duty to prepare the Shah to face his enemies."

"Like who?" Ashur said.

"Remember how I said that it's dangerous for leaders to believe they're untouchable? Well, by 1973, the Shah believed he was in-

vincible—and more importantly, the rest of the world was starting to worry he might be right. He'd built one of the most powerful militaries in the world and controlled access to a great deal of oil. When the oil crisis hit, countries like the United Kingdom and the United States grew even more concerned about the Shah's power. And then he gave an interview—"

"Wait," Ashur interrupted. "Another interview?"

"This one came first," Odishoo said. "He laid out his plan—Iran would become one of the most prosperous and powerful countries, and soon. He criticized Britain, too—in spite of them being one of his best customers and allies. He called their culture 'permissive' and 'undisciplined' and said the British would go bankrupt because they didn't work hard enough. They never forgot what he said."

Ashur shifted in his seat, trying to fit all the pieces together. "But why do you remember it?"

"I snuck out of bed to watch it. Your grandfather had some colleagues over to our house. I eavesdropped. I should have known better, but I was curious. Maybe you can understand that."

Ashur blushed, thinking of all the nights he'd strained to hear his parents arguing, trying to understand what could make them so angry with one another.

"My father and some of the other men were concerned," Odishoo said. "The Shah had been popular in the sixties, even in America and Britain. But by the seventies they saw him as a threat. Iran had become a nation you wouldn't want to go to war against. Allies may be friendly when a country is small and weak, but things change when that nation grows powerful. That is what my father was worried about, and why he wanted the Shah to be more careful about what he said openly."

Ashur shook his head. "But, Dad, if Iran was so powerful and feared, how could it fall?"

"Good question." Odishoo fiddled with the CD player for a moment. A song by Moein, "Isfahan," began to play. Odishoo sighed.

"I went to Isfahan. With my parents. I was a kid, and we took a vacation. Those were good times. I miss them."

He looked back at Ashur. "What causes empires to fall?"

Ashur thought hard, going back in his mind through all the books he'd read over the last year—books his father had picked out for him, telling him he thought he was ready to understand them now. It had filled Ashur with pride, receiving those books, and made him concentrate hard even when the reading was challenging.

"When they lose a war?"

"Is that a question or an answer?"

"Answer."

"Excellent. What else?"

"The military can turn on the rulers."

"Good. And then there are financial crises—I don't think you've read about that yet. But know that hungry people are angry people. But here is the strange truth: none of these things happened in Iran."

Odishoo paused here, took a sip of tea. Ashur followed suit and wondered what happened next.

"There is an old military strategy," Odishoo said. "One that is very effective at overwhelming a strong enemy, if done subtly. It has caused many wars, destroyed countries, families, even religions. It's a method that creates an imaginary enemy, drawing attention away from whoever has created the deception. Then the deceiver is free to act, unnoticed, against the enemy."

"What's the method?" Ashur asked.

"Psychological warfare," Odishoo answered gravely. "That's exactly what they did to one of the most beautiful places in the world."

CHAPTER FIVE

The guard at the gate took a long look down at Ashur's ID, and then back up at him. Ashur stared back, meeting the man's eyes—he'd had enough of men in uniforms trying to intimidate him for one day. The guard glared for a moment, and then laughed before handing back the license.

"Found yourself another live one, Zaya," he said before waving them through.

They were at a little airstrip inland, a few hangars and a long stretch of asphalt, scrubland as far as the eye could see beyond the chain-link fence. Ashur had said nothing the whole drive as Zaya guided the sleek sedan over the California highways. He felt his shoulders tighten as the adrenaline of the robbery and the interrogation room slowly seeped from his body.

Zaya drove over the tarmac toward a waiting jet, its engines already thrumming. He parked just beyond the steps leading up to the cabin and turned off the car.

"Promise me something before we get on that plane, Ashur," Zaya said.

Ashur nodded—of course there would be conditions, given what Zaya was promising him. He waited to hear what the man would ask, or perhaps he would offer some words of advice or explanation for how all of this had happened.

"Please don't bother the pilots with questions," he said. "They won't tell you anything, and it gets old for them to be pestered by new recruits."

Zaya led Ashur up the steps to the jet.

I woke up this morning not knowing where I was going to be by the end of the day, Ashur thought to himself. *But if you had told me that I was going to be heading there on a private plane? I wouldn't have believed it.*

But then again, nothing else about the day—the robbery, the interrogation, and Zaya's mysterious appearance—had been normal. Why would this be any different?

"Where are we going?" Ashur said as they settled themselves into the luxurious leather seats. One of the pilots pulled up the door after them and grinned back at the passengers, Ashur's reflection doubled in the man's aviator sunglasses.

"Texas," Zaya said. "Now get some rest. After the day you've already had, and what's still to come, you'll need all the energy you can get."

Zaya pulled on a pair of oversized headphones and leaned his seat back. Ashur stared out the window as Los Angeles receded in the distance.

"Why have I never heard of the Academy?"

They were somewhere outside of Dallas now, Zaya driving once again.

"But you have," Zaya said, a small smile at the corner of his lips. "By a different name, perhaps."

"What do you mean?"

Zaya took one hand off the wheel and pointed up at a bill-board by the side of the road. John Glenn was smiling down at the passing motorists, young and handsome in his flight suit, with the old Apollo flight helmet tucked under an arm. Helping the Dreams of Mankind Soar to the Heavens.

"Worldcorp?" Ashur said.

"A forgettable name, no? Almost so as to be practically invisible if you aren't paying attention," Zaya said. "The Academy was the start of all of it."

"So this is, what, some corporate training program?"

"It can be. For some. If you aspire to a life in industry. And, who knows, I've been surprised before. But something tells me that is not your path."

Ashur briefly pictured himself in a suit, seated behind a desk, with a giant stack of papers waiting for his stamp. He shivered slightly. Zaya laughed.

"I thought not."

"So then, what will it be for me?"

"That is for you to decide," Zaya said. Ashur began to ask another question, but Zaya reached forward and turned the CD's volume higher, his fingers tapping along on the steering wheel. Ashur slumped back into his seat, waiting, until they reached another gate.

The building at the end of the long, sprawling driveway was smaller than Ashur would have expected. Tasteful red brick, large ornate windows, and a few columns out front. It looked like the sort of building that belonged on a college campus, housing some minor department—the sort that tour guides would hurry past, leading prospective students on to other, more obviously impressive structures.

"That's it?" he said as Zaya drove past the high gates. He looked out the rearview window of the sedan to see the high-rises of downtown Dallas just barely visible on the horizon.

"Not what you were imagining?"

"Not exactly."

"Remember what I told you about the name World-corp," Zaya said, stepping out of the car and leaning back with his hands against his lower back. "Sometimes it can be an advantage not to attract attention. Make it so that someone would need to look very, very closely to see you for what you really are."

The door to the building opened for them, and Zaya ushered Ashur inside. They were in a sort of lobby area, with dark wood and a few low-slung, comfortable-looking leather chairs. A woman was waiting behind a desk with a small tablet in her hand, smiling up at him.

"Ashur Yonan," she said. "You made very good time. We were worried we might have to start orientation without you."

"I've never had a late recruit, Sam," Zaya said, and Ashur thought he noticed the man puffing out his chest slightly with pride.

The woman—Sam—reached back behind her and produced a small metal box. "The gun, please?"

Ashur frowned. "The gun is in a sheriff's office in California."

Zaya reached behind him and produced the pistol, along with the spare clip that Ashur had left back in the office of the Big Boy. He smiled as he handed them over to Sam.

"How did you—" Ashur started.

"It was your father's, I understand," Zaya said. "I know how much it must mean to you. Your bike will also be waiting for you, whenever you are ready to return to California."

At the mention of his father, Ashur felt a pang of something go through him. What would Odishoo make of all this? He wished his father were still alive, so he could share this with him and tell him how he was feeling.

"Thank you," he said softly.

"Orientation is about to begin," Sam said. "Otherwise, I'd have someone take you to your room to…freshen up."

Ashur attempted a subtle sniff of himself—his shirt was a sweat-crusted mess and his hair probably a tangle of dark curls at this point. He tried to think whether there were any clothes in his backpack that would be suitable for something like this orientation. When he had packed his bag, he hadn't planned on going to anything like this anytime soon.

"You'll want to be there for all of it," Zaya said. "And there will be time later to impress people with how well you can dress and how nice you smell."

"I believe you'll find we've taken care of everything you could need during your time with us," the woman said with a small smile, as though she could read Ashur's mind. "Including a wardrobe suited to your needs."

"Okay," Ashur said, his head still reeling from all the new information. Of course they knew his clothing sizes—they seemed to know everything about him. How long, exactly, had they been watching him?

"One last thing," the woman said, reaching down behind the desk and retrieving a small, vaguely metallic square card that she held in her palm. "Hold out your hand, please."

The card was heavy for such a small object. Ashur expected it to be cold but found instead that it emitted a gentle heat. As it continued to warm up, the card seemed to unfold, thrumming slightly, like a bird that had settled down to roost in his hand. Before long it was no longer a card but a fully three-dimensional cube, with a faint light now glowing from somewhere within it.

"A quick pairing," the woman said. "That's a relief. I've had some recruits who need to spend all day with one of the techs to get their Cubes working right, and even then there are lingering issues."

"What is it?" Ashur said, holding the device up to his face and feeling the vibration flow from his palm down his arm and into his body.

"One of the great achievements of the Worldcorp engineering department," Zaya said. "The most advanced bit of personal electronics that we've ever produced. And your new best friend for as long as you remain on campus."

A small light began to glow on the top of the cube. When Ashur held it closer, he saw that a thin band of writing had formed, the words seeming to float just above the surface of the device.

HIYA, ASHUR! ☺ WELCOME ABOARD!

"Is it always so chipper?" Ashur said.

"It'll adapt to you soon enough," Zaya said. "Its tone will change rather quickly, I suspect, once it gets to know you a bit better."

"Keep it on you at all times," Sam said. "It's your ID card, room key, and access point to all of the Academy's technology."

Ashur nodded, marveling at the little cube in his hand.

"It's been a genuine pleasure, Ashur Yonan," Zaya said.

"You're leaving?"

"I'm a recruiter, not an instructor. And I have successfully delivered my recruit, on time and on cycle. Now go before you make me look bad."

Zaya smiled and extended a hand. Ashur stood with his back straight and felt the warmth of the man's grip.

"I don't know what would have happened to me if you hadn't shown up."

"You would have managed," Zaya said. "The way you always have. It would have taken longer, perhaps, but you still would have made something of yourself. Of that I have no doubt."

"Zaya," Ashur said, hesitating for a moment. He had decided to leave home before he'd known where he was going; he had been so mad at Rose that the thought of her not knowing where he was felt good, an appropriate punishment for her. But now he felt a slick of guilt—it was one thing to put up with her abuse, but another to make her wonder whether he was still alive, or if she had driven him away so thoroughly that she would never see him again. "I know this is meant to be some kind of secret. But…if there is any way you could let me mother know that I'm all right."

"I'll make sure Rose understands," Zaya said.

The men shook hands again, and then Zaya was out the front door and on his way, Ashur assumed, to find another lost teenager in need of a chance to show who they really were.

"This way, please," Sam said, coming from around the counter. She led Ashur through a set of thick wooden doors, holding her own metallic card up to a small device that gave a small beep as they passed.

Ashur gasped as the doors closed behind him.

A campus the size of a city block stretched before them, the entire complex encased in a giant glass geodesic dome. A stone pathway cut through a lush green lawn, and buildings rose up on all sides. Tall towers of glass and white marble soared toward the blue sky, and shorter buildings with peaked roofs crowded in front of them. Everything was set at a slight angle, so that Ashur saw a triangle as he looked out over this marvel, terminating in a fountain that rose majestically at the end of the lawn.

"It's impossible," he said.

"Merely unlikely," the woman said. "And extremely well hidden."

"But how?"

"Some classic play of the light, a little advanced polymer design, and a few other tricks that require a PhD in nanotechnology before they're even worth talking about. Now follow your Cube to orientation—you don't want to be late."

Ashur was about to ask what she meant, but the cube began to very gently float off his palm. If he hadn't been the one holding it, Ashur wouldn't have been sure the thing was levitating.

"Whoa. How does this thing float?" Ashur thought out loud. "There's no magnet, and it's not blowing any air out."

"It's a *bit* more complicated than that," Sam said with a hint of pride.

"Try me," Ashur said.

The woman sized Ashur up and down for a second, as though deciding if she was interested enough to see how sharp he might be.

"Alright then. Enclosed in that tiny device are particles of newly discovered, superdense quantum matter, spinning around each other quite naturally and at nearly the speed of light." Ashur's eyes widened. Sam continued, "Like tiny black holes, their fierce interaction emits a gravitational wave that we can calibrate to be perfectly out of phase with Earth's gravity and therefore counteract it."

"That's exactly what I thought you were going to say," Ashur said with a grin. "Okay, without the jargon now?"

"Think of how a hovercraft floats above the ground by creating a cushion of air," said Sam. "The Cube does something similar, but instead of air, it's creating a 'cushion' of altered gravitational forces."

After a long pause to process this information, Ashur studied the cube closely and concluded, "That's got to require a lot more energy than can fit inside of here."

"More than you can imagine. But the source of the Cube's energy isn't *inside* it. The device harnesses energy at a quantum level—and a strange feature of the quantum world is 'entanglement,' where particles become linked and the state of one can instantly affect the state of another, regardless of distance." Sam pointed at the heart of the cube and continued, "So the charged particles in *that* Cube are *entangled* with those of a much larger power source far, far away from here," Sam gestured toward the horizon, "giving the Cube all the energy it could ever need."

"That's…terrifying." Ashur's eyes darted from the cube to the sky and back again. After a few seconds of shaking his head, he asked, "And who created them?"

Sam paused, as if trying to decide whether she'd said too much already. "Actually, one of our faculty members did," she said.

"Impossible. How does one person invent a thousand years' worth of science in one lifetime?" Ashur said.

"Ah," the woman smiled, "be patient. All will become clear soon enough. We need to keep moving or you'll be late."

The cube began to push forward, and Ashur followed, the speed of the little device modulating with his pace as he made his way down the lawn and toward the nearest building, trying not to openly gawk at everything around him.

As he stood in the Grand Hall for orientation, listening to the talk of the other recruits around him, it was hard for Ashur not to wonder if there had been some mistake after all.

The three women gathered around the high table to his left were talking about the summer research they were planning to do. Ahead of him, two chemical engineers were chiding a third for her focus on civil engineering projects, despite her good-natured protests that the world needed bridges, too. A Black man with a warm smile and a laugh that boomed across the room was demonstrating the difference between his approach for a kickoff and how he took field goals—apparently, he was heading to the University of Miami in the fall on a full ride, a degree in marine biology an even bigger draw for him than the school's legendary football program. Two men were huddled over a chess board in the corner; neither, as far as Ashur could tell, had made a move since he had arrived at orientation, but that hadn't stopped a crowd from gathering around them, whispering among themselves as they debated the board position and the vulnerability of white's bishop.

Zaya had seemed so sure that this was where Ashur belonged. But who was he, really? A high school dropout, a teenage runaway, and nearly a felon as of that morning, if Zaya hadn't shown up to spring him. For all this talk about his potential, what did he actually have to show for it? He wished Kiki was there with him now, telling him that she believed in him and reminding him of all the promise he had. He couldn't believe that she would be heading to college so soon, without him. It made his heart ache even to think about it.

And then he smelled something.

It was subtle, hard to distinguish at first in a room full of people. The top note was light, jasmine and something citrusy, but there was a lingering…something that made him want to take another sniff. Something musky, and a little sexy. He had never smelled anything like it before, and he began to look around the room, trying to find the source.

As he searched, he saw a woman beginning her descent from the top of the stairs opposite where he was standing. The first thing he noticed was her thin ankles atop a pair of tasteful heels. She took another step down, revealing a black skirt that showed off plenty of leg. The material clung to her hips and then cinched into a tight waist. She was wearing a baby-blue shirt, the material rich and silken. As she continued to descend, he saw her hair, a warm brown that cascaded in waves over her shoulder. He kept watching her, noticing the delicate features of her face, the high cheekbones and full lips, as she scanned the room, looking for a familiar face. Their eyes met, just briefly, and she smiled and looked down before heading off in the other direction.

"She's something, isn't she," said a voice from behind him.

Ashur turned around, slightly ruffled at the idea that someone had been watching him. The young man behind him was short and slight, his glasses smudged and askew. Ashur had felt self-conscious in his T-shirt amid the more formal wear of the other recruits—most of whom, he assumed, had been given time to properly change into the clothing the Academy had provided specifically for them. But this man somehow made his own clothing seem sloppy and ill-fitting, with the collar of his shirt flipped halfway up and the tails sticking out of the back of his pants. There was, already, an archipelago of stains on the man's shirt, mapping out the places where various dipping sauces had failed to make it all the way to his mouth.

And yet, despite the man's schlubby appearance, there was a cool intensity about him as Ashur met his glance. The man didn't shy away from his look, the way so many of the other students in high school had when he passed them in the hall. This man seemed to be appraising him, almost impassively, as though they were sitting down together to play cards. There was, Ashur could tell, a fierce intelligence at work here.

"You have excellent taste," the man said. "But not much of a chance."

Ashur felt himself bristle at the man's comment. A part of him wanted to walk over to her at that moment and prove the man wrong. But he thought, again, about Kiki, and the sting of her leaving for college. Was he really ready to try with someone else, no matter how good she smelled? Open himself up to that kind of hurt again?

"We'll see about that," Ashur said, standing as tall as he could—he had a good half a head on this man.

The man grinned and gestured around the room.

"Half the cohort is male, so start with a base case of one out of fifty, knowing nothing. Assume some of them have partners. You're a good-enough-looking guy. Seems like you work out...a lot. And maybe the ethnically ambiguous look does it for her.

I'll be generous and put you in the top ten of candidates, based solely on physical appearance."

"What the hell are you talking about?" Ashur said.

The man held up a finger. "But! She is—and I mean this objectively—the most beautiful woman in this room. Maybe on the planet. But for the purposes of this analysis, we only need to worry about the room for now. Which means that her selection of a mate is as much a question of social signaling as it is raw sexual desire. You've been standing alone at the periphery of the room, trying to figure out where you fit in. And now you're stuck talking with me, who will never be worth any social points whatsoever. So, sorry to say, I think you've blown it already."

Ashur looked back over at the woman, holding court in a small circle, everyone's focus on her no matter who in the group was speaking. Did all these people know each other already? Or did they just assume—in a way that he had never been able to—that they belonged in a place like this? The right schools, rich parents, access to the best of everything: why *shouldn't* they be in a place like the Academy? Maybe they could just sense it in one another, that feeling of belonging.

"Who are you?" Ashur said, turning back to the man.

"Me? I'm Boris. And if you want any shot with Cassandra, you'll walk away quickly and find a more socially desirable group."

Cassandra. It was a perfect name for her. Ashur felt a small smile creeping over his lips.

"I don't know, Boris. I sort of like the challenge."

Boris smiled and shrugged. "Suit yourself."

A chime began to ring out in the room, and slowly the recruits began to make their way over to where rows of seats had been arranged in a semicircle around a dais. Behind the lectern was a large banner in a rich purple, with a lion sewn on in silver thread. Ashur stared at the banner—the lion was eerily similar to the tattoo on his forearm. He shook his head and tried to dismiss the coincidence; the big cat was one of the most popular emblems for any organization, from nations to sports franchises, trying to project strength and power. Though he thought he could see, just behind the animal, the faintest trace of wings.

Ashur sat near the back, next to Boris, watching the other recruits as they found their seats. He craned his neck, searching the crowd for another glimpse of Cassandra. When he finally found her, he held his breath—she really was as beautiful as Boris had said, with piercing green eyes and full lips that curled down slightly into a frown when she noticed Ashur looking.

"What?" she mouthed at him as a speaker moved to the front of the room.

Ashur grinned. "I'll tell you later," he mouthed back. Cassandra cocked her head to the side, and then took a seat a few rows in front of him, turning around for one last look before the speaker began to talk.

"Congratulations, recruits," the man said. Ashur, distracted to this point by Cassandra, looked at him for the first time. His hair was salt and pepper, the suit trim around his body, and his face weathered but still vibrant. Again Ashur felt a pang of recognition—was this his body's way of trying to convince him he belonged, or something else?

"We have spent years, in some cases, considering each of you. Trying to find the rare few who contain within them the potential to become a world-changing leader. Some of you knew of us already and have aspired to sit in these seats for a long time. Others..." and here he smiled and seemed to look directly at Ashur, "have only known of us for the last few hours. However you arrived here, and however long you've known about us, be assured that you are here for a reason. And that reason is greatness.

"I am the Director of the Academy and responsible for its mission: to develop future world leaders and teach them what we have learned in our many, many years of training promising young talents. Most people don't ever take the time to identify their true calling in life. And even if they do, they don't put all of their energy into fulfilling that calling. Every one of you has different skills and abilities, different strengths and passions. In this room are artists and politicians, future military leaders and corporate titans. We have brought you here because we believe in you, and in your promise.

"We aren't here to tell you how to think, or what to do. We are here to help you build the skills to know how to make decisions for yourself—and determine the path that will allow you to have the greatest impact. There is no greater waste than potential gone unfulfilled. We will help you identify your true calling and put you in an environment to use your gifts and talents as well as possible. But it will always be up to you to do the work…and make the most of the opportunities presented to you.

"The coming days will be some of the most difficult, and rewarding, of your lives. The lessons you learn on this campus, and the relationships you form, will stay with you forever. Not all of you will graduate from the Academy—competition is at the heart of how we determine who has what it takes to become the next generation of leaders. But every last one of you will leave this place better for having been here—and having tested yourself against the best minds of your generation.

"We live in dangerous and turbulent times, with freedom under great threat. Times when many would rather see the world return to some imagined better past than forward to a place of progress and greater freedom. I feel as though I issue this warning every year I address a new class of recruits, but every year I believe it to be true. Just yesterday, I received a report of a credible threat against the Academy from an adversary that would want nothing more than to see all of this torn to the ground. I say this not to frighten you but to urge you to be on your guard, and to make the stakes clear. Now more than ever, we require people with not just the aptitude for leadership but the wisdom to know what's right, the courage to pursue that course even when it becomes difficult, and the strength to see it through. These are the core tenets of the Academy: Courage, Strength, and Wisdom. And tomorrow, you will learn what it is to be truly tested.

"So congratulations again, recruits. I am honored that you've chosen to accept a place at the Academy and inspired by your resolve and determination. I expect great things from all of you. And I suggest you get a good night's sleep tonight. The morning will be here sooner than you know it."

As the Director left the stage, Ashur felt his heart rate rising. What did it mean that not all of them were going to make it? And what were these tests going to be?

"Did you know about the tests?" he asked Boris.

"I didn't even know this place existed before yesterday," Boris said. "To be honest with you, I thought it was a prank before I saw the jet. And even then, I thought, maybe this is just a very, very expensive prank."

"Did you have something to say to me?"

Cassandra was standing right in front of them now, one hand on her hip, a very small smile playing at the corner of her lips. Ashur cleared his throat.

"I just wanted to say hello. Now that I know I'm talking to a future leader with great potential."

"I noticed you weren't as quick to introduce yourself to the other future leaders with great potential," Cassandra said. "Even the ones who were closer to you."

"I'll get to them, I'm sure," Ashur said. "But I would have kicked myself if I left here without introducing myself to you."

Cassandra laughed and rolled her eyes. "Do those lines ever work for you?"

Ashur grinned. "Sometimes. It helps that they're not lines. They're just the truth. There's a difference."

He reached up to run a hand through his hair and noticed something change in Cassandra's face. She reached out and took his arm into her hand.

"Your tattoo…" she said, pushing up the sleeve of his shirt so she could see it more fully. Boris was peering at it, too. A few of the other recruits wandered over, whispering among themselves as they stared at him. Ashur took his arm back from Cassandra and pulled the sleeve back down.

"It was the same tattoo my father had," Ashur said.

"Was he involved with the Academy?"

Ashur shook his head and stared at her. "No. I got it in his memory."

"In his memory," Cassandra said, and then frowned in understanding. "Oh. I'm sorry. I'm sure it's hard, losing a father. And then having some stranger ask you personal questions that are none of her business. Like someone coming and pressing on a bruise."

"It's all right," Ashur said quietly. Then, smiling at her: "I had the same thought when I saw the logo. But it's not like the Academy has a monopoly on lions, right?"

"Go Lions!" she said with a grin. "My mom is from Detroit."

Ashur laughed.

The same chime as before sounded, and the recruits began filing out of the room. People took their Cubes out of their pockets, the metal cards expanding as they held them in their palms, leading them back to the different rooms around the campus.

"What's your name?" Cassandra said.

"Ash," he said. "Ashur Yonan."

"I've never heard that name before."

"It's Assyrian."

"Interesting."

They stood there for a moment as the other recruits streamed around them.

"Aren't you going to ask me my name?" she said.

Ashur grinned. "Your reputation precedes you, Cassandra."

"Yeah? What's that?"

"The most beautiful woman at the Academy."

She scoffed and looked away, but Ashur could tell that she liked to hear it.

"Enough of that, Ashur Yonan. Go to bed before you get yourself in trouble. It sounds like we're in for hell tomorrow."

"Good night, Cassandra," Ashur said as her Cube led her off in the other direction. He watched as she walked, admiring the subtle swing of her hips as she went, until his own Cube began beeping with polite impatience.

"All right, all right," he said, and began walking to his own room.

The room was sparse but comfortable: all blonde wood and glass, with a bed, a desk, a bathroom, and a small kitchenette stocked with food and drinks. The closets, as promised, were filled with clothing tailored exactly to him—everything from a suit to athletic apparel, perhaps in advance of some more physical trials tomorrow.

In the center of the room was a small pedestal, and the Cube, as soon as he came into the room, seemed to guide itself over to it. Ashur placed the Cube on the pedestal, and it anchored itself in with a satisfying *thunk*.

The lights dimmed and shades came down over the windows as the room was transformed into a three-dimensional monitor, images coming from all directions as the Cube relayed its information. Ashur took a bottle of water from the small refrigerator and flopped down onto the bed.

WOULD YOU LIKE TO READ YOUR MESSAGES? read the prompt on the far wall.

"Do I have to?" Ashur said.

IT'S A REALLY GOOD IDEA!

Ashur sighed—he was bone-tired and knew he needed sleep. But what if there was important information about the trials tomorrow, things he needed to do to prepare? It was funny, the way he could go from not knowing anything about the Academy to now wanting to do whatever it took to secure himself a spot in the organization. He couldn't remember ever feeling like this before—like he had a real chance to do something. He didn't want to blow it, now that it had arrived.

The first several messages were short and perfunctory—a welcome message from the Director, instructions for how to use the Cube, and where to go for different things around the campus. Ashur closed his eyes briefly, letting the sound wash over him. He opened them again when he heard his Cube giving another insistent beep.

PERSONAL MESSAGE—FROM ADMIRER

Admirer? Ashur thought. That was odd. Maybe it was Cassandra, trying to flirt with him? The message was short—a single line of text—but the contents sent chills up Ashur's spine.

Odishoo would be proud.

SEND RETURN MESSAGE?

"Who are you!" Ashur said, leaping from the bed. "And what do you know about my father?"

MESSAGE SENT.

He stood there in the middle of the room, confused and angry. Was someone else trying to mess with him? Maybe this was part of a test—trying to get to the thing that upset him most. If that was the case, it was working. Ashur paced in small circles around the little room, waiting for his pulse to slow. He knew he needed to calm down—needed to sleep before tomorrow. But he just kept staring at the wall where the message from Admirer was still displayed, wondering what the hell was going on.

"Who was dividing people?" Ashur said.

"Son," Odishoo said, "remember that this is not the story you're going to read in school. People will get angry if you try to discuss it with them, so keep it to yourself. But I want you to know the truth.

"You need to remember, Eisenhower had instituted an agreement back in 1954, giving US companies control over how much

oil Iran pumped and how much they could sell it for. But the Shah said in 1973 he wasn't going to renew the agreement; he wanted to control Iran's oil, to make Iran stronger. But the countries that had benefitted—the US, the UK, and France—didn't like this idea at all.

"The United Kingdom in particular, concerned about Iran's rapidly growing strength, needed American help to bring down the Persian Empire. And that's exactly what they got when Jimmy Carter was elected the president of the United States in 1976.

"Although President Carter was a man of faith, sincere in his intentions, and extremely intelligent, he was a naïve leader. Weak. Leaders like him try to please the majority instead of doing what's best for the country and making it stronger. America actually ended up paying a big price later on for voting him into office."

Ashur leaned forward.

"What do you mean?"

Odishoo held up a hand.

"We'll get there. But what you need to know is that Jimmy Carter emphasized the importance of human rights. It sounded like an honorable cause during his campaign, but he didn't fully realize the negative consequences—especially in the Middle East.

"Carter accused the Shah of torturing three thousand political prisoners. He demanded that the Shah release them or else threatened to withhold military and social aid. And that was just the beginning of the problems for the Shah. His popularity plummeted during the Carter administration. He was demonized as an imperialist dictator who only cared about his own wealth and not the average person living in Iran. I don't even think President Carter knew the possible consequences that the world could face if those political prisoners were freed, but he kept at it."

"So the Shah was holding political prisoners?"

"Yes."

"Isn't that bad?"

"Just because a prisoner is a political prisoner doesn't mean he's also not extremely dangerous."

Ashur felt a ripple of trepidation in his stomach.

"What happened?"

Odishoo took a deep breath.

"Iran's enemies, who didn't want to see Iran powerful and in control of the region's oil, needed to find a candidate who was capable of leading the fall of the Persian Empire. This wasn't easy to do at that time because the Shah had SAVAK—his secret service—in place all over Iran, working diligently to preserve the country's progress and keep it safe from dangerous elements." Odishoo shook his head. *"But Ayatollah Khomeini was a perfect candidate. Khomeini could create a feeling of 'us against them' within his following like you wouldn't believe.*

"Propaganda came first, to get the attention of the people and to make the Shah look like a weak leader. Khomeini was originally arrested in 1963, after claiming to the people that the Shah was a miserable man who was planning on destroying Islam in Iran. His words created havoc all over the country. Thousands rioted, and many died. Khomeini supporters claimed afterward that nearly fifteen thousand people were killed by local police and SAVAK. The real numbers were much lower, but no one listened to the truth. People believed the propaganda, which created more supporters for Khomeini.

"Things got pretty ugly. Khomeini was eventually released after almost a year of house arrest, with the hope that he had calmed down. But the exact opposite happened. He said the Shah was a puppet of the US government and criticized him for extending diplomatic immunity to American government personnel in Iran.

The Shah believed in giving the people freedom, but Khomeini felt the people needed to be controlled, that under the Shah too much Western influence was seeping into Iran. He was exiled, but his influence only grew."

Odishoo looked his son in the eye.

"Ashur, I pray that you will never see such turbulent days in your lifetime, but I hope that if that happens, you will face challenges head-on, like a Yonan, like your grandfather did. I know that greatness will find you and that you will rise to meet it. That is why today I speak of our family's history, our people's history, with you man to man. I want you to remember this afternoon for the rest of your life."

Ashur nodded solemnly.

CHAPTER SIX

Ashur didn't remember falling asleep—his mind had been so full of questions about everything that had happened in the last day, and that strange message, that he had been sure he'd be awake all night. But his body was exhausted, and even as his eyes opened, he could feel his muscles aching, resisting his attempts to sit up in bed. The curtains parted on their own, flooding the room with morning light. And his Cube, seeing that he was awake, spun around atop its pedestal. Ashur couldn't dismiss the thought that the Cube looked *happy* to see him, somehow.

GOOD MORNING ASHUR! read the words displayed on the far wall. BIG DAY TODAY!

"Any new messages from Admirer?" Ashur said, cracking his neck as he let his arms stretch up over his head. Who could possibly know he was here—and that he was Odishoo's son?

NO…BUT DON'T GET DISCOURAGED!

"Yeah, yeah," Ashur said, trying to hide his disappointment, before shuffling off to the bathroom.

As he brushed his teeth, the Cube continued to relay information to him, the words displayed on the mirror just above his head. He was due down at the testing facility in half an hour.

"Can I have a little privacy?" Ashur said, scowling at the mirror.

NOT REALLY, the Cube replied. BUT I CAN PRETEND IF IT WOULD MAKE YOU MORE COMFORTABLE!

He stood in the shower, feeling the hot water over his sore muscles, as the Cube continued to explain the day to him. There were three tests, one for each of the school's core tenets: Wisdom, Strength, and Courage. The results of the initial tests would be used to sort the students into teams—and strong test scores, the Cube said, were usually a good indicator of who would still be around by graduation.

The closet doors were open when Ashur came out of the shower.

DRESS TO MOVE! read the note that seemed to appear organically on the paneling, as though burned into the wood. Ashur leafed through the clothing until he came to a tracksuit in deep purple, the back emblazoned with the same lion he had seen on the banner the day before. He slipped on a soft black T-shirt and then put on the tracksuit, along with the pair of new dark sneakers that squeaked a bit against the floor of his room. The Cube chirped.

LOOKIN' GOOD!

"Come on," Ashur said, picking up the Cube from its pedestal. It spun itself around and began to float just above his palm before leading him out of the room and out into the complex.

Outside his room, the hallways were filled with other recruits hurrying around. Ashur could hear the sound of nervous laughter and shouts as people called out to familiar faces. He scanned the crowd, hoping to find Cassandra, but she was nowhere to be seen.

"Did your Cube thing tell you anything useful?"

Ashur turned around the find Boris walking up behind him, looking slightly green. Ashur shook his head. "Ah, 'dress to move'?"

Boris grimaced. "The last time I ran a mile was in the seventh grade. And you can guess how that went."

"What do you think they'll have us do?"

"Who knows?" Boris said. "But if it isn't chess, or coding, I'm a goner."

Ashur couldn't help but smile. It was nice to find, among all the other recruits who seemed so certain that they belonged, someone who seemed just as mystified about everything that was happening as he was.

"Come on," Ashur said. "We'll jog over."

"Why the hell would we do that?"

"To warm up!" Ashur said, slapping Boris on the shoulder and leading him out the door of the dormitory into the bright morning beneath the dome. He heard Boris curse, but when he turned back to check, Boris was dutifully running behind him, the other recruits watching them as they made their way over to the testing facility.

A little while later, Ashur was waiting in line behind two other recruits, watching as one by one they were led to a door and ushered through. They had been told not to speak while they waited, and despite his best efforts, he had been unable to hear what the administrators of the test whispered to each recruit before beckoning them through the waiting door. The large golden letters over the door, though, made it clear that the first test was WISDOM.

Ashur hoped that he'd have a chance to take all three tests, and that the Academy wouldn't eliminate him on the basis of just this first test. He knew he was strong, and he had courage to spare—his actions at the Big Boy, facing down the armed robber with nothing but an unloaded gun, were proof enough of that. But wisdom was a different quality entirely. His father had been wise—Ashur could hear it when Odishoo told him stories about Iran, and the careful way he tried to teach his son about the world and what to expect from life. But Ashur knew that he was sometimes too quick to act, hot-headed, and prone to rage. And while he was smart, he had never really applied himself in school. He did *fine* on tests, but he never truly worried about them the way he saw the best students in high school carefully preparing and drilling themselves. Would this test let him show the Academy who he really was? And if it did, would they still like what they found, or would they realize this had been a mistake all along?

When it was his turn to go, he recognized Sam, the woman who had greeted him when Zaya brought him to the Academy the day before, as the woman administering the test. She gave him a small, professional smile and entered a few notes into her Cube. There was a light above the door, currently glowing amber. As they watched, it suddenly flipped over to a deep, soothing blue.

"Looks like they're ready for you," Sam said, leaning in close to whisper in his ear. "Here are your instructions. You may spend as long as you need. Nothing you do inside the testing room will have any bearing on your score. The only thing you'll be graded on is your answer to this question, given once you leave: What is the rule?"

"What is the rule?" Ashur repeated.

"Precisely," Sam said. She keyed something into her Cube and the door slid soundlessly open. Leaning in even closer, she whispered, "Good luck, Ashur."

Ashur nodded. He could see nothing through the doorway. He took a deep breath and strode in. As soon as he was through, the door slid shut behind him, and Ashur Yonan was standing alone in the darkness.

For a few moments, he couldn't see anything at all. But gradually his eyes began to adjust to the intense darkness. Ashur stood in the middle of a chamber that appeared to be made entirely of black glass. A thin band of light began to shine upward from where the walls met the floor, and he could dimly see his reflection back against the wall. On the far side of the room was a dark hollow, gaping like the maw of some deep-sea creature. The Cube in his palm was urging him on, and after a moment's hesitation he went over and inserted it into the hollow with a satisfying *thunk*.

A shimmer spread along the surface of the glass like a ripple across a pond, and the room filled with the distant hum of machinery coming to life. On the wall opposite him, a white box appeared. As Ashur watched, the box began to fill with different numbers: two, four, eight, sixteen.

In the center of the room, now glowing, was a single large white button atop a short pedestal. Ashur stood for another moment, waiting to see if anything else was going to happen. Waiting, he assumed, was the sort of thing that wise people were always telling him to do. But it didn't come naturally— Ashur preferred action, and movement, to quiet contemplation.

But when nothing changed, he went to the button and pressed it down. Suddenly the chamber lit up with warm, comforting light, streaking around the room like he had just won some sort of arcade game. Happy, soothing music played. It was, Ashur had to admit, extremely pleasant after the darkness of the room.

He looked back at the far wall: the white box was now empty. In a panic, he tried to remember the numbers that had appeared. There were four of them, he remembered that much, but the specific numbers evaded him as he tried to concentrate on them. The first number had been a two. But what were the others? There was some kind of rule governing which numbers were supposed to appear in the box—Sam had made that much clear. But how much complex math could they expect him to do? The last two numbers came back into his mind—an eight and then a sixteen. Was it something to do with doubling? Or some kind of multiplication? He briefly thought of Boris, and how happy he would be to discover that this was the first test.

Okay, maybe it's something simple, he thought. *All the other numbers doubled. Maybe that's the pattern?*

"Ah, three?"

A three appeared in the box.

"And six?"

Three, six.

He kept going until the box was filled: three, six, twelve, twenty-four. The white button before him was glowing again. Ashur pressed it.

Again the chamber lit up with soothing light and happy noises. Ashur grinned—it felt good to get this right, and to have the test show him that he was doing well.

He spent a few more minutes testing the pattern. Every time he put in a set of numbers that doubled, he got the happy, friendly lights. He wondered if he had figured it out—was this really all there was to it?

"There has to be something more," he said quietly to himself.

He tried to think of some way to test the pattern. *What if,* he thought, *the numbers cut in half each time, instead of doubled?* He spoke aloud a set of numbers to test: "Forty, twenty, ten, five. The button was shining again. Ashur pressed it.

His hands shot up to his ears as a sound like an air raid siren began to ring out in the chamber. The lights, tinged a bloody red, strobed painfully against his eyes. The whole room seemed to shake, though Ashur couldn't tell if that was real or just a sensation created by the noise and the lights.

After a few moments the noise suddenly stopped and the room returned to its previous dark state. Ashur could feel his heart beating faster and heard a distant ringing in his ears. It was a deeply unpleasant feeling, having the chamber assault his senses like that.

He put in another set of doubling numbers, just to hear the happy sounds again. He felt himself calming as the room confirmed that he had gotten the pattern correct. A part of Ashur was tempted to just stop there, be done with the test and tell the admin that he had figured out the doubling pattern.

But as the happy chirping noises subsided, Ashur began to nod to himself. *They want to make it painful to guess wrong. But guessing wrong is the only way to figure out what the rule is.*

For the next hour, Ashur tried every combination of numbers that he could think of—rising and falling, repetitions, the jersey numbers from the Los Angeles Lakers and Dodgers. He braced himself each time for the siren and the strobing lights; once you were expecting them, they weren't really so bad. And more importantly: they meant that he was getting more information—and coming closer to the rule.

There were, Ashur was sure, other recruits who were better than him at math—better probably than Boris, even, who would recognize every obscure pattern and probably derive some kind of proof for why it *had* to be the rule. But Ashur would put in the time, no matter how unpleasant, to give himself a fighting chance against them. He spoke aloud another set of numbers—Kiki's cell phone number—and grimaced as the siren wailed once again.

But as time stretched on, Ashur began to doubt his approach. The only thing even close to a "rule" that he had been able to come up with was that the chamber seemed to like it when the numbers went up each time and disliked it when they didn't. He kept trying different combinations, trying to go deeper...but nothing else appeared to him. Ashur sighed— maybe there was some grander pattern at play in the different combinations. But if there was, then maybe he just wasn't smart enough to see it.

"I'm ready to give my answer," he said, fighting off the feeling of defeat. A question mark appeared in the white box on the far wall.

"The numbers...go up."

His words appeared in the box, and looking at them, it was hard for Ashur not to feel a little stupid. It was so basic—so rudimentary—that he was sure there was something he was missing. *I'm sorry, Dad*, he thought. *I blew it.*

The white box on the wall disappeared, and another door slid silently open. There was no indication of whether or not his answer had been right, or whether it would be worth anything when the administration reviewed the test results later. Ashur took up his Cube and exited the black chamber.

Ashur emerged to the familiar sound of sneakers squeaking on a hardwood court. He was in a massive gymnasium now, with maybe a dozen basketball courts. Most of the recruits were huddled around a far court, so pressed together that Ashur had a hard time seeing what was going on. He made his way quickly over there, listening to the sound of shouting and laughter.

At first he thought it was half-court basketball—the long arc like a three-point line, the way the players dribbled and passed the ball around the court to one another. But as he continued to watch, he noticed there was no hoop. Instead, there was a small net, the size of a hockey goal, set along a baseline. The game was rougher than basketball, too, with the defenders actively jostling and crashing into one another. The way the players moved and battled with one another reminded him of the rough pickup games he used to play in Glendale—the kind where calling a foul was more or less forbidden unless someone drew blood. Ashur grinned. This was more like his kind of test.

The players moved fluidly around the court, passing the ball to one another, making quick in-cuts and trying to work their way closer to the net. Ashur noticed that the defense had one more player than the offense—maybe there was some kind of a penalty, like in hockey? But it didn't seem to matter much. It was obvious who the best player on the court was: a man with broad shoulders and thick, dark hair who none of the defenders could keep up with. There was, Ashur thought, something familiar about the man, but he couldn't put his finger on it. The player barreled his way through the defense, turning his back now and then to prevent anyone from stealing the ball, before hurling a powerful shot that sank into the upper-left corner of the net. He pumped his fist and then jogged back out to the arc as a scoreboard above the net completed a quick set of tabulations, the scores flipping over as though announcing arrivals at a train terminal.

"Is that…" Ashur said quietly.

"Can you believe it?" said a man standing just in front of him. "Jim Thorpe! Insane athlete. Two Olympic golds, pro football, pro baseball. One of those guys who can just play anything."

As Ashur watched the player begin some sort of negotiation with the others, he noticed a very faint flickering around the edges of his skin. As he looked at the court more closely, he began to recognize some of the other players as well—a woman he remembered from an Olympic volleyball team, Pelé, Magic Johnson, Wayne Gretzky, and Bo Jackson.

"They're holograms?" he said.

"Wild, right? I had seen the ads and all…but this is something else."

Ashur shook his head and then turned his focus to the man speaking to him. He recognized him from the orientation—he was the Black man with a warm smile who talked about going to the University of Miami on a kicking scholarship. He wore tight, dark-purple gym clothes that highlighted his physique—and made Ashur wonder how he had decided on kicking instead of playing another position.

"You are *ripped!*" Ashur said, with sincere appreciation in his voice. "You must have a killer workout routine."

The man laughed.

"To take care of the spirit, you must take care of the body," he said. Then he extended his hand forward. "I'm Jahi."

Ashur introduced himself.

"Did I hear that you were going to Miami?"

The man nodded and put his hands up in the school's famous *U* shape. "It's a good education. And my mom's a huge fan. But I'm really thinking about the seminary."

"Like, to be a priest?"

"Youth minister is what I'm thinking. But I figure that can wait a bit until I see what's going on here. They keep saying the experience will be useful regardless of what we end up doing—let's see if they really mean it."

Ashur nodded and fought down a tiny tinge of jealousy. Jahi seemed so confident in his purpose, so sure of what he wanted to do with his life—what would it be like, Ashur thought, to know what you were meant to do?

"So what's the deal with this game?" he said.

"Test number two—Strength," Jahi said. "I've been watching for a little while. Think I'm getting the hang of it. But I'm telling you, it's nuts. I've never seen a sport like this before."

"What do they call it?"

"Traitorball."

"Why?"

"Watch."

Jim Thorpe was standing behind the line, holding the ball impassively in his right hand and staring at the other six players on the court.

"Declare allegiance!" came a shout from a referee standing just behind the line.

Four of the other players took a step across the line, now facing in toward the goal. But Ashur noticed that they looked nervous—not how he would have expected Jim Thorpe's teammates to look.

"They don't look too happy," he said to Jahi.

"That's because they're not going to play with him."

"What do you mean?"

The referee blew one quick whistle burst.

"Captain! Accept or decline allegiances!"

Jim Thorpe looked down the line at the other athletes who had tried to team up with him for the round. One by one he shook his head, only taking on the sinewy volleyball player as his teammate.

"See, the more players on his team, the less valuable the goal is for him," Jahi said. "But the really crazy part? His teammates can steal the ball and become the captain. So even though she's not the strongest player, necessarily, he thinks he can trust her. And then he just needs one more goal to win—and she goes from being in last place to middle of the pack. It's a good deal for her."

Play began—two on five—with four of the defenders swarming Jim Thorpe. He stayed around the perimeter of the court, cagy, daring the defenders to come out to him and expose a lane to goal. The volleyball player set up on the opposite side of the court against the remaining defender, using her length to box out and try to position herself for a pass. One of the defenders faked toward Jim Thorpe but misjudged the angle. It was all the space Jim needed, and suddenly he was through, barreling through defenders and warding them off with his other hand as he rhythmically and fluidly pounded the ball against the court. The other defender left the volleyball player to come help—just in time for Jim Thorpe to loft a pass across the court. She caught it…but hesitated.

"What's she doing?" Ashur said.

"Deciding whether or not it's worth it for her," Jahi said.

The defenders weren't even running toward her now—she had a clear shot on goal. Instead, they were arguing with her, gesturing up toward the scoreboard and again at Jim Thorpe, who was standing there with his hands on his hips and a look of fierce concentration on his face. After a few moments, though, the volleyball player shrugged and threw the ball in for an easy goal as the other players on the court groaned. The referee blew a long blast on the whistle: game over.

As Jim Thorpe went over and shook the woman's hand, Ashur watched as the scoreboard shifted to reflect the final scores.

"Apparently they play a new season every month," Jahi said. "Goal is to get as many points as you can in that time. If she screwed over Jim, he's not letting her on his team the next time he needs her. It's like that old saying: you can shear a sheep many times, but skin it only once."

"A repeat game," Ashur said. Jahi grinned.

"Exactly."

"So when do we get to play?"

A sudden sound came from the scoreboards arrayed above the courts up and down the gymnasium—names being displayed as the boards flipped through their sets of mechanical letters. The recruits who had been spectating began to run around, trying to find their court.

"Looks like now," Jahi said. "Let's play."

THE ACADEMY

As he put his shoulder into the thin kid's chest and hurled the ball toward the goal as the guy collapsed in a heap, Ashur was beginning to suspect that he might like Traitorball.

He had never been a big team sports player—he didn't tend to see eye to eye with the coaches, who called him standoffish and rude. Too many rules, too many asshole teammates, and a jock culture in high school that he hated. Kiki had tried to convince him to try out for a team—he was strong and fast, good with his hands, and she had been raised to believe in the value of sports by her dad. But even if Ashur hadn't been too busy with work, it felt like he had missed the chance to go out for any of the teams—and his mom would never have signed the consent forms, even if he had asked.

But here he was, plowing his way through the defense and then high-fiving his teammates as they all ran back out to the Allegiance Line (which, the referee had explained to them, was apparently what they called the arc that looked like the three-point line in basketball). He and Jahi had ended up in the same game together, and it was immediately obvious that they were the two strongest players. Before long they settled into their team—the two of them, together with a small, shockingly fast woman named Naomi with a strong arm and the ability to seemingly disappear into a cloud of defenders and emerge on the other side. They were dominating the game: every time another person declared for their team, Ashur would shut them down, sending them trudging back to play defense again. It was enough to make him wonder if he could have been good enough to go to college on an athletic scholarship himself if he had figured out early on that he liked playing sports. Maybe not Miami like Jahi, but somewhere good.

After the teams were declared, Jahi called Ashur and Naomi over, the three of them standing in a huddle before the next round started. Jahi had been calling plays all morning, noticing what the defense was doing to try to stop them and coming up with new counters to use against them. Ashur couldn't remember seeing this kind of real-time strategy and adjustment in sports before—maybe, he thought to himself, not all jocks were the meatheads he'd always assumed they were.

"They're going to send two at Ashur, because they have to," Jahi said. "And if you pass out of that to me, the woman they've got on Naomi is going to cheat over towards me to keep me from driving. That means you'll be open for a long pass and a shot, Naomi. You up to put the game away for us?"

"You know it!" Naomi said, grinning and reaching forward to bump fists with Jahi.

The referee blew the whistle to start play, and Ashur dribbled the ball in. He waited patiently just inside the line, surveying the defense. Then he started to charge forward, making a beeline directly for the goal with his head down. Two of the defenders—a gangly redhead and a squat kid with a thick neck—ran toward him, arms raised, bracing for impact. Just like Jahi had predicted.

Ashur saw Jahi standing in the corner, hands up, waiting for the pass. Ashur cocked back his arm and hurled a quick bounce pass that skipped across the gymnasium floor with the satisfying thud of leather against wood. The defense was scrambling now—even with their numbers advantage, four of them to three of Ashur's team, they were having trouble covering the whole floor. Jahi feinted forward, making like he was driving, and the woman guarding Naomi glanced back and forth between the two of them before taking a few steps toward Jahi.

Damn, Ashur thought as he watched this. *Jahi really knows what he's doing!*

Jahi waited another half second, for the woman to take one last step toward him, before lofting a high, soft pass above the heads of the defenders and into Naomi's waiting arms. Ashur grinned—the game was theirs. Maybe his performance in the strength test would be enough to make up for what had happened in the wisdom challenge, and ease his nagging sense that he hadn't been smart enough, or known enough math, to understand the complicated pattern. Then it would all come down to courage, however they planned to test that.

There was just one problem: Naomi wasn't taking the shot.

"Shoot it!" Jahi shouted. "Take the shot!"

But Naomi was turning her back on the goal now, dribbling back out towards the Allegiance Line.

"What are you doing?" Ashur called after her. He was confused—if she had scored, they all would have shared the victory. Naomi said nothing, didn't even look at him, as she crossed the line.

The referee blew his whistle and the other players looked around, most of them as confused as Ashur was. Naomi reached down and placed the ball on the ground, hands on her hips.

"The rest of you come play with me against them," she said, pointing to Ashur and Jahi, "I'll boost your scores on the strength test."

"You can't be serious!" Ashur said, seething now. "The only reason you have any points is because of me and Jahi."

"We had a deal, Naomi!" Jahi said.

Naomi smirked at them, and then looked at the rest of the players.

"Well? What will it be? Tank your chances at advancing at the Academy, or come help me win?"

Ashur felt his hands ball into fists at his side and a familiar rage course through him, white-hot and crackling.

"*That's not fair!*" he shouted.

Naomi shrugged.

"The game is called Traitorball, Ashur. I don't think they wanted it to be fair."

One by one, the other players crossed over the Allegiance Line and stood uncertainly on the other side. Naomi accepted all of them, leaving only Ashur and Jahi as the defenders. The two men looked at one another. Jahi shook his head and sighed, and then lowered himself into a defensive crouch, arms outstretched.

"Hit 'em hard, and hit 'em fast," he said quietly to Ashur. "If they're going to betray us, let's make them pay a price."

But there were simply too many of them. It was five against two, and even if Jahi and Ashur were the strongest players, it didn't take long before the offense realized they could just keep themselves spaced out, pass the ball around, and wait for Jahi or Ashur to commit before finding an open player. By the end, Ashur was exhausted from chasing the ball around the floor, his shoulder sore from crashing repeatedly into the other players.

The referee blew the whistle to signal the end of the game. Naomi stood atop the leaderboard, with Ashur and Jahi behind her and the other players much closer to them than they would have otherwise been.

"No hard feelings, boys," Naomi said as she walked off the court. Ashur ran after her, looming over her. But to his surprise, she didn't seem scared of him, staring up impassively.

"You screwed us over," Ashur said.

"Yes, I did," Naomi said.

"I would never lie like that."

"Well," Naomi said, putting a hand on his chest and stepping back, "maybe you should think about that. Or else I bet you're going to have a hard time here."

Then she turned and walked away, leaving Ashur standing there, watching her go.

"We'll get them next time, Ashur," Jahi said, putting a hand on his shoulder.

Ashur picked up the ball where it lay on the gymnasium floor and hurled it as hard as he could across the room. It didn't make him feel any better.

After Traitorball they sent the recruits back to their rooms to wash up and wait for the third and final test: Courage. They would be called down individually to the testing facility. Ashur stood under the hot water of the shower for a long time, leaning his head against the wall and wondering if he was already too far behind for the last test to make any difference.

How had he let Naomi betray him? Why hadn't he been more drawn to the math classes at his school? Here was this opportunity, dropped into his lap out of nowhere, and he felt like he was blowing it before he even had a chance to show them his potential. He didn't know where he would go if the Academy cut him, what he would do. He would be starting over completely.

Half an hour later, his Cube lit up, all excited: they were ready for him. Ashur took a deep breath and stepped out of his room. But immediately he was greeted by a familiar smell, the musky, sexy scent that had so captivated him at orientation the day before.

"Cassandra!" he called out, recognizing the woman's back just before she turned the corner.

He hurried after her—he had been hoping to see her all day. He grinned involuntarily at the thought of having another chance to talk with her. She was standing still, her back turned to him, shoulders held in tight.

Ashur said her name again. When she turned to look at him, her face was streaked with tears. She looked exhausted.

"Hey, what is it?" he said. Ashur reached out a hand to touch her softly on the arm, but she carefully shrugged it off.

"I'm fine."

"You don't look fine."

"I just need to rest."

"What happened?"

Cassandra looked up, a long sigh exhaled out her nose.

"You'll find out soon enough," she said.

"You took the last test?"

"I can't tell you anything."

Ashur frowned. "Can't, or don't want to?"

"Both," Cassandra said, and there was something fiery in her eyes as she glared back at Ashur.

He nodded. "Okay. I can respect that. But, Cassandra…"

"What?"

"I just want to make sure you're okay."

"I told you, I'm fine. Now go take the stupid test."

And then she was gone, walking fast down the hallway in the opposite direction as his Cube urged him on toward the test. But Ashur stood there, watching her until she turned a corner and disappeared, wondering what had happened to her, and what was waiting for him now.

It felt like he was in a hospital from the future. The room was spotless and white and silent, as though something was sucking all the noise out of it. Ashur was sitting in a large padded chair, leaned back like he was at the dentist. Two technicians were attaching sensors to him: a small oximeter on his finger, stickers with wireless diodes on his temples and neck, and a cuff around each arm slightly snugger than was comfortable. After a few minutes, a man wearing a bowtie and a white lab coat strode into the room, his Cube in tablet format as he flicked through it for information.

"Ashur Yonan!" the man said with a small smile. "I'm Dr. Smith. Welcome to the Emotional Resilience Testing Center."

One of the lab techs was now restraining his wrists against the padded armrests of the chair.

"This is the test?"

"It's perfectly safe, I assure you. I've never lost a recruit before. Well, not with this test anyway!" The man chuckled to himself, but Ashur couldn't tell what was meant to be funny.

"How does this work?"

"We're going to be measuring how you respond to pressure. A *lot* of pressure. A bombardment of audio and visual stimuli designed particularly with you in mind. Now, the helmet, please."

One of the lab techs produced a large helmet with a thin, nearly translucent screen extending downward and wrapping around the sides. Dr. Smith made some minute adjustments and then fastened it over Ashur's head. It fit snugly, and Ashur watched as the screen began to slowly move in toward him. The screen, more like plastic wrap than glass, fitted itself neatly over his skin as Dr. Smith hummed in approval.

"Life is all about handling crisis," Dr. Smith said as he adjusted the strap under Ashur's chin. "The more pressure you can take, the better equipped you are to deal with challenging situations. Your file says that you've already faced a lot of challenges. That's good for you—that profile tends to do better on this test than people who haven't had a particularly tough life. Deep breath now, Ashur."

Ashur sucked in a lungful of air and felt the screen fully press itself onto his face. The feeling was disorienting at first, but after a moment it was as though the screen wasn't there at all.

"A perfect graft," Dr. Smith said, nodding approvingly down at his tablet. "Now, keep in mind, Ashur, we can stop whenever you want. If it ever gets to be too much, just say the word. The experience can be…intense. Do you understand?"

Ashur took a deep breath. Here was his last chance to make an impression on the Academy and convince them that he had what it took to be part of their organization. He wasn't going to take any chances; he'd hold on as long as he could.

"I'm ready," he said.

"All right," Dr. Smith said, his fingers waggling as he scrolled through the tablet. He looked up one last time, a more serious expression on his face now. "Good luck, Ashur."

And then the room disappeared.

Ashur found himself on a dusty street with a charred Humvee smoldering beside him. At first all he could hear was a high-pitched whining. But then the sound of automatic gunfire began to ring out in its familiar *ratatat* pattern, mingled with the sounds of shouting coming from behind him. Bodies littered the ground as soldiers clutched the bloody wounds of their comrades. Ashur could feel his pulse rising. The images themselves weren't any worse than what he'd seen on TV or in war movies, but the immersion into this world was unlike anything he had ever experienced. It felt *real*, like all of this had really happened or was happening even now, and he was there amidst it.

Suddenly Ashur was in a car hurtling down the freeway. The shift from the battlefield to the driver's seat was enough to make his head spin as he tried to get a sense of what was happening. When he looked down at the steering wheel, the hands gripping it were his, but he had no ability to steer. It felt like being in a hyper-realistic dream, his body fuzzy and incapable of responding to the signals his brain was sending. The light at the intersection turned from yellow to red, but still Ashur kept speeding forward. A semitruck leaned on its horn as it came across the road, and Ashur could feel the tendons in his forearms straining as he tried as hard as he could to turn the wheel. But it was no use: the car smashed into the truck in an explosion of glass and metal as he felt his body rock forward. He gritted his teeth and braced for impact.

And then he was in a cave somewhere, a sliver of light dimly visible in the distance and the sound of running water behind him. When Ashur looked down, he could see that the chamber he was in was quickly filling with water. He was going to drown.

It kept on like this for some time, the scenarios becoming more graphic and intense with each new situation. Ashur could feel his heart beating fast now; he focused on breathing easily and tried to stay relaxed. How long, he wondered, had the other recruits managed to make it before giving up?

But then suddenly, Ashur was on a front lawn somewhere. The sudden quiet and serenity were disorienting after the percussive violence of the last few minutes. Ashur braced himself—surely this was some kind of trick meant to lull him into a false sense of security. He turned to look…and saw his father, laughing.

"You run so fast, Ashur!" Odishoo said, the familiar smile plastered across his face. "How can I possibly catch you when you run so fast?"

Ashur saw his mother behind them on the porch, a drink in her hand, glaring at him as he ran through the grass. He felt confused—was this a home video he had never seen before, or some kind of a recreation? More than any of the other scenarios, this one felt real, like a memory he had managed to forget.

And then a voice began whispering softly in his ear.

You've let your father down, Ashur, the voice said. *You're a failure. A disgrace to him and his memory.*

"That's not true," Ashur heard himself say softly, his voice muffled.

No wonder your mother drinks the way she does. No wonder she hits you.

"Those are her own issues," he said.

It's your fault that your father is dead.

A cold sweat formed on Ashur's skin.

"No—"

Suddenly he was on an unfamiliar city street, a crowd thronging around him and chanting in a language that sounded so familiar. He looked around and saw people carrying signs with the face of Khomeini on them, and others showing the Shah with his eyes gouged out or a giant red *X* over his face.

Your father wanted you to learn from history. He wanted you to change the world. But what have you done?

Ashur could feel himself trembling, the exhaustion of the last few days settling over him heavily. He tried to fight off the feeling, tried to stay present there on the streets of Iran even as the sinister voice continued to whisper in his ear.

Odishoo was wrong. You're not destined for greatness. You're not destined for anything.

"That's not true!" Ashur roared.

Then everything was very dark again. Ashur could feel the momentum of being wheeled down a hallway somewhere, and after a time realized there was light coming faintly through the sheet that blanketed his face. Everything hurt. He could feel slicks of wetness over his body, and hear the sound of sirens and an intercom. Someone lifted the sheet from his face, and he looked down at his body, bloodied and bruised beyond all recognition. His femur was sticking out of his leg, and Ashur felt himself close to vomiting. The only identifying feature he could see was the lion tattoo on his arm. But as he looked more closely, Ashur could tell the body wasn't his, and another wave of nausea hit him. It was Odishoo.

"*Dad!*" Ashur screamed, feeling the wetness on his face as he began to sob uncontrollably.

And then everything went black.

Odishoo puffed on his pipe meditatively. Ashur waited in silence. He could see how difficult it was for his father to tell this story— the end of his homeland as he had known it. Odishoo sighed and leaned back in his chair.

"*Jimmy Carter came to visit Iran. This is the end of 1977, while things were still somewhat under control. The idea was to show that there was still an alliance between him and the Shah.*

"*But the moment he left, things started to crumble. Students and religious leaders organized militant anti-Shah demonstrations. It wasn't safe to be in the streets—my mother kept me home from school. And when they sent the army to stop the demonstrations, several of the protesters were killed. In response there were even more protests—and riots across the country. By the summer, every city in Iran was seeing protests, with tens of thousands of people taking to the street. Khomeini had been calling for change in Iran's leadership for years, and now he finally had the perfect opportunity.*

"*The Shah asked the US for help—Kissinger especially. But he told the Shah he had nothing to worry about. Never mind that the media in the US and the UK made him look like a terrible leader who didn't care about his people, while making Khomeini look like the next Gandhi. One of my father's good friends, a man who worked closely with the Shah, advised him to ignore the Americans and move to quash the protests before they grew too strong. But the Shah waited, assuming that the protests would burn themselves out.*"

"*Who was Grandpa's friend?*" Ashur asked.

"*He would never share names with me,*" Odishoo said. "*But I do know that he was an extremely powerful and influential voice in the Shah's regime. He was tall, and very serious, I remember that much. Less likely to laugh than my father. But laughter was rare in those days.*"

Odishoo took another puff on his pipe.

"*By the end of the summer, the protests were attracting hundreds of thousands of people. Driving home from school with my* mom, protesters would hit the windows and scream, 'Marg bar Amrika'—death upon America."

"Why would they say that?" Ashur asked.

"Propaganda. They hated the Shah. They thought he was a puppet for the American government. They blamed the CIA for teaching SAVAK different torture methods and how to control the population. Some of the accusations were even true, to an extent— but almost every great nation has its own intelligence agency. I don't think that SAVAK was any worse than the rest of them.

"The violence kept getting worse. And then something happened. Something that was the point of no return. For the country...and for our family."

Tears sprang suddenly to Odishoo's eyes. Ashur saw that his fingers gripped the pipe so tightly that they were turning white. It frightened him to see his father so sad.

Odishoo swiped at the tears in his eyes and took a deep breath before continuing.

"Cinema Rex was a well-known movie theater in the city of Abadan—theaters had become a very common place for Islamist demonstrations. And that August, the theater was set on fire.

"They intentionally locked the doors of the theater so the people couldn't get out. Over four hundred people were killed. It was the largest terrorist attack in world history before 9/11.

"Khomeini's people blamed SAVAK. And the news spread across Iran like wildfire. Many of the Iranians who were still loyal to the Shah abandoned him after that. But right after the Shah fell, they identified who was behind the attack. The arsonists had been working with Islamist clerics, trying to turn the population against the Shah. And it worked. But by the time the truth emerged, it was too late."

"That's awful, Dad," Ashur said. "But...why was it the point of no return for our family?"

Odishoo wiped again at his face.

"My father's younger sister—my aunt Shamiran—was seven months pregnant the evening she and her husband decided to go see a movie at Cinema Rex. Both of them burned to death that night. She's the woman in the small picture in the upstairs hall—the one with the beautiful eyes, and a gorgeous smile."

Ashur knew that picture well. He had often wondered why there were no pictures of his own mother smiling like that.

"My father was devastated," Odishoo said. "And the only reason they were in Abadan in the first place was because my father had gotten a job for Shamiran's husband at the refinery there. He had thought it would be safer for them there.

"My father got a call in the middle of the night. I raced to the phone before he did. It was my grandmother. I could hear her screaming, 'She's dead! She's dead! They killed her!'

"My dad tried to calm her down, find out what she was talking about. But she was hysterical. Finally she settled down enough to tell him. My father fell to his knees crying. We didn't know what to do—not even my mother. She had never seen him cry before.

"He went up to his room after that. He made a few calls—even now I don't know who. But he came out after a few minutes and left for his mother's house. That was the night I truly understood that there was no going back. We were in a fight for our lives—and for our freedom.

"Our family didn't even have the chance to mourn because things were so unstable. And they only got worse, until my father sent us to America. And then he went missing."

THE ACADEMY

Ashur nodded. He had always known that his grandfather had been missing during his childhood, but only today did he start to understand why. They sat quietly for a time, the songs from Odishoo's playlist filling the air around them. For the first time, Ashur felt like a man, felt the weight of that responsibility as he sat in the backyard with his father, learning this great and terrible history.

CHAPTER SEVEN

"He lasted *how* long?"

"Ten minutes and twenty-two seconds."

"That's impossible. It's too much pressure. Something must have malfunctioned."

"I have the results right here. Look for yourself. And he didn't pass out without a fight, either."

Everything was black and fuzzy. As consciousness gradually came back to him, Ashur kept his eyes closed. It took him a minute to remember where he was: the testing facility.

"There's real potential here," he heard an unfamiliar voice say.

"If he lives long enough," said Dr. Smith. "Lasting as long as he did might just mean he's suicidal and reckless. We know he can withstand pain...and seems willing to push himself. He's willing to go to the limit. But will he do that for some higher purpose, or only because he has nothing to believe in?"

Still weak, Ashur could feel an old familiar anger begin to course through him. They had used his history to torture him, essentially, all in the name of finding out how much pain he could withstand. It seemed that he had done well, from the way the men were discussing his test results. But were they right, about him having nothing to live for? He had people he loved, like Kiki, and ideals he believed in.

But I don't have a cause that grips my heart, he thought to himself. *I still don't have a calling, or a purpose.*

Ashur felt lost all over again.

He let his eyes fall open. The room was full of activity as lab techs bustled around, adjusting sensors and whispering to one another as they took readings off the various monitors now arrayed around the room. For a few moments it was quiet, Ashur still too weak to move from the chair even if he hadn't been strapped in. But then Dr. Smith noticed that he was awake and came over to where he sat.

"Well, Ashur Yonan," he said, a small smile playing across his lips. "You seem to be full of surprises."

As Ashur made his way back to his room, physically and mentally drained, he noticed some other recruits in the halls carrying backpacks and duffel bags, looking dejected. One boy was openly crying. The tests were done; apparently some of the others were already heading home.

Suddenly, the thought of going back to his room—and finding out his scores—didn't seem so appealing. He was pretty sure he had done well on the last test, based on what Dr. Smith and the others had said when he woke up. But he was still sure that he had messed up the wisdom test, and he'd let that girl trick him and Jahi while playing Traitorball. He wasn't sure if he had done enough to make it into the Academy.

Ashur held his Cube up to the door of his room, took a deep breath, and stepped inside.

He settled the Cube into its dock and braced himself as the far wall illuminated with new messages.

CONGRATULATIONS, ASHUR YONAN. YOU ARE NOW AN APPRENTICE AT THE ACADEMY. REPORT AT 8:00 A.M. TOMORROW MORNING TO MEET YOUR TEAM.

Ashur heaved a tremendous sigh of relief and collapsed onto the bed. He felt like he could sleep for a year. But as his eyes closed, he heard the chirp of a new message coming in and pried open his right eye to read what it said.

Well done, read the message. *You have achieved some of the highest scores the Academy has ever seen. We are expecting great things from you, Ashur. I'm proud of you. And I know Odishoo would be, too.*

The message was again signed only by a single name: Admirer.

Ashur shot up in bed, his exhaustion gone now that his mind was whirling. Was it really possible that this "Admirer" had known his father so well, as he seemed to be implying? Was this some additional test meant to try to break him all over again? It seemed so cruel, but after the final emotional test earlier that day, anything seemed possible.

He hated that Admirer could contact him anonymously, hated that whoever it was ignored his messages back. And he hated the way that, even as he doubted what the message said, his heart still swelled at the notion that Odishoo would have been proud of him if he could have been there to see him. He balled his hand up into a fist and slammed it back against the headboard of the bed, feeling the wood crack beneath his blow and the pain that began to spread through his arm with the impact.

"Tell me who you are!" he shouted across the room to where the words were still suspended on the opposite wall.

SEND MESSAGE? the Cube asked, spinning around in its pedestal. If Ashur didn't know better, he would have sworn the Cube looked nervous as it waited for his answer.

"Sure. Whatever," Ashur said, feeling himself deflate. He needed to find out who this Admirer was—but at a place as secretive as the Academy, it seemed like anyone who wanted to stay hidden could do so pretty easily. He let out a groan and fell back to sleep.

Dawn came too quickly. Ashur felt like he had just closed his eyes when the curtains to the room were thrown back and sunlight came streaming in. His Cube was practically dancing as it spun in its pedestal, chirping happily as it prepared the room for Ashur to get ready for the day.

YOU MADE IT THROUGH THE TESTS! read the message. NOW THE FUN STUFF CAN START!

Ashur felt like he'd been run over by a truck. The last test especially had drained every last bit of energy from him, and he felt like he had just barely had time to recharge anything. Still, after all the uncertainty of recent days, it was gratifying to know that he had made it this far—and earned the right to see what came next for training with the Academy. He pushed himself out of bed and got ready for the day.

Half an hour later, showered and wearing new clothes that fit him perfectly, Ashur was following his Cube down the halls of the main building at the Academy. Every other apprentice he passed nodded and smiled at him. Any of them, he thought, could potentially be his new teammate...or bitter rival, keeping him from what he wanted. Still, the mood was hopeful, mixed with the anxieties of the first day of school.

His Cube led him to a plain wooden door off the main hall. Ashur took a breath and then walked in.

The room looked like an old college classroom, with steep seating rising up around a podium in front of a vast array of chalkboards. It smelled like chalk dust and leather and the faint scent of old pipe tobacco. Three heads turned to look at him at the sound of the door opening.

"My man," Jahi said, smiling wide and coming over with his hand extended. "I thought we were toast after yesterday."

Ashur grinned, happy to see a familiar face.

"I did, too. Maybe they want to see whether we can learn from our mistakes."

"Yeah, well, I'm not sure I'm ready to have 'trust nobody' be my motto," Jahi said. "But I'm going to choose my teammates much more wisely going forward."

"That's smart thinking," Boris said. Ashur hadn't noticed him at first, sitting meekly in the first row of seats.

"You made it," Ashur said, coming forward and shaking his hand.

"Yeah, somehow," Boris said. "I almost screwed up that first test, too. I came up with some crazy polynomial theory for what was going on with all those numbers before realizing it was actually just a simple N-plus-one situation. So much for higher-level math."

Ashur cocked his head to the side.

"What do you mean?"

"That first test? With the flashing strobe lights and happy music when you got things right? Trick question, basically. The only rule was that the numbers have to go up sequentially."

Jahi muttered something under his breath and shook his head, but Ashur kept looking at Boris.

"Are you sure?"

"Positive. They wanted you to overthink it. Get too cute."

I got it right, Ashur thought, still not believing he had actually managed to stumble upon the correct answer. It still felt like a fluke, but maybe luck was on his side more than he realized.

"They wanted the negative feedback to scare you," said a woman sitting high up in the stands, away from the others. She had her Cube in tablet mode and was typing away furiously, not bothering to look up as she spoke. She was tall and thin, with bright red hair she wore back in a tight ponytail. She looked slightly alien to Ashur, like someone who had crash-landed on Earth and was trying to figure out how to behave around other humans. "Humans crave positive reinforcement. But the only way to properly test the patterns was to try everything. Learn to crave those strobe lights and sirens, because they mean you're learning and getting closer to the truth."

"You're trying to tell me you *liked* having those strobe lights flash in your face?" Jahi said, looking up at her. The woman finished keying something into her Cube and then peered down at where the rest of them were standing.

"I hated it. I'm photosensitive and dislike loud noises. It was torture for me. But I told myself that none of it mattered, because the satisfaction of getting the answer right was greater than any momentary discomfort."

"Damn," Boris said. "That's hardcore."

"I'm Ashur," Ashur said, climbing up the steps to where the woman was now standing, even more spindly now that she was out of her seat. When he held out his hand, she looked down at it uncertainly, as though she wasn't entirely sure what to do with it. Eventually, though, she grasped it briefly and then released it.

"I'm Brodi," she said.

"What was that you were doing on your Cube?" he asked. This was enough to draw a smile from Brodi.

"Just exploring. For a place that's super secretive, most of their infrastructure is pretty open. If you know the right questions to ask, you can poke around the network. It's beautiful—so elegant. I can't wait to learn more."

Ashur smiled—and made a note to himself to ask Brodi whether there was any good way to track down who was sending messages through the network. Maybe she would have an idea for how he could figure out who was really sending him things from the Admirer account.

"I thought I was going to be the nerdy one," Boris said. Jahi chuckled and shook his head.

The door to the room opened again, and they all turned to look. Ashur felt his heart leap in his chest as he watched Cassandra come into the room. The last time he had seen her, she was crying in the hallway, still shaken up by her experience of the final test. He wondered what it had been like for her, and what the Academy had used to bring her to the edge. He resolved to ask her about it, once they had a minute alone. But now, Cassandra looked perfectly collected in a smart pantsuit that tastefully showed off her elegant body, her warm brown hair tied back in a bun and a little smile on her face as she looked around the room.

"Am I late?" she asked.

"Right on time."

A man had entered the auditorium through a door that Ashur hadn't noticed before and was making his way toward the podium. He was a slight man, wearing a tweed suit. His black hair was combed back from a widow's peak, and his face sported a neatly trimmed salt-and-pepper beard. He had the avuncular vibe of a favorite college professor, or someone's friendly uncle. But already Ashur thought he could sense a fierce intelligence in the man as he surveyed each of them in turn. Cassandra took a seat in the front row as the man placed a worn leather briefcase beside him and cleared his throat.

"I suspect you're all a bit sick of welcome speeches by now," he said, chuckling a little to himself. "But if you'll indulge me for a few moments, I'll introduce myself, and our mission for the precious time we have to spend together.

"I was recruited to the Academy when I was your age. This was back in 1976, and I had no sense of what I wanted my life to be. My time here helped me find my first passion, in law. After practicing for several decades, the Academy gave me the great honor of promoting me to be a full-time instructor. And nothing has given me a greater sense of fulfillment than giving young people like you the tools to find your own path, and your own purpose."

He looked down briefly, as though remembering something from long ago, then looked back up with a smile.

"If you graduate, you may get to learn my real name. But here, I am known as Cicero."

Cicero had the apprentices go around and briefly introduce themselves. Ashur already knew most of what Jahi said: he was from South Florida, on his way to Miami on a football scholarship, and then on to the seminary to become a youth pastor. Boris had come to the States from Minsk when he was a baby; he competed with the top team in the Math Olympiad when he was fourteen years old and was playing his way through Bach's

Goldberg Variations on the piano just for fun. Brodi won a bracelet on the World Poker Tour on her eighteenth birthday, playing an obscure poker variant called Razz; she also claimed to have hacked into at least one major governmental agency and accepted their reward for white-hat coders who show vulnerabilities in their systems. Cassandra was from Connecticut, a champion Lincoln-Douglas debater who had been on her way to Harvard before the Academy recruited her. She had also been a nationally ranked squash player until a hamstring injury put her out for the year, but she still hoped to play for fun.

"Sounds WASP-y as hell," Boris said with a shy smile. Cassandra turned back and playfully stuck out her tongue at him.

"Your turn, Ashur," Cicero said. "Tell us a little about yourself."

Ashur was quiet for a moment, not sure what to say. All the other apprentices had already accomplished so much—what did he have to show for himself in comparison? It was difficult, in moments like this, not to feel all over again like the Academy had made some mistake in choosing him. But then again, other recruits had already been sent home, unable to pass the initial tests. That had to mean something, didn't it?

"I'm Ashur Yonan," he started. "I got kicked out of high school for fighting. Until a few days ago, I worked at the Big Boy in Burbank. I broke up an armed robbery there, with my father's gun, but the police brought me in for not having a license to carry. But instead of going to jail, I got sent here. And I'm still trying to figure it all out."

It was silent in the auditorium for a time after that, everyone else taking in what Ashur had told them.

"Woah," Boris said. "Was your dad angry at you?"

"My dad's dead."

"Oh. I'm sorry."

Ashur felt something catch briefly in his throat and nodded to Boris.

"Thanks."

Cicero clapped his hands together once, bringing all the attention in the room back to him. Ashur was grateful—he wasn't sure how much more he would have been able to say.

"Now that we all know each other a little better, why don't I give you a little taste of what you can expect during your time here at the Academy? If you would all just follow me…"

Cicero strode briskly to the back of the auditorium, the apprentices rising and following him. He held his Cube up to a small panel on the wall that Ashur hadn't noticed before. There was a brief chirping noise and then a deeper vibration, the sound of machinery moving deep beneath the earth. Slowly, the floor began to give way, and Ashur found himself peering down a long series of steps extending down so far that it was impossible to see where they led.

"Cool," Jahi said.

"Very cool," Cassandra said. "But where do they go?"

Cicero stepped back and held out a hand.

"To the Vault."

The humming sound came to an end with a slight shudder. No one moved for a moment. But then Ashur stepped forward and began his descent, the gentle lights and bright collegiate smell of the auditorium giving way to the still air of a dark passageway as he made his way further and further down.

At the end of the stairs was a door that appeared to be made of obsidian, smooth and so black that it absorbed what little light filtered down from the auditorium. Cicero brought his Cube up to the door and it slid open.

"Everyone in," he said, and then closed the door behind him.

Other than a faint humming sound, there was no sense of motion as they stood in the room. But it was clearly an elevator, and Ashur found its smooth descent uncanny—it was impossible to guess how far down they were traveling.

"How far below ground are we?" Boris asked. His eyes, Ashur noticed, were clamped shut. He wondered if the man was afraid of enclosed spaces.

"A very long way indeed," Cicero said.

"Oh, great," Boris groaned.

"For protection?" Ashur asked.

Cicero nodded. "The Vault stores our most important knowledge and technology. We needed the space, somewhere that wouldn't attract too much attention. And we built it to withstand a nuclear attack, though hopefully it will never come to that."

The elevator glided to a halt and the doors slid open. The space was massive—Ashur couldn't see a ceiling above them, just white pillars that seemed to rise indefinitely from the polished concrete floor until they disappeared into the gloom above. As Cicero led them forward, they passed by a number of glass cases, each displaying different artifacts: ancient maps, swords and pistols, statuettes, and bits of machinery that Ashur couldn't identify. There were a number of elevator doors like the ones they'd just taken down, leading, he assumed, to other places on the campus.

Cicero approached another door, this one designed in the style of an old bank vault with a metal wheel affixed to it. Emblazoned on the front of the vault door, and seeming to glow faintly against the dark metal, was the same lion that Ashur had seen when he first came to the Academy.

"Take out your Cubes, please," Cicero said.

The five apprentices produced their Cubes and held them forward in their hands. One by one, the Cubes began to glow, lights of different colors passing between them as they synced.

"Through this door is our true classroom," Cicero said as the process finished. "And your best instructors will be some of history's greatest and most fascinating minds. But I'll warn you now—the experience can get intense. If you ever need, for any reason, to stop, use the Blink function on your Cube to stop the interaction."

"Interaction?" Brodi said.

Cicero smiled. "You'll see."

He showed them the small groove on the Cube that had subtly jutted out from the metal, holding his finger briefly over it and looking around to Ashur and the others to make sure that they understood.

"So, are you ready?" he said.

"Yes," Ashur said.

"Then let's begin."

The Cubes suddenly all began to glow a bright, brilliant white, the little devices turning around just above the palms of the five apprentices. The door groaned open, and Cicero stepped through.

"Don't you know it's rude to keep a girl waiting like this, Cicero?" said an oddly familiar voice. Ashur followed into the room and found a voluptuous blonde woman in a pair of black pants and a tight-fitting sleeveless blouse unbuttoned to show off her ample cleavage. The peroxide-blonde hair, the pouty red lips, the unmistakable beauty mark—there was no question who this was.

"My sincere apologies," Cicero said with a small bow. He turned to the apprentices with a smile on his face. "Class, I'm pleased to introduce you to Marilyn Monroe."

"By November of 1978, it was all over," Odishoo said. "People who supported the Shah were afraid to speak out, because of the consequences. The Shah himself reached out to the US for support, but it was no use. They knew it was over—and weren't going to do anything to stop it.

"On December second, two million people showed up in the streets of Tehran, in what they now called Azadi square, chanting for the removal of the Shah. They really felt like they could do anything. Within a week the protests had grown to five million, all over Iran. Imagine that, in a country with forty million people. It was enough to make the French and Russian revolutions look small.

"The Shah took his family into exile in Egypt in January. It was a sad day for those who loved the Shah…and years later, the day that Khomeini's supporters look back on and realize what a mistake they'd made.

"With the Shah gone, the prime minister was forced to free political prisoners, order the army to leave demonstrators alone, and dissolve SAVAK. Just a few days later, on February first, he allowed Khomeini to return to Iran. No pope has ever received the kind of welcome that Khomeini got: millions at the airport to welcome him, chanting 'Islam, Khomeini we will follow you.' He had

become a divine figure. And we were terrified—we didn't know how he would choose to retaliate against the Shah's supporters."

"But, Dad, I don't get it," Ashur said. "How could everyone hate the Shah after what you told me about how he made Iran so much stronger?"

Odishoo leaned forward to pause the CD player.

"Human nature has a weakness, Ashur: we take things for granted before we lose them. And people took for granted their individual freedom. But it only took a few days for Khomeini to declare himself the Supreme Leader of Iran and start issuing decrees. The people no longer had a voice in their own governance. It was terrifying. Can you imagine, being afraid to live in your own country?"

Ashur shook his head.

"It all sounded good, initially," Odishoo continued. "How great Iran could be with the overthrow of the Shah—the man who had killed and tortured all those people. But Khomeini and his religious regime made the Shah look like a saint compared to the bloodshed they brought to Iran—and countries all over the world."

Odishoo turned the CD player back on and leaned back in his chair.

"Khomeini and his people had no experience running a nation. The whole economy was soon in shambles as inflation soared— what you could buy with seven toman now cost a thousand. People who had been well off under the Shah left the country. They didn't have much money anymore, but they were happy to sacrifice their wealth to give the freedom they'd once had back to their children. The people who had bought into the idea that the rich were too rich and the poor were too poor were the ones who paid the biggest price. The rich, who made the economy function, all left for other countries. And the people in the middle no longer knew what to do.

Tourism completely dried up. No one was thinking about bringing their families to Iran for vacation, and the days of watching beautiful girls at the beach were over.

"And Khomeini hated anyone who had ever supported the Shah. His regime executed ten thousand innocent Iranians: police officers, liberal intellectuals, military leaders, and any high-ranking individual they could get their hands on who supported the Shah. Churches and synagogues were destroyed. The gay community, which had existed before in a 'don't ask/don't tell' environment—there were even beloved gay celebrities—was persecuted. Khomeini considered gay people to be mentally ill, and had thousands executed. Citizens could be arrested merely for owning satellite dishes that might tune into Western programs.

"People were afraid to say anything against the new regime. My family stayed inside as much as possible, afraid of being harassed—or worse—by Khomeini's thugs, the hezbollahi.

"In the end, the 'change' that Khomeini had promised the Iranian people was an exchange: freedom for control. Women in particular. My mother went from being able to wear comfortable clothes to suddenly having to cover her entire body with a chador. *If any hair or skin was shown, even by accident, women would be arrested and whipped seventy-seven times."*

Ashur shuddered. "Why would women stay there?"

"Many didn't," Odishoo said. "Khomeini and his people considered women second-class citizens. Before the revolution, women in Iran had the same freedoms as men. But things changed quickly. They had no right to voice their opinions about anything. Husbands and wives were not allowed to hold hands or kiss in public. And if a wife cheated on her husband, or lost her virginity before marriage, she would be stoned to death. Does that sound like a place people would want to live, want to raise their families?"

"Not at all," Ashur said.

"Do you think most people knew this was going to take place when they supported Khomeini?"

"I hope not."

"That's why we must educate ourselves carefully about politics, instead of simply accepting what others tell us."

Ashur tucked his father's words away carefully in his mind.

"But none of what I just told you about was even the worst part of the revolution's effect on Iran…and the world."

CHAPTER EIGHT

Ashur couldn't believe his eyes. Sitting right there, perched on a desk on a small stage at the front of the room, with her shapely legs swaying gently beneath her and a coy smile on her face, was Marilyn Monroe. She noticed him staring and gave him a sly wink, then threw back her head and giggled.

"Looking as lovely as ever, Ms. Monroe," Cicero said with a smile.

"You old flatterer," she said breathily. She stood up from the desk and put her hands on her hips, turning to look over the apprentices. "My, aren't you an attractive group—best-looking apprentices I've seen in years."

"Um, ma'am?" Jahi said. Ashur thought his friend looked deeply uncomfortable, glancing back and forth between Marilyn and Cicero. "Aren't you, ah. Well, you know…"

"Dead?" Marilyn said, giggling again and hiding her mouth behind her hand. "Of course, cutie. I've been dead since 1962. But I'll tell you the truth: I'm not sure I've ever felt better than I do being here today with you all."

"Is she a clone?" Brodi asked, leaning in closer so she could get a better look.

"I don't think so," Boris said. "A hologram, maybe?"

Brodi scoffed.

"No way. There's no flicker at all, and no projection source that I can see. Technology like that would be…"

"Rather advanced, indeed," Cicero said, with a smile on his face. He stepped toward the desk, and Marilyn extended her arm toward him. Cicero held a hand aloft, and then passed it through the woman as though she was made of air. The apprentices gasped.

"All of us in the Vault are holograms," Marilyn said, and Ashur thought he could see a touch of wistful sadness in her eye.

"Like the Worldcorp billboards I've been seeing all around LA," Ashur said.

"Precisely," Cicero said, stepping down off the stage. "We've been rolling out the technology to the public, slowly but surely, over the last few years. We've found that if we show off everything at once, people tend to be…unsettled."

"So it's, what, some kind of informed artificial intelligence?" Brodi said.

Cicero raised his eyebrows.

"Well, let's see now. Unpack what you mean by that, Brodi."

Brodi leaned back and put her hands behind her head.

"Obviously you use all available data sources that exist on the person and the life they led—videos of the individual, if they're available, books, journals, recordings, every writing and first-hand account you can find. Triangulate across every possible read on the person to most faithfully recreate their response."

With lips flatted, Cicero asked, "Would all that impress you?"

"Honestly? Not really," Brodi said. "Anyone can feed their own Large Language Models with the same data and recreate the responses of a historical figure."

For a moment, Brodi looked hard at the voluptuous blonde, briefly mesmerized by the woman.

"Of course, that doesn't explain how she appears so life-like, almost down to the pores on her skin and the hairs on her head," she said. Cicero smiled.

"Ms. Monroe is, in actuality, *exactly* how she looked in real life. But setting aside Marilyn's appearance, I can offer but two small hints as to what makes our holograms' brains tick."

Boris shook his head.

"It's not so different from the neural nets they're building in the labs," he said. "I bet MIT could make a version of Marilyn that works just as well."

"Not exactly," Cicero said, bristling a little at the suggestion.

"Why? What's so special about what you do?" Boris said.

Cicero's eyes lit up and his chin rose slightly. "First, I can disclose that the Academy's holographic faculty are imbued with *astonishingly more* information about their real-life counterparts than exists *anywhere* else on the planet today."

The apprentices all processed this. Finally, Asher said, "I saw holograms of Abraham Lincoln and Cleopatra back in Glendale. Where do you get more information about the real lives of Lincoln, Cleopatra, and Marilyn Monroe that doesn't already exist publicly?"

"That's the second and final hint I'm able to offer," said Cicero. "In 1946, the Academy's archaeology team made a remarkable, unpublished discovery in northern Iraq: the ruins of one of the Seven Wonders of the Ancient World, the Hanging Gardens of Babylon."

Cicero scanned the stunned faces with pride. "Except, they weren't in Babylon and they weren't built by Nebuchadnezzar," he said. Cicero then seemed to give the slightest of glances to

Ashur and continued, "They were located in ancient Assyria, and they housed the tomb of King Ashurbanipal, who built the great library at Ninevah."

Ashur straightened up in his chair. "What did it all look like?"

"Flattened, and oddly fossilized," Cicero said. "But the organic remains made it possible to identify two hundred species of flora, from all over the world, as well as species that we can't identify or explain to this day."

"Oooh," Marilyn cooed, "get to the good part, about what we found in the tomb."

Cicero seemed to enjoy being bossed around, smiling wide at her.

"Indeed. There was an artifact preserved beside Ashurbanipal's remains—a small, intricately designed metallic object with an unusual sheen. The archeology team's field equipment began to behave erratically; even their watches malfunctioned," he said. "And, as they tell the story, they all began experiencing a sense of vertigo when they stared straight at the artifact."

"Some say that I have that same effect on men," Marilyn said.

The apprentices were silent, ignoring Marilyn's quip. Even Brodi had a puzzled look on her face.

Cicero cleared his throat.

"So, we sent it to our top physicist, at Philips NatLab in the Netherlands, and he made some remarkable discoveries."

Finally, Boris got his voice back.

"Amazing. Now what does this have to do with training these holograms with 'astonishingly more information about their real-life counterparts than exists anywhere else on the planet today'?"

"Great memory," Cicero said. "Photographic?"

Boris flushed.

"Let's just say that that artifact has allowed the Academy to become *exceptional, one-of-a-kind* gatherers of information," said Cicero. "And that information has made our holographic instructors as genuine as the real thing."

At that moment, Marilyn stood up, rolled her eyes, folded her arms, and stomped her high heels. "Any day now, Cicero…"

"Still a work in progress, as everything is. Though our patents ensure that we are several steps ahead of anyone else—and will stay that way for some time. But I think you'll find Ms. Monroe a more than capable teacher."

"She's going to be our teacher?" Jahi said. Ashur noticed that the man still seemed uncomfortable—while the other recruits seemed unable to take their eyes off the hologram, Jahi was looking down at his feet, shy in a way that Ashur couldn't remember seeing his friend before.

"For your first lesson," Cicero said.

"Which is on, what, makeup and cleavage?" Cassandra said. She was standing with her arms folded across her chest and seemed largely unimpressed.

"Those are only the tools," Marilyn said, apparently unfazed by Cassandra's standoffish attitude. "But the goal—and the danger—is its own thing entirely."

"Sex?" Boris said.

Marilyn tittered. "Close. Seduction."

"I don't get it," Cassandra said. "Why should sex—or seduction, whatever—have priority over all the other things we could be studying?"

"What's wrong with sex?" Ashur asked.

"Nothing's *wrong* with sex," Cassandra said, rolling her eyes. "But this is, like, some totally male fantasy."

Jahi shifted uncertainly, his mouth still twisted into a frown.

"Cicero, sir," he said. "I'm not really sure if this is, um, appropriate…for me to be studying."

"Not all of your lessons at the Academy will be comfortable, Jahi," Cicero said. "Often, the goal is explicitly to push you outside your comfort zone. But I assure you, there is reasoning behind the curriculum. Everything we do is in the service of helping you grow and achieve your potential."

"It's interesting that you describe this as a male fantasy, Cassandra," Marilyn said, a small smile on her face. *She knows our names*, Ashur thought to himself. "Tell me, have you ever been seduced?"

"That's a personal question," Cassandra said.

"Oh, very personal," Marilyn said. "Don't worry. It's just between us girls."

Cassandra huffed, and then shook her head. "I don't think so."

"Oh, you'd know. It's the greatest feeling in the entire world," Marilyn said, sweeping her arms out wide and then smoothing down the pleats of her billowy skirt. "Imagine someone you like—someone you find yourself thinking about constantly—but who you don't think even knows that you exist. And then, all of a sudden, they've trained the entirety of their attention on you. Like a spotlight on a stage, everything else in darkness. Like you're the only thing in the world that matters—or has ever mattered. That you're the most beautiful, most interesting, most captivating woman in the world, in their eyes. And you let yourself believe it, because you want to—and because it feels so good."

Marilyn Monroe turned now and looked right at Ashur.

"How about you, handsome? Has anything like that ever happened to you? Or maybe you've done it to someone else?"

Ashur paused for a moment, considering the question. Things with Kiki had felt a little bit like what Marilyn was describing—how good it felt to have her believe in him, to give him her time and attention and energy. But he was pretty sure that wasn't a seduction. He felt more like they were equals, each of them invested in the other. All of a sudden, he felt a sharp pang of longing for Kiki. He thought about their last trip up the coast and the night they had spent together. He wasn't sure if he would ever see her again.

He shook that thought from his mind and tried to focus on the question at hand. Sex had always come easily for him—but did that mean he had actually seduced his partners? He was rigorously honest and up-front with the women he slept with, making sure they understood where he was coming from and what he was looking for: a little fun, some physical release, but nothing more than that. It hadn't been his intention to seduce anyone. But if someone asked these women now, "Were you seduced by Ashur Yonan?" maybe some of them would say yes. Was it possible to seduce someone without really trying? Or maybe it was the fact that you weren't really trying, and that you didn't particularly seem to care, that made you all the more irresistible.

"Is it possible to seduce someone by accident?" Ashur said. In the row behind him, Brodi snorted.

"Okay, player," she said. Ashur shook his head and felt himself flush slightly.

"I didn't mean it like that."

Marilyn smiled at Ashur. She leaned back to prop herself up on her hands, slowly uncrossing her legs to recross them at the ankle.

"In a way. I was always attracted to men who didn't throw themselves at me. The ones who I couldn't seduce easily—they always caught my attention, because my spell didn't work on them. Not fully, at least."

"Who could resist *you?*" Boris asked. Ashur and Brodi chuckled at him, and his face flushed red.

Marilyn smiled and touched a hand to her hair, her eyes looking briefly off to the side. "Well," she said softly, "there was one man who did, even though we knew each other for many years and felt so much love for one another...not to mention attraction."

"Who was he?" Boris asked.

Marilyn looked back at the apprentices, her face aglow. "John."

"John Kennedy?" Cassandra said.

Marilyn shrugged, still smiling. "I just think of him as John. We never did get together, but I loved him wholeheartedly until the end. I wish we'd had a chance, but...that's how it goes sometimes."

"I'm sorry, but what's the point of all of this?" Cassandra said. "Are we just going to sit here and talk about all the men that Marilyn Monroe did or didn't sleep with?"

A hurt expression came over Marilyn's face, and Ashur felt himself filled with unexpected anger.

"What kind of a question is that?" he asked Cassandra.

She looked at him over her shoulder. "Seems pretty straightforward to me."

"Straightforward—and mean!"

Cassandra sighed and rolled her eyes. "She's a hologram, Ashur. A simulation. Computer programs don't have real feelings."

Ashur looked back over at the desk. Marilyn was swinging her legs back and forth, with a small, sad smile on her face, looking expectantly at him.

"Oh, don't worry about me, Ashur. I'm a big girl. It's not the first time people have been nasty to me."

Cassandra looked back at Cicero.

"Look, can you just explain to me why this is where we're starting? I feel like I would get more out of the lesson if I understood the thinking behind it."

Cicero put a finger to his chin and looked off into the distance, as though considering her request. Finally he closed his eyes and nodded.

"Very well. Marilyn?"

"The usual presentation, Cicero?" Marilyn said.

"I think so."

Suddenly the far wall was lit up with the picture of a man, handsome and wearing robes, with a crown of gold on his head. Soon, his image was replaced with one of another man, this one wearing the ruffled collar of an Elizabethan courtier. The procession of images began to go faster and faster, until there was barely enough time to see any particular individual. Ashur watched closely, trying to place the figures as they flickered before his eyes. The effect was overwhelming, almost nauseating.

"Stop," Cicero said. The image suspended on the far wall was of a politician Ashur recognized who had been undone by a sex scandal a few years earlier.

"We are evolutionarily programmed to pursue sex, at any cost," Cicero explained. "The more children we have, the better our odds of genetic success. It's how our species survives. But in the process, countless people—people with great potential who otherwise could have changed the world for the better—have destroyed themselves."

"We start here because, of all the ways in which you might not be able to achieve what we believe you can, the most likely is that you fall victim to your own lust," Marilyn Monroe said. "Kings, presidents, generals, spiritual leaders, inventors, entertainers have fallen because of it. Entire empires have fallen. So we want to teach you to recognize it, guard against it when necessary, and use it to your advantage when the opportunity arises."

"Like, counterintelligence stuff?" Brodi said.

"Sure," Marilyn said. "But, you know…more fun!"

"I know it seems like a strange place to start, Cassandra," Cicero said. "But I want you to trust me."

"You really think I can't keep it in my pants?" Cassandra said. Cicero grinned and looked down.

"I think you have no idea what you're capable of. You, or anyone else in this room. And that's what we intend to show you during your time here."

"Shall we introduce the other instructors?" Marilyn said. "It's not a party when it's just little old me."

Cicero nodded. "I think that's an excellent idea."

A sudden flash of light, and then four other figures were standing up on the stage flanking Marilyn Monroe. One woman in particular caught Ashur's attention: deep olive skin and almond-shaped eyes, her face elaborately painted and a headdress resting on top of her jet-black hair. She had golden bangles up and down her arms and thin, delicate wrists. When she noticed Ashur looking at her, her eyes narrowed slightly as she stared back at him. Ashur felt something in his stomach flip slightly.

"Time for practice," Cicero said.

A few minutes later, Ashur was sitting at the front of the room, the eyes of the other apprentices on him. Across from him was the woman who had caught his eye, looking impassively at him, as though waiting for him to bark or perform a trick. There was something intimidating about the way she was looking at him, a feeling that Ashur usually never had in the company of a beautiful woman. But it wasn't just that she was beautiful—she had been, at one time, arguably the most powerful woman in the world.

He took a deep breath. It felt slightly awkward to have everyone else watching him, as though he were on a first date being observed by an audience. But he told himself that this was no different than talking with any other woman.

"May I call you Cleopatra?"

The woman stared at him for a long time. He couldn't tell whether she was bored, offended, or amused by his presence and his attempts to engage her in conversation.

"Who are your people?" she said.

"My people?" Ashur said, looking back at the other apprentices and Cicero.

"Not them. Your kin. Of what land are you?"

"I am Assyrian," Ashur told the woman, remembering his father's stories about their ancient lands. At the mention of this, Cleopatra's lips curled into a smile.

"An old people. Once great. No longer. Pity."

Ashur felt a hot flash of something between anger and embarrassment—who was this woman, dead now for millennia, to tell him anything about his people?

"We are still great."

"You are a people without a land of your own to rule. Doomed to wander. Oh, pretty, sensitive Assyrian boy."

Ashur tried to fight down the feelings welling up within him. But he knew that, in some ways, she was right. By the time Cleopatra had ruled over the Egyptian empire, the Babylonians had been ruling Assyria for centuries already. He snuck a glance up at Cleopatra—she was smiling at him, a wicked sort of smile, knowing that she was getting under his skin. He took a deep breath, and imagined he was back in high school, noticing a girl across the hallway he thought was halfway cute. He was fearless then, willing to talk to anyone, not worrying what they thought of him or whether they liked him yet. They would come around to him. They always did.

He put on a cocky smile and leaned back in his seat, trying to look at relaxed as possible.

"You think I'm pretty?" he said to Cleopatra. He watched as a look of surprise passed over her face, and then a very small bit of color ran through her cheeks beneath the layers of elaborate makeup. He leaned forward, grinning, and waited to see what she would have to say.

By the end of the day's lessons, Ashur was exhausted. He had done well in his back-and-forth with Cleopatra. She hadn't come all the way around to him, but he was pretty sure that if she were real, he could have convinced her to go out to dinner with him, if not to bed. The other students hadn't fared nearly as well: Jahi had stared at his feet the whole time he tried talking with Helen of Troy; Boris had tried to discuss chess with a Chinese princess from the Han dynasty; and Cassandra had been openly hostile toward Lancelot, to the point where the knight had asked her if anything was the matter. Brodi, however, had done unexpectedly well, though she had requested to practice on Frida Kahlo, the two women chatting more like friends than potential lovers.

Cicero told them it had been a good first day and dismissed them back to their rooms until lessons the next morning. At Jahi's suggestion, the team had gone to dinner together in the cafeteria. Despite how awkward and fumbling Jahi had been during the seduction lesson, Ashur could tell that he was a natural leader—quick to seek consensus among different kinds of people, trying to forge points of commonality. It didn't feel forced, the way it sometimes did with others who tried to establish themselves as authority figures. Ashur thought that he would make a good youth pastor.

Jahi tried to convince Ashur to go play another round of Traitorball after dinner, but Ashur was wiped—he was looking forward to being back in his room, thinking over his first day and resting up for the next day's lesson. But as he was getting into the elevator, he heard a voice calling out his name. He turned around and found Cassandra, hurrying after him.

"Hey," she said, the door to the elevator closing just after she stepped inside. The small space was quickly filled with the scent of her perfume, and Ashur had to work hard not to take a deep inhale.

"That was...intense, today," she said.

"Yeah," Ashur said. "Though, to be honest, it didn't really seem like you wanted to be there."

Cassandra shook her head and looked up at the ceiling of the elevator.

"It was different from how I thought it was going to be. Weirder. I don't know."

"Does sex make you uncomfortable?"

She laughed, but it sounded awkward to Ashur. "No. Sex is fine. But I never would have thought that's where they'd have us start."

Ashur nodded—he had been surprised, too. "I guess we have to trust them? Believe them when they say they have a plan?"

"Oh, sure. Defer to authority. You seem like you're great at that."

Ashur grinned as the elevator doors dinged open at their floor. "Yeah. Not exactly my typical MO."

"Look," Cassandra said as they walked down the hall, their Cubes leading the way back toward their respective rooms. "I sucked today in the practice. I know that. And if I keep sucking, I'm going to drag the whole team down. I don't want that to happen."

"I wouldn't worry so much about it," Ashur said. "It was only the first day."

"But I was thinking. It seems like you know what you're doing. Maybe you could show me some pointers sometime? Make it so that I'm not just scowling at various historical figures?"

Ashur stopped walking for a moment. After how Cassandra had performed all day during the lessons, the last thing he expected was for her to admit she'd been bad and come to him asking for help. But more than that, she was asking for help in the art of seduction. Was she coming on to him, or genuinely asking for him to make her better? *And why*, he thought, *does it have to be one or the other?*

Ashur again felt something course through him, the same way it had earlier in the day when he had been listening to Marilyn and his thoughts had turned to Kiki. He couldn't believe their trip had only been a few days earlier. It felt like so much had changed since then. Was he ready for someone new—if that was really what Cassandra wanted? And if he wasn't, would he be helping a rival get a leg up on him when it came time to choose which apprentices got to advance to the further levels of the Academy?

"Sure, Cassandra, I'd be happy to."

"Cool," she said. "I'll message you."

She gave him a quick wave and then walked down the hall toward her room, Ashur watching as she went. He wondered if she could feel his eyes on her, tracking her shapely body as she moved away from him. He wondered if she liked it. When she turned the corner, he shook his head and followed his Cube, more insistent now than before, back to his own room.

An hour later, Ashur was lying on the bed, reading a book about Xerxes I, the Persian king who had invaded Greece. The bookshelves in his room seemed to have been stocked specifically with his interests in mind; they were filled with histories, with a particular emphasis on military history. In school, it had been a slog to make it through the required reading that he found uninteresting, but he would stay up all night with a book that grabbed his attention and opened his mind. Ashur wondered how the Academy had known what he would find compelling.

He heard a knock on the door. He glanced up from his book as his Cube did a little spin on its pedestal.

"Who is it?" he said.

"It's me," came a voice. "Boris."

Ashur frowned and got up to open the door. Boris was standing in the hallway, hair disheveled and glasses smudged.

"Is everything all right?" Ashur said.

"What? Oh, yeah. I just, you know. Wanted to talk about today. Can I come in?"

Ashur hesitated—he was tired and had been looking forward to a quiet night after all the excitement of the last few days. There was something edgy about Boris, too. But he thought about how out of place the guy had looked at orientation, and how he had recognized someone else who didn't automatically assume they belonged. Maybe he was lonely and wanted someone else to process everything that was happening. Ashur held the door open, and Boris came in and started pacing around the small dormitory room.

"It's just incredible, isn't it, seeing that technology up close? I'd seen bits and pieces of it, just from all the Worldcorp demos, but the real capabilities are so, so much more impressive."

"It was cool," Ashur said, nodding. Boris looked at him like he was crazy.

"Cool? Ashur, cool doesn't even begin to describe it. This is the most powerful, advanced technology in the history of the world. And they're letting us use it!"

Boris flopped down onto the easy chair next to the desk, his limbs splayed about like some sort of rag doll.

"Did you hear how pissed Cicero got when Brodi suggested this was just run-of-the-mill AI stuff? I've bet they've got crazy ways to map a person's brain. Though how they're doing it with historical figures, I have no idea.

PATRICK BET-DAVID

"I don't understand why everyone isn't freaking out about all this," Boris said, his eyes nearly closed. "It's all I've been able to think about since they brought us down to the Vault. I mean, think about being able to talk to anyone, at any time in history. It's insane! And this is just the stuff they're showing us apprentices. Imagine what other stuff Worldcorp is doing with it."

Ashur nodded. He hadn't thought about it that way, but it was true: there were probably so many secrets, so much impressive technology, that it would take years for him to see it all…if he could earn the trust of the Academy—and Worldcorp.

"This is just the tip of the iceberg," Ashur said.

"Exactly," Boris said, nodding his head so vigorously that his glasses jostled up and down. He sighed and then laid back in the chair. "You were good today, by the way."

"Decent first day," Ashur said. "If they'd had us talking with chess masters, I would have looked like an idiot."

"I don't think it's going to be that kind of lesson. I think they want us doing practical things—the kind of stuff they didn't teach us in school. It turns out that linear algebra doesn't come up that frequently in day-to-day life."

Ashur perched on the side of the bed. Maybe today hadn't been a fluke, just a lucky first lesson that he happened to know a thing or two about. Maybe it wasn't just some freak chance that had landed him at the Academy. Everyone else seemed to assume they could hack it here—why shouldn't he?

"You want to know what I can't stop thinking about?" Boris said.

"I have a feeling you're going to tell me either way."

Boris laughed and nodded.

"Who I would bring back. All the great chess masters, like you said, to teach me their games. Galileo and Copernicus.

174

The greatest minds in history! I don't even know where to start. What else is possible?

"How about you, Ashur? If you had the power to create a hologram of anyone—literally anyone who's ever existed—who would you want to meet? If, you know, you could choose."

The answer came to Ashur with a speed and clarity that he hadn't been expecting. He knew exactly who he would want to see as a hologram, if he had the ability to bring anyone back. He wondered if it would work like this—if it was possible that regular, everyday people, and not just the most famous and notable figures from history, could truly be reanimated in the way they had seen so impressively done in the Vault. But he put that thought aside for the moment, so fully absorbed in the feelings that were overcoming him that he worried he might lose it in front of Boris. He took a deep breath.

"My father, Odishoo."

"Your...oh, right. How long has he...?"

"Six years now."

Boris nodded, suddenly more solemn, the restless energy from before hardening as he watched Ashur. Ashur took a deep breath and wiped at his face quickly—it was no use thinking about things like this. His father was gone, as much as he wished otherwise. He lived only in Ashur's memories, in the occasional voice that came to him, reminding him of the things that Odishoo had said while he was still alive.

"I'm sorry, Ashur," Boris said. "I didn't mean to bring all that up."

"It's all right," Ashur said.

"I'll, ah, see you tomorrow. Okay?"

And then Boris was gone, leaving Ashur alone in his room. He looked back down at the book on the great Persian king he had been reading, knowing that he wouldn't be able to focus for the rest of the night. He sighed and laid back in the bed, his hands beneath his head, staring up at the ceiling.

Ashur woke from a deep, dreamless sleep to the sound of his Cube chirping on its pedestal. It was pitch black, save for the small bits of light coming from the Cube. When he looked at the clock next to the bed, it read 2:47 a.m.

"What is it?" he said groggily. The Cube began to whir, projecting a message onto the far wall. Ashur groaned—he had set the Cube so that it should have known not to disturb him while he was sleeping, intent on being fresh for the next day's lessons. He wondered if it was Cassandra, unable to sleep and making good on her promise to message him. Maybe she wanted to see if he was still up…

But as the words appeared in stark white against the dark of the far wall, Ashur could see that it was nothing like that at all.

You don't know the truth about Odishoo's death.

The sender was, once again, Admirer.

Ashur sprang from the bed, suddenly full of rage. Who was this person to tell him anything about his father, and then hide behind their anonymity? None of the messages that Ashur had sent back had been returned—whoever it was, they didn't seem interested in answering any of Ashur's questions. He felt like screaming, *Who are you?!* But he knew the Cube would only send his message back into the void, and he had no reason to expect anything would echo in response.

He kept staring at the message, trying to make sense of it. His father had died in a car crash—he knew that. What were they talking about? He wondered if this was all part of the training—some cruel, extended version of the testing they had subjected him to. He had been able to withstand tremendous psychological pain; did they want to keep pushing him, to harden him, or to see where his limits were?

He thought of asking someone—Cicero, or some other administrator at the Academy—what was going on with these messages. If Ashur reported it, surely they would have some way to track through their system who was actually sending things to him. But even as he considered this possibility, he could feel that he wouldn't be reporting Admirer. As frustrating as it was—as much as it made him churn with anger—there was still the possibility, remote but there nonetheless, that the nameless, faceless voice was right. That they actually knew something he didn't. And the possibility of finding something out about his father that he didn't know was too intriguing to dismiss.

SEND RESPONSE? the Cube queried.

"What's the point?" Ashur said. He collapsed back into bed as the room retreated into darkness, and waited for a sleep that he knew would take a long time to come.

"It's important that you understand exactly the consequences of the plans—by the UK and the president—to defeat the Shah," Odishoo said. "They never saw it coming. I know that one day you will lead people, Ashur, and I want you to be prepared. Be careful when mapping out your strategy, and do your best to imagine possible consequences, even unintended ones, of your decisions. Or else you'll be doomed to suffer the same fate.

"After the revolution, Khomeini only focused on controlling the revolution. He assassinated hundreds of the military leaders who

had been advocates for the Shah. He thought this would help to keep him in power. But it meant that the military became very weak, with few leaders with any real military experience.

"Saddam Hussein saw what was happening, and he smelled an opportunity. For him, a revolutionary Iran was a weak Iran. So he only waited a year. The war between Iran and Iraq started in 1980, and it didn't end until 1988. And it was terrible. Just terrible.

"We were living in Tehran when the city was bombed over two hundred times in just one day—one day, Ashur. My father put tape in the shape of an X on every single one of our windows, so that the bomb blasts wouldn't send exploding glass everywhere in the room. Some of my closest friends and relatives were killed in this war. Sometimes we didn't have a body to bury.

"Five hundred thousand people died in the war." Odishoo lowered his head. "All of it could have been prevented if Carter and the UK had just left the Shah—and Iran—alone. I sometimes wonder how they feel, knowing that they caused this war, and that the blood of so many is at least in part on their hands."

Odishoo fell silent again. Ashur shifted anxiously in his seat, waiting for his father to tell him more.

"I need you to understand something: just because someone is a good person does not mean he will make a good leader. I think about this with President Carter. I believe he was a good man, with good intentions when it came to human rights in Iran. But the final result was devastating.

"Remember how I told you about the three thousand prisoners freed as a result of his human rights policies, because he believed that SAVAK was using illegal torture tactics against them? Well, the last part is true—they were. But SAVAK learned these methods in the first place from the CIA, who used them against their own prisoners. Such hypocrisy. And these were no ordinary prisoners. The prisoners the Shah was forced to free were the most radical religious fundamentalists, communists, and terrorists. Some of them are now part of Al-Qaeda. These prisoners who Carter helped free are the same people who killed three thousand of America's own people on 9/11.

"Remember this, the unintended consequences. Plato once wrote: 'Those who believe it's foolish to study politics are usually governed by fools who do.' It's always your choice to study politics yourself, and not let yourself be easily swayed by politicians or the media. It's important to take this responsibility seriously. Very seriously. Do you understand?"

"I think so," Ashur said. "I need to do my own thinking, not let others do it for me."

Odishoo smiled and clapped him on the shoulder. "Yes," he said. His smile faded, and his fingers tightened on Ashur's shoulder.

"Right before we left Iran, my mother took me to see the Shah's old home. It was lavish—several mansions really—a place of extreme wealth. I could see why people would be angry that he had so much when so many had so little. But it had been meant to show the power of Iran. They never understood that.

"Khomeini's people had intentionally turned each and every one of his photos upside-down. To represent the fall of his empire." Odishoo shuddered. "I hated that. Even today I hate seeing pictures put upside down. It brings back memories of what happened to our Shah. To our country. It was turned upside down, and it still hasn't been put right. Not yet."

Odishoo paused the CD player. As he reached back, his tattoo peeked out of his shirtsleeve. Ashur had always admired the tattoo: a lion in crisp black ink on his forearm, with a pair of wings spread wide behind it. Whenever Ashur had asked about it before, his *father had said that he would explain its meaning when he was older. Maybe today he might finally be ready.*

"Dad?" Ashur said. "What does your tattoo—"

Suddenly they heard the sound of breaking glass coming from the kitchen. It sounded like someone had thrown something against the wall.

Before they could stand, Rose was at the back door, skin flushed, hair disheveled, face twisted in fury.

"I am so sick of you teaching our son all this nonsense!" she shrieked. "You think I can't hear you out there? Do you want him to go through the same thing your father did? Do you?"

Odishoo looked away. Ashur glanced quickly between his parents, hoping that Rose's anger would go away quickly and that things would calm down. His mother's rage was unpredictable; sometimes it lasted only for a few minutes, and other times it roiled the house for the entire day. But today was special—the day he became a man—and he couldn't bear the thought of her ruining it. He knew his father usually tried to avoid fighting with his wife, especially in front of Ashur. But Rose seemed intent.

"Answer me!" she screamed.

CHAPTER NINE

Life at the Academy began to fall into a rhythm. Workouts in the morning before breakfast: long runs around the campus, doing laps inside the massive dome and then darting back and forth among the various buildings, Boris huffing and puffing behind the rest of the group. Then on to breakfast, where the five of them huddled around a table in the cafeteria—Brodi sometimes put her head down on the table and slept right next to her oatmeal, her eyes all red like she hadn't gotten any sleep the night before. They took their lessons down in the Vault, with Cicero guiding conversations with some of the most august and interesting figures in history. Ashur talked to George Washington about politics and morality, Martin Luther King about organizing and changing minds and hearts, Ayn Rand about using art to make political arguments, and the importance of individual freedom and excellence.

In the afternoons he played Traitorball with Jahi, and sometimes took on Boris at chess or Brodi at poker, though both of them were much better than he was. But so far, every time he'd asked Cassandra whether she wanted to try practicing their first lesson with Marilyn Monroe—the way she'd suggested the first day of class—she begged off, claiming she had reading to do or some other urgent task. Ashur wondered if she had lost her nerve, or if there was something else going on. Either way, he fell asleep exhausted most nights, his mind still whirling from everything he'd learned that day and all the questions that still remained.

But Ashur was still dogged by the question of the Academy system user who went by Admirer, and what they had said about his father. The user hadn't tried to contact him again since their last message. Ashur didn't know which was more frustrating: getting messages from this anonymous voice, or when the voice went silent, leaving him to wonder whether the user actually knew Odishoo—and more about his death. He tried asking the other members of the team whether they were getting any strange messages in the system, without telling them about Admirer, but no one seemed to know what he was talking about. In a world as controlled as the Academy, it was the one thing that stood out to Ashur—and made him wonder whether it was some kind of secret Academy test, designed to see how he would react to more emotional stress. He tried not to think about it too much, but it was hard. Even all these years after his death, Odishoo was still never far from Ashur's mind.

Dad would have loved it here, Ashur thought to himself as Cicero led the class down for another day's lesson in the Vault. Odishoo had such an inquisitive mind and had constantly told his son to think critically about everything around him and probe deeper to understand the "why" behind things. School had never felt like this—everything had been rote memorization, or basic talking points that the teachers expected the students to regurgitate back to them on multiple choice quizzes. Ashur never really felt like he was learning or having his way of thinking challenged. Here, he was encouraged to keep pushing when things didn't make sense to him, balancing his own innate sense of how the world worked against being open-minded enough to allow new ideas and perspectives in. It felt like a workout for his mind, and he could feel himself growing stronger with each passing day.

The elevator silently reached the Vault level and the doors slid open. Cicero led the five apprentices through the hall filled with memorabilia and priceless art before coming to a stop outside the massive Vault door. Ashur and the others held out their Cubes, but Cicero held a finger up.

"Before we begin our lesson today, I want to remind you of something. All of you are bringing your own life experiences, and your own values, with you. Diversity of thought is important. So is standing up for what you believe is right. But I would urge you to work hard to consider different perspectives—and ask yourself whether there might be anything you're missing, no matter what you start out believing. Do you all understand?"

The apprentices looked around at one another and nodded. Cicero smiled.

"Good. Because things get messy when we start to talk about money."

"Money?" Boris said.

The five Cubes began to glow in unison, and the Vault door opened. The apprentices stepped inside.

Two figures were standing at the head of the classroom, on opposite sides of the desk, and neither, Ashur noticed, appeared to have any interest in the other. On one side was a man in a black suit, with long white hair, a bushy white beard, and inquisitive eyes that scanned the apprentices as they filed into the room and took their seats. On the other was a woman, patrician in her bearing, wearing a navy-blue pantsuit and a high-necked white blouse, a sapphire brooch affixed prominently to her lapel. She held her head high, chin jutting out slightly, coolly appraising the room.

"Class," Cicero said. "Please allow me to introduce our two guest lecturers today: Mr. Karl Marx, and the Baroness Margaret Thatcher."

Ashur sat up a little bit straighter in his seat. *No wonder they don't want anything to do with one another*, he thought to himself. *These two must hate each other and what they stand for.*

"Good morning, children," Thatcher said to the room. Ashur could see Cassandra bristling in the seat in front of him, though he couldn't tell whether it was because the Iron Lady had called her a child or if there was something deeper at play.

"Have you two decided who will speak first?" Cicero said, a small smile playing on his lips. Thatcher and Marx looked at one another. Marx sighed.

"If Mrs. Thatcher will promise not to interrupt me when it is my turn to speak, I will happily yield to her first," Marx said. "Though she has given me little reason to expect such civility."

"Civility is indeed a virtue, Herr Marx," Thatcher said. "One not shared by so many of your followers. The floor is yours if you would like. I pledge only to interrupt if some egregious error demands it."

Marx sighed and looked at Cicero, who nodded for him to continue. Margaret Thatcher took a seat in the front row, and Marx strode to the front of the stage.

"I'd like to start today with a simple question," Marx said. "Please raise your hand if you've ever held a job before."

Ashur put up his hand and looked around the Vault. Jahi and Boris had their hands up, too. Cassandra, Ashur noticed, kept her hand down.

"Does poker count?" Brodi said from the row behind him.

"Not for our purposes, no," Marx said with a small smile.

"Then I'm out," Brodi said. "Suckers."

"You there, Jahi," Marx said. "What was your work?"

"I was a summer camp counselor," Jahi said.

"Shaping the minds of young people," Marx said with a nod. "Keeping them safe. Allowing their parents the time and energy to engage in activities other than childcare. Tell me, what were you paid for these valuable services?"

"Eight dollars an hour," Jahi said, looking a little sheepish as he said it. "And, you know, lunches and stuff."

"And do you feel as though you were compensated fairly for the work you performed?"

"I mean, I don't know," Jahi said. "If I wasn't a counselor, they would have hired someone else and paid him the same amount."

"Maybe so," Marx said. "Unless, of course, you and your fellow counselors all demanded more money together."

"You're talking about a union," Ashur said.

"Specifically, yes. A small action in an attempt to rebalance power between those actually doing the work and those accruing the benefits—the profit—of that labor. But even such an action still operates within a capitalist system. And what I want to suggest to you today is, what if it didn't have to?"

Ashur heard a groan from the front seat and looked over to see Margaret Thatcher rolling her eyes. Marx gave her a sharp look, and she held up a hand.

"Go on, go on," she said.

"I spent my life studying the history of human societies," Marx said. "How people have lived and worked and existed together for millennia. A complex thing, a society. But at its core, I believe that this is the history of class struggles. Slaves and masters in ancient Rome. Serfs and kings in the Middle Ages. Workers and factory owners, the latest version of this dynamic which began in my time and has persisted, in some form or another, ever since. In each case, the system of economic organization is the root of everything in a society—the way people organize themselves, how they pray and eat and marry, the ways in which power and violence are used in the name of preserving those systems.

"So much of human history is the story of power, concentrated in the hands of the few, benefitting from the toil of many. But does it need to be this way? Is it some immutable law of nature, like gravity or relativity? I think not."

"But why would it change?" Ashur said. "If it's always been like that, what makes you think anything different will happen?"

"Technology changes," Marx said. "Our knowledge and our understanding improve. In years past, the working classes could be kept down with all manner of tools: fear of violence, fear of hunger, a religion designed so that the rewards of the next life are considered greater than those in this world."

Ashur looked over at Jahi and saw that he looked uncomfortable as Marx made this last point about religion. Jahi was a man of deep faith and probably didn't like the way Marx was describing it.

"But we have seen what happens when the working class begin to understand their lot, and the intolerability of their conditions. When they begin to imagine the possibilities of a different kind of world. At some point, they revolt. The power of many, rising up against the few. Freeing themselves from an oppressive, extractive regime to create something better. A world where goods are produced not with profit in mind but with consumption. Where labor is not exploited but celebrated—and valued. Where work is performed by each according to his own ability, and the material wants of all are met according to their own needs. A just and equitable society.

"This is my belief of what the future must look like. How many times have societies destroyed themselves through the desperate clawing of the few with so much to keep themselves in power, at the expense of everyone else? The only sustainable society is one based around a communal approach to an economy, once the shackles of the old power structures have been thrown off. This is my vision, based on my study and understanding of people. And this is the world I believe we will reach some day, once its potential, and its possibilities, are more fully known."

As Marx finished his speech, Cassandra and Boris both began to clap loudly. But Ashur kept his hands down by his sides. He knew what it was like to work a shitty job—he was only making eight dollars an hour at the Big Boy, even after working there for several years. It had been hard, after Odishoo's death, for him and his mother to make ends meet. It would have been nice to know that they would be cared for, rather than Ashur having to worry about whether his salary, and whatever assistance Rose qualified for, would be enough. And yet something kept him from embracing the vision that Marx had laid out. He wanted to wait and hear what Margaret Thatcher had to say.

Marx took a seat, and Thatcher stood up on the stage. She was, Ashur had to admit, a commanding presence—there was an intensity to the woman that was palpable. She said nothing for a moment, instead looking in turn at each of the recruits. When her eyes met Ashur's, he returned her gaze and noticed the small nod that she made.

"It is so interesting that you use the word *freedom*, Herr Marx," Margaret Thatcher said. "You spoke about the importance of freedom. On that point, both of us can agree. In fact, I would hold that freedom in a society is perhaps the most important value. The freedom to love whoever it is that you happen to love. The freedom to pray to whichever God you choose—or none at all, if that is your preference. The freedom to dream, and to work to make those dreams a reality. I think we can all agree that this sounds like the sort of a society we would all want to live in."

"I think I know where you're going with this," Boris said quietly from his seat. Thatcher turned to him, a little smile on her face.

"You do, Boris? Then, by all means."

"You're going to say that capitalism is the economic system that offers the most freedom," he said. "And that socialism or communism are all about control. That for those systems to work, the individual needs to give up freedom for the sake of the collective."

"And tell me, what do you make of all that?" Thatcher said.

"I think if you tried to tell most people working under capitalism now that they are free, they would laugh in your face," Boris said. "They're working jobs that don't pay them enough to provide for their families. They're saddled with debt and can't even pay down the principal. They can't afford a house; they can't afford a good education for their children. They're trapped. That doesn't sound like freedom to me."

"Do you come from a wealthy background, Boris?"

Boris shook his head. "Not really, no."

"And yet I think your presence here—together with what I know about you—suggests that your future ability to make a living for yourself is rather high."

Boris shrugged. "Just because things might work out okay for me doesn't mean it's that way for others. We shouldn't let a couple of success stories blind us from the reality of what it's like for most people. Capitalism is its own kind of a religion—if you make people believe that one day they might hit it big, it lets them keep toiling along, underpaid and exploited, instead of actually trying to do something to change the system."

"So you would sacrifice everything that makes you exceptional—and your ability to use those exceptional talents to make things better for you, your family, and perhaps even the world—in exchange for…what exactly?"

"Equality," Boris said. "Fairness."

"Well, now," Margaret Thatcher said. "Equality and fairness are two *vastly* different concepts. Is it *fair* if someone who does no work at all, and contributes nothing whatsoever to a society, gets the same rewards as someone who works hard and has the vision necessary to produce great value?"

"Is it *fair* if fat cats sitting on their asses all day collecting rents make a thousand times as much as their workers pulling in minimum wage?" Cassandra said. "If we're talking about fairness, then I'm sorry, I don't see your point."

"Is that really what you think of most business owners? Idiots who do nothing but count their money?"

"I know it is," Cassandra said, her arms folded over her chest.

A tea pot appeared on a table behind Margaret Thatcher. She reached back, poured herself a cup, and blew gently over the lip before taking a sip.

"I notice one thing that has been missing from this discussion," she said. "A concept that Herr Marx seems to have conveniently left out of his schema. And that is the idea of risk."

"Risk I can get," Brodi said from the back row.

"Yes, our poker player," Thatcher said. "This is right up your alley. Tell me, when you make a bet at a game of cards, why is it that you do so?"

"Because I want to win," Brodi said.

"Of course. But when you make that bet, most of the time, are you certain of the outcome?"

"Not usually," Brodi said. "I'm playing the odds."

"But you are accepting that there is some chance that you lose, yes? Your read on the other person might be wrong. The cards might be unlucky. All manner of things might transpire that result in you losing that money."

"I mean, yeah, that's how poker works."

"Not just poker, Brodi. That's how the *world* works."

Ashur heard Cassandra scoff in the front row, and Margaret Thatcher focused her attention on her.

"Cassandra. Earlier, when you were talking about those 'fat cats,' as you put it, making more money than their workers, do you believe that profit is amoral?"

"I think it's wrong to make so much money when so many others have so little."

"But then, tell me, what incentivizes someone with money to do something risky with it? Like, say, build a factory? Or open a business? Or invest in research for a new piece of software, or a new drug? Things that employ people, things that move society forward. All of those things involve risk. And profit is the incentive that encourages them to take that risk. Without profit, why would someone risk their own money?"

"Because it's the right thing to do," Cassandra said.

"Oh, my," Thatcher said.

"I mean it," Cassandra continued. "Why couldn't it be the government doing all of that? Or professors in universities, doing research to drive technology forward? That's happening already—before others swoop in to take all the money and credit from their hard work."

"You really think it's only businesspeople who are selfish?" Ashur said. "I don't know about you, but I trust them a lot more than politicians. At least the businesspeople are honest about what they're doing and why they want to do it. Politicians just want more and more power, to control people."

"It doesn't have to be like that," Cassandra said, turning around to glare at Ashur.

"Yeah? And what happens if it does? Are you just going to march right into the Politburo and demand action? Too bad—they're not accountable to anyone but themselves."

"Better to just let corporations pay the politicians directly, right?" Cassandra said. "Dark money and buying votes and all the other bullshit that already happens?"

"At least now you have a say," Ashur said. "Who you vote for. What products you want to use. Rather than being just another nameless, faceless cog in a machine."

"Try telling a worker in a warehouse that they're not some faceless, nameless cog right now, just waiting for a robot to come in and replace them!"

"That's enough," Cicero said, standing now and moving toward the front of the room. When Ashur looked back up at the stage, Margaret Thatcher was smiling at him and nodding. "I think that's about as far as we're going to get with theoretical discussions. A quick show of hands, although I think most of us know the answers already. Who in this room thinks that what Karl Marx is saying makes more sense?"

Boris and Cassandra both stuck up their hands.

"And who thinks Margaret Thatcher here has the right idea?"

Ashur put his hand up and saw Brodi do the same.

"What about you, Jahi?" Cicero asked.

Jahi had a hand on his chin and was looking thoughtfully down at the stage.

"It's a hard question," he said. "I believe in equality of opportunity. And I know that doesn't always happen now—I've seen how hard it is for people to make something of themselves from nothing. But how hard someone works, how good they are at something—that has to matter, doesn't it? And I've seen how Marxists feel about religion. The spiritual life is always undervalued and debased. So if I had to choose, I guess I'd go with Mrs. Thatcher."

"An excellent choice, Jahi," Margaret Thatcher said.

"All right, then. Those will be your teams," Cicero said. "Boris and Cassandra, you'll spend the rest of the day with Mrs. Thatcher. The other three of you are with Karl Marx. You'll both have an opportunity to argue in defense of your constituency."

"What constituency?" Ashur said.

"You'll be representing miners, Ashur," Cicero said. "Boris and Cassandra will speak on behalf of the owners of the mine. We are going to run a historical simulation—the United Kingdom, in 1984. Mrs. Thatcher has plenty of thoughts for why some of the mines need to close. And the rest of you have your work cut out for you. You have the rest of the day to do your research. We'll meet back here tomorrow morning to hear your arguments."

"Cicero," Cassandra said. "Let me switch teams. Please."

Cicero looked at her, not unkindly, and shook his head.

"I understand this will be difficult for you. But like I told you at the beginning of the lesson, it's important to learn to see things from the other side. Even if you don't end up agreeing, your arguments will be stronger, and your ability to convince people greater, if you understand where people who disagree with you are coming from."

"But…" Cassandra started.

"The decision is final," Cicero said. "Now I suggest you all get started. There's a lot to learn—and not much time."

Ashur and his team spent the rest of the day going back and forth between the austere Academy library and the Vault to stress-test their ideas with Marx. Brodi proved especially adept at the research, directing her Cube to pull up old editorials and on-the-ground reporting to try and give them a sense for the stakes, and the way things had gone back in the early 1980s, when Margaret Thatcher had swept into power.

"It's a tough position," Brodi said, looking up from where her Cube was displaying videos of the picket lines, and the violent confrontations between the miners in Northern England and the policemen sent to break up the strikes. "It wasn't like there were some rich assholes trying to squeeze the miners dry.

It was all nationalized; the government is the one who owned the mines in the first place. It was just getting harder to mine the good coal, and new machines meant you needed fewer miners. And in response to all that, the miners basically wanted to make coal really, really expensive for everyone in the country, holding the UK hostage until the other side gave in to their demands."

"Yeah, but think about it from the miners' perspective," Jahi said. "It was the only employment in a lot of these places. And it's not like it was making them rich. They're basically fighting for their families."

Ashur nodded. "We can't make this a technical argument about efficiency and yields," he said. "If we do that, we'll lose. This has to be about what society owes its people, especially its most vulnerable people. An emotional appeal. Put the listener in the miners' shoes."

"Do you think Cicero will really go for that?" Brodi said. "He seems like a pretty logical guy."

"Logic and reason aren't the only ways to win arguments," Ashur said. "Politicians have always known that. We need to take a page from their book."

The three of them stayed up late into the night, sketching out their plan for how to make an argument on behalf of the miners. Every hour or so, Brodi would leave for a few minutes and come back smelling like smoke and something skunky.

"Are you smoking pot, Brodi?" Ashur finally asked her. Brodi coughed and nodded.

"Yeah, of course. Why, you want in?"

"No way!" Jahi said. Brodi began to laugh.

"Chill, Jahi. It helps me concentrate."

"Aren't you worried about getting caught?" Jahi said. Brodi shrugged.

"I mean, I figure they know everything we're up to, right? If they wanted to kick me out, they would have done it already."

"Look, as long as you're doing the work, I don't care," Ashur said. "But let's focus. I want to get at least a little sleep before we have to present tomorrow."

"Fine, fine," Jahi said, holding up his hands. "But when you die of lung cancer at fifty, don't tell me I didn't warn you."

"Who wants to live all the way to fifty?" Brodi said. Then, laughing, she pulled up an old BBC documentary and began scrolling through the footage, looking for anything the team could use.

Down in the Vault the next morning, all five apprentices looked haggard. Ashur had managed only an hour or two of sleep—he still felt groggy, despite the cold shower and strong coffee he'd had that morning. Boris looked the worst of all of them, his hair completely disheveled and his eyes only half open. Cassandra seemed both furious and exhausted—Ashur thought about her objection the day before and wondered why she was so dead set against representing the owners of the mine.

Marx and Thatcher were sitting off to the side of the stage, grinning at one another in a faux friendly way. Once the apprentices were in their seats, Cicero introduced them to their panel of judges: Abraham Lincoln, Saint Augustine, and Elizabeth Cady Stanton. All of them, Cicero explained, were renowned debaters and orators in their day and would be deciding which team won.

"And they've promised to put any personal feelings on the matter aside for the day," Cicero said, giving Elizabeth

Cady Stanton a long look as he mentioned this. She sighed and nodded.

"Fine, yes," she said. "On the merits of the arguments only."

"Very good," Cicero said. "Would the team representing the miners please present first?"

Ashur and the other two rose from their seats and made their way to the front of the stage. Ashur and Brodi had agreed to let Jahi lead the presentation—though it went against Ashur's nature to wait in the background, he recognized that his style was more combative. He was like a boxer when he debated, looking to jab at his opponents, find their soft areas, and then go for the knockout punch. But that wasn't what their team needed. Jahi had a natural charisma and a way of connecting with an audience—people trusted him, believed in his goodness, and wanted to hear more of whatever he had to say. Ashur thought he would make a very good pastor, if that was still what he wanted to do once his time at the Academy was over.

"We could stand before you today and make a number of different arguments as to why the government plan to close down so many of the mines is wrong," Jahi said. "We could cite the various promises made by this government—economic support, job retraining, education—that haven't been kept in good faith. We could remind you that we are the backbone of the Northern English economy—and have been for more than one hundred years. We could invoke the short-sightedness of the conservative government in their attempts to privatize, enriching their friends at the expense of the common working man. All of which is true.

"But this isn't an economic issue," he said. "It isn't even a labor issue. It's a moral issue, and one that I'm not best equipped to make."

At this, Jahi nodded back at Brodi, who began to key something into her Cube. Ashur stepped forward for his part.

"In a few moments, we're going to have a chance to hear directly from Robert Smyth, a miner in Northampton who's worked the black seam for twenty years."

A man appeared, relatively short and gaunt, his back arched from years of work. He was wearing what looked like his best clothes—his church clothes—which were nevertheless threadbare and a little tatty. He held a hat between his hands and seemed at first uncomfortable standing on the stage. But as Ashur asked him questions—about the physical toll of his work, the importance of the mine to the economic life of the town, and his children's prospects if the mine were to close—he stood straighter and began to talk with more confidence. There was a decency about Robert Smyth, and an honesty, and Ashur watched as the judges leaned in a bit closer to hear what the man had to say through his Midlands accent.

It had been Ashur's idea, late the previous evening, to have a real miner appear via the Vault to make their argument.

"There's nothing we could say that would have the same emotional impact as actually hearing from a person," he said to Brodi and Jahi.

"Are we allowed to do that?" Jahi had said.

"Only one way to find out," Brodi said. "Let's try it."

Ashur watched with pride as Robert answered the questions they'd prepared. It was no longer an abstract economic argument, the way it had sounded when Marx lectured them the day before. Now it was a human standing before them, pleading for his life and the lives of his family. When he was through speaking, Ashur extended a hand for the man to shake and watched as the hologram's hand passed briefly through his fingers before Brodi flickered it out.

"A society has an obligation to its neediest people," Ashur said. "It isn't charity. It's an investment in the future, and the social fabric. Work gives meaning. Work gives dignity. These men aren't asking for a handout—they're asking to be able to do their jobs, or to find other work if necessary. We don't believe that's an unreasonable request—and we urge the government to reconsider the closures."

The panel of judges clapped politely at the conclusion of their presentation, and Ashur nodded to Brodi and Jahi. They had worked well together. He wasn't sure there had been enough substance—maybe Cicero would ding them for not bringing more in the way of data and figures. But when they had rehearsed the night before, the numbers had seemed cold and abstract, in a way that hurt them more than helped. Ashur sat down, feeling satisfied that he had done a solid job.

Boris and Cassandra got up from their seats now and stood at the front of the stage. Boris fiddled with something on his Cube, and then suddenly a red line was projected on the wall behind him. The line was jagged, running down from the top lefthand corner of the wall toward where Boris stood below. He took a deep breath and then began.

"This is the graph of coal employment in the United States," he began. He clicked on the cube, and a blue line appeared, almost identical to the first. "This is the graph of coal employment in Europe writ large. And this…" he said as he keyed in a final number and a green line appeared, almost the same as the others, "is coal employment in the UK.

"Coal miners have been the backbone of English working men for a century. But the era of coal is coming to an end. This is not because of greedy prospectors desperate for profit. No one is trying to squeeze another dollar from the pocket of a working man. But the position has become untenable. We can't keep pretending that times aren't changing. We're paying too much for too little coal, and all of England—including the miners—are suffering. Something needs to change."

Ashur noticed Margaret Thatcher nodding in the corner. Boris turned to Cassandra, urging her forward. She stepped up, looked at the panelists, and then shook her head.

"I'm sorry. This is wrong," she said. She turned to look at the former prime minister. "Your policies destroyed the working class in England. You made the rich richer and the poor poorer, and it doesn't matter what kind of pretty words or clever data we use to try to justify the decisions. What you did was appalling, and I won't be part of anything apologizing for it."

Cassandra stepped down off the stage and headed for the door.

"Wait!" Boris shouted after her.

"Let her go," Cicero said as Cassandra's footsteps echoed on the floor outside the Vault, heading for the elevator. "Are you prepared to finish the presentation on your own?"

"He is more than capable, I'm sure of it," Margaret Thatcher said. "Adversity is a powerful force. I have no doubt it will sharpen him even further."

Ashur shook his head in wonder. What had happened to Cassandra that she would walk out in the middle of a lesson—and possibly risk her place at the Academy? He could understand that she disagreed, politically, with capitalism, but as an intellectual exercise it didn't seem like all that much to ask her. *Something must have happened to her*, he thought. *Something bad.* Once they were done for the day, he thought, he would try to find her, and see if there was anything he could do to help, or at least understand. After all, they were still a team. He half-listened to the rest of Boris's presentation, distracted by thoughts of Cassandra and trying to imagine what could be wrong.

Despite Boris's best efforts, Ashur's team won easily—the panel was unanimous. Afterward, Ashur went up to Cicero.

"What will happen to Cassandra now?"

"She'll receive no credit for the lesson, and her scores as an apprentice will be lowered significantly as a result," Cicero said. "It isn't quite a death blow, but something remarkable will have to happen now for her to make it through."

"Let me talk to her," he said. "See if I can help."

Cicero nodded.

"Tell her I'll be expecting her, when she's ready for a conversation," Cicero said. "She has some explaining to do if she wants to keep her place here at the Academy."

Ashur told him that he understood. The mood, even among his team, was somber. Boris looked like he was ready to fall asleep standing up. They all left the Vault together and took a long, quiet ride back up to the ground level.

"Answer me!" Rose screamed at the top of her lungs.

Ashur put his hands over his ears. His mother had a piercing voice when she was upset; if it was any louder, Ashur thought, it could shatter all the windows in the house.

"Mom, please stop," he begged. "I hate it when you two fight. It's my birthday. Dad was just telling me some stories."

"Stories?" Rose said. "More like lies. About how great the Shah was. Don't believe anything your father tells you. He thinks the

Shah was a God! Why don't you ask him what that monster did to his father."

"Don't go there, Rose," Odishoo said.

"Why? You don't want your son to hear how your precious Mohammad Reza Shah Pahlavi killed your father?"

"My father didn't die because of him," Odishoo said, struggling to keep the emotion out of his voice. He glanced at Ashur. "No one knows what happened to my father, but it had nothing to do with the Shah."

"That's what they said about all of them," Rose said. "The people the Shah had tortured, just because he could. Or SAVAK, which killed more innocent people than anyone else in the world at that time. I swear the Shah was the devil himself! My only regret about him is that he died naturally, without being stoned to death."

Ashur gasped.

"How could you say that, Mom?"

"You have no idea what you're talking about," she said. "All you know is what your father told you. But ask my family what the Shah did to them. Uncles with missing fingernails. Cousins who never came home from work, or school. The Shah was an evil man."

"Not again with this, Rose!" Odishoo snapped. He walked over to her. "You've been drinking—I can smell it."

Rose slapped him across the face, so hard that his head jerked to the side.

"Did you tell your son who gave me my first drink? Who encouraged me to start? I bet that wasn't one of your little stories."

Odishoo's face darkened. He glanced at Ashur.

"Go up to your room, Ashur—you shouldn't have to watch this."

"Stay where you are!" Rose said. "I want you to hear this. I want Odishoo to tell you who his father really was. He was no

hero, that man. Did you tell him about how he killed every single member of a family because he believed one of them killed his sister? Thirty-nine innocent people! Oh yes, I know about that, Odishoo. I know all about it."

Ashur looked back at his father.

"Dad?"

"You're out of control, Rose," Odishoo said.

"Tell him!" Rose said. "Look Ashur in his face and tell him I'm lying. Or else tell him what a brutal family he comes from."

"You're scaring your son," Odishoo said. "Why don't you go upstairs and take those sleeping pills you like so much?"

"Do you know why I take those pills, Odishoo? Because when I'm asleep is the only time I can forget that I'm married to you." There were tears in her bright eyes as she turned to Ashur. "I was the most beautiful girl in our town. I had my choice of men. But I fell for your father. I didn't know he came from a line of killers. Or that he cared so little for anyone else. Only his heritage, and his ego, matter to him."

She turned back to Odishoo.

"You Assyrians. Full of it—all of you. But God disowned you. He killed nearly two hundred thousand of you in a single day. The famine—I'm sure you told your son about that. And yet you wake up every morning and pray, thinking God is on your side. But he isn't. He abandoned you and your people. You don't even have your own country. Just a bunch of bastards, scattered across the world. I know your father had some grand plans for the Yonans. Look how that turned out. And I won't let our son get caught up in the same danger, and failed dreams, that brought him down."

She knelt down next to Ashur and took his face in her hands. He could smell the alcohol on her breath.

THE ACADEMY

"Look at me, Ashur. Your father is a disgrace. The last thing I want is for you to end up like him."

Ashur's eyes began to burn.

"Please don't say that, Mom. I don't like it when you do this. Please stop, please."

His palms were sweating. A part of him wanted to go upstairs, but he was so afraid of what might happen if he left. Something bad, he feared.

But Rose didn't seem to notice the pain she was causing him, or else she ignored it.

"But you're a man now. Isn't that right? So it's time to learn the truth about your father. He's had his time for stories, and now it's mine."

Rose sat down heavily in the chair where Odishoo had been sitting, while Ashur's father paced in front of them, looking anxiously at his wife.

"Your grandfather had grand plans for your father. He was going to be a super soldier, a real killer. But instead, he was a disappointment. I met him just after he left Iran with his mother —right before your grandfather disappeared. Odishoo was young, handsome, strong—he was going somewhere. He talked about honor and duty, about changing the world. My family hated what he stood for, and I knew he supported the Shah and SAVAK, who had my relatives arrested and tortured. But I still fell in love with him. I will never forgive myself for that.

"Then he disappeared. For weeks. To this day he won't tell me where. He only came back when he heard that I was pregnant with you. He'd always been a drinker. But it was worse when he came back. He was drinking so much, whatever he could get his hands *on. Completely out of control. He couldn't stop until you were born. Every one of my friends, every member of my family, told me what a mistake it would be to marry him. But I felt sorry for him. What a waste.*

"Now look at me! No friends, no homeland, no life. And I can't stand to listen while he fills your head with his nonsense. Those crazy beliefs of his father, the man who abandoned all of us."

"That can't be true," Ashur whispered. He looked at Odishoo. "Dad?"

Odishoo hung his head.

"Go ahead!" his mother screamed. "Tell your son!"

CHAPTER TEN

The rest of the team staggered back to their rooms after the lesson. But as tired as he was, when Ashur reached the hallway that led to his room, he turned in the other direction. He walked down the corridor, thinking back over the lessons that had set Cassandra off the most. It wasn't just her outburst earlier in the day with Margaret Thatcher. She had also seemed so angry during their first lesson with Marilyn Monroe, especially when she was talking about her affair with the president. Something was clearly bothering her—something that went beyond any intellectual objection. And if she didn't get herself right, then according to Cicero, she wouldn't have much time left at the Academy.

Ashur rapped three times on the door.

"Go away," came a voice from the other side.

"It's me," Ashur said.

"I said go away."

Ashur sighed.

"Look, it's none of my business," he said. "If you want to throw away your shot at doing something great, go ahead. But I don't think you do. I think you care. Or else you wouldn't be here. So do you want to talk to me about it?"

"What does it matter to you?"

"You're my teammate," Ashur said. "Teammates help one another. Especially when someone's down."

This was true—Ashur felt sure that he would be doing the same thing if Jahi, or Brodi, had stormed out of a lesson and endangered their place in the Academy. It had been so long since Ashur had been part of a team like this, surrounded by people who were as smart and capable as he was. But he also knew there was more than just loyalty that had brought him to Cassandra's door, even as every muscle in his body was crying out for rest. Since that very first day of orientation, when he had seen her walking down the stairs and into the reception, Ashur had been unable to stop thinking about Cassandra. She was beautiful, of course—that was part of it. But there was something about her that made him want to know her better, understand her mind and who she really was. Other than Kiki, Ashur couldn't remember ever feeling like this before, and the time he and Cassandra had spent together since being at the Academy had only confirmed that initial tug he'd felt somewhere deep inside him. He had been so excited when he discovered that she would be on his team, and that he'd get to spend every day alongside her, learning and growing and discovering their true potential together. He hated the thought of her being gone from this place, and hated even more the idea that he might never truly understand why.

"Cassandra, please," Ashur said. He waited. After a moment, he heard the lock sliding to the side, and then the door opened. Cassandra was standing in the doorframe, her eyes red and puffy, in a white T-shirt and a pair of sweatpants. Ashur still thought she looked amazing.

"I didn't take you as the type to beg," Cassandra said.

"Only when it's important," Ashur said with a small smile. "Can I come in?"

"I'm not in the mood."

Ashur jerked his head to the side. "Then how about a walk? Might do you some good."

Cassandra rolled her eyes, then sighed. "All right. Fine."

For a while they walked together in silence around the perimeter of the dome. It was twilight in Dallas beyond the massive geodesic structure, the sky gone purple and orange. They saw a few other apprentices and faculty members strolling around the grounds, hurrying to dinner or typing furiously into their Cubes, too absorbed in their own lives and their own dramas to notice the pair ambling on their own. Cassandra seemed intent on walking quickly, as though hoping that moving faster would solve whatever it was that had been bothering her. Ashur had to work to keep himself from asking all the questions that had been bubbling in his head since the end of the lesson—Cassandra had barely agreed to the walk, and if he pressed her too hard, she might turn right back around. He had always been able to read people well, to know what they wanted.

"What did Cicero say?" Cassandra said finally.

"You're not out yet," Ashur said. "But you've made it hard on yourself, by leaving the Vault without finishing the lesson."

"What, is he worried I hurt some hologram's feelings?"

"I think he's concerned that whatever's going on with you is keeping you from actually engaging with the lessons. Thinking critically—and logically."

"Why is it that whenever a woman shows any sort of passion, men start talking about thinking logically? And if a man has some fiery speech, he's standing up for his principles and being a bold leader?"

"You really think that's what's happening here?"

"Maybe. I don't know."

Cassandra heaved a deep sigh.

"Look, I know I screwed up, okay? It's just…Margaret Thatcher is so full of shit. Thinking that unfettered capitalism is going to solve everything, with no downsides? I mean, come on."

"Okay, but I think this is more than some political disagreement," Ashur said. "You're too smart for that. I bet you could make a brilliant case for free markets right now—one that would have the prime minister on her feet applauding—even if that's not what you believe. So what's really going on?"

"It's complicated," Cassandra said. Ashur nodded.

"Something to do with your family?"

Cassandra turned and looked at him, her eyes narrowed. For a moment Ashur thought she might turn right back around. But then she let her head sag down and nodded.

"Yeah. Something like that."

"You want to talk about it?"

"You wouldn't understand."

"Maybe not," Ashur said. "But you're not the only one with a screwed-up family, whatever's going on. My dad is dead. My mom's an alcoholic who hates me. I was running away from home before I came here, with no real idea of what I was going to do. I might not understand your life. But I know how complicated things can be. And how it can affect you at times you don't expect."

Cassandra was quiet for a moment. Ashur hadn't expected to say all of that, and he waited to see how she would take it. Was it too much, telling her about his family?

"My dad," Cassandra said finally. She let out a long exhale. "He was—is—a brilliant businessman. I mean *brilliant*. Not just some guy who got lucky on a few stock market bets, or a rich kid's son who inherited everything and thinks he earned it himself. Totally self-made. Worked his ass off. He's been a CEO since he was thirty. Billions of dollars. And he's good at it.

"He understands people. What they want, how to motivate them. People love working for him. He's as comfortable talking with junior employees as he is chatting up the board members after quarterly earnings are reported. He makes people feel like they're playing for the winning team. And he loves it. Really loves it, Ashur. I know so many people are just in it for the money, but for my dad, it's everything.

"I grew up in Connecticut, one of the rich suburbs by the water. Lots of friends had parents who worked in finance, had more money than they knew what to do with. I saw how miserable so many of them were. So many divorces, kids raised by nannies who barely saw their parents. I felt lucky. My mom worshipped my dad. They seemed to have a good thing going. Like they really got each other. And my dad was so smart, and funny, and even if I thought he worked too much, I knew that he was doing it to provide for me and the family. He talked about how amazing it was to live in a country where someone like him could rise to the top and make something of himself. He really believed in all that American Dream stuff. And I did, too."

"So what happened?" Ashur said. Cassandra took a deep breath.

"When I was thirteen, I came home early one day. I was supposed to be at a tennis lesson, but the teacher was sick, so they sent me home. My mom was on the couch when I got inside. Just sobbing. She didn't hear me come in. I thought someone had died, Ashur. Sometimes I wonder if that would have made things easier.

"She didn't want to tell me what was happening at first. Said that she was fine. But eventually she broke down and told me. She had found out my father was having an affair. Not the first one, apparently. She had forgiven him before, but this time was the last straw. She was leaving him.

"I couldn't believe it. I had never realized before then how selfish he was. How much he believed his own bullshit about how great he was, and how smart he was, and how he earned absolutely everything. Like there was nothing in the world that didn't belong to him, because of who he was.

"The next time I saw him, he tried to explain to me. He looked sad, like he was showing me a part of the world he'd hoped I'd never have to see. I told him that he made me sick, and that I never wanted to see him again. He didn't argue. I heard his car driving off a few minutes later. He left me there.

"I hated what he was doing, and everything he stood for. I hated the way he treated selfishness like a virtue. I don't know if he was always that way, or if decades of having people kiss his ass convinced him he really was that great. But I saw the way that he was corrupted. He was a great businessman—honest, ruthless, always seeing the next move before anyone else. But it made him a really shitty person, and an even worse father. And I promised myself I would never become someone like him."

Ashur thought for a moment of his own father's shortcomings—all those things Rose had said to him about how he would never amount to anything, just like Odishoo. He was grateful to have always had a good relationship with his father, no matter the troubles between him and his mother. He could imagine how much it would have broken his heart to have something like that happen—and discover that the man he loved and respected so much wasn't worthy of those feelings.

"You could never be like your father," Ashur said. "No matter what path you pursue. You're too good to ever stoop that low, or let your sense of self get that distorted."

"I still worry about it, though," Cassandra said. "That's why I sort of flew off the handle in the lesson. I could just hear all the things my dad told me, echoing through Thatcher's speech. And it made me so mad...to hear all of that again."

"I can understand that," Ashur said.

"It's something I'm always going to be dealing with," Cassandra said. "But that's not a good reason to give up on being here. I don't want to spend the rest of my life blaming my dad for everything."

Ashur reached out an arm and put it around Cassandra's shoulder. He could feel her stiffen for a moment, surprised by the intimacy of the gesture, and then her body relaxed as she leaned into his embrace. They walked that way for a time, not saying anything, Ashur feeling her body against his. How long, he wondered, would they have to keep paying for all the ways their parents had screwed up?

Later, back in his room, Ashur kept thinking about that walk with Cassandra. He had dropped her back off at her room afterwards, lingering in the doorway for a moment, wondering if she would invite him in. But Cassandra seemed exhausted, and he didn't want to push it. She had been so vulnerable with him, and so honest. He appreciated everything she'd told him and hoped that talking about her past would allow her to move beyond it for a little while and focus on their lessons while she still had a chance at the Academy.

Across the room, his Cube chirped with the sound of an incoming message. Ashur braced himself—it had been days since he'd heard anything from Admirer, since that cryptic message about his father and the truth of Odishoo's death. He'd started to wonder if he was ever going to hear anything again. But when the Cube projected the message on the wall, it was from Boris.

Meet me in the halls tonight at 2am, the message read. *I think I've figured something out.*

Ashur groaned—he had barely gotten any sleep the night before, and the thought of sneaking out late with Boris didn't have much appeal. Still, he was intrigued. He couldn't imagine what the small, strange man had come up with that was so urgent. But he could sense a fierce intelligence in Boris, the sort of probing mind that often led to exciting ideas. So he set his alarm for a few hours later before closing his eyes.

"Over here!"

Boris was standing in the shadowy corridor, illuminated only by the light of his Cube, whispering to Ashur. Ashur shuffled over to where the man was and couched down low.

"What was so important that it couldn't wait until morning?"

"I think I've figured something out."

"You said that. About what?"

"Just follow me, okay? I'll explain along the way."

It felt strange, being out and about in the Academy at night. Everything was stilled and empty, as though the dome itself was somehow holding its breath until morning came again. Boris led Ashur to what looked to be a dusty storage closet, but on closer inspection, he could see it contained a metal plate covering something in the floor.

"Help me with this, will you?" Boris said, straining against the metal. Ashur lifted it up neatly—and saw beneath it a long metal ladder descending into the floor.

"Okay, I'm going to need more before I just go climbing down into the ground with you," Ashur said. Boris nodded.

"I think I've figured out a way for us to build our own holograms."

"What?" Ashur said. "How?"

"I've been studying them," Boris said. "A lot of it they keep hidden, but we're around them so much that over time I've sort of put it together. What you really need is two things, I think: enough knowledge about a person to put together a sort of personality matrix, and then a little bit of the actual person's DNA. That's the only way to recreate them authentically, I think."

"Boris, what are you talking about?"

"Remember our conversation? When I asked who you would bring back, if you could make a hologram of anyone?"

Ashur nodded—his answer, Odishoo, had been so immediate as to be almost painful.

"Well, I couldn't stop thinking about it after that," Boris said, "trying to figure out the mechanics. I've got it all worked out, theoretically. But I'm going to need your help to actually do some testing."

"Are you serious?" Ashur said. "You want to sneak around the Academy, behind the instructors' backs, and hack into the Vault to try and build our own holograms?"

"Well, it sounds bad when you say it like that," Boris said. "I'm thinking about it more like an extra-credit assignment. An experiment. Showing some initiative! I think Cicero would be pleased."

"Though I assume you're not going to ask him?"

Boris grinned. "What's that old line about forgiveness instead of permission?"

Ashur nodded—he had never been big on asking permission himself. If he wanted to do something badly enough, he usually just went ahead and did it, no matter what other people thought—or the potential consequences. Still, this felt dangerous and came with the risk that if they were discovered, they might get thrown out of the Academy altogether. After everything he'd said to Cassandra about overcoming her own feelings if she valued her spot at the Academy, was it worth risking everything for this?

"How sure are you that this will work?" Ashur said. "That we could actually create our own holograms?"

"Theoretically it should work," Boris said. "But there's so much we need to do first. Figure out a way down to the Vault. Figure out access to the computer core where they design the things. Find the DNA for whoever we want to recreate. I'm not promising it will work, and I know we have lots of stuff to do as it is. But I saw the way you reacted when I asked you who you would bring back. I wouldn't be bringing you into this if I didn't know how much he meant to you. Tell me the truth, Ashur: if you had a chance to see your father again, wouldn't you do anything?"

"Yes," Ashur said, not even hesitating before he said it.

"Well, okay then," Boris said, beginning to descend the ladder. "Now watch your step. This isn't the world's greatest ladder, and if you fall, you'll definitely kill me, too."

They climbed down in the dark for what seemed like forever, Boris pausing every once in a while to examine something on his Cube.

"What are we looking for?" Ashur asked.

"Maintenance shafts," Boris said. "I think they used to cool the computers with giant air vents and fans. Now they've probably got them all liquid cooled or something we've never even heard of. But the shafts are still all here; I pulled up the old blueprints in the library. I don't think anyone even uses them anymore."

Ashur and Boris spent the rest of the night mapping out different routes down to the Vault, tracing their way between the dorms and the various buildings on campus. The maintenance shafts were a truly sprawling network—Ashur was sure they could get anywhere they wanted to go, provided they had it mapped out well enough. He had to keep crouched as he moved around, breathing in the dust as his Cube illuminated the area directly in front of him and nothing more. It was hard going, but at last Boris held a hand up for him to stop.

"Here," he said, pressing a metal panel out and snaking his body through. Ashur followed him.

They were standing in a small, dark chamber, the thrumming of machinery all around them. It was like being in the beating heart of a computer. Boris clapped his hands together and let out a little whoop.

"Where are we?" Ashur said.

"Deep," Boris said. "I wasn't sure we could actually make it down this far."

He went over to a small display on the far wall and held his Cube up.

"Analog," he said, slipping the Cube back into his pocket. "Air gapped."

"What do you mean?"

"I mean it isn't linked up to the other computer systems at the Academy. For protection, I guess. Very cool. Very smart."

Boris hesitated for a moment, his fingers waggling, before keying something in. A glowing red *X* appeared on the screen, and Boris stepped back for a moment. He sighed and turned around.

"Come on."

"What, that's it?" Ashur said. "After you made me come all this way?"

Boris grinned.

"That's science. You have a hypothesis. You test it. And then the results tell you something about the world, whether or not it's a success. We know how to get down here. We know the system they're using. And now we just have to figure out how to access it. But that's not going to happen tonight."

The rest of the way back to the dorms, Boris told Ashur all about the piano teacher he was hoping to recreate. The woman had apparently been the most celebrated concert pianist in all of St. Petersburg, had enthralled audiences across Europe. All he wanted, he told Ashur, was a chance to study with her.

"It had always been a dream of mine, but I never thought it could actually happen," he said.

"But how are you going to get her DNA?" Ashur said. Boris smiled.

"I bought a piece of sheet music she used once. Cost me, like, a whole summer's salary, which was not money I could afford to spend. But, I don't know, I had a feeling about it, a calling. Like, if I could have that in my presence, just hanging in my room, it would make me a better player by osmosis. And now I know why I wanted it so badly."

"And you brought it with you?"

"Of course not," Boris said. "I had my grandmother send it to me."

Ashur thought about whether there was anything he could use for Odishoo, if Boris's plan really worked. The motorcycle was all the way back in California, and it was hard to imagine there being anything of Odishoo left on it after all this time. There was no way Rose was going to send him anything from home. The Beretta was locked up in a safe somewhere, and he couldn't exactly ask for it back without attracting attention. He kept thinking. And then he remembered what he'd used to wrap up the gun.

"Boris?"

"Yeah?"

"How long do you think DNA lives on a T-shirt?"

"Long enough, buddy," Boris said. "Long enough."

Ashur had never seen Boris like this. Despite the hour, and the physical toil of their journey, he seemed almost hyper with energy. Ashur thought he would make a good academic, the sort of guy who would stay up late with a hard problem on a whiteboard, using everything in his power to get at the right answer. Maybe the Academy would push him in that direction and show him the right way to reach his full potential.

When they got back to his dorm, Ashur was wiped. Boris started to head back the other way.

"Hey," Ashur called out. Boris turned around.

"Thanks for thinking about me," Ashur said, "with, you know, all of this."

"Sure, Ashur," Boris said. "And hey, no promises. Maybe we'll get both our sorry asses kicked out. But if you're willing to try, then so am I."

The men shook hands, and Ashur made the walk back to his room.

There were only a few hours left until the next morning's lessons. Ashur was desperate for a bit of sleep. But as he was closing his eyes, his Cube lit up with another chirping indication of an incoming message.

"Damn it, Boris," he muttered to himself. "What could possibly be that important?"

The Cube lit up to display the message, and Ashur quickly saw that it wasn't from Boris.

You still don't know the full truth about Odishoo's death, the message read. *But the Director does....*

"The Director?" Ashur said. He thought back to the man from orientation—trim, older, with close-trimmed gray hair. What would the Director of the Academy possibly know about his father, and the circumstances of his death? Ashur wondered again if this was all a prank, or some test by the Academy.

The Cube asked if he wanted to respond, but Ashur knew well enough by now than to try and talk directly with Admirer. He lay down and tried to sleep.

But sleep would not come—he kept thinking about the message, and what it might mean, and all the different ways that a young apprentice like himself might find a way to speak privately with a man as powerful as the Director. Tomorrow, he resolved, he would start trying.

On hearing Rose's challenge, Odishoo's body started shaking. He clenched his fists, and for a moment Ashur worried he might hit his mom. Rose saw the same thing, her eyes moving down to where his hands were balled by his sides.

"Go ahead, you crazy man. Hit me! Isn't that what you want? Hit me!" She stepped up until she was mere inches from his face. "Show your son how to treat his future wife!"

Tears began to stream down Odishoo's face. He stepped back from Rose and then slumped down into his chair. He looked down at the floor, not meeting Ashur's eyes as he began to talk to his son.

"Your mother is right, Ashur. About everything. I blamed myself when my father disappeared because I knew I had let him down. I was a drinker, an alcoholic, and I only quit the night you were born because I didn't want to let you down, too. Your mother was the most beautiful woman in the world, and I let her down. I took her away from her family, showed her how to drink, ruined her life. Just like she says. The only reason I keep living is to continue my father's legacy through you, Ashur. You are the great hope for me. I still believe that."

His chin dropped down onto his chest, and he heaved a tremendous sigh.

"But I need to make a change."

Odishoo looked up at Rose.

"I'm sorry for everything I've put you through. It's all been my fault—I blame myself each day for everything that has gone wrong.

I never wanted this for you. I don't know how to make it up to you, but I am going to try."

Ashur could see that the anger had left his mother's face. Rose didn't speak—she seemed stunned, looking through her husband and into the distance. Ashur looked between his parents, waiting for one of them to say something more. When neither did, he jumped up and threw his arms around Odishoo's shoulders.

"I love you, Dad," he said. "Please don't cry. This hurts. I don't like to see you like this."

Without lifting his head, Odishoo squeezed Ashur tightly against him.

"I will always love you, Ashur," he said quietly. "You're the greatest gift God ever gave me. You are good—and strong. Just like your grandfather. He wasn't a perfect man. But he was a good man, and so are you. You are going to do something very special with your life."

He pulled back for a moment and looked Ashur square in the eye.

"I pray you keep God very close to you, because it will be difficult at times, and without Him it will be even more painful. But you will persevere. Forgive me for today. And forgive your mother, too. She is a good woman who has a lot of pain inside her—most of it caused by me. But she still loves you—and wants the best for you."

Ashur's stomach dropped.

"Why are you talking like you're leaving?"

Odishoo leaned forward and kissed Ashur's forehead. Then he stood for a moment.

"Just for now," he said. "There's something I need to do."

"Where do you think you're going?" Rose said, her voice suddenly harsh again.

Odishoo didn't say anything. Ashur and Rose followed him as he moved through the house. He walked silently to the front door and took his keys off the hook in the entryway.

"Where are you going?" Rose said again. This time, Ashur could hear her panic.

"I really am sorry, Rose," Odishoo said. "For everything I've put you through. I hope that someday you find it within your heart to forgive me."

As his father stepped outside, Ashur pushed past Rose and followed Odishoo to his car.

"What's going on, Dad? Where are you going? Can I come?"

He hated the thought of being left behind with his mother. But Odishoo shook his head.

"No, son. I need to do this alone."

Ashur grabbed his father's hand.

"Please, Dad! Please don't leave!"

Odishoo knelt, and for a moment Ashur thought he might stay. But then the man shook his head.

"I have to."

Odishoo stood and opened the car door.

"Your life is about to change, Ashur. Remember: you became a man today. And I know you won't let any of us down."

He climbed into the driver's seat and closed the door, but Ashur put his hand against the window.

"Dad! Please don't!" he said, tears blurring his vision. But without another word, Odishoo backed out of the driveway and into the street. As he pulled away, Ashur ran behind the car, screaming in the middle of the street for Odishoo to stay.

But his father was gone.

CHAPTER ELEVEN

The next day, after his morning run with the team, Ashur begged off breakfast, telling everyone that there was something he wanted to finish reading before their lesson for the day. But instead of going back to his room, he headed straight to the administrative building.

He had only seen the Director once before, when the man made his opening remarks during orientation. But he still lingered powerfully in Ashur's memory. And now that Admirer had suggested that the Director had something to do with his father's death, Ashur was determined to talk with him...and discover whether there was any truth behind the strange, cryptic messages he kept receiving.

The administrative building was sleek and modern, constructed of large panes of glass that let in the abundant morning light. Ashur walked confidently down the central corridor, trying hard to look like he was supposed to be there and knew where he was going. The men and women in the conference rooms around him seemingly paid him no mind as he pushed deeper into the building.

At the end of the corridor was a large, imposing wooden door, seemingly out of place with the contemporary design of the rest of the building. It looked to Ashur like the entrance to the office of a business titan from a century earlier—he imagined Andrew Carnegie or John Rockefeller directing their empires from a similar perch. He took a deep breath and went to open the door.

"Can I help you?"

He turned and saw a small, older woman seated behind a desk in an alcove off to the side, looking up at him from her Cube. The placard on her desk said her name was Cheryl.

"I need to speak with the Director," Ashur said.

"Do you have an appointment?"

"It's important."

Cheryl keyed a few things into her Cube.

"Ashur Yonan. New apprentice. I hope you're enjoying your time at the Academy, Ashur."

"So, can I speak with him?"

The woman shook her head.

"I'm afraid he's unavailable."

"Well, when will he be available?"

Cheryl removed the small pair of glasses from her nose and let them hang, suspended from a thin golden chain around her neck.

"I'd be happy to give him a message."

Ashur shook his head. "No. I need to talk with him directly."

The woman sighed. "I hope you won't take this the wrong way, but that isn't possible. The Director is an extremely busy man. Especially right now, given the threats facing the Academy. And it's my job to protect his time, as much as I can. You understand that I can't let every new apprentice who wants to get a little face time with the most powerful person at the Academy just walk in and chat with him."

"But this is urgent."

"Then I suggest you leave a message," Cheryl said. "And I'll be sure to relay it."

Ashur groaned. The woman was being impossible, but he couldn't figure out how to make contact with the Director without going through her.

"Fine. Will you tell him that I want to speak with him?"

"I was going to do that anyway. Anything else?"

Ashur thought for a moment—he still didn't know where the Admirer's messages were coming from, or truly what they meant. Something told him he needed to keep that information to himself for now, until he had a chance to speak with the Director and figure out what was really happening.

"No," Ashur said. "Nothing else."

"I'll be sure to let him know," Cheryl said, keying something into her Cube. "Now hurry along. You don't want to be late for today's lesson. It's a doozy."

"Our theme for today is control and deception," Cicero said from a podium by the stage in the Vault. "And our instructors are…perhaps more unorthodox than some of the others you've heard from so far. But to me, these are some of the most important lessons, so I want you to put aside whatever preconceived notions you might have and pay close attention. Even people you might not agree with still have plenty to teach you.

"Our first instructor is a man I expect to be familiar to all of you, though today you're going to be hearing from him in a very different context. The man is self-educated, passionate, and driven. He has read and thought more about political theory and history than many more traditional instructors, and he has a unique perspective that I believe is particularly valuable. So please listen with an open mind."

On the stage materialized a Black man in baggy jeans and a tight black T-shirt, wearing a bandana tied tight around his head. He wore a heavy gold chain around his neck that glinted in the lights of the Vault. He looked over the apprentices with a coolly appraising eye. In the seat next to Ashur, Jahi gasped. The man turned with a slight smile and looked at him.

"Y'all know me?"

"You're Tupac Shakur," Jahi said.

Ashur was in awe. How many times had Kiki played *All Eyez on Me* in her car, speeding down the freeway? He wished she were there to see this.

"What is it," Tupac said. "You know why my mom named me Tupac? Huh? Any of y'all?"

Ashur looked around the room. This was arguably the most famous rapper ever—everyone here had heard his music, and the music of generations of musicians that had followed in his footsteps. Surely someone would know. But the group stayed silent. Tupac let out a quick, barking laugh and shook his head.

"Shit…every time. When you gonna get yourself some *educated* recruits, Cicero?"

"That's what you're here for," Cicero said with a small smile. "Otherwise, they'd put us all out of a job."

"I was named for Túpac Amaru," the rapper said. "The last descendant of the last Incan ruler. A legend, man. Tried to rebel against the Spanish in Peru and lost his damn head for the trouble. But of course y'all ain't never heard of him. Because they don't *want* you to."

"Who is 'they' in this case?" Boris said with a hand halfway raised.

"Shit, who is 'they'? Open your damn eyes. The government. Corporations. The media. And not just the faces you know. The *real* power players. The ones with the cash who can make things happen. Who use institutions as tools to inject their beliefs—and control more people. Those in power who plan on keeping it that way and are willing to do whatever it takes. You think they want you hearing about people fighting back? Hell no, man."

Ashur thought this sounded a little familiar—he had heard his share of old men at the restaurant, swapping conspiracy theories like they were baseball cards. But at the same time, the basic structure of what Tupac was saying made sense. People want power, and once they have it, they will use every possible tool to preserve it. The question was how they achieved it—and what to do about it.

"So how do they do it?" Ashur said. Tupac flashed a grin.

"You ever heard of Friedrich Hegel?"

Ashur shook his head—he'd read a lot, but he'd never come across him.

"Listen up, 'cause this is the truth. That shit they don't want you to know. So this dude, he's got this thing, the Hegelian Dialectic. I got real into him a few years back. He says you create a problem, then you create opposition to that problem, and then you create a solution. Thesis, antithesis, synthesis. Sound a little familiar? Introduce crack to the inner cities. Start the war on drugs to stop it. And then lock up more people than any other country in the history of the world. All for control."

"You really think crack is some government conspiracy?" Jahi asked.

Tupac looked at him. "Where you from?"

"Miami," Jahi said.

"Yeah, but you ain't from Liberty City," Tupac said. "You ain't from Brownsville. I bet you from Coral Gables or some shit."

Jahi looked down and didn't say anything.

"Yeah," Tupac said, nodding his head. "Bet you had a dad too, right? You had your pops telling you how to be a man, how to treat women right, about hard work and discipline. You never see people getting shot at—your friends, your family, the people you love. You never see your Auntie on the corner tryna cop a vial. You don't see the way that shit tears people up."

"But that doesn't mean it's some big government conspiracy," Cassandra said.

"You think that shit's an accident, shorty? Shit, you look smarter than that."

"I think sometimes we want to believe there's some grand plan," Cassandra said. "When really there isn't."

"Forget crack, then. The financial system. Health care. Pick whatever you want. Crisis after crisis, and the government stepping in to try and play the savior. Making people dependent on them, stopping folks from thinking for themselves. Because politicians, the media, businessmen—all experts in the art of deception. You know what Hitler said? 'Make the lie big, make it simple, keep saying it, and eventually they will believe it.' He was a real bad dude—the worst—but he wasn't stupid. And I spent my life trying to liberate people from deceptions—the deceptions of their minds, the deceptions of their government. I tried to bring them freedom."

Boris huffed a sigh. "Cicero, sir, with respect, this seems a little ridiculous. A rapper peddling conspiracy theories? Why aren't we hearing from someone like Lenin?"

"The hell you talkin' about?" Tupac said, striding toward Boris with long, menacing steps.

"I'm sorry, I just don't see what the point of this is."

"Boris, please," Cicero said. Tupac was still walking toward the apprentice.

"You think you smart, huh? Smarter than me. Too smart to listen. You must have it all figured out, huh?"

A sneer came across Tupac's face as he stepped down from the stage. He reached into the waistband of his jeans, and the apprentices gasped as he pulled out a gun.

"How 'bout now, huh? You respect me now, white boy?"

Cassandra screamed as Tupac lifted the gun in Boris's direction. Boris cringed and looked over at Cicero, and Ashur leapt up—he wasn't entirely sure what was happening, but he instinctually felt the need to do *something*.

But before Ashur could reach him, Tupac's voice began to skip, like he was nothing more than a scratched CD. His body froze, his face a mean mug trained on Boris. He flickered in and out of sight, once and then again, before suddenly, he was gone.

"Aw, man, it was just getting good!" Brodi said, waving an arm down toward the stage. "Which one of you babies hit your Blink?"

"The what?" Jahi said. Brodi rolled her eyes.

"The Blink. The kill switch on the Cube? You didn't actually think a hologram could shoot you, right?"

"Hey, I didn't hit anything," Boris said, holding up his hands.

"Me neither," Cassandra said. One by one, each of the apprentices confirmed that they hadn't used the Blink on their device.

"Is there some kind of automatic stop if the holograms become violent?" Jahi said. Cicero shook his head. Ashur noticed the man looked extremely concerned.

"No," he said. "It isn't necessary since holographic weapons aren't real. Whatever damage they could do, they'd do with their words. Just like how Tupac managed to get under Boris's skin."

"Then what happened?" Ashur said.

Cicero was frowning down at his Cube. "I don't know. The system appears to have gone offline."

"Does that happen often?"

"It's got to," Brodi said. "Any system that complex."

Cicero looked up and shook his head. "Not this system, Brodi," Cicero said. He looked as though he wanted to say something more, but then clammed up, cognizant of the apprentices. Ashur wondered what he was afraid of saying.

Ashur felt a chill run down his spine. Something weird was happening, between the messages from Admirer and now Tupac suddenly disappearing. Things that weren't meant to be happening. He thought again about the Director—if only he could talk with him, then maybe all of this would make sense.

"I need you all to get out of here as quickly and calmly as you can," Cicero said. "Hopefully this is nothing, and we'll have things back up and running by this afternoon. But just in case…"

"In case of what?" Brodi said.

Cicero shook his head.

"Go, please. Now."

Boris came and found Ashur after lunch.

"You up for a little more exploring tonight?" he said quietly, looking around first to make sure no one could overhear them. "I've been thinking through different ways we can get around the firewall, and I've got a guess that I think might work."

Ashur sighed. "You really think this is a good idea, after what's been happening?"

"What do you mean?"

Ashur paused. He wished he could tell Boris and the others about Admirer, and all the strange messages. But instead, he mentioned the Tupac hologram flickering out.

"I'm sure Cicero is overreacting," Boris said. Stuff like that must happen a lot. It just doesn't feel that way when you're used to it working."

"You really think so?"

"Trust me. I might not be Brodi-level, but I understand computers. Now, what do you think? You want to see your dad again or not?"

Ashur sighed and nodded. He'd do anything for a little more time with Odishoo, even if it was only a hologram.

"All right. I'm in."

"Great!" Boris said. "I'll come find you tonight."

On the way back down to the Vault, Ashur caught Cassandra looking at him. He wondered if she had been watching him and Boris or had heard anything they were talking about. But she didn't say anything, so they rode down to the lower level together in silence.

Cicero was standing at the front of the Vault lecture hall, looking sternly down at the apprentices.

THE ACADEMY

"The diagnosis for what went wrong during this morning's session is ongoing," he said. "Given the fluid nature of the situation, certain voices within the administration counseled that we pause our lessons with the simulations. But I believe that this is the core of the Academy education—while I consider myself an able speaker and educator, I know that my own abilities pale in comparison to the perspective you can gain by talking with the historical figures whose life experiences far exceed my own. Thankfully, they listened to me. But I urge you all to appreciate the opportunity before you and make the most of it. For some of you, your time at the Academy will be coming to an end soon."

Ashur nodded along with the rest of the apprentices. They had known since their first day on campus that most of them wouldn't be continuing with the Academy once they were done with their lessons—they were under constant evaluation to see whether they merited a chance to stay. Still, it cast things in a starker relief to hear Cicero speak so frankly about their remaining time together. Ashur had enjoyed the lessons so far, but he still didn't feel like he was close to understanding his true purpose. He needed to keep going.

"With that in mind," Cicero continued, "this afternoon's speaker might alarm you. But I assure you we have selected him for good reasons. Still, I will understand—and perhaps even encourage—if you refrain from a warm welcome."

He keyed something into his Cube and then offered up his palm for a final authentication. A few moments later, a small man wearing tall black boots and an olive-green uniform appeared onstage. He scowled beneath a familiar mustache, and Ashur could see the swastika-emblazoned band wrapped around his arm.

"Dear God," Jahi said softly. Revulsion filled Ashur's stomach.

Adolf Hitler stared at the recruits coldly, then clicked his heels together and began to speak in clipped German. In front of him, holographic letters appeared: *Good day, apprentices.*

"Hitler insists on speaking German," Cicero said. "It is inconvenient, I know, but it's directly tied to the hologram's accuracy."

"Why would you ever choose such a monster?" Jahi said.

"Hitler was responsible for starting World War Two," Cicero said as Hitler glared at the young Black man. "He would have ended it, too, if he could have, even if it meant the end of the world. He's the best primary example we have for you to learn from, to know how he operated, and hopefully watch for examples of others like him. Averting World War Three isn't the only goal of the Academy, but we believe it is our duty to do everything we can. Because all our other projects together won't amount to very much at all if the world is destroyed."

"Armageddon," Ashur said.

"Precisely," Cicero said. "This lesson is of particular interest to you, Ashur, given your possible future in the military."

Ashur was a little surprised—he had never actively discussed his interest in the military with the instructor. Still, he could feel a certain rightness in what Cicero said. History had always fascinated him, military history especially. He was physically fit and enjoyed work that allowed him to use his body as well as his mind. And he had been thinking about enlisting after leaving home—though that was about as far as he got before everything had happened. He sat up a little straighter in his seat.

Cicero turned back to Hitler.

"If you wanted to start World War Three, how would you do it?"

"Very easily," read the subtitles accompanying Hitler's staccato German speech. "Create a problem, blame and vilify someone else, and then come in as the hero to fix the problem. I would become the savior so that the population would believe in me and follow me blindly into whatever I wanted. That would give me power to begin the war, and the mandate to finally see it through this time."

"That's the same thing Tupac was talking about," Brodi said from the back row. "Hegel."

"*Ja*," Hitler said, nodding his head. "An eminent German thinker. Interpreted poorly by that fool Marx. But his dialectic gives those who understand it the tools necessary for control."

"Don't you think we're a little past all that now?" Cassandra said. "No one really wants war now. Everyone just wants world peace."

Hitler sneered at her.

"Peace is control. Peace requires a single worldview. Until such a time that those with aberrant views can be brought back into the yoke—or purged, if necessary—there is no such thing as peace."

"There has to be a way to have different opinions *and* peace," Boris said. "It's the foundation of liberal democracy."

"And it, too, will crumble," Hitler said. "Too many grudges between nations, between brothers. Too much bad blood. The cycle of war and violence will always persist, until it is ended by domination by a single entity!"

Hitler had become more and more animated as he made this last point, bringing his fist down dramatically on the desk behind him. Ashur noticed the other apprentices jump a little at the sound.

"First, you must control the population," Hitler said, striding now back and forth on the stage with his hands tucked behind his back. "Drugs are good. Media is even better. Did you know that the first movie ever about the *Titanic* was a German film? Back in 1943. I hired the director myself. The hero of the picture is a Nazi soldier. I allowed people to see the truth: that Nazis are the *heroes*, not the villains! The greatest men in the world—*pure Aryans*, the best-built, the most intelligent. Once you saw this golden man on the screen, you could not help but understand that *we* are the master race."

"Let's continue, if you would, with the question at hand," Cicero said with thinly veiled disgust.

"You make people believe you," Hitler said. "And then you lie."

Ashur recalled Tupac earlier that day, quoting the loathsome man now standing on the stage before him: *make the lie big, make it simple, keep saying it, and eventually they will believe it.* That squared with his own perspective—people really will believe anything they hear, often without thinking at all critically about it.

Hitler swung his arm rapidly through the air, as though slashing at an unseen foe with a sword. "Then you divide and conquer! Turn children against parents, and siblings against siblings. Turn the congregations against the clergy. Divide marriages, families, businesses. Make people believe that those around them don't know anything, especially if they oppose *me*, for *I* am the one who is always right. Their moral compass—and the direction of the nation—will be dictated by *me*, their almighty leader, not by God.

"The most difficult type of nation to control is one that believes in a higher power. A nation that has faith and hope is a difficult nation to control. You have to gradually undermine that relationship and eliminate those who keep preaching. And all the while you act as though you are the one trying to bring everyone together, being the magnanimous hero, standing between the good people of the nation and the threats—internal and external—that would otherwise tear them apart.

"Begin to eliminate those threats, the people within the nation that would challenge you—dissenters, radicals, troublemakers. And then move on to those beyond your borders who would oppose you. And be sure to remind everyone of your glorious goal as you do it. Keep telling your people the direction you are moving in. Have them feel morally righteous in your quest. Make them believe in the rightness of what you are doing. They will sacrifice for you, *bleed* for you, *die* for you—if they believe truly in your cause. And with them behind you, you can begin your conquest."

"You really believe people would make the same mistake again?" Cassandra said, frowning at Hitler. He turned to her and smiled.

"My sweet Aryan princess," he said. "Of course they would. They always do. And they always will."

"But things are different today," Boris said. "Everything is so much less centralized."

Hitler nodded.

"It was easier to censor in my time. But great communicators must be demonized and censored. Now you have big virtual governments that need to prevent great communicators from selling faith and hope. Instead, give the platform to fools who demonize God and build up the leader of the nation. These naïve fools are easy to buy. They seek attention. Very easy to control. The key is to publicly undermine the influential leaders who have strong faith and values, to create false narratives about them using media: your virtual governments. Then…you get dirty. Use women, deception, seduction, drugs. Invite them to parties where they'll do something embarrassing—and keep recording them. It's easier than ever to control people. Believe me."

Hitler scowled and looked briefly up toward the ceiling.

"Technology is the key. If *I* had obtained the proper technology in my time—been given the tools I needed to see my work through—then all of you would be living in a *very different world*."

"What kind of technology?" Brodi asked. "Like social media, you mean?"

"Something far more powerful," Hitler said.

"Nuclear weapons?" Boris said. Hitler looked at the man, then took a few steps toward him.

"If the timing had been different," he said. "If the Jews hadn't behaved like rats scurrying from a sinking ship and fled for New Mexico. Then perhaps yes, the bomb would have been enough. The ultimate tool of coercion, as the Americans learned in Japan. But I wanted to rule a glorious empire, not a world reduced entirely to radioactive dust. No…what I wanted was something far more powerful."

Hitler's lips pursed into a small, terrible smile as his fingers reached for the Cube sitting on Boris's desk. Instinctively, Boris drew the device back toward his chest. Hitler stamped his foot.

"*Scheisse!* I was so close—*so close!*—to having everything I needed."

"You're saying that this," Brodi said, holding up her Cube, "is more powerful than a nuke?"

"I tried to tell you," Cicero said, with a satisfied smile playing at the corner of his mouth. "But you seemed more interested in probing the limitations of a technology you didn't yet understand."

"It's the energy, right?" Ashur said. The others in the room turned to look at him. "Sam explained it to me. Something about quantum entanglement. That's how they levitate, and do…whatever else they can do."

"Enough energy to build whatever I needed," Hitler said. "Enough energy to *control* whatever I needed. With this technology, I could have ruled the world!"

"But you let it slip through your fingers," came a gentle voice, speaking in lightly accented English, from the back of the room. Ashur turned around to see an older, grandfatherly figure with a familiar mop of hair, sitting cross-legged in a chair with his pipe tucked thoughtfully into the corner of his mouth. "Didn't you?"

At the appearance of Albert Einstein, the little dictator's face began to turn so red that Ashur half-expected steam to start spilling out of the man's ears.

"*Juden* scum!" he screamed, stamping his feet. "Thieves! Traitors! Stealing from me what was *mine!*"

Einstein rolled his eyes.

"Yes, hard to imagine why we would leave, why we wouldn't stick around to help build your empire. Quite the project manager you turned out to be, Herr Hitler."

Hitler began to scream in German, but the subtitles that had so far been translating his words in real time no longer accompanied his diatribe. Ashur wondered if this was some sort of glitch until he noticed Cicero looking down at his Cube with intense concentration as he keyed in a few commands. The next moment, the dictator went quiet, still frothing at the mouth as he hurled silent invectives at the scientist sitting at the back of the room. And then, in an instant, Hitler disappeared from view—without, Ashur noticed, the usual courtesy and appreciation that their teacher typically extended toward their guest lecturers. The instructor shuddered slightly and took a deep breath before he turned to the class.

"It never gets easier to listen to that man," he said. "But I wouldn't do it if I didn't believe it was important."

"He seems to get madder every time he sees me," Einstein said with a small chuckle. "You would think, after all this time… but no, it seems to only stoke his hatred that much more."

"Why is he so angry with you?" Jahi asked. "Is it because you're Jewish?"

"I'm sure that doesn't help," Einstein said. "But his is a more delicate, and personal, complaint."

"It's because of this," Ashur said, holding his Cube aloft so that it floated just over his palm. He turned to look at Einstein. "You built this, didn't you?"

"*Einstein* built the Cube?" Cassandra said.

"Sam told me a professor here was responsible for the technology," Ashur said. "But I didn't realize it was a hologram."

Einstein raised his bushy eyebrows.

"You make it sound like it was me alone," Einstein said, a twinkle in his eye. "But scientific progress is almost never the work of one man. I did play my role, yes. I made the mathematics work, but Hendrik was the one who deduced the Garden artifact's wonderfully negative trait, and reverse-engineered more of them. And let me say, it brings me such joy to see you all putting them to such use. For good, not evil."

"Thank you, as always, Dr. Einstein, for making the time," Cicero said. "Even when we're hosting unsavory company."

"On the contrary, I enjoy these visits the most," he said. "There is a satisfaction that comes from knowing you've made the right choice. And, in doing so, helped keep the world safe."

Einstein rose from his chair, gave the class a brief wave, and then blinked out of existence.

Cicero stood at the front of the room, looking out at the apprentices.

"None of us ever believe something as awful as the Second World War—with all its death and suffering—could happen again. But, like Boris asked, imagine if the Nazis had gotten nuclear weapons first. Or, worse, if they had somehow kept the scientists from fleeing Europe and coming here to build the Cube. And yet history tells us we would be wise to give the possibility real consideration, if only to allow us to do everything we can to avert such a terrible outcome."

"Yeah, but did it have to be Hitler?" Jahi said. Cicero gave a very small chuckle.

"Believe me, we have tried just about every dictator in history. The internet is wrong about many things, but in this regard our data suggests it is right: you really can't compare anyone to Hitler."

Behind Ashur, Brodi let out a loud laugh. Ashur turned and looked at her—she was shaking her head and nodding at the same time.

"You've heard two very different perspectives on the subject of control and domination today," Cicero said. "Now it's time to put that learning to practical use. Each of you will be put in charge of your own country in the following simulation. And the goal will be to see how quickly you can bring about World War Three."

"Wait, you want us to *cause* World War Three?" Jahi said. Ashur could see how uncomfortable his friend seemed with the idea.

"I know it seems counterintuitive," Cicero said. "But this really is the best way to gain an understanding of the mechanisms and levers available to those who would seek to bring about this magnitude of destruction. If you all would proceed to your stations, please?"

The desk at the front of the room had transformed into a map of the world—Ashur thought about the movie *Dr. Strangelove* as the screens all around the Vault began to display different statistics and information. At the top was the DEFCON level, currently showing four, which meant that things were more or less peaceful. There were other screens listing casualties, radiation levels, and the military capabilities of the world's largest nations. Ashur took a seat and looked down at the map.

Jahi, however, was lingering uncomfortably off to the side of the stage. Cicero saw him standing there.

"Is something wrong, Jahi?"

Jahi nodded and then took a deep breath. "Cicero, I can't participate in today's lesson," he said. "I can't allow myself to be involved in the bloodshed of innocents, even if they're simulated lives. It goes against everything I believe in: mercy, faith, the goodness of God."

"C'mon, man," Brodi said, not looking up from the screen as she quickly scrolled through her Cube and oriented herself with the simulation. "You know this isn't real, right? Didn't you ever play, like, Risk or anything?"

"As a matter of fact, I didn't," Jahi said. "And don't act like this is Scrabble."

"I appreciate your concern, and your faith, Jahi," Cicero said. "But you understand that I'll have to mark down your overall score if you choose not to participate? Is it worth risking your place at the Academy over an exercise like this?"

Jahi closed his eyes and took a deep breath. "I understand, Cicero, and I appreciate your concern. But I need to listen to my moral compass, even if—especially if—there are consequences."

Cicero nodded and made a quick note on his Cube. Ashur looked at Jahi, trying to understand why his friend would jeopardize his place at the Academy over a philosophical exercise. This felt different than Cassandra storming out of their debate with Margaret Thatcher—he couldn't detect any sign of personal trauma or anything else that might push Jahi toward what felt like an irrational decision. If anything, Jahi seemed at peace with his decision. Ashur couldn't comprehend his choice, but he had always known Jahi to be a man of faith. If this was part of that, even with the consequences, then there was something noble, if possibly misguided, about Jahi's decision.

"Would you stay and observe, at least?" Cicero said. Jahi nodded and went to sit in the front row.

"All right, apprentices," Cicero said. "You've listened to what Tupac and Hitler had to say. You have all the tools of a leader of a modern state available to you. It's up to you to decide how best, and most quickly, to bring about World War Three. And please note that just indiscriminately attempting to deploy your nuclear arsenal will not work—though someone still tries every year, bless them. Your time begins…now."

Ashur looked down at his Cube, reading the basic information about his country—he was playing as India—and trying to remember everything he'd heard that day. Divide and conquer sounded so easy in theory, and he could remember Odishoo telling him the story of how Ayatollah Khomeini had managed his rapid ascension to power in the wake of the Shah. But how was he actually supposed to do that?

A loud *ping* rang out in the room, and the apprentices turned to watch a news headline scroll across the Vault's screen: REPORTS OF MASS MURDER IN SAO PAOLO AS PURGES OF BLUE-EYED CITIZENS BEGIN; GOVERNMENT UNWILLING TO INTERVENE.

"What the hell?" Boris said. Across the table, Brodi began to laugh.

"You think murdering innocent civilians is funny?" Cassandra said.

"It is when the citizens are just bits of digital code," Brodi said. "And when I made it happen. And hey, you know who has a bunch of blue-eyed traitors? Colombia. *Vamanos, muchachos!*"

If Ashur hadn't understood Jahi's desire to sit out the exercise at the beginning, after an hour he wondered if there might have been some wisdom in his friend's choice. The apprentices began to make more and more depraved decisions as they urged their citizens on to greater atrocities. Ashur tried to play things straight, forming an alliance with Cassandra to try and stave off the aggression of the NOA (No Ojos Azules—the name that Brodi had gleefully given her coalition of murderous countries) in the Pacific while Boris attempted an incursion from Canada. But after Boris double-crossed them with a maneuver to take Manchuria for himself, suddenly all four apprentices were fighting among themselves. But it was quickly becoming clear that no one could match Brodi when it came to the speed and invention with which she accumulated power and used it to ever-more-terrifying ends.

"It's just a game," she said as she laid waste to Oceana and sank New Zealand into the ocean as a warning to others who might try and cross her. "Did none of you ever play, like, *StarCraft* or anything?"

"You don't have to commit genocide in *StarCraft*!" Boris said.

"Tell that to the Terrans," Brodi said as she continued her push toward Scandinavia.

Then, all at once, the screens became pixelated, as though someone had hit them with a baseball bat.

"Hey!" Brodi said, jumping up from the table. "Who's doing that?"

The map continued to shimmer, and then, with a snap that sounded like a lightbulb breaking, everything blinked out and the Vault was plunged into darkness.

"God dammit!" Brodi yelled.

"Stay where you are, everyone," Cicero said. Ashur could barely see the man illuminated by the subtle glow of his Cube as he frantically looked for an answer to what had happened.

"Jahi, did you do this?" Brodi said.

"What?"

"Did you hit the damn Blink? Come on, man. I know you're uncomfortable. But that doesn't mean you have to drag the rest of us down with you."

"Hey, that's not fair," Ashur said. Emergency lighting was illuminating the Vault now with an eerie red glow.

"Easy for you to say," Brodi said. "You're doing fine. Me? I needed this. *This* was the place for me to show I belonged here. And Mr. Jesus Freak had to come along and ruin everything."

"I didn't do anything, Brodi," Jahi said. Ashur was furious with Brodi for accusing Jahi, but he noticed that Jahi sounded more concerned than anything.

"Yeah, right," Brodi said.

The doors to the Vault creaked open, and lighting from the lower level flooded the room.

"My records don't show anyone activating their devices to override the simulation," Cicero said. "But two glitches in the same day? Something is clearly going on. I think it's best if we all head back up to the surface."

"Whatever. I'm out of here." Brodi stalked off, leaving the rest of the apprentices behind. Ashur started after her but felt a hand on his shoulder. It was Boris.

"Leave her for now, Ash," Boris said. "She's going to go smoke a bowl and then she'll get over it. Stuff happens. She's just like one of those gamers complaining about lag or something stupid, you know?"

Ashur turned back and watched as Brodi nearly ran to the elevator. She was usually so unflappable—always cracking jokes, half-stoned most of the time, but able to beat him at basically any game he tried to play with her. He'd never seen her this upset, and he was worried about her.

"I'll give her some time," he said. "But I'm going to check on her later."

"You guys know I didn't do anything, right?" Jahi said. "That would be crossing a line."

"We know, Jahi," Cassandra said. They all stood and watched as Brodi got into the elevator and headed up toward campus. "We know."

A weird ache filled Ashur's stomach. Why was his father leaving? His forehead was sweating and his whole body began to tremble as he stood in the middle of his street, staring after the car. He began to sob. It had been a long time since Ashur had cried, and this sounded nothing like the little-boy sound he remembered making when he was hurt or afraid as a child. This was a cry that seemed to come from his very soul.

Odishoo was his hero. Even if his mother was telling the truth—even if he now knew all the mistakes Odishoo had made—Ashur still worshipped his father.

He turned and walked slowly back to the house, trying to keep his sobs hidden from his mother. Rose was standing in the doorway.

"Are you okay?" she asked. She seemed softer now, quieter than she had been—she usually got this way after a fight, as though all the energy had been drained from her.

"You did this," Ashur said. He never talked back to his parents. But defiance suddenly seized him—he hated the way his mother fought with his father, hated the hurtful way she had spoken to him, hated how she had ruined a day he had been looking forward to for years. "Are you finally happy?"

The concern on Rose's face quickly vanished, replaced instead with a look of shock.

"I did this?" she said. "You must be crazy, like all the other Yonan men. You heard him say it himself—he told you this was all his fault. Your father is a quitter. He gives up on things when they become too hard. I don't know why you would be surprised that he would quit on his family, too."

"You blame him for everything!" Ashur shouted. "And I'm sick of it! Have you ever thought of taking any responsibility yourself? Or will everything always be someone else's fault? I listen to the way you talk with your friends on the phone every day, all of you

complaining endlessly about your husbands. All competing to see who has it harder. It's pathetic."

"Don't you talk to me that way, Ashur Yonan," she said. "I am your mother!"

Ashur could hear the anger in her voice—usually that would be enough to keep him from going on. But there was something inside him now, a growing rage that made him want to tell her all the things he'd been keeping to himself for years.

"You're blind, Mom. You've convinced yourself you're sick because that's the only way you can keep going. Because you don't ever want anything to be your fault."

Rose looked shocked. She held a hand to her face as though he had slapped her.

"I am *sick*. You don't understand the pain I'm in. Your father doesn't, either. Do you know how that feels?"

"This is all getting old," Ashur said. "You just want an excuse to stay home, sit around, not do anything. I don't call that sickness. I call that laziness."

"What did you say?" Rose said. She was still standing in the doorway, Ashur just below her on the step leading into the house.

"I said you're lazy!" he screamed in her face.

Rose's hand flew without hesitation, hitting Ashur across the face. The first thing he felt was shock. Rose had never touched Ashur before—never—though she had slapped Odishoo plenty of times. But as the shock faded, it was replaced by a growing pain. Ashur reached a hand up to touch his face. A hot pain was spreading, especially near his right eye. When he drew his hand away, it was covered in blood. Ashur looked from his hand to his mother's. Her gaze followed to the ring she wore on her finger, covered with large, faceted jewels. A bright splash of blood shone on the stones.

"Oh God."

Rose dropped down into a crouch in front of Ashur.

"I'm so sorry, baby. I didn't mean to do that. I didn't mean it. Look up. Let me see your face."

Ashur could feel, by the pain and the blood now obscuring his vision, that the cut was deep. But seeing Rose's expression told him just how bad it was.

"What's wrong with you?" he said. His face was turning numb.

"God, why did you make me do this?" she said. Tears were streaming down her cheeks. "We have to get you to a hospital."

"I wish Dad had taken me with him," Ashur said.

CHAPTER TWELVE

O nce they were back up to surface level, Cicero strode purposefully away from the apprentices, making his way quickly toward the administrative building. As he turned the corner, Ashur thought he could see their instructor—usually a model of unflappable calm—break into a run.

"Anyone feel like they have any idea what's going on here?" he said, looking around at his classmates. "Because I get the feeling that something is very wrong."

"It's just some glitch," Boris said. But Ashur couldn't help but notice that his friend seemed less than sure as he said it, rubbing the palms of his hands against the front of his pants until the fabric was shiny with his sweat.

"That was totally unfair to Brodi," Cassandra said, her brow furrowed. "She was destroying all of us."

"I know," Jahi said. "I feel awful. She really needed a win."

"Like you really feel bad for her," Boris said. "You couldn't even be bothered to participate."

"I told you, it went against my faith!" Jahi said, looming over Boris. "You got a problem with that?"

"Oh, so you won't blow up some pixels on a screen, but you have no problem beating up a real person? What kind of faith is that?"

Ashur stepped quickly between Boris and Jahi and gently laid a hand on each of their chests. "Easy, now," he said. "It's been a weird day for everyone."

Boris pushed Ashur's hand away, gave Jahi one last stare, and stalked off in the opposite direction. Jahi let out a long, slow exhale and looked up at the ceiling.

"Lord, give me strength," he said, rolling back his shoulders. "Because that man does not make things easy."

"You're all sure you didn't do anything to mess up the exercise?" Ashur said. "Even by accident?"

Cassandra and Jahi both shook their heads.

"I was too busy figuring out how to keep Brodi from wiping all of Finland off the map," Cassandra said. "Did you know that almost ninety percent of the population had blue eyes? It was basically a Nordic genocide."

"I didn't do anything," said Jahi. "Like I said."

Ashur nodded slowly. "Okay, I believe you."

"So what do we do now?" Cassandra said.

Ashur looked down and shook his head. "Nothing to do until Cicero figures out what's really going on and lets us back into the Vault."

"Traitorball?" Jahi said. "I get the sense that it would feel pretty good to truck through a few defenders right about now."

Ashur smiled and nodded.

"Yeah," he said. "I'm going to go check on Brodi first. Keep a spot open for me?"

"You know it," Jahi said, flashing Ashur the first smile he could remember in days as he headed off.

"I'm coming with you," Cassandra said as Ashur turned to go.

"You sure?"

"She's my teammate, too," Cassandra said. Ashur nodded, and the pair walked quickly over to the dorms.

The hallway reeked of weed. Cassandra wrinkled her nose at the smell as soon as they stepped off the elevator.

"You think that's her?"

"Usually she goes outside," Ashur said. "Or at least cracks the window."

"It's like she's trying to get caught," Cassandra said. Ashur shook his head.

"She seemed pretty sure they weren't going to kick her out. But maybe she just doesn't care anymore. Either way, I don't like it."

"Me, neither," Cassandra said.

The smell grew danker and more potent as they got closer to the door. Ashur's Cube, held aloft before him to lead them to the proper room, began to spin in his hand.

ENVIRONMENTAL READING WARNING, the display read, emitting a low amber glow. CONSIDER AN ALTERNATE ROUTE.

"It must hate pot smoke, too," Ashur said. He ignored the device, folding it back down and slipping it into the pocket of his pants. They rapped on the door.

"Brodi?" Cassandra said. "It's us. Me and Ashur."

There was no answer. Cassandra put her ear up against the door.

"You hear anything?" Ashur said.

"Maybe?" Cassandra said. "It's hard to tell. The doors are thick."

Ashur took a step forward and pounded with the side of his fist against the door.

"Brodi, c'mon. Open up. We just want to make sure you're doing okay. And then we'll leave you alone, all right?"

Still there was no answer.

"Maybe she isn't in there?" Cassandra said.

Ashur shook his head. "I don't think so."

The Cube, now in his pocket, began to chirp insistently. Ashur sighed and took it out. The ENVIRONMENTAL WARNING was still displayed on the screen, but the amber light had darkened to a deep red.

"Ashur," Cassandra said. She was looking down toward the ground, where a thin tendril of smoke was now snaking out from beneath the door to Brodi's room.

Ashur pounded on the door again.

"*Brodi!*"

No answer. More smoke was filling the hallway, the acrid scent of synthetic material burning mingling with the previous smell of pot.

"Stand back," Ashur said. He took a step back and then threw himself at the door, shoulder first. He collided with the solid wood but didn't feel it give way. He crashed into the door again, aiming for the space just above the knob. He heard a faint *crack*, but still the door wouldn't give.

"Go get help," Ashur told Cassandra.

"There isn't time," she said. "We need to get her out of there."

The two of them looked briefly at one another, Ashur noticing the desperation mounting in Cassandra's eyes.

"On three, okay?" he said. Cassandra looked at the door and then nodded and stepped back. "One, two, *three!*"

The two of them hurled themselves at the door. Ashur could feel the wood beginning to give. They stepped back and crashed forward again. Cassandra was clutching at her shoulder, teeth gritted in pain. Ashur wanted to ask her if she was okay, but before he could, she fixed him with a hard look and began to count again.

"One, two, *three!*"

The door splintered, the top breaking free from the jamb. Ashur kicked it hard, and the door finally swung open. Smoke came billowing out from the room, briefly blinding him. Cassandra was coughing, her shirt pulled up to cover her nose and mouth. Ashur did the same and then went into the room.

Brodi was lying on the bed. Her lips were blue. Cassandra ran to their classmate as Ashur searched the room for the source of the fire. A trashcan next to the bed was in flames, and Ashur stuck a boot inside and stomped hard. From somewhere down the hall, fire alarms began to blare. He twisted open a window and looked back through the haze at Cassandra.

"I don't think she's breathing!" Cassandra said. Other apprentices were streaming out of their rooms now, the hallway reverberating with the sound of their footsteps and confused yells. Ashur went to the bed and felt for a pulse. It was there, but faint.

"She doesn't have much time," he said. Without thinking, he hoisted Brodi up from the bed and draped her limp body over his shoulders. "Come on!"

Ashur and Cassandra charged out of the room together, yelling as they went for people to get out of the way, Ashur praying the whole way that they weren't too late.

"Damn it, Brodi!" he said.

He pushed his way out of the building, his grateful lungs filling with oxygen, and watched as medical personnel from the adjacent buildings sprinted across the delicately manicured lawns toward where he laid Brodi gently in the grass.

"Help!" he yelled as loudly as he could. "*Help!*"

His whole body smelled like smoke as he sat in one of the stiff plastic chairs outside the small hospital room where Brodi was being treated. The staff at the medical center had told him four times already to go back to his room and get some rest, or at least shower. But Ashur wouldn't budge until he heard that Brodi was going to be all right. Cassandra was there alongside him, the two of them sitting next to one another in a deep, knowing silence. They knew there was nothing to say until they heard the news.

A man in scrubs finally emerged from the room. He looked tired and shook his head slightly as he came out into the hallway. Ashur stood without thinking and stepped forward. He braced himself for the worst.

"Is she going to be all right?" he said.

The man sighed...and nodded.

"We were able to reverse the overdose," he said.

"Overdose?" Cassandra said. "From pot?"

The doctor shook his head. "We'll need to wait for the blood-work to come back, but the pot was just the start of it. Looked to me like an opiate of some kind. Nasty stuff."

Opiates? Ashur thought. He wondered about all the times he'd seen Brodi high, and the way he'd written it off as harmless.

She'd always acted like it was no big deal, and he'd believed her. Had she been using the other stuff the whole time? Or was there something about that day, and the disappointment of not finishing the exercise, that finally pushed her over the limit?

"She's suffering from smoke inhalation, too," the doctor said. "Basically did everything she could to keep oxygen from getting to her brain. We'll have to keep her for observation for a while. There may still be some lingering effects, but the most acute danger seems to have passed."

Next to him, Cassandra let out a single choked sob as the emotions of the day flooded over her. Ashur felt the tension he'd been holding in his body ebb just slightly as he slid back against the wall and down into the chair.

"I probably don't need to tell you that things would have gone very differently if you hadn't been there," the doctor said. "Even with the fire, who knows if we would have found her in time. You saved your friend's life."

"Can we talk to her?" Cassandra said.

The doctor shook his head. "She's sedated, and will be for some time. As soon as we think it's safe, we'll make sure you have a chance to see her. But for now, there's nothing more for you to do."

"Thank you," Ashur said, looking up from where he was sitting. The doctor nodded, held his gaze for a moment, and then continued on down the long hallway of the medical center.

"Why would she do that?" Ashur said once the doctor was out of earshot. He could feel his blood rising. Now that he knew that Brodi was going to be okay, the fear was leaving him, replaced instead with anger. "Why?"

"I don't know, Ash," Cassandra said, shaking her head.

"Did you know she was using?"

"Pot, sure. Nothing else. I don't think anyone did, or else we would have tried to stop her."

"I can't believe it," Ashur said. "How can someone so smart be that dumb? She almost died, Cassandra. And left us to find her."

"I don't think she meant it," Cassandra said.

Ashur stood from his seat and ran a hand quickly through his hair. He took a deep breath and turned to look at Cassandra. Her mascara had run, leaving light black streaks down her cheeks. Even so, she was beautiful.

"You were great back there," he said. "I don't know if I could have gotten that door down alone."

"We got lucky," Cassandra said.

Ashur nodded. He couldn't shake the feeling that their luck could have easily gone the other way—and if it had, what would have happened? He couldn't stand to think of a world where Brodi was dead. He stared hard at the wall, trying to ignore the feeling.

"Ashur," Cassandra was saying. He turned around to discover Cheryl, the small woman who sat outside the Director's office, waiting patiently in the hallway for him to notice she was there.

"Seems like you've had a hard day, Ashur Yonan," Cheryl said. Ashur nodded. "It would be understandable if you need to rest. I imagine I would, after everything you've been through. But I wanted to let you know that the Director would like to speak with you, whenever you're ready."

"The Director?" Cassandra said, looking between the small woman and Ashur. "What's going on?"

"I'll come find you after and explain," Ashur said. He turned back to Cheryl. "I can speak to him now."

"Are you sure? He would understand if—"

"Now, please," Ashur said. The comment came out more forcefully than he had intended, and he tried to calm himself down. "If that's all right."

Cheryl hesitated for just a moment, as though considering his request. Ashur thought about how he must appear to her: sweaty, exhausted, still reeking of smoke. But he wanted to talk to the Director, as soon as he could. Things were getting stranger, and whether or not Admirer had anything to do with it, he suspected the Director would be able to help him make sense of everything.

Finally the small woman nodded, and Ashur followed her, ignoring the look of concern and confusion that Cassandra offered in his wake.

Music was playing softly in the Director's office. That was the first thing Ashur noticed after Cheryl closed the door and told him to wait. Soft music, with a woman singing quietly. There was something familiar about the music that he couldn't quite put his finger on. He stood before the large imposing desk, now empty, and listened, waiting for the Director.

A door on the far side of the office slid open and the Director strode into the room. He was an older man, trim and toned. His hair was gray, and his goatee salt-and-pepper-flecked. On his lapel was the Academy's lion logo, rendered this time in gold. Ashur had only ever seen it in silver before. The man walked quickly, frowning down at something on his Cube before placing the device in the cradle on his desk with a sigh.

A powerful man, no doubt, Ashur thought, but one perhaps grown weary of all the obligations placed upon him.

The Director stood for a moment behind his desk. For the first time since coming into the office, he looked at Ashur. This was not a gaze seeking to understand what the apprentice was doing there, but instead a look of appraisal. It felt to Ashur as though the man could see down into his very soul. He wondered what it was he found there.

"I hear you saved a life today," the Director said finally, taking his seat and motioning for Ashur to sit as well.

Ashur nodded as he took his seat.

"Yes. Though I wish I didn't have to."

"We can't control the behavior of others. People make their own choices. Perhaps we should have kept Brodi on a tighter tether, or listened to the concerns of those in the recruiting process who thought her penchant for recreational drugs augured poorly for her ability to make something of herself. But if we only accepted those with flawless resumes, we would miss giant swaths of human potential, including those individuals who might not have a chance otherwise to achieve everything they can."

It was impossible for Ashur not to hear himself in the Director's description. All the questions that he'd wondered about since Zaya had come into the interrogation room came flooding back to him now.

"Like a recruit picked up on weapons charges in California?"

A very small smile crossed the Director's lips.

"Your instructors speak highly of you," the man said. "Cicero tells me you have an interest in the military. Tell me, what appeals to you about that path towards leadership?"

Ashur thought about this for a moment before answering.

"I've always been interested in history," he said. "The rise and fall of empires. How wars are won and lost. So much of human society has been shaped by conflict. But more than that, I see it as a chance to be part of something greater than myself. I believe in duty, and honor, and bravery."

"Though your personal history suggests that following the rules has never been a strength."

Ashur felt himself bristle at the suggestion, though he knew that anyone looking at his file would come to the same conclusion.

"No, sir. Though, in my defense, many of those rules were stupid."

The Director chuckled lightly.

"I'm sure they were. Though I feel I have to warn you that you might not find all the rules of the military to be paragons of wisdom and discretion. A military is, in the end, just a collection of human beings. All of them fallible and imperfect, as much as we might wish it to be otherwise."

"Did you serve, sir?" Ashur said.

The Director nodded. "Yes. In a sense."

"What branch?"

The older man shook his head. "It was a long time ago. In a very different sort of world. That's all I'll say about that for now."

Ashur felt to urge to press the man further but suppressed the impulse for the moment. He could sense that there were limits to what the Director would be willing to share with him, and he didn't want to waste his questions on personal history that had nothing to do with what brought him to the office in the first place.

"Cheryl said you came to see me this morning," the Director said. "She said that you were unusually insistent, for an apprentice with no appointment. And when Cheryl tells me that someone is insistent, I trust her. She is extremely good at protecting my time."

Ashur nodded.

"But given the way the day has gone, I thought I owed you a meeting. Considering what you've done for the Academy. So tell me, Ashur Yonan. What is it you wanted to speak to me about so badly?"

Ashur took a deep breath before answering.

"My father, sir."

For just a brief moment, Ashur thought he saw something pass across the Director's face—some look of concern, or unease. But quickly the man regained control of himself.

"Your father," he said.

"Odishoo Yonan."

The Director nodded. "Your file mentioned that he had died. I'm sorry for your loss."

Ashur wondered if now was the time to mention the strange messages he had been receiving from the account that called itself Admirer. If anyone at the Academy would know what was happening, it was the Director. All Ashur had to go on were the anonymous messages suggesting that the Director knew something about his father. But then again, if Admirer was right, what would Ashur be giving up by revealing his source?

"Did you know him?" Ashur asked. He looked across the desk, locking eyes with the Director. For a few moments, neither man said anything, and Ashur waited for the Director to excuse him from the office. But instead, the man issued a very small nod.

"I knew your father," the Director said. "Odishoo Yonan was a promising student."

"My dad was here?" Ashur said. "At the Academy?"

"Yes. A long time ago."

Ashur could feel his mind churning with the new information. Why hadn't his father ever told him about the Academy? Did Rose know anything about it? And why had the Director pretended as though he only knew about Odishoo from a file? The man hadn't lied, exactly—in fact, as Ashur thought back through the exchange, he noticed that the man had worked carefully to avoid lying. But even so, he had managed to withhold the essential core of the truth, saying barely anything at all.

"I never knew about that," Ashur said.

"We work hard to keep it that way," the Director said. "Most people don't know we exist at all. Those who do know, for the most part, have a cursory understanding of our organization at best. Very, very few have the opportunity to see the full picture of who we are—and what we do."

Ashur wondered, not for the first time, how much of the Academy he would ever have the chance to understand himself.

"So what happened?"

The Director sighed. "Not everyone who attends the Academy is able to achieve their full potential. No matter how much we might wish it to be otherwise. Your friend Brodi, whenever she wakes up, will be experiencing that sting of disappointment."

"Are you saying my dad got kicked out because of drugs?"

The Director shook his head. "No, I'm saying that there are all manner of ways to go astray. This is difficult work, Ashur. The opportunity before you is tremendous, but so are the risks."

"So what happened?"

"I'm sorry. But that's all I can say for now."

Ashur narrowed his eyes as he looked at the older man.

"Perhaps someday, when you've had a chance to understand more, we can talk again about him. But there is nothing more I can tell you about Odishoo at this time."

"Not even about his death?" Ashur said.

The Director froze. "What did you say?"

"Are you telling me you have no information about the death of my father?"

The two men stared at one another as though locked in a battle of wills. Most people shrank before Ashur when he looked at them that intensely. But not the Director. There was within his eyes not only a fiery intensity but also a reserve, as though he was merely watching to see what happened next, with no emotional involvement whatsoever. *Has he always been like that*, Ashur thought, *or did he train himself to be so impassive?*

"It's time for you to leave this office, Ashur," the Director said finally. He spoke no louder than his typical speaking voice, and yet there was an edge to his words now that came laden with warning.

Ashur stood and then looked once more at the Director. He could feel his anger at the man growing. This person knew something about his father—and his death. He needed to know what that was.

"What is it that you aren't telling me?"

"I don't have enough days left to tell you everything you don't know," the Director said.

"He is my father," Ashur said. "Not just some name in a file. I deserve to know."

"To know what?"

"The truth!"

"The truth is that the world is a complicated place. And that people are complicated animals. And understanding either is difficult work that never stops. Nothing I tell you, today or otherwise, will change any of that."

The Director pointed a finger toward his door, now open, and nodded. Ashur thought for another moment if there was anything else he might say to change the man's mind. He was so hungry for information about his father, desperate to learn anything that he hadn't known before. But he could sense that this conversation was over, and that pushing any further would only risk his spot at the Academy. He did not sense that the Director was a patient man. He had allowed a certain amount of pushing, perhaps out of deference to everything that had happened to Ashur that day. But he was the kind of man who had a clear limit, and Ashur was close to reaching it.

As he left the office, stalking purposefully out the door and past Cheryl, he made a point not to look back. Already in his mind he was composing his response to Admirer, ready to tell him he believed him when he said the Director knew more about his father's death than he was letting on. The only question was, what would it take to learn what it was? Information, as Ashur was beginning to understand more and more, was never free. And rarely was it cheap.

Before he turned the corner at the end of the hall, he thought once more of the music that had been playing in the Director's office. That soft, lilting voice.

Googoosh, he thought. His father's favorite.

Ashur held the towel to his face. He could feel the wound throbbing beneath the thin fabric as his mother raced through the midday traffic. He tried to keep his head up to stop the blood from getting all over the worn fabric of the car seats, but when he looked down at himself, his T-shirt was soaked with blood, the rain staining in rusty rings as it dried.

Rose darted in and out of traffic. Usually his mother was a lethargic, cautious driver, but today she drove faster than he had ever seen her go before. When she came to a light, she dialed Odishoo again on her cell phone, but again, no answer.

She pulled into the hospital parking lot with a screech of tires, parking her car across two handicapped spaces. An orderly smoking behind the emergency room bay started to yell something at her. But when the man saw Ashur emerge from the car, he threw his cigarette butt to the ground and rushed over to help.

The whole ride over, Ashur hadn't said a word. He remained silent as the orderly talked with Rose and as he was processed and rushed into surgery. When the anesthesiologist told him to count backward from ten, he stared at the man with his one good eye, still not saying anything, until the world faded to black.

Ashur woke to the sound of his mother praying. He hadn't heard her pray in a long time. But now she sounded like she was pleading, desperate as she asked God for a miracle. He kept his eyes closed.

After a time, he heard the door open. His mother was talking with a doctor now, begging him for information. He told her there would be a permanent scar above Ashur's eye but that he would keep his sight. Ashur heard his mother's choked sobs as she thanked the doctor. There was a pause before the doctor responded.

"Do you have other children, Mrs. Yonan?"

"No. Ashur is my only child. Why?"

"I tried to speak with Ashur before the surgery," the doctor said. "About what had happened. But the boy wouldn't say a word. Maybe he's like that, but I wasn't sure."

"What are you saying, Doctor?"

"Now, listen. I don't have any evidence for this, and I'm not trying to get anyone in trouble. But something, call it doctor's intuition, tells me Ashur was trying to protect someone."

There was silence for a few moments.

"This is your only son, Mrs. Yonan. Treasure him. Let this situation be a reminder of that. Do you understand?"

"I would never hurt my son."

"Of course not," the doctor said. He told her that Ashur would be able to go home later that night and that he needed to come back in a week. Ashur heard the door close again, then drifted off to sleep once more.

"What are you doing here?"

Ashur woke and cracked his good eye open. There was a man in the room, unfamiliar to him. But it was clear that Rose knew him.

"I was here already. Waiting on an old friend. What happened?"

"Odishoo…he left. And then Ashur…there was an accident."

He could see his mother beginning to shake. The man patted her arm and then reached into his coat and produced a flask.

"There, there, Rose. I'm sure everything is going to be all right. Here, have a bit. After the day you've had, you deserve it."

Ashur closed his eyes as his mother took a drink.

"I must be going," the man said. "But I'll be sure to check back in. You can always count on me, Rose. No matter what happens."

As he heard the door close, Ashur shut his eye tightly before Rose could see that he was awake. Who was this man? There was something strange about him—how could he have found them, and what was he doing in the hospital already? It seemed like too much of a coincidence to believe. And yet his mother had clearly known him. Ashur wished he could ask her point-blank to explain herself but knew that it would be useless.

When Ashur woke up again, he could feel his eye throbbing. Whatever pain meds they had given him must have worn off. He groaned and put a hand up to the injured eye.

"Don't touch that, honey," he heard his mother say.

"Where is Dad?" Ashur asked. His eye was covered with a patch, and his stitches covered by gauzy bandages.

"He isn't here yet. But I'm here."

"Can you get him?"

"I'm trying, honey. I'm sure he's going to come as soon as he can."

Ashur lay back against the pillow and sighed.

"This is the worst birthday ever," he said. There were a few soda crackers on a tray next to the bed, and he picked up one and crushed it in his hands until it crumbled into tiny pieces.

After a short while, a nurse arrived with a wheelchair. Ashur groaned as he pushed himself out of bed and into the waiting chair. It was dark outside; he couldn't tell how long they'd been in the hospital.

"You must be happy to go home!" the nurse said with a cheerful smile as she pushed Ashur out of the room.

"Not really," he said. The nurse ignored him, and they continued down the hall.

As they rolled into the waiting room, a crowd of nurses and orderlies rushed toward the doors. Outside, an ambulance was waiting, its lights refracting into the emergency room. With his one good eye, Ashur could see a patient on a gurney being wheeled in toward the entry doors.

"Coded patient!" a nurse shouted. "Coded patient!"

"What does that mean?" Ashur asked.

"I don't know," Rose said. The nurse who had been pushing Ashur was running toward the entry.

The automatic doors of the emergency slid open and a crowd of medical personnel pushed the gurney into the hospital. Ashur heard one of the EMTs as he passed.

"T-boned. Big freakin' sedan. We had to rip the door off to get him out. No sign of the other driver, but this one's in critical condition."

Ashur watched as they passed. The gurney and sheet were soaked in blood, which dripped onto the floor in dark streaks. His mother pulled his wheelchair back against the wall to give the EMTs more space.

"Don't look, honey," she said. But Ashur kept watching.

From beneath the sheet, the man's arm slipped off the gurney as they rushed past. Ashur's one good eye went wide in horror.

"Mom," he said, with such urgency that his mother started. "Did you see his arm?"

"What?"

"That guy," Ashur said. "He had the same tattoo as Dad."

CHAPTER THIRTEEN

Back in his room, Ashur paced back and forth like a caged animal. His anger at the Director wasn't going away. If anything, it was growing stronger. The man clearly knew something about Odishoo and wouldn't tell him what it was. Didn't he understand how badly Ashur needed to know? The lengths to which he would go to know anything more about his father? And still the Director had denied him. The music in his office, too—had he played that in anticipation of Ashur's arrival, as a way to taunt him? It was all too much.

"Bring up the messaging service," Ashur said to his Cube. The little device spun around on its pedestal and then projected the inbox on the far wall.

Ashur looked back at the most recent message from Admirer: *You still don't know the full truth about Odishoo's death. But the Director does....* He hadn't responded yet, not knowing who to trust or what to say. But now that uncertainty had hardened into conviction.

"I believe you," Ashur said, watching as the Cube transcribed his words. "Tell me everything."

The message was sent with a small, chipper sound that in no way reflected how Ashur felt. He wondered if Jahi was around—and still up for a game of Traitorball. It would feel good to run around and hit something, push his body hard until the troublesome thoughts were gone from his mind, however brief the respite. But as he cued up the new message, he heard a knock at his door.

Boris was standing in the hallway, looking awkward as he slowly shifted his weight from one foot to another.

"I heard about everything," Boris said. "You okay?"

Ashur nodded. "Yeah. Brodi's going to be…well, not fine, but not dead either."

Boris nodded, his eyes not quite meeting Ashur's.

Ashur cocked his head to the side. "What's up?"

Boris took a deep breath, then turned to Ashur with a newfound intensity. "We need to go back to the Vault. For the hologram. Tonight."

Ashur couldn't believe what Boris was saying. After everything they'd just been through, how could he still be talking about that?

"Are you crazy?"

"Let me come in," Boris said. "I'll explain everything."

Ashur stood there for a moment, looking at the small man standing uncertainly in the hallway. Smudged glasses, thick brown hair, and a look about him like he was constantly wincing in anticipation of a blow he was sure was coming. Ashur sighed and stepped aside as Boris came into his room.

"I think I know what's been happening to the Vault," Boris said. "What happened today with the lecturers. The glitches. Everything that seems to have Cicero and all the other instructors so freaked, okay?"

"Okay," Ashur said. "So what is it?"

Boris took a deep breath.

"Us."

Ashur frowned. "What do you mean, 'Us'?"

"I mean what we've been doing," Boris said. "Trying to get down to the Vault level. Trying to gain access. Trying to build our own holograms. Everything we've been working on."

"But why now?" Ashur said. "We haven't been down there for a while."

"*You* haven't," Boris said quietly.

Ashur took a step back.

"Boris…," he said. "What have you been doing?"

"Building on our work," Boris said. "Trying to figure out how it all works. Some of it gets pretty complicated, and I needed time to work it out on my own."

"And you did something that triggered some kind of alarm?"

Boris shrugged. "I don't know for sure. I don't have access to the right logs to see what's actually causing the errors. But the thing takes so much damn power, Ashur. *Huge* amounts of energy. Hard to do that without someone noticing. My guess is that they built the Vault with the technology to defend itself from unauthorized users trying to gain control, and it must not have liked something I was doing."

"You're talking about it like it's alive," Ashur said.

Boris's eyes got wide as he nodded. "Sometimes it feels like it is," he said.

"Okay, so now you're worried they're going to figure out it was us?" Ashur said.

"No, not that," Boris said. "I mean, maybe they do, maybe they don't. That ship has already sailed. But if it's building up its defenses, it's only going to get better, and more tightly protected, as the process keeps going."

Ashur tried to imagine what this would look like. He pictured a walled city receiving the first reports of distant raiders, calling its peasants in from the outlying fields and sealing the gates tight as it prepared for the onslaught. Maybe the glitches with the instructors were the equivalent of the farming tools and personal effects that got left behind in the rush to get within the walls, the regular day-to-day work and operations suddenly abandoned in the face of a looming existential threat.

"That makes sense," Ashur said.

"Right," Boris said. "So we have to do it tonight."

Ashur nearly laughed out loud as he let his head loll back until he was looking up at the ceiling. "You are actually insane," he said, stretching his arms behind his head.

"I can't be sure any of the work we've done will be any use at all after tonight," Boris said, as though he hadn't been listening at all. "We might be too late as is it. But once they get in there and diagnose whatever's been going on, and patch up the system to stop it from happening again, we're toast. There will be no way we can get access before the end of the apprenticeship."

"Boris, think about the day we just had," Ashur said. "The Vault failed, not once but twice. They cancelled classes, which apparently never happens. And if Cassandra and I didn't try to go see Brodi, she'd be dead! She almost didn't make it as it is. And you want to talk about messing around more with the Vault technology?"

Ashur hadn't realized how loud his voice was getting until he was done talking to Boris. He was breathing a bit heavily, the smaller man almost cowering as he talked. Ashur took a deep breath and tried to calm himself, but it was difficult after what had already been a much longer day than he had planned for when he woke up that morning.

"I'm sorry, Boris, but I just don't see why, compared to all of that, this is so important right now."

Boris waited for a moment before saying anything. For a moment, Ashur thought he might just leave.

"I'm not as strong as you, or Jahi, physically," Boris said. "There will never be a sport I can beat you at, unless you include chess, which no one does. I don't have any of Cassandra's charm, or the way she so effortlessly and naturally draws people in to her. I thought I was the best systems engineer I knew, until I met Brodi. And even laid up in a hospital bed, I bet she could figure out the architecture of all this more quickly than I could.

"But you know what I am, Ashur? I'm persistent. I don't give up. When I get a problem I can sink myself into, I keep scratching at it until I figure it out. I don't stop when other people would. It's the one thing that makes me special, more than anything else. It's why I'm here. It's what my potential looks like.

"This is how I stay here, Ashur. My chance to show that I belong at the Academy. You've seen my scores for the in-class exercises. They're fine. Middling. Average. Do you know what a curse it is to be *average* in a place like this? It's a death sentence. Average people don't stick around at the Academy. Extraordinary people do.

"So I'm doing this tonight. Whether you're with me or not. To be honest, I'm not even sure that I need you. But after everything we've been through—all the times you looked out for me—I thought I owed it to you to give you a chance."

"A chance to do what?" Ashur asked. He had never seen Boris speak this passionately before and was oddly moved by the small man's heart.

"To see your father again," Boris said.

Something inside Ashur leapt up into his throat. He thought about Admirer, and the Director, and all the things he didn't know about Odishoo. Would the hologram be able to give him the information the Academy had about his father that no one else would? It seemed possible, if the Vault really was as powerful as Cicero and the others were suggesting. But even if it wasn't, he longed to see his father again, to hear his voice and listen to him share his stories of life in Iran before the revolution.

"I understand if you don't want to," Boris said. "After everything that's happened. But if you want the chance to see Odishoo again—"

"Yes," Ashur said, interrupting his friend before he could finish his sentence. "Yes. I'll do it. I'll go with you."

"All right," Boris said. He reminded Ashur what they would need for the project, if they made it all the way down to the Vault: his father's DNA. Instinctively Ashur turned to look at the drawer where he kept his father's T-shirt, the one he had used to wrap Odishoo's gun. Would there really be enough of Odishoo left on it to bring his father back to life in whatever spectral, digital form the Worldcorp technology had created? There was only one way to find out.

They waited until it was dark outside. The campus was unusually quiet that evening, with classes cancelled for the day and the news about an apprentice's overdose spreading among the ranks of the other students. Ashur had spent most of his time at the Academy with the other apprentices in his own section, only interacting with the others at mealtimes and when playing Traitorball. He wondered what they must think of Brodi if the only thing they knew about her was that she had overdosed and nearly burned down the dormitory. Did they know how brilliant she was, the way she saw the innate structures of things beneath layers of complication, her ability to make people believe they were beating her at a hand of cards when in truth she'd had the nuts the whole time? Of course they didn't—how could they? Ashur wondered, not for the first time that day, what would become of Brodi after she recovered.

He tried to push those thoughts from his mind as he slipped from his room and made his way quietly to the same maintenance shaft that he and Boris had used before. He kept his father's T-shirt tucked carefully into the back pocket of his pants. Boris showed up a few minutes later, a backpack slung over his shoulder and a determined look on his face. He gave Ashur a nod and then jimmied open the entrance to the maintenance shaft.

Even though Ashur had been in the shaft before, there was still something disorienting about climbing back down into the darkness. The air was cool and slightly moist, like they were going from the surface down into a cave. As he went, Ashur noticed new markings on the concrete walls—small lines and annotations made in chalk.

"What are these?" Ashur said. Below him, Boris grunted.

"Research," he said. "I've been mapping out new routes, trying to find the most efficient way down into the Vault. This place is a maze, Ashur. I'd love to meet the mad genius who came up with the structure."

As they continued to descend, the extent of Boris's explorations became clear. This was nothing like the halting, methodical pace at which they'd previously made their way cautiously down into the Vault. Now they moved swiftly, and Ashur could sense the confidence as Boris navigated the long maintenance shafts and narrow corridors that connected them. The small man moved quickly on the ladders and through the low passageways, where Ashur was forced to crouch and wedge his muscled body through the tight spaces. The glow of their Cubes illuminated their path, the faint blinking of distant red emergency beacons the only other light in the darkened spaces.

Boris was uncharacteristically quiet as they went. Ashur had expected a little bragging about how much Boris had managed to do on his own, but the man stayed silent except for the occasional direction or word of warning when there was a tricky section of the descent. Ashur thought back to what Boris had told him about this being his one shot to make something of himself at the Academy. He wasn't sure that was true, but Boris was certainly treating it as though this was his best chance at sticking around.

Finally, after nearly an hour of wending their way through the cool, damp shafts, Boris brought them to a stop. Beneath their feet was a square metal plate about the size of a manhole cover. Boris crouched and tapped on the metal lightly with his hand, then looked up at Ashur and nodded.

"Okay, this is it," he said.

Ashur frowned. He remembered the other room they'd been in, and the question of how to gain access. This was clearly something different. "What about the other access point?" he said.

Boris smiled for the first time in a while. "I figured that out some time ago," he said. "I've just been getting myself closer and closer to this."

"What is it?"

"You kind of have to see it for yourself," Boris said. "Careful now."

Together they lifted the metal plate out of the ground, and Ashur was nearly blinded by the glow coming from the space beneath it.

"Drop down feet first," Boris said. "And, uh, try not to freak out."

Ashur tried to peer down into the room, but all the light after the darkness of the descent was too much for his eyes to make out anything clearly. With an arm braced on either side of the hole, Ashur lowered himself into the room.

He was dangling now as his eyes adjusted. The space was flooded with the most brilliant white light he had ever seen. It was a glass cube, extending seemingly to infinity. He looked down and couldn't see anything below him.

"Boris?" he called back up.

"There's a floor, I swear," Boris said. "It's just an optical illusion."

Ashur stared hard below him. The light seemed to extend into nothingness, and he could see no reflection or any other indication of a surface. His arms were starting to ache from holding his body in suspension. He took a breath and let go.

For a moment, Ashur experienced the sensation of freefall, his body hurtling through the air. And then his feet hit the ground and he landed in a crouch, one knee down and his off-wrist bracing against the floor.

Even now that he was in the room, it was difficult for Ashur to make out its dimensions or the material it was built out of. Even the ceiling he'd just fallen from was barely perceptible. The only thing he could clearly make out was the little square hole he'd dropped through, Boris's face looking down at him through it, beaming.

"You survived!" Boris said.

"You told me there was a floor."

"And I was right," Boris said, turning around now to position his body to come down. "But it's always nice to have someone else to really test your hypotheses. Now help me down."

Ashur got to his feet and positioned himself beneath the opening. He grabbed Boris's legs as they dangled and helped him down into the room. Boris dusted himself off and then turned around, staring wide-eyed at their surroundings.

Now that his eyes had fully adjusted, Ashur could see more clearly what was all around him. Suspended in that dim and seemingly infinite void were nodes of light, pulsating with an intensity he had never seen before. There were thousands of them, if not more, some looking as massive as suns and others just little pinpricks of light. It was impossible to get a sense of the scale or scope of everything around them. The room was completely silent, but Ashur could almost *feel* a hum coming off the pulsating nodes, energy coursing around him and passing briefly through his body as it went.

"What *is* this place?" Ashur said. Boris was still looking around, wide-eyed in wonder.

"It's a massive quantum computer," he said. "The only thing in the world capable of coming up with renderings as intricate as the Vault holograms."

"This thing is a computer?"

"Maybe just part of one," Boris said. "This could be like one of those server farms or something. It's like we're ants, Ashur, and we just happened to crawl into one of the processors on a desktop PC. Would we have any sense of what was happening there, either?"

Even though Ashur knew his feet were planted, the room still gave him the vertiginous feeling of being suspended in mid-air, floating through the cosmos. There was something awesome, and terrifying, about the whole thing.

"They built a few of these rooms into the structure for maintenance, or as manual shut-off if anything ever went wrong," Boris said. "It's the only way to access the system directly, instead of going through one of the programs that's just calling on part of the computing power."

"It's incredible," Ashur said. "How big is it?"

"Who knows?" Boris said. "It could be underneath most of Dallas for all we know. Or maybe they've figured out a way to bend space-time, so it's not taking up any space at all. These people are way more advanced than they're letting on, Ashur. We're just seeing the tip of the iceberg."

Boris reached into his backpack and produced a device that looked like his Cube. But this one was clearly different from the Academy-issued Cubes the other apprentices carried around—it was matte black and larger, turning slowly as Boris brought it to life.

"Where'd you get that?"

Boris turned to Ashur. "This will be easier if you don't ask so many questions. Do you have the information I asked for?"

Ashur nodded and took the T-shirt out of his back pocket. He passed it over to Boris, along with the biographical info about his dad that he had scraped together and uploaded to his own Cube. Boris had told him that wasn't necessary—that the Worldcorp databases had access to all the data they needed to recreate anyone with the proper DNA input—but Ashur wasn't leaving anything to chance.

"Okay now…" Boris said. He was typing quickly into the terminal that the black Cube had presented to him. Ashur watched as a small scanner descended from the Cube, and then a tiny laser began probing the T-shirt. Boris kept typing, his eyes behind his smudged glasses focused on the work before him.

"What is—"

"Would you just shut up, Ashur? Not now. Not when we're so close."

Ashur resisted the urge to shove Boris. He tried to focus instead on the prospect of seeing Odishoo again. How would they do it, once his father's avatar was uploaded to the Vault? Would they need to sneak down into one of the Vault classrooms where they had interacted with the other holographic instructors? Or would Boris find some way to bring Odishoo to life right here? Ashur could imagine his father staring with wonder out into the void and brilliance of the quantum computer, marveling at how far his son had come. Would this Odishoo know where he was? Would he remember his time at the Academy?

"Come on, come on," Boris said, wiping his shiny forehead with the back of his hand. The dark Cube began to make strange sounds, chirping as it spun with increasing urgency. "Almost there…"

Ashur imagined his father standing before him, laughing—he could still remember what that sounded like, though the sound had grown fainter over time. Would he be proud of Ashur for how far he had come, and all the promise that now lay ahead? Would he have advice for him, tell him where he thought Ashur had the best chance to fulfill his potential? There was so much for them to say to one another, so much he wanted to tell his father.

"*Yes!*" Boris said. Ashur looked over at his friend, who had a maniacal grin on his face and both arms raised in triumph.

"So where—" Ashur started. But before he could say anything else, everything was plunged into darkness.

It was entirely enveloping, that black. Like being nowhere at all. Like he had never existed. Ashur had the feeling that he was floating in a void. Time and space seemed to have no meaning here. When he looked up for where they had come in, the square that led back to the rest of the world was gone. All around him was nothing but total darkness. He could hear the blood moving through his body, the pounding of his own heart. Beyond that, there was nothing. Maybe there had never been anything.

"Boris?" Ashur tried to say. But he couldn't tell if he had spoken the word aloud or merely thought it, for in this place, sound didn't seem to carry the way it normally did. Either way, no reply came.

Suddenly, painfully, the room was flooded once more by light. Ashur clenched his eyes shut and put an arm over his face. He forced one eye open and squinted against the brightness. It was different than before—the glowing nodes were gone now. In their place was a harsh illumination, like fluorescent bulbs lighting up an office hallway. The illusion of infinity was gone, too. Ashur could see the architecture of the place more clearly, the way the different rooms were suspended at regular intervals.

He found he could now stand and turned to see if Boris had come through everything alright. But his friend was gone.

From somewhere above him, Ashur heard a distant sound like sirens wailing. Slowly the noise grew louder, and the white lights were gradually replaced by a pulsating red. Ashur could feel a bit of dread in the pit of his stomach.

Something had gone horribly wrong. And the fact that he didn't yet know what it was made it that much worse.

Ashur could see the panic spreading over his mother's face as the meaning of his words began to hit.

"What?" she said.

"It was covered in blood," Ashur said, hoping as he spoke that he would find a reason why it couldn't be his father. "But...it looked just like it. And it was on the same arm. And...and..."

His mother grabbed the arm of a passing nurse.

"That man who just came in," she said. "Who was he?"

The nurse jerked free of his mother's grasp. "I can't share that kind of information, ma'am."

Rose grabbed hold again. "Tell me his name!"

The nurse's annoyance shifted to a mix of anger and fear. She tried to free herself again, but Rose held tight. The nurse looked around for help.

"Ma'am, if you don't let go..."

"Please, nurse," Ashur said. The woman turned to him, and something inside her seemed to soften at the sight of him. "He has the same tattoo as my father. What's his name?"

All the irritation disappeared from the woman's face.

"Oh, honey. I don't know. Really. But if you sit tight, I can try and—"

Ashur was out of his wheelchair before the nurse could finish. Rose followed him as he walked past the nurses' station and pushed open the double doors they'd taken the gurney through. In the hallway, a bloody trail led to a cluster of doctors, nurses, and EMTs.

"Whoa, hang on there, big guy," a man in scrubs said as Ashur tried to walk past him. He put an arm gently but firmly on his shoulder. "You guys aren't allowed back here. Hospital policy."

"Please," Ashur said. "I just—"

A sob cut him short. Tears streamed down his face and leaked out from under his eye patch.

"What's that man's name?" he asked. "The one in the accident? I think he might be my father."

The doctor looked at Rose with a startled expression. "What's your husband's name, ma'am?"

"Odishoo," she whispered. "Odishoo Yonan."

The doctor stepped toward one of the nurses and whispered something in her ear. Her eyes went wide, but she nodded and quickly started down the hallway.

The man returned to Rose and Ashur.

"It'll just be a second. Can you step back into the waiting room for me?"

"Please just tell me," Ashur said. He was shaking a little now. "Please don't make me wait. Is that my dad?"

"I don't know. We're finding out." He looked at Rose. "Please take your son and go sit down."

Ashur allowed his mother to lead him back into the waiting room.

"Honey, I'm sure it wasn't him," Rose said. But Ashur couldn't listen to her. He refused to sit back down, and instead paced back and forth, his one good eye glued to the double doors.

After a few minutes that felt like an eternity, the doors swung open. Ashur held his breath. But it was just an old man with a cast on his leg, being wheeled out of the hospital.

But then, through the doors, Ashur caught a glimpse of the nurse Rose had asked about the accident. Her face was flushed and *she was shouting something at the doctor, shaking her head. She was clutching something in her hand. It looked like a wallet.*

"I can't!" the woman was shouting.

Without a word to his mother, Ashur headed back into the hallway, ignoring the shouts of the orderly who was following him now, trying to stop him.

The doctor and nurse stood there, talking animatedly to one another. Both turned to look at Ashur.

"What's that?" he whispered.

"What's what, buddy?" the doctor asked.

"That," Ashur said, pointing to the wallet in the nurse's hand.

The nurse looked like she was about to cry. She handed over the thick leather bifold to Ashur.

"I'm sorry," the doctor said. "We did our best. But your father passed away."

"But that's impossible," Ashur said. Quietly, at first, but then his voice began to rise as the reality of the moment set in. "That's impossible! No way! He's my best friend. The only person in the world who believes in me. He can't be gone!"

The doctor pulled Ashur into a hug as he began to sob.

"I just want my dad," Ashur said through his tears. "Just for a little longer."

CHAPTER FOURTEEN

The sound of the sirens was getting louder. Ashur stood in the suspended chamber, pulsating red lights all around him. He took a moment to assess the situation.

He and Boris had infiltrated the Vault. Boris had done… something. And now he was gone. Leaving Ashur behind to deal with the consequences.

Ashur didn't like any of it. Not one bit.

He pulled out his Cube and wondered if its range extended this far down into the bowels of the Academy. To his immense relief, the little device hummed to life with a quick, happy spin above his palm. Whatever was happening, it was clear he was going to need help. He cued up the messaging function on the Cube and sent a fast note to Jahi and Cassandra.

NEED HELP. FIND BORIS, he wrote. DON'T TRUST HIM. POSSIBLY DANGEROUS.

Ashur looked up at the hole he'd dropped through into the chamber. He reached up as far as he could but still couldn't quite get hold of the edge. How the hell had Boris—puny, unimposing Boris—managed to get out so quickly? Ashur took a few steps back. He bent low into a crouch, like a sprinter at the starting blocks, then ran forward and leapt as high as he could.

The tips of his right-hand fingers just barely found the lip, gaining slight purchase, and for a moment Ashur hung precariously, his body twisting around and a grunt of exertion escaping his lips as he struggled to keep himself aloft. Then he reached up with his other hand and hoisted his body up and through the gap. He allowed himself a moment to sprawl on the floor of the ventilation shaft before he pushed himself back up and began to run.

He kept his body crouched and moving quickly as he made his way through the labyrinth of maintenance shafts and cramped air ducts. He watched for the small markings Boris had made along the walls on his previous excursions down into the Vault and tried to remember which way they'd come before. Boris had seemed so certain on the descent that it had been hard for Ashur to follow entirely where they were heading. But as he pushed his way toward the surface, Ashur's mind was occupied with questions about Boris—and what had happened.

When the lights first went off, Ashur had been worried for Boris's safety. It was now clear that the Academy had technology on a level that was like nothing he had ever seen, or even heard about, before. He was pretty sure a quantum computer couldn't just blink someone from existence, but what did he really know about its capabilities? But the more he thought about it, the more certain Ashur became that Boris had known exactly what was happening. What was that strange Cube-like device he'd produced once they were down in the chamber? What had he been so excited about? And—this was the worst part—why had he really brought Ashur along with him? He had told him it was for a chance to resurrect his dead father, even if only in holographic form, and Ashur had been so seduced by the possibility that he hadn't thought to question it. Now he couldn't escape the feeling that Boris had been using him, though how, exactly, he didn't know. But whatever was happening, Ashur was sure that it meant trouble—for him, but also for the Academy. He thought back to the Director's speech at the orientation all those weeks ago, about the forces that wanted to stop the work they were doing. Ashur didn't trust the Director, but did that mean he automatically agreed with his enemies?

It was all so much to try and process as he fought his way back up toward the dorms.

After what felt like an hour of climbing ladders, but couldn't have been more than ten frantic minutes, Ashur burst through the maintenance door and back into the dormitory hallway. The flashing lights and siren's wail he had heard all the way down in the Vault were now echoing across the campus, students milling around outside their rooms, unsure of what was happening or what to do. Outside a window, he saw security personnel dressed in black uniforms fanning out across the grounds. He wondered if he was too late.

"What's going on?"

Cassandra was down the hallway, outside his room, with a look of intense concern on her face.

"Where's Boris?" Ashur said, panting slightly.

"I haven't seen him. I just got your message. Ashur, what is all this?"

Just then, Ashur spotted a familiar figure making his way calmly across the lawn. He seemed to be moving deliberately slowly, so as not to attract security's attention. His hands were actually in his pockets. He might as well have been whistling. Ashur began running down the hallway.

"Wait!" Cassandra shouted, and soon Ashur could hear her following him as the pair raced down the stairs and outside.

Once they were out on the grounds Ashur pushed forward, oblivious to the noise and the occasional shouts of the security personnel. He saw Jahi across the lawn, his friend moving so impossibly fast that it was easy to imagine him on a football field, leaving defenders in his wake as he weaved his way toward the end zone. Jahi saw them and came over fast.

"What is all this, Ash? The place is going crazy!"

Ashur tried to explain what was happening as best he could without losing any speed as the three of them now sprinted in the direction he'd seen Boris last.

"Boris…Vault…bad…stolen…"

"What are you talking about?" Cassandra said, her voice higher-pitched than usual.

"Don't know…what he's doing," Ashur said with effort. "But it's…no good. And we need…to stop him."

"From what?" Jahi said.

"I don't know!" Ashur yelled. "But whatever it is, it's my fault, too. And this is my chance to fix it."

By now they had attracted the attention of several of the security personnel. Ashur ignored their yells—there was no time to explain. If he stopped for them, then Boris would be gone for sure. He felt certain of that much.

He rounded the corner of the administrative building and saw his former friend fiddling with a door along the low base of the massive dome that extended over the entirety of the Academy. The campus was clearly in lockdown—what else could the sirens and the security presence possibly mean? But Boris had his black Cube out again, the same device he'd used to do whatever it was he was doing down in the Vault.

"*Boris!*" Ashur yelled, his lungs now burning. Boris turned, looked briefly over his shoulder, and then continued to fiddle with the Cube. Ashur and the rest of the team were gaining on him, the security forces not far behind them. But before they could reach him, Boris pushed open the door and disappeared through the translucent barrier that separated the Academy from the rest of the world.

Ashur reached the door just before it managed to close. He forced it open with his shoulder and found himself in an alleyway among a long row of dumpsters. Boris was nowhere to be seen.

"Where did he go?" Jahi said.

"I don't know!" Ashur said, slamming a fist down on the top of a dumpster.

From behind them came the sudden, ominous growl of a very large engine. Ashur turned and saw a car coming toward the three of them, its headlights huge and menacing as it gained speed.

"Look out!" he yelled. Without thinking, he threw himself to the side, pushing Cassandra down as he did. They hit the pavement hard, with Ashur's shoulder bearing the brunt of the force. He grunted and got back up to his feet, running briefly after the car as it pulled away, its taillights dwindling against the evening sky before it turned the corner and disappeared.

"Damn it!" Ashur yelled.

"Ashur!" Cassandra said.

He turned around and saw Jahi crumpled on the ground. Both of his legs were bent at impossible angles, his face against the pavement. Already blood was beginning to pool, a dark red slick against the black of the ground. Jahi wasn't moving at all.

The security forces spilling out through the door to the Academy had their guns drawn, aimed at Ashur and Cassandra. There were repeated calls for them to get down on the ground. Cassandra was collapsed against one of the bunkers, sobbing. Ashur was kneeling over his fallen friend, a hand on his back, hoping desperately to feel any sign of life.

"*Help!*" he shouted at the approaching figures in black, as one came behind him and pushed him down. "*We need help!*"

As he lay there with his cheek against the rough ground, the smell of blood and burnt rubber from the screaming tires filling his nostrils, Ashur felt a familiar anger: at Boris for betraying him, at whoever it was who was driving that car, and at himself, for being so naïve as to believe Boris and for getting his other friends involved. But mingled with that anger was an unfamiliar feeling: fear. Not for himself, but for the people he loved. It had been a very long time since Ashur had felt this kind of fear. He lay there with a bitter taste in his mouth, listening to the commotion around him as the security personnel called for backup medical attention and began administering to Jahi.

Ashur and Rose drove home from the hospital in silence. Ashur kept his head against the window and his eyes closed. It was almost possible, if he let his mind go blank, to forget momentarily what had happened, and why it felt like he was being cleaved apart from the inside. But then he'd remember all over again, and somehow that was even worse.

He went straight to his room when they got home, slamming the door behind him. He lay down on his bed face first, his cheeks buried in the familiar fabric of his blanket. His father was dead.

The impossibility of this kept washing over him. He kept waiting to wake up from what had been a long, terrible nightmare of a day. But he knew he wouldn't.

After a time, he heard voices coming from the kitchen.

"Rose," he heard a man say. "I'm so sorry."

"You…" his mother said, seemingly shocked. "You're alive? How—"

Ashur sat up in bed, wondering for a moment if it was his father, somehow magically returned to them from the dead. Maybe the doctor had been wrong; maybe his father had fought through, after all. But no—while this man's voice sounded similar to his father's, it wasn't Odishoo who was speaking, no matter how badly he wished for that to be true.

"That's not important," the man was saying. "Ashur is important—he's so special, Rose. We need to take care of him, now more than ever. Let me help him. Help you both."

"Like you helped Odishoo?" Rose said. "He's dead. Because of you! He couldn't live up to the warrior you wanted him to be. You abandoned him! And now he's abandoned us."

Her invective broke off as she began to sob.

"I don't think he abandoned you," the man said. "I think someone came after him. Someone who wanted to hurt me."

"He knew you were alive?" Rose said. "Lies! Always lies! These secrets and killings and spies—that's your life, and that's all you are. I won't have my son in that world. I won't! Leave us alone. And don't you dare come near me or my son again. Ever!"

There was a long silence.

"If you ever need me, Rose…" the man began.

"I don't need help from a killer," Rose said. "Now go, and never come back."

Ashur heard no more dialogue. In the driveway, a car engine started. He watched out his bedroom window as the black sedan cruised down the street, nearly silent. In the years that followed, he would wonder sometimes if this had really happened, or if it had been some sort of a strange dream, the mixture of exhaustion and grief and the drugs from the hospital all playing with his mind. But he never forgot the sound of that man's voice, or the way his mother had spoken to him, an acid in her words that, even at her angriest, she had never managed when talking to Odishoo.

CHAPTER FIFTEEN

There was no more of the familiar music coming from behind the imposing door of the Director's office as Ashur sat outside and waited. Only the sound of Cheryl tapping away at her Cube and the hush of a campus stunned into silence beyond the walls of the administrative building. As darkness fell over Dallas, Ashur could see the security teams continuing their sweeps of the school grounds, the white beams of their flashlights mingling eerily with the glowing reds and greens of laser sensors, scanning for who knew what: other vulnerabilities, listening devices, anything that could have pierced the bubble of the Academy that Ashur, like so many others, had assumed was impregnable. But now Boris, and whoever else he was working with, had managed to do just that—and with that realization came the sinking sense of being forced to confront just how little was actually known about what was going on.

Jahi was still in surgery at Methodist Dallas—the medivac chopper had airlifted him to the nearest Level One trauma center once the security services and EMTs realized the full extent of his injuries. He still had a pulse when Ashur had watched them take him away, but only barely, and he didn't seem to be breathing on his own. Even if Jahi survived, it was hard to imagine he would ever play football again with his legs so horribly mangled. His athletic career was over. And Ashur held himself at least partly responsible.

Ashur felt something on his leg. It was Cassandra's hand, pressed firm down against his thigh. Security had tried to send her back to the dorms, once Ashur had made clear that she hadn't been involved with Boris and had come to his aid only at his request. But she had refused to leave his side. They were in this together now, for better or for worse. Ashur thought back to the first time he had seen her, walking down those stairs at the Academy orientation. He had been so full of hope for this new beginning, and for the chance to finally realize his potential. If he had known everything that would happen to him, and all the ways he'd manage to screw things up, would he have still accepted Zaya's offer?

"Ashur?"

Cheryl was looking at him from across her desk, her eyes full of concern. Ashur couldn't tell if the worry was for him or for everything else that was happening.

"The Director will see you now."

Ashur and Cassandra both stood.

"I'm sorry, Cassandra," Cheryl said. "Just Ashur."

Cassandra began to protest, but Ashur put a hand on the small of her back. She seemed surprised by the intimacy of the gesture.

"It's okay," he said.

"I'll be here when you're done," she said. "No matter what happens."

The door to the Director's office swung open, and Ashur nodded and walked through it.

The Director was sitting with his back to Ashur. He could see the gray of the Director's close-cropped hair. He heard the click of the door shutting behind him and stood there, waiting for the man to say something.

"Sit."

Ashur took the chair in front of the desk. Slowly, the Director wheeled around and took a long, hard look at Ashur, his eyes narrowed.

"Can I trust you, Ashur?" the Director said. Ashur sat up a little straighter in his chair. It wasn't the question he had been expecting.

"Sir?"

"If you live for too long in an equilibrium, it becomes tempting to imagine that stasis is the permanent state of things. That just because something hasn't changed, it won't. But things are moving now. Quickly. In ways that are difficult to predict. At times like these, the decisions you make are amplified. They echo through not only your own life but also, sometimes, all of history. And now you find yourself, for whatever reason, at the heart of the chaos. So let me ask you again, Ashur, and be careful how you answer: can I trust you?"

Ashur looked at the man across the desk from him. He had been so frustrated with the Director and his unwillingness to tell him anything more about his father. Trust was a two-way street, and the Director had so far given him little reason for that. But even so, Ashur understood that he had chosen incorrectly when he put his own trust in Boris.

"I didn't know what Boris was planning to do," Ashur said. "I still don't really know what he *did* do, to be honest."

"Then what were you doing down in the Vault with him?"

"He told me he was working on something," Ashur said. "Like an extra-credit assignment. I understand now how incredibly stupid that sounds. But at the time...I don't know. I thought it would be seen as us taking initiative."

"And what was the assignment?"

Ashur let out a deep sigh.

"He told me he had figured out a way to use Vault technology to build our own holograms. Of anyone we wanted."

Ashur watched as his words sank in with the Director. The man leaned back in his seat and was silent for a few moments.

"He told you that you could see Odishoo again," the Director said finally. Ashur nodded.

"How did he know about your father?"

Ashur frowned and tried to think back to his early conversations with Boris. It had felt so innocent at the time—the two of them talking about who they most wanted to see again in the world, or what historical figures they might choose to meet for the first time. But now Ashur wondered if there had been more than that behind Boris's questions. Had his friend—no, he had to stop calling him that now—known all along about his father? Had he been manipulating Ashur into helping him, using the one thing he knew that Ashur was helpless to resist?

"We talked about him," Ashur said. "When he asked me who I would bring back. I didn't hesitate. I knew who I would, if I could."

The Director pursed his lips and pressed his fingertips together, his fingers forming a small tent above his desk as he considered Ashur.

"We are still putting together all the details of how Boris was able to gain access so deep into the Vault network," the Director said. "I don't believe that he was working alone. Someone with an intimate knowledge of the system—someone who has been studying the Academy, and our network, for a long time—must have been helping him."

"When we were down there," Ashur said, "in the—I don't know, Boris said it was part of a quantum computer—with the lights and the nodes, he had some kind of device with him. It looked like a Cube, but it definitely didn't come from the Academy."

The Director nodded. "The core that Boris stole is an advanced simulation engine. It's at the heart of what you've witnessed in your lessons, interacting with the various guest lecturers throughout history. With the correct inputs, the engine is capable of producing remarkable simulations of any figure in history, as you've seen."

Ashur frowned. "It's incredible technology. But why was Boris so intent on stealing it?"

"You tell me. If you were in my seat, what motives would you assign to Boris?"

Ashur thought for a few moments. "You could sell it," he said. "I'm sure it's incredibly valuable as a piece of technology. Sell it to one of Worldcorp's competitors, or some foreign government. You'd be set for life."

"If Boris is only intent on getting rich, then I will be able to go back to sleeping through the night," the Director said. "Greed is dangerous, but not so dangerous as some other motivations. Keep thinking."

Ashur thought back to the lessons at the Academy, the hours spent with his fellow apprentices listening to the greatest minds in history challenge their beliefs and ideals. The technology was amazing—as a learning tool, it was unparalleled. But who would want it so badly that they would risk everything that Boris had? What did he want to do with it?

"He would have access to everyone in history," Ashur said.

"Yes," the Director said. "Boris now has at his disposal the most advanced, evolved council in the history of humanity, capable of advising him on whatever it is he intends to do. Imagine drawing up battle plans with Napoleon on one side of the table, George Washington on the other, and Cyrus the Great watching over all of it."

"But he would still need an army," Ashur said. "Advice without the means to act upon it is only academic."

"So. What else?"

Ashur was quiet for a few moments as he considered. Boris was now in possession of an immensely powerful, immensely valuable simulation engine. He could, hypothetically, talk to anyone, at any time, about anything. But money and potential alone weren't what had motivated him to infiltrate the Academy, deceive Ashur and everyone else, and work tirelessly to steal the Vault technology. So what was it?

"Is there someone in history he really wants to speak with?" Ashur said. "Someone who knows something that other people don't?"

A very small smile passed over the Director's lips, and he nodded.

"The Vault is not only a simulation engine. It's an encryption engine as well. Capable of storing the Academy's—and the world's—deepest secrets. Protected in special holograms that only a few have access to or could possibly hope to recreate."

"Who does he want to talk to, then?"

The Director shook his head. "I can't tell you that. It's too dangerous. I trust you, Ashur. I believe that you didn't know what Boris was doing, and that you were brought into his plot unwittingly. But with every additional person who knows that information, the risk of its exposure grows exponentially."

"What kind of secrets, then? And what would he want to do with them?"

"It's too early to say for sure. But I have found it a good policy to prepare for the worst-case scenario at times like these, given how wide the aperture is and how quickly things can change. I believe that whoever Boris is working with is intent on the destruction of the Academy. And plans to use our own technology against us."

"What kind of information would be dangerous enough to bring down the Academy?"

The Director inhaled a quick, sharp breath through his nose and held it for a moment. "If you stop a random person on the street in LA and ask them what Worldcorp is, odds are that person wouldn't really know anything at all. Maybe they'd mention seeing one of our holograms. If they're a businessperson, they might say something about our public holdings, or our market cap. But to most people, we barely exist at all. We have worked very hard to keep it that way, Ashur. As I told you on your first day here, our mission is to keep the world as safe and free as possible. And that requires a certain degree of secrecy.

"There are certain avatars that have access to the full extent of our organization's operations. Including the true and full membership of the Academy. All the people through time who have passed through the Academy and devoted themselves to the betterment of the world, doing their work, in and out of the public eye, as individuals."

Ashur frowned. "What's so bad about people knowing they were affiliated with the Academy?"

"If you seek to destroy the Academy, the first thing to do is tell people about it. The full extent of it. Make them fear it. Make them question it. Give them something to blame for what they perceive as all the problems in the world, all the ways in which their lives feel small and inadequate. The heart of every conspiracy theory come vividly to life, and with the proof that cranks online always claim to have but never actually do.

"We have enemies, Ashur. Those who try to tell stories about what we do here. That we buy presidencies. That we meddle in elections worldwide with the technology we have. That we control people's lives. Often these rumors are started by those who know just enough about us to make their claims credible. Former apprentices who left under less-than-ideal circumstances. Imagine the kind of chaos that kind of information would unleash, if allowed to gain purchase."

"Divide and conquer," Ashur said. "Like in Iran."

"What did you say?" the Director said.

A hardness had come over the man's face. Ashur couldn't quite tell what had set him off, but he continued.

"My father used to tell me a story. About Iran, when he was a child. What happened there, in the revolution. All the ways that the people were convinced to rise up against the Shah, and all the terrible things that happened after they did. What you're describing…it sounds to me like that."

The Director nodded. "Yes. Only this time, it won't be just one country. *It will be the whole world.* And there is a chance that we never recover from it."

Ashur felt a chill run down his spine. "Where is Boris now?"

"We don't know. We believe he's still somewhere in Dallas— if he tried to board a plane, or cross any borders, we'd know about it, and none of that has triggered yet. He must be hunkering down somewhere nearby."

Ashur frowned. "Why wouldn't he try to get as far away as he can?"

"Either he knows he's watching him, or..."

"Or what?"

"Or he doesn't have everything he needs."

"You mean...?"

"Yes. For the hologram to have its full capabilities, you need the proper inputs. The data component is one half of the blueprint. But the biological marker—the DNA—enables us to engineer a digital replica of the historical figure's unique mental faculties, and that is almost impossible to create synthetically."

"So he's going to try to get back in, unless you find him first."

The Director offered a curt nod in response.

"I'm sorry, sir," Ashur said. "About everything. I should have known better. I should have listened to the part of myself that wondered why Boris was so hell-bent on the Vault, especially after everything that started happening. I let my desire get the better of me."

"You loved your father," the Director said. "A son's love is a powerful thing. You made a mistake, Ashur. But don't compound that error by taking the wrong lesson from all of this."

Ashur took a deep breath, thinking about everything that had happened. His time at the Academy felt simultaneously like it had just begun and as though it had already lasted a lifetime. He had never expected to find himself in a place like this, to have this kind of chance to make something of himself. And now, because of him, all of this—and maybe all of the world, if the Director was right in his analysis about what Boris intended to do—was in danger.

"I think I need to leave," Ashur said.

"Of course," the Director said. "It's been a difficult day."

"No. I think I need to leave the Academy."

A look of grave concern crossed the Director's face. "What are you talking about?"

"I've caused too much damage. I don't know if I can risk staying and causing even more."

"Ashur…"

"I understand what I'll be giving up," Ashur said. "But after everything that's happened, I don't think I can be here anymore."

Ashur stared across the large desk at the Director. It was true that his time at the Academy had been turbulent, but that wasn't why he wanted to leave.

Boris was still somewhere in Dallas, and Ashur was going to find him. He was going to fix the mess he'd made, no matter the consequences to himself. He was going to save the Academy. And he knew he'd never have another chance like the one before him now.

The Director sighed. "I can't make you stay. Though I hope you might reconsider. Sleep on it, perhaps?"

Ashur shook his head. "I'm sorry. I've made my decision."

Another long look across the desk at one another.

"Your father left the Academy," the Director said finally. "Under very different circumstances. The pressure of this place was too much for him. It was difficult for him, extremely difficult. But as a result, he was never able to achieve his full potential. Do you understand what I'm saying, Ashur?"

Ashur looked down for a moment.

"I think I may have had something to do with that, sir."

"What do you mean?"

"My father had me young. Both of my parents were young. If he'd had more time, if he could have discovered himself more before the responsibilities of fatherhood and needing to provide for his family. I've always wondered if things would have been different for him. If his world could have been bigger."

The Director shook his head.

"You don't understand. Ashur, before you, Odishoo was a mess. He was not cut out for the Academy, or any other kind of serious life. He was drinking too much, floundering, utterly without a direction. Without you, I don't know how much longer he would have lasted. Your being born saved him, Ashur. You were the best thing that ever happened to him."

Ashur frowned.

"How do you know so much about him?"

The Director paused for a moment before answering.

"We monitor everyone who passes through the Academy. Whether they complete their time here or not."

Ashur said nothing. He believed this was true, that the Academy did in fact monitor everyone who came through it—and probably just about everyone else on earth. But, like so much the Director said, this wasn't the whole truth.

"I understand the risk I'm taking by leaving now," Ashur said. "The possibility that I may never achieve my full potential."

"You will always be a man with great potential, Ashur Yonan," the Director said. "Whether you choose to cultivate it here or not. And I have faith that you will discover whatever it is you're meant to do. I only wish it could have been here at the Academy."

Both men stood now, and the Director extended a hand across the desk. Ashur reached out and grabbed it, surprised by the rough, calloused pads on the base of the man's fingers.

As he was leaving, he turned around before he made it to the door.

"The music that was playing the last time I was here?"

The Director looked up from his Cube.

"Yes?"

"Googoosh, right?"

The Director nodded.

"That was Odishoo's favorite, too," Ashur said, and then walked out the door.

"What do you mean you're leaving?"

Cassandra and Ashur were in his room, Ashur hastily packing a bag. He had been quiet after the meeting with the Director, telling Cassandra only a skeletal outline of what the two men had discussed. But he had waited until they were in private before telling her what he planned to do.

"Don't you get it?" he said. "This—everything that's happened—is all my fault."

"That's crazy," Cassandra said. "You had no way of knowing what Boris was going to do. None of us did!"

"You weren't the one he was taking on these expeditions," Ashur said. "Luring you down into the Vault with the promise of seeing your dead father again. He used me, Cassandra. He knew exactly what I was going to do. And I did it, like an idiot."

"So now, what? You're just giving up? Abandoning all of this?"

"It isn't like that, and you know it."

"It sure looks like that, Ashur. It looks like you're running scared."

Ashur slammed a hand against the wall, the sound reverberating through the small dorm room. But Cassandra didn't look startled or scared. She looked furious.

"And you're abandoning *me*. Did you even think about that? Brodi is gone. Boris is gone. Jahi may not survive. And when you leave, it will be me on my own, listening to Cicero and whoever else he dredges up from the past to talk about honor and duty and whatever other pretty words are on the menu that day."

She and Ashur stared at one another across his bed. He had seen her angry before, but never furious like this.

"I care about you, Cassandra," he said. "I really do. I think we could have something together. And when all of this is over, maybe we can. But I need to do this."

"Why? Explain it to me."

"Because it's my fault, and I have a chance to fix it, okay?"

He watched as the expression on her face changed from anger to surprise.

"You're going after him."

Ashur nodded. "I'm going to try."

"What makes you think he's even still around?"

"The Director said he was still in Dallas. Probably. I think they could track him otherwise. I don't know how long I have."

"Let me come with you."

"No."

"Ashur…"

"I could never forgive myself," Ashur said. He reached across the bed and took Cassandra's hand. "You have the chance to do something amazing. Here, and wherever else you decide to go afterwards. I've seen how brilliant you are, and how much you've grown. After everything else I've done, if I managed to screw that up too, I couldn't live with myself."

"It isn't your choice to make," Cassandra said.

"No," Ashur said. "So I'm asking you. Stay here. Graduate. Do everything I know you can. And then, maybe once all this is over, you can tell me all about what I missed."

"Ashur..." Cassandra said. She came around the bed, ran a hand softly down his cheek, and then kissed him.

Ashur had been thinking about this moment for weeks now—the feeling of her lips, the warmth of her body as she pressed up against him, the intoxicating smell that followed her wherever she went. He had wanted it all so badly. But now there was something bittersweet about it, knowing that his time at the Academy had come to an end, and all the darkness and uncertainty that now swirled around them. But just for a time, he tried to push all that from his mind as he kissed her harder, trying to stay in this moment for as long as he could manage, trying to remember it even as it was happening.

It was nearly midnight by the time Ashur made it back to the front desk where Zaya had left him all those weeks earlier. He had packed a bag with the clothing the Academy had provided for him and then left Cassandra back in her own room, with the promise to be in touch as soon as he knew anything. In the meantime, she would keep him apprised as best she could about what was happening at the Academy. If Boris really was planning to return for something, it would be good to have someone on the inside keeping an eye out.

THE ACADEMY

Sam, the woman who had handled his intake when he first arrived at the Academy, was waiting for him at the desk. It felt strange, coming here from the other side now, knowing the immensity of the world that he was leaving behind.

"Sorry to keep you up so late," he said.

"And I'm sorry that you're leaving," Sam said. "But I trust you have your reasons."

Ashur nodded.

"Your Cube, please."

Ashur produced the device from his pocket and handed it across the desktop to her. If the little machine had any indication that it was being abandoned, it made no sign of it. He had grown fond of its beeping and interactions in recent weeks, and realized, with a small and funny pang, that it would be one of the many things about the Academy that he would miss once he was gone.

Sam reached down beneath the desk and produced a small black case in made of hard plastic, with a lock on the top. She pushed it across to Ashur.

"What's this?" he asked.

"Your possessions," she said. "Go ahead and open it up."

Ashur fumbled with the lock for a moment, and then the case snapped open. Inside, laid against a bed of soft textured foam, was his father's pistol.

"We took the liberty of having it serviced, cleaned, and registered to you," Sam said. "After what happened in California, we wouldn't want you running into any more trouble."

Ashur looked at Sam, the shock on his face clearly registering as she smiled back at him.

"Zaya told me how important it was to you," she said. "I wanted to make sure we took good care of it."

"Thank you," Ashur finally said, the words nearly catching in his throat. Sam nodded, snapped the case shut, and then handed the key to Ashur.

"Your motorcycle is waiting for you back in California. Yours to pick up at your convenience. Will you be needing a ride to the airport?"

Ashur slid the case with his father's gun into his bag, hefted it over his shoulder, and shook his head.

"No," Ashur said as he turned to leave. "I'll be making my own way."

CHAPTER SIXTEEN

Ashur sat on the bed in a dingy motel room on the outskirts of Dallas, trying to plot his next move. Somewhere in the city, Boris was hiding out, waiting for an opening to get back into the Academy. Ashur had to find him first and convince him to give back the Vault technology that he had stolen. But where was he?

He thought back over everything Boris had ever told him about himself, searching the biographical details and personal history for anything that might give him a clue. His family was from Belarus—was there anywhere in the city he might go that would feel like home, some restaurant that would serve him a dish that reminded him of family? He loved music, particularly classical piano—would he risk trying to make it out to see a concert while he was biding his time? None of it seemed particularly likely; Boris was too smart to go for anything like that, especially when he knew that the Academy was likely searching for him. A city like Dallas was a big place to hide, especially if the person looking for you—like Ashur—didn't know it at all.

Ashur sighed and wiped a hand over his face. Over the bed was sprawled the map of the city he had picked up at the front desk when he'd checked in. It was the witching hour now, the sky not yet light but not a soul outside and only the occasional distant rumble of semitrucks on the highway coming in above the high whine of the A/C unit.

He figured he would take a quick shower, get a little sleep, and then head out into the city in the morning. It was like that old riddle: If you need to meet a stranger in New York but don't know where or when, what do you do? You go to Grand Central Terminal at noon and wait under the massive, famous clock—the most recognizable spot in the city at the time all the hands on the clock touch one another. The problem was that Boris wasn't trying to meet him; he was trying to hide. Still, it would feel better to do *something* other than sit around his motel room, waiting to get word from the Academy that he was already too late. He would start at first light tomorrow.

Ashur shuffled into the bathroom and flipped on the light. He froze—and reached for the gun he now kept tucked into the back of his waistband. Scrawled on the mirror in black ink was a message:

ASHUR YONAN.

YOU'RE SO CLOSE TO THE TRUTH.

TIME TO MEET YOUR ADMIRER.

Beneath that was a time and a set of numbers that Ashur recognized as GPS coordinates. He pulled back the shower curtain with a violent tug, half-expecting Admirer to still be waiting for him—nothing. He made a quick search of the rest of the room—empty—and packed up the few things he had brought with him.

How had they known he was coming here? And what did they want with him? Ashur didn't like the feeling of being followed, being watched, knowing less than they did. Admirer had been keeping him in the dark, feeding him just enough to pique his interest and make him keep going. He knew it might be a trap, but at this point it was worth it. He keyed in the coordinates, found the address, and headed out into the city.

Ashur stood in an abandoned lot surrounded by warehouses, some of them with their windows smashed and boarded up. It was a desolate place, especially at this hour. He had scaled a chain-link fence to get in. He wondered if this was the right place, or if he had messed up the address somehow. Weeds pushed up through cracks in the concrete. As far as he could tell, he was alone. Was Admirer messing with him? Leading him on a wild goose chase around the city for their own amusement?

Suddenly, in the dim recesses of an alley on the far side of the abandoned lot, he saw two headlights illuminate like the eyes of a jungle cat shining in the dark. The headlights flashed once, then twice. Ashur felt the muscles of his neck tighten briefly, then made his way over to the car.

The passenger-side window rolled down as he approached. Boris was sitting there, calmly aiming a pistol right at Ashur's chest. Back at the Academy, Ashur would have guessed that Boris had never held a gun before, but something about the cool way his former friend was handling the Glock suggested that was yet another thing Ashur had misjudged about him.

"We were starting to worry you wouldn't show," Boris said. "Did it really take you that long to find us?"

It was all Ashur could do to stop himself from lunging through the car window and putting his hands around Boris's neck, squeezing until he felt the life leave him. He deserved that, after what he'd done.

"You put Jahi in a coma!" Ashur said through gritted teeth. "You stole from the Academy and left me behind to take the blame. You betrayed me, and everyone else! Why would I ever listen to you?"

"Because I have a gun trained on you at point-blank range," Boris said. "And even if I didn't, aren't you curious to know why I did it? Why I sacrificed everything for it?"

"You're a coward and an animal!" Ashur said.

"Boys, please."

The voice came from the man sitting in the driver's seat, his face cloaked in shadow. The voice was deep, and calm, and there was something familiar about it. Ashur strained to get a better look but couldn't make out the man's features.

"If you would take a seat, Ashur, and give me an opportunity, I think you'll begin to understand," the man said.

Ashur felt the metal of his father's gun against the small of his back, cold in the early morning air against the heat of his skin. Boris was armed; the other man probably was, too. He was outnumbered and outgunned. But worse than that, Boris was right: he did want to know what was going on, why they had done this. And if there was a chance that this man actually did know something about his father and his death—even if that chance was small—then Ashur wanted to hear what he had to say. He stared at Boris for another moment, watching the way the man's mouth curled into a small smile, and then jerked open the car door and sat down on the soft leather seat.

Boris kept the Glock pointed at his chest as the man in the driver's seat began to speak.

"Thank you for coming, Ashur. I mean that sincerely. And while I know this will be difficult for you to believe, you find yourself among friends."

Ashur felt his chest grow hot with rage.

"Friends?" he said. "You tried to kill Jahi. You've been stalking me since I first stepped foot at the Academy. What the hell kind of friends are those?"

"I understand you're upset," the man said. "I would be, too. And I *am* truly sorry for the unfortunate incident with Jahi. It was not our intent to hurt him, or anyone else. But…casualties, even of innocents, are a part of war."

"What are you talking about? What war? And why have you been following me?"

"Maybe try just listening?" Boris said. "You learn a lot more with your mouth closed."

"That's enough, Boris," the driver told him, and there was something cold and sharp in the way he said it that made Boris recoil.

"Yes, sir."

"Did you even know my father?" Ashur said after a moment. "Or was that all part of your trap to get me to listen to you?"

"You don't remember me, do you?" the man said.

"How would I remember you?"

The man turned around in his seat, his face gradually illuminated by the light from the street. He was a big man, broad-shouldered, with dark olive skin, wrinkles near his eyes, jet black hair, and a neatly trimmed goatee. Ashur thought back to what felt like a lifetime ago, visiting his father's grave on the anniversary of his death. Was this the same car that had been at the cemetery that day?

"Dobiel," Ashur said.

"I've gone by that name, yes," the man said. "But most people call me Namirha."

"So you've been following me even since before the Academy?"

"Ashur Yonan, I've been following you your whole life."

"Why?"

"I've been waiting for this day to come. For a long time now. Because you hold the fate of the world in your hands, Ashur. And soon, you're going to have to make a choice, and I need you to know the truth before you make that decision."

"What are you talking about?" Ashur said. It felt like the man was talking in riddles. "The truth about what?"

"About the Academy. About your family. About what really happened to Odishoo Yonan."

At the mention of his father, Ashur stiffened.

"My father was killed in a car accident."

"Do you believe that's the whole story, Ashur?"

"I was there in the hospital," Ashur said. "I saw them wheel him in on the gurney. I heard everything they said. It was a car accident."

"Have you ever really believed that? Odishoo was just in the wrong place at the wrong time?"

Ashur could feel the hairs on the back of his neck standing up. His father's death had felt so random, so unfair. Even sometimes still, Ashur found himself waking in the night, forgetting just for a few moments that his father had been taken from him. Would it make things better or worse to know that something other than the vagaries of a California highway one day all those years ago had sealed the fate of Odishoo?

"Your father died that day because of what happened during his time at the Academy," Namirha said. "They used him, Ashur. That's what they do. They brainwash people, and then they use them. And when they are no longer of use to them, they dispose of them."

"Are you saying the Academy killed my father?"

"They broke him, Ashur. Promised that they'd help him find his potential. And when he resisted their attempts to brainwash him, they spit him out. Do you know the mortality rate of those expelled from the Academy? Too high to be random. Because when you're keeping a secret as big as the Academy, it doesn't pay to have disgruntled ex-apprentices on the outside running their mouths."

"My father had gone to the Academy years earlier," Ashur said. "Why would they still care about him?"

"For all their talk of logic and reason, I've found the choices made by the Academy have little to do with either. They operate on the whims of the powerful, hungry for more control and willing to do whatever it takes to keep it, no matter the cost. Maybe your father said the wrong thing to someone. Maybe they'd been waiting. But his death was *not* an accident."

Ashur slumped back in his seat, trying to process what Namirha was telling him. Was it true? Was the Academy really behind his father's death? The Director had been resistant to talk about Odishoo, but when he finally did, Ashur had thought he sensed real warmth when the man described how Odishoo had changed after Ashur was born. Could the Director really have stared at him across the desk and lied to him in cold blood? He didn't want to believe it, but at this point, he didn't know who to trust.

"They didn't want you there, Ashur," Namirha said. "After everything with your father, the last thing that Academy wanted to deal with was one more Yonan. But you were too much for them, as I knew you would be. Beneath that rough exterior and aimless teenage life was a beating, pulsing heart full of the purest raw potential and power I had ever seen. They had no choice but to take you, once they saw that for themselves."

Ashur stared at the man, trying to make sense of the words.

"You...did something."

Namirha smiled. "Yes."

"Convinced them to take me?"

"Indirectly. It was you who did all the work, Ashur. If I had been wrong about you—if you hadn't proved yourself to be as fearless as I knew you would be—then you wouldn't be here today, talking with me."

The realization came over Ashur all at once: the strange behavior of that one gunman at the restaurant the day of the robbery, the way the cops seemed puzzled by the whole thing, the sense he'd had, even at the time, that something was off.

"You sent them," Ashur said. "The robbers at Bob's Big Boy. That was you."

"You were leaving California," Namirha said. "I didn't know where you were heading, or what you were going to do. I merely gave you the opportunity to show the rest of the world what I already knew about you."

"You sent two armed robbers after me. I could have died!"

"Those men were never going to shoot you, Ashur. They had strict orders."

"I can't believe you did that! What kind of craziness is that? And why did it matter so much to you that I get into the Academy?"

"Because I believe there are great things in your future. With the technology that Boris liberated from the Vault, we are so close to having the tools to finally fight back. And you are the last piece of the puzzle."

"I still don't understand," Ashur said. "What do you want to do?"

"I want to destroy the Academy," Namirha said. "And give you the chance to avenge your father."

"Think about it, Ashur," Boris said. "*Really* think. What has the Academy been trying to do since the day we got on campus?"

"Help us achieve our potential."

Boris scoffed and rolled his eyes. "Get real. You believe that? They've been brainwashing us this whole time."

"The Academy doesn't brainwash people."

"No?" Namirha said. "You've found all your lessons to be fair, balanced among various viewpoints? You've never felt as though you're being pushed in a particular direction ideologically? That beneath all that lip service to 'thinking for yourself' and 'questioning your beliefs,' your dear Cicero was actually waiting to hear one answer in particular?"

Ashur didn't want to admit it, but he could see some truth in that. They heard viewpoints from all different sides with the historical instructors, and Cicero made a big deal out of everyone thinking for themselves. But over and over, the same kind of thinking was held up as a paragon—the strong, free individual, striving to maintain their rights.

"So the Academy has a viewpoint," Ashur said. "How does that make them different from any other school?"

"Because other schools can't possibly imagine the power and reach of the Academy," Namirha said. "Worldcorp is the largest public corporation in the world—but that's a mere fraction of their actual holdings. The Academy here in Dallas is one of dozens of similar institutions around the world, all intent on creating the next generation of world leaders. Leaders…*who the Academy can control.*"

"Academy students are everywhere," Boris said. "In every country, every movie studio, every major military, every newspaper and cable talk show—*all* of them beholden to this one organization. It's a cabal, Ashur. These guys are secretly controlling the world, and everyone is either too dumb or too disengaged to care."

"And you represent, what?" Ashur said. "True freedom against this control?"

"I have no desire to rule the world," Namirha said. "Unlike the Academy. I just want to show the rest of humanity who's really been running their lives all these years and see what they think of it. The truth—no more, no less. Sunlight is the best disinfectant, and the Academy has operated in the shadows for too long. Things have been allowed to fester out of sight. I think it's time to bring that to an end."

Ashur didn't want to believe him, especially given the snide, superior look on Boris's face. But even still, there was something compelling about what he was saying—it did seem wrong, if the Academy and Worldcorp were really as powerful as Namirha claimed, that most people didn't know about it. Ashur was honest to a fault; he couldn't help himself, he hated to lie. He believed in giving people the facts and letting them decide for themselves what they thought and how they felt about things. But it was hard to square the cool, rational tone of Namirha's voice with the things he'd done.

"And you're willing to hurt people—even innocent teenagers who've done nothing wrong—to get what you want?"

Namirha sighed. "I'll say it again. Jahi's accident was unfortunate. But it *was* an accident. We didn't mean to hurt anyone. Ours is an ideological war, fought with weapons far more powerful than guns or missiles. And with Boris's help, I now have almost everything I need."

Ashur turned to Boris now. He seemed so proud of himself, practically preening as he sat in the passenger's seat. Ashur once again felt the powerful urge to lunge forward and hurt him, but he resisted.

"What is it that you took?" Ashur said, playing dumb.

"The core engine," Boris said. "The tools to make anyone come to life. I wasn't messing with you, Ashur. With this technology, if we get what we need, you can bring your father back to life. As a hologram if nothing else."

"I've heard that line before," Ashur said. "It didn't work out so well."

"I'm not trying to bribe you, Ashur," Namirha said. "Seeing a hologram of your father isn't the same as bringing him back to life, no matter the peace and closure it might offer. I don't want you to do this because you have to, or because someone is pointing a gun at you. I want you to join me. I've seen the potential you have—Yonans have always been strong leaders, for millennia now. I'm sure Odishoo told you about your history. *This* is your chance. The opportunity to decide for yourself what your potential is, rather than be forced into it by some shadow organization offering only the illusion of free will."

Ashur looked at the faces of the two men staring back at him in the car. Boris was almost gleeful with expectation; Namirha was calm, impassive, though Ashur could sense the tension within him. Ashur still didn't know what to believe. He thought it was likely that they were right about the size and scope of the Academy and Worldcorp—had he been enmeshing himself in something that he hadn't fully understood? He'd been so amazed to find himself at the Academy, excited for the opportunity to prove himself. There had been so much he hadn't known at the start that he'd never stepped back and questioned the purpose of the organization. If it was a choice between the world knowing about the Academy or not knowing, then he liked the world where more people knew. Then maybe other kids like him would have a chance to find out and try to apply—a way out of crappy homes and bad schools and tough situations that didn't involve stopping random robberies engineered specifically for them.

But Boris had lied to him—lied to everybody. After all that, could he really trust him? He mostly believed what Namirha had told him. But there was something about the story with Odishoo that wasn't adding up. What was he missing?

And then, of course, the biggest question of all:

"Why do you need me?"

Namirha smiled a very small smile.

"Because we need something only a Yonan can get," he said. "We need the Director's DNA."

"There's a hidden avatar," Boris said, "with the names of everyone who's ever been associated with the Academy. The Master List. It's the proof we need to show the world just how deep all of this goes."

"Will you help us, Ashur?" Namirha asked. "Achieve your potential? Do something truly consequential with your life? Join me in showing people there's a different way? Together, we can do great things. I know we can."

Ashur looked back and forth between the two men. For just a moment, he closed his eyes. *Dad, what should I do?* he asked the ether. For a time there was nothing, just the quiet of the void and his own mind. And then, all at once, as though Odishoo had reached out from the grave, he had an idea. It was as though all the thoughts and facts that had been percolating in his mind for weeks now had finally come together—the pieces rearranged so that, for the first time, they made sense. And he knew what he had to do.

"I'll go see the Director," Ashur said.

Namirha allowed him a smile and reached back to place a large hand on Ashur's shoulder.

"I knew you would," the man said.

CHAPTER SEVENTEEN

The car sped along a deserted stretch of highway. Boris kept the gun trained on Ashur while Namirha drove, narrating as he navigated the car around Dallas in the early morning dark.

"We need anything that has some trace of the Director's DNA," the man reminded him. "A coffee cup his lips touched. A stray hair you find. Anything that contains his essence should suffice. But remember, it must be his."

"Won't they be suspicious of me showing up again?" Ashur asked. He could still feel his father's gun pressing against the small of his back as he leaned against the padded leather seat.

"They would be," Boris said with a nod. "Which is why you're sneaking in."

With the hand that wasn't holding the gun, Boris brought out the same black Cube that Ashur had seen him use down in the Vault. He keyed in a few things and then laid it flat on the center console. A holographic image of the Academy appeared, suspended in midair inside the car, its giant geodesic dome rotating slowly in ghostly white.

"Security was pretty tight, even before the lockdown," Boris said. "Now they've got everything totally sealed up. Or so they think."

"Overconfidence is not the greatest sin of the Academy," Namirha said coolly. "But it is their greatest weakness. Arrogance—that will be their downfall."

Boris quickly walked Ashur through all the conventional security measures in place at the Academy, as well as several precautions that Ashur had never even heard of before. There were armed guards performing regular patrols both inside the dome and along the perimeter outside. Geological monitoring would discourage anyone who might try to burrow under the enclosure. The dome itself was designed to withstand a direct nuclear hit.

"It might look delicate, but the material they're using is like nothing the world has ever seen before," Boris said. He put a finger on one of the holographic dome's panels, and Ashur watched as the impact rippled out along the other panels, dispersing the force so that the whole structure quivered but never broke.

"Imagine the benefit to the rest of the world if their technology was shared, rather than hoarded behind dozens of shell companies and corporate obfuscations designed to keep everything hidden and secret," Namirha said. "All of humanity could make such an amazing leap into the future, if only these breakthroughs could be pried from the cabal's grasp."

Ashur shifted in his seat. There was, even now, something compelling in how Namirha described the Academy and his vision for bringing it down. For someone like Ashur, who hated secrets and abhorred liars, the notion of spending the rest of his life beholden to such a shadowy organization was not particularly appealing. And yet there was something about the man that kept him from giving himself over completely. Despite the calm, even tone of Namirha's voice, his vision of the world felt manic—a true believer's absolute faith in their own version of the truth, unwilling to imagine any of the ways in which their model world might not be reflected in reality. For all his reservations about the Academy, Ashur did appreciate that one of its core tenets was that everyone should think for themselves—and question their preconceived notions. They might have been pushing an agenda, but Ashur never felt like it was dogma—he was always allowed to ask questions and try to figure out things that didn't make sense to him. He couldn't imagine Namirha ever allowing that sort of heresy, or anything short of undying loyalty to his cause.

But the only way to fix his mistake—to recover what he had helped Boris steal—was to show them that he was capable of being useful. That was the only thing keeping his captors from shooting him and leaving him by the side of the highway. The rest he would figure out later.

"So if I can't break through the dome, and we can't dig our way there, and I can't just walk up to the front door, how am I going to get in? Dress up like a guard and hope they don't notice the new recruit?"

Namirha and Boris quickly exchanged a glance in the front seat, and then Namirha started to chuckle. Boris sighed and looked at the roof of the car.

"That was my first idea," Boris said. "You know, like how Luke Skywalker dresses up like a stormtrooper to rescue Leia?"

"They'd make you in a heartbeat," Namirha said. "They're arrogant, but they're not dumb."

"So then, what?"

Boris grinned and then rotated the hologram so that Ashur was now looking at it from the bottom. "You see all these pipes feeding into the dome?" he said. Ashur nodded—it looked almost like the root system of some massive tree. "When you have a computer network as powerful and complex as the Vault, it's going to generate heat. A *lot* of heat. And you need something to deal with all that heat, or you're going to melt down the precious supercomputer you spent so much time and treasure building. So what do you do? Forget that little fan whirring in the back of your laptop—air isn't going to cut it at the scale you're talking about. You need liquid coolant. You need water, and lots of it."

"You want me to scuba into the Academy?"

Boris grinned. "Even if we put you in a frog suit, the water pressure is too high. You'd either get pushed out into an aquifer or go crashing into the treatment plant on-site and get smushed to death."

"It sounds like you're trying to kill me."

"Ashur," Boris said, shaking his head. "If we wanted to kill you, you'd already be dead."

Ashur felt himself stiffen at these words, his eyes narrowing as he glared at Boris across the hologram of the Academy.

"Boys…" Namirha said. Boris nodded and put up a hand in apology.

"It would never work if the pipes were working normally. But guess what?"

"They aren't," Ashur said.

"And for extra credit, can you tell me why?" Boris asked.

Ashur thought about it for a moment. If the Academy needed the water to cool the Vault, then why would they have shut off the water now?

"They took the Vault offline," Ashur said.

"Ten points for House Yonan!" Boris said. "A precaution, given recent events that have revealed particular security vulnerabilities."

"And opened up new ones they still don't know about," Namirha said.

"So you want me to get in through these pipes, make my way undetected to the Director's office, steal some of his DNA, and then make it back out without anyone noticing?" Ashur said.

Boris and Namirha looked at one another and grinned.

"I think he might be starting to get the hang of this," Boris said.

"And if I do all that," Ashur said, "How do I know you won't just shoot me once I give you what you want?"

"You don't," Boris said. Namirha reached across the center console and smacked him—harder than anything playful—across the back of his head. Boris yelped a little and then cowered away from him.

"Ours is a relationship built on trust, Ashur," Namirha said. "And like any new relationship, trust can be a precarious thing. I wish we had more time together to build that trust, but things are moving quickly now, so that isn't possible. But you've heard my vision, and why I believe so deeply in this mission. And I believe you could be a core part of what we do, moving forward. So the question for you is, do you want it? Can you achieve your potential here, with me, doing the work to bring down the Academy?"

Ashur closed his eyes for only a moment. He heard again the voice of his father, saying the same thing that had come to him as they sat in the abandoned lot earlier that night. He knew what he had to do, even if the idea of it went against everything he stood for and everything that felt right. It was the only way.

"Yes," Ashur said. "I want that."

"Good," Namirha said.

"And everybody knows," Boris said, "that Ashur Yonan never lies."

"I hope the same is true for you," Ashur said, as the car came to a stop on an abandoned stretch of highway, the strange feeling of his false words still rolling around his mouth like poison.

The sewers were dark and damp, Ashur's feet struggling to find purchase on the slick stones. He wondered how long it had been since another human had been down here. The little flashlight Namirha had given him illuminated only the stretch of the tunnel immediately in front of him. If he got lost down here, he imagined no one would ever find his body.

He pushed on through the dimness, the sound of water dripping all around him.

He tried to remember the last time he had lied about anything. It had been so long ago now. He had an almost physical revulsion when it came to falsehood, his body rejecting lies like they were some unfamiliar organ. It had not been natural to lie to Namirha and Boris, but it had not been difficult either. Was this the way it always began? Convincing yourself that a lie was necessary for the greater good, and then allowing that falseness to seep into your heart until it became a part of you?

Boris had said what everyone else knew: Ashur Yonan never lied. He hated to betray that part of himself. But there was more at stake than his reputation now, more than merely his righteous sense of self. He had found himself in a game where the stakes were incomparably high, with opponents who had been playing far longer than he had and rules that seemed to be shifting at all times. He still didn't know who to trust, or what to believe. But he knew this much: he had made a mistake when he helped Boris, and now it was his mess to fix.

He wished once more that Odishoo was there for him to talk to. His father had come to him in the car, filling him with a certainty that he could not explain. Maybe that was what faith really was: the belief in action when rational thought alone was insufficient. He knew who he had to go see once he made it back into the Academy, what he had to try to do. He just hoped he was right.

Ashur kept moving, keeping a hand skirting along on the slick walls of the tunnel as he went. Boris had said it would be about half a mile until he reached the subsurface of the Academy. It shouldn't take too long.

He felt the vibrations before he heard the sound. And then it came into his ears, a whooshing sound like something angry, coming from behind him. His shoes, already damp from the puddles that dotted the tunnel, began to splash now as he walked. He wondered briefly if it had begun to rain outside, the runoff from the storm drain where he had entered the tunnel filtering the water away from the surface.

And then he heard the roar. And he started to run.

He could not see the wall of water behind him when he looked briefly over his shoulder. He could only feel it in the rising moisture and the mounting pressure pushing against his back. There was no time to wonder what had gone wrong or whether Boris and Namirha had lured him into a trap. His mind was focused on the only thing that mattered: survival.

Ashur kept his knees high as the water level rose, pumping his arms and pushing himself forward even as he felt his pants become slick with water. Up ahead, the tunnel split off in two directions—Boris had said nothing about a fork. It was a hard thing, having your life reduced so unexpectedly to a coin flip. The water was almost up to his waist now, and the flashlight slipped from his grasp, plunging the tunnel into complete darkness.

Ashur pushed on to his right, wading through the water as the tunnel continued to fill. But then he saw it: a little rectangle of light in the distance, on the roof of the tunnel near the opposite wall. He couldn't tell if it was a drain or an exit or just a trick of his mind, desperate for survival. It didn't matter. He moved toward it, groping through the water now.

The water was nearly up to his neck, the whooshing sound becoming louder as the tunnel filled. He could see the little opening up above him, but there was no way to get to it—no ladder along the wall, no rungs on which to climb, the stone walls too slippery for him to gain purchase. He could feel himself being sucked backward as the flow of water continued on beneath him. It felt like he was in the ocean, a tremendous riptide keeping him away from the shore and pulling him further out.

It took all his strength to fight against the tide and keep himself close to the wall. The water continued to rise until there was just a narrow gap left along the roof of the tunnel; he could only breathe if he kept his head tilted to the side, taking small sips of air before he was plunged back under. He reached out his arm, groping for the little opening at the top of the tunnel. His fingertips found the slick edges, but then lost his hold, forcing him back down again.

He kicked hard against the water, pushing his way up one more time. Now both hands found the lip of the opening, and he held on for dear life as he punched the rusted grate covering the hole out of the way. With all his strength, he hoisted his body up through the raging water, legs pumping behind him and shoulders screaming as he went. The opening was narrow—too narrow for his body? It didn't matter. He contorted himself to be as small as he could be, pushing the bulk of his muscly body against the stone, ignoring the way the edges scraped and cut against him.

He was part of the way through now, his head nearly clear, when he felt his shoulders wedge firmly against the stones. He wriggled as hard as he could, but to no avail. Ashur was stuck, his head through the opening and the rest of his body still dangling, being pounded by the raging water and the hard stone sides of the tunnel. Whatever light he had seen had now been extinguished; he couldn't see a thing. He considered calling out for help but stopped himself before he could. He wasn't supposed to be there, and anyway, there didn't seem to be anyone around.

For a time—he couldn't tell how long, as things were oozing through his mind in a way that made the regular flow of time irrelevant—he struggled there, trying to free himself while also trying to make sure he didn't slip back into the water. He had used up so much strength that he wasn't sure how long he could keep fighting against the ravages of the watery tunnel. It seemed impossible that this would be how things ended for him, drowned like a rat in some sewage system, unmissed and unfound for who knows how long. He would do anything to keep that from happening.

Suddenly, a light switched on. He could now see the tile floor beneath him, and the row of stalls along the far wall. Then he saw a familiar pair of legs—shapely and elegant in tight spandex shorts, padding across the tile. He thought for a moment that he might be hallucinating. But he decided to try calling out anyway.

"Cassandra?" he yelled. The legs stopped moving for a moment, then doubled back. And then he saw her, wearing a sports bra, with her hair pulled back tight in a ponytail, a little dopp kit in her hand that she let fall to the ground as she quickly knelt beside him.

"Ashur!" she cried. "What are you—"

"Help!" he said, wriggling now. Cassandra dropped to her knees and grasped one of Ashur's hands. She smelled sweet, her face knotted tightly in concern. She began to pull as Ashur thrashed hard against the water. For a few moments, nothing. And then as Cassandra strained, his arm finally cleared the hole, followed by his shoulder. It was excruciating work. But slowly, Cassandra pulled and he pushed himself through, until all at once he was sprawled out on the tile, lying lightly atop her, his clothes soaked and bloody, and both of them just laughing in surprise and exhaustion.

Ashur shook the water out of his hair and looked down at Cassandra, sprawled and lovely on the floor beneath him. A part of him had hoped he would have a chance to see her again, before everything went down, but he hadn't figured out how without risking someone discovering him on campus. Her hair billowed against the tile floor and she smiled up at him, and he cupped her face in his hand and kissed her.

She seemed momentarily surprised, her eyes wide open, and then she let her lids fall closed and brought both hands up to the back of his head. Ashur ran his hand along the curve of her leg and then up her back, feeling the way she shivered lightly in delight as he touched her. After a few moments she pulled back, putting a hand against his chest.

"What are you *doing* here?" she asked, lightly scolding as though angry he hadn't sent word ahead of his arrival. "I thought I might never see you again."

"It's a long story," Ashur said.

"You're soaking wet," she said, pulling at the damp fabric of his shirt. "And cold."

Ashur peeled off his shirt, the muscles of his torso hard and glistening beneath. He liked the way Cassandra watched him, the hungry look in her eyes.

"I think we need to get you into the shower," she said. She stood, shook herself, and then helped Ashur to his feet.

They were in an old locker room somewhere on campus. It was still very early morning, everything quiet. The runoff from the water here had to feed back into the system for the Vault. He wondered what Cassandra was doing down here, since all the dorm rooms had their own shower. As though she could read his mind, she smiled as she led him to the shower stalls.

"I couldn't sleep," she said. "I was going to get a workout in."

"Sorry to interrupt," Ashur said with a small smile.

"Don't be," Cassandra said. She reached into a stall and turned the water on full blast, so that Ashur could feel the steam rising off the spray. How long had he spent thinking about this moment, when Cassandra and he could finally be together like this? How different this felt now, with everything so heightened and strange and the fate of the world seemingly at stake? But here she was, this beautiful woman who had saved him, smiling at him as she stepped out of her sneakers and into the shower. He watched the spandex shorts flip over the partition, and then her sports bra. He peeled off his jeans, grinned to himself, and then stepped under the spray to join her.

They snuck back up to her room afterward without anyone noticing. It was easier than Ashur thought it would be, the guards so worried about external threats that a couple of students getting up early for a workout and then wandering back to the dorms didn't arouse any suspicion. He lay on her bed in a towel, running a finger up and down her back, knowing that before too long he would have to leave her to do what he had come back to the Academy to do. But it felt so good to lie there with her, laughing about the strange turn the morning had taken.

"What would you have done if I hadn't gone to work out?" Cassandra asked.

Ashur shook his head. It was such an odd turn of luck—first the water being there when Boris had assured him it wouldn't, and then Cassandra happening by the exact spot on campus he needed to escape. It could feel sometimes like the world was random and indifferent, uncaring and cold. But on a morning like this, it was hard for him to believe that.

"My hero," he said. Cassandra smirked at him and punched him on the arm.

He had told her the broad outlines of his plan—the need to speak with the Director, and his plan to recover what Boris had stolen.

"I'm coming with you this time," Cassandra said. Ashur groaned.

"We've talked about this."

"Yes, we have. I let you go alone once, and look what happened. You came running right back to me."

"That's not really what happened."

"Looks that way to me."

Ashur rolled over so that he was looking Cassandra square in the eyes. She really was beautiful. But more than that, she was loyal, capable, and strong. It had taken both of them to break down Brodi's door and rescue her; he might still be bouncing around the water system beneath the Academy if it weren't for her. His instinct was always to go alone, knowing he was self-sufficient and the best man for the job. But this was bigger than just him now; he'd need all the help he could get.

"All right," he said.

Cassandra brightened with surprise and delight. "Yeah?"

"Let me talk to the Director. See how that goes. But I have a feeling I might need you."

Cassandra leaned forward on the bed and kissed him once more, and for the first time in many days, Ashur felt his heart fill with something other than dread determination.

The sun was barely rising as Ashur came into the administrative building and made his way to the Director's office. At this hour few of the offices were occupied. Security around campus was tighter than usual, but no one paid Ashur much attention. He had been an apprentice until the night before; he was wearing Academy clothing; few people even knew he had gone. Getting into the Academy had been difficult, but now that he was here, he could move about freely.

Cheryl was already at her desk, head down and tapping away on her Cube. Ashur froze when he saw her—how was he going to explain his presence here? He thought about retreating, trying to find some other way to see the Director. But before he could decide, Cheryl held up a finger for him to wait, then looked up from her Cube.

"He's waiting for you," she said.

Ashur frowned. "How did he…"

"I'm sure he'll explain it all to you. In you go now."

Ashur cleared his throat and marched through the oversized door that led into the office, feeling a slight change in the air as they closed behind him. The Director was pacing back and forth behind his desk.

"You found him," the Director said. "Boris."

"They found me," Ashur said.

"They?" the Director said.

"Boris and Namirha."

Ashur saw the Director take a sharp inhale through his nose, then gesture to the seat across the desk. Ashur sat down, keeping his eyes on the older man. There were dark circles under his eyes now; Ashur wondered if he'd slept.

"I wasn't sure if he'd reveal himself to you or stay hidden," the Director said. "They must believe themselves to be closer to their goals than I anticipated."

"How did you know I was here?"

"Namirha believes that we are arrogant to the point of thinking us stupid," the Director said. "It isn't the first time he's made the mistake of underestimating his opponent. And I do all I can to encourage that line of reasoning. But just because I don't act on information in the same way that he would doesn't mean I don't have it. Inaction is so foreign to Namirha that he mistakes it for ignorance."

Ashur nodded, taking in this information.

"He sent you here to collect my DNA?" the Director asked.

Ashur hesitated a moment. "Yes," he said finally.

"Is that what you came here to do?"

"I came here to speak with you," Ashur said. "I want to help. To clean up the mess I've made. But I need to know that I can trust you."

The Director nodded, and for a time the two men regarded one another across the table.

"Do you know who I am, Ashur?" the Director said.

Ashur thought about everything that had passed between them—their conversations about Odishoo, the older man's knowledge of Ashur's family, and the music that was playing the first time the two met. All that information had been simmering in his mind before it finally coalesced into the truth. Now all he needed to do was say it aloud.

"You're my grandfather. Sargon Yonan."

A small smile came over the Director's lips.

"Well done, Ashur."

Ashur felt a jolt of something electric go up his spine. There was so much he wanted to know. But there was something he needed to ask first.

"I want to trust you," he said. "But I need to know something first. Namirha told me the Academy had a hand in my father's death. Your son's death. I need to know the truth."

Sargon sighed. For the first time since he'd met the man, Ashur thought he looked old.

"Would your father still be alive if he'd had nothing to do with the Academy?" Sargon said. "I believe the answer is yes, unfortunately. It's why I tried so hard to keep you from this place, despite knowing how well you'd do here. The Academy has many enemies, Ashur. You've now met the most powerful of them. People who would do anything to hurt me, and this place, no matter how horrible. I did everything I could to protect him. And in the end, I failed. I consider your father's death one of the great failures of my life. And nothing I can say or do will bring him back."

Ashur frowned.

"If the Academy didn't kill him, then who did?"

"Ask yourself—who had the most to gain from Odishoo's death?"

"Do you mean…?"

"Yes. There is nothing Namirha would not do to hurt me. Odishoo's death was my great shame. But nothing would hurt me more than seeing my own grandson used to undermine the Academy. He intended it as his final triumph, the capper on his life's work."

"He lied to me!" Ashur yelled, feeling heat surge through his body as the rage spread.

"And you to him," Sargon said. "Or else you wouldn't be here now, talking to me like this. That must have been very difficult for you. From what I understand, Ashur, lying does not come easily to you."

"Why does he hate you so much? Why is he so intent on bringing down the Academy?"

Sargon sighed.

"Your father told you about Iran, yes? About the revolution, and everything that happened in those terrible years?"

Ashur nodded.

"Namirha and I served in SAVAK together. We were two of the five directors of the Shah's intelligence service, trained by the CIA. I recruited him. His mother was Russian. Stalin wiped out his entire family. He hated communism and everything it had done—and was willing to do whatever it took to keep Iran safe from the same fate that had befallen his mother's country. And when I say whatever it took, I mean it.

"Those accusations you've heard of SAVAK killings? Namirha was behind many of them. He had watched the rise of Khomeini and even offered to assassinate him personally. But the Shah refused. Because I advised against it."

"Why would you do that?" Ashur said.

"I felt at the time that it would be worse to kill Khomeini—and create a martyr. The Shah was worried about being perceived as a ruthless dictator, after the pressure from the United States and other countries on human rights. Khomeini was an older man; I didn't imagine he would last much longer on his own. I was wrong."

"If you could do it again, would you have supported Namirha?"

"Ashur, I wish I could tell you for certain how things would have changed. But life is not black and white—so much is shades of gray. I made the choice I made, and I've had to live with it ever since."

"So Namirha was angry with you for what happened in Iran," Ashur said. "What does that have to do with the Academy?"

"Namirha knew about my involvement with the Academy," Sargon said. "He sees it as the reason for my weakness—the role of the elites in not doing enough to protect Iran. He knew that I safeguarded the True List of all the Academy members, now and through time. These days I can't tell how much is his personal vengeance against me, and how much is his true belief that the Academy is evil. But whatever the reason, he wants the List and to see me—and the Academy—destroyed."

Ashur was quiet for a moment, taking in all of the new information. Something still didn't sit right with him.

"How could you leave?" he said finally.

Sargon furrowed his brow. "What do you mean?"

"You abandoned your family. My father and my mother. You abandoned me. I had never met you before I came to this place. And even then, you did everything you could to keep me away from here and hide your true identity. How could you?"

He hadn't meant to, but Ashur's voice had grown louder, until he was almost shouting. His words echoed in the Director's office, reverberating against the silent walls.

Sargon wiped a hand across his face. He seemed more tired than before.

"When it became clear to me that Iran would fall, I had two responsibilities," he said. "I needed to keep my family safe. And I needed to keep the List safe."

"So you chose the List over your family?!"

"No. I went in to hiding to protect my family. I believed at the time that the only way to keep them safe was for me to disappear—so that my enemies would think they had nothing to gain from harming Odishoo or anyone else related to me. You asked me if I regret my actions, Ashur, when it comes to Namirha. I don't know. The only true regret I have is that my absence seems only to have made things harder on you and your family. I did what I did because I thought it was for the best, but you're right. I abandoned you. And for that I am truly sorry.

And worse yet, nothing I say can change that. I can only ask for your forgiveness and, hopefully, your understanding."

At this, Ashur felt some of the anger that had coursed so powerfully through his body with the heat of a wildfire begin to ebb. He could see how much the tragic events had weighed on his grandfather, having to live all those years with the choices he'd made, having to watch their impact on those he loved. He might not agree with what Sargon had done, but Ashur could begin to understand why he had once thought it was right.

"I eventually made my way to Dallas," Sargon said with a small chuckle. "The last place I figured anyone would look for me. I established a new chapter of the Academy here. I grew it from a small provincial outpost into something truly great. And not a day went by when I didn't think of my family. And once you were born, that included you, Ashur. I only tried to make contact once—after Odishoo's death. Your mother made it clear, in no uncertain terms, that she wanted nothing to do with me. And I didn't blame her. I couldn't have trusted me, either, after everything that happened."

"I heard you that day," Ashur said, sifting back through those painful memories, "when you came to visit my mother."

"Don't blame Rose. She did what she thought was best for you. Your mother is a complicated woman who has lived a hard life. But she loves you."

Ashur thought about his mother, all their fights, all the anger through the years. Yet still, he believed that, at her core, some piece of her truly did love him, no matter how difficult it was for her to express it in those words.

"Once the Vault technology became advanced enough, I transferred the physical copy of the True List to a hologram. I believed it would be more secure that way. I used my own DNA as a key. I believe that was why Namirha killed your father: he believed his DNA might be close enough to create a replica. A foolish notion, but consistent with the beliefs of a zealot blind to logic and science."

"Which is why he needs your DNA."

"Precisely. Without it, the True List is beyond his grasp."

"But he still has access to everything else in the Vault," Ashur said. "All those avatars the Academy has already created. All that knowledge and power."

"Yes."

"So we have to stop him!"

The Director shook his head.

"Namirha is a master of deception. He is too nimble, too clever, for us to hope to track him down. There's a reason for his nickname, you know. It's what made him such an effective agent, and such a difficult enemy. I don't make the same mistake as he does—I never underestimate my opponent."

"What if I bring him what he wants?" Ashur said.

Sargon frowned. "What do you mean?"

"Your DNA. He believes I'm here to recover it. What if I bring him exactly what he wants?"

"Ashur, have you been listening? The True List is the most closely guarded secret in all of the Academy. Revealing that would cause pandemonium. We've run the simulations. If Namirha does what he's planning to do, the odds of World War Three are above ninety percent. Do you understand? Nuclear holocaust. Bioengineered pandemics. Cyber warfare that shuts down essential infrastructure. The end of civilization."

"What if there was a way to stop him?" Ashur said. "Destroy the technology before he has a chance to use it?"

"Namirha is a killer," Sargon said. "He will discard you the minute he no longer has any use for you."

"I can do this," Ashur said.

Sargon sighed. "I already lost your father, Ashur. I don't think I could live with myself if I lost you, too."

"You always talk about my potential," Ashur said. "You and everyone else. It's why this place exists. I know I'm young. I know how much I still have to learn. But this is our chance to keep the world safe. To keep the Academy safe. If we let it slip past, who knows what else Namirha might do? Who knows what we might regret if we don't act now?"

Sargon leaned back in his chair with his hands behind his head. He reached down for the Cube on his desk and keyed in a few instructions. Music began playing softly over the speakers. The familiar strains of a woman singing in Farsi. Sargon swayed lightly back and forth, his eyes closed.

"I always think better with this music," he said softly.

"Dad did, too," Ashur said.

"It would be dangerous, Ashur."

"I know."

"Are you afraid?"

Ashur thought about this. For so much of his life, he had been unafraid. He'd had nothing to lose—his family all but gone, no friends, no future or dreams to hold on to. Now there was so much to lose. True courage, he realized, doesn't come when you have nothing to lose. It comes from being willing to risk everything for the people you love and the things you believe in.

"Yes," he said. "But I'm ready."

Sargon opened his eyes.

"Then let's discuss the plan."

CHAPTER EIGHTEEN

The instructions from Namirha had been clear: make it out of the Academy with what he'd been asked to get and find someplace to lay low for a while. The Academy would be looking for him, no doubt, but Namirha would find him first.

This hotel room was nicer than the one he'd hidden out in last time; Cassandra was paying for it. Ashur paced across the rug while Cassandra looked out the window at downtown Dallas. In his pocket was a glass vial with a few strands of Sargon's silvery hair. He knew now what Namirha intended to use it for, and how dangerous it would be in his hands. Ashur was hoping that Namirha's desire would blind him to everything else. But it was still a massive risk.

"Are you hungry?" Cassandra asked.

Ashur shook his head, incredulous at the question. "How can you possibly think about food right now?"

As soon as he said this, his stomach gurgled, loud enough for Cassandra to hear it from across the room. She laughed as he tried to remember how long it had been since he'd eaten something.

"Come on," she said, standing up. "I'm taking you out."

"We can't just *go out*," Ashur said. "Not now."

"Why not?" Cassandra said. "If this Namirha is really as powerful as you say he is, I'm pretty sure he'll be able to find us if he needs to. And who knows how long he's going to make us wait around until he's ready to see us?"

Ashur started to say no again, but then he thought about it a little more. He liked the idea of sitting across a table from Cassandra, talking and laughing and feeling the way her foot brushed against his shin. Who knew what would happen after their meeting with Namirha? Even if they made it through, he had a feeling that everything would be different.

"All right," he said with a reluctant smile. "Where are you taking me?"

Fifteen minutes later they were in a cab, Cassandra looking beautiful in a tight skirt that showed off her legs, Ashur's broad shoulders perfectly contained within a blazer he'd "borrowed" from his closet at the Academy. He would miss the tailoring at the Academy—and all the ways they had made his life easy enough that he could focus only on learning. It was amazing now to think back on everything else that he'd been forced to focus on since his father's death: making sure the family had enough money, his never-ending arguments with Rose, assholes at school looking to pick fights, and the lingering question of what his future really held. His time at the Academy had felt like such a luxury; he wondered if he would ever get to feel like that again, or if life would go back to being the sort of struggle he'd known for years.

The cab driver had a neatly trimmed mustache and deep olive skin; the taxi permit posted on the dashboard said his name was Tanvir. He asked them where they wanted to go, and Cassandra grinned at Ashur.

"Take us to your favorite restaurant in town," Cassandra said. "The kind of place you'd bring family when they came to visit."

The driver's surprised eyes met Cassandra's in the rearview mirror, as though wondering if she really meant what she had said. She gave him a warm, winning smile in return. The man thought for a moment, then nodded and began to drive.

The little Pakistani restaurant didn't look like much from the outside. It was tucked into a strip mall, with a pet store on one side and a shuttered martial arts studio on the other. But as soon as they stepped inside, Ashur was greeted with the familiar scent of spices bloomed in oil. The restaurant was pleasantly bustling: families seated around large tables, groups of friends laughing over tea, efficient waitstaff bustling around with plates of food, stopping every once in a while to check in with a table or share in a small joke. Cassandra and Ashur sat at a small two-top, sipping tea while Ashur looked over the menu. It was different from the Persian food he had sometimes eaten with his parents at restaurants in California, but looking around at the other tables, he saw some similarities, too. The woman who came by their table gave him a knowing smile as he ordered.

"So, how often do you pull that trick with cab drivers?" Ashur asked as the first plate of food came out. Cassandra laughed and shook her head.

"That's what my dad used to do. Whenever we were traveling somewhere as a family. It drove my mom nuts, but we found some great places we never would have seen if we stuck to the resorts and guidebooks. My dad could be an elitist asshole, but he really felt comfortable with all kinds of people. I think that's what made him a good CEO."

"My dad would have loved it here, too," Ashur said, looking around the room. "I'm sure he'd tell me why Persian food was better, and about all the recipes the Pakistanis stole from Iran. But these were his favorite kind of places."

For a little time after that they were quiet, Ashur thinking once again of Odishoo and Cassandra of her father. He felt so comfortable talking to Cassandra, in a way he hadn't with anyone other than Kiki. There was romance there, of course, the sort of powerful erotic charge he'd felt from the first time he'd seen her. But now there was friendship, too; he hadn't been expecting that.

"What happens after all of this?" Cassandra said. "After tonight, after the Academy?"

Ashur shook his head. "I don't know. We go back to our lives, I guess."

"Just like that?"

Ashur reached under the table and put a hand on her knee. She looked down and then covered his hand with her own, holding on tightly. "I don't know what the future holds, Cassandra. For us, or for anyone else. If Namirha is as dangerous as the Director says, we might not even make it that far. But I'm not ready to say goodbye yet. And as long as we both feel that way, I think we can figure it out."

Cassandra nodded, and smiled, and clung even more tightly to his hand beneath the table.

The meal passed pleasurably. The food, as Ashur had suspected when they first walked in, was delicious—warming and homey, with a rich depth of flavor and familiar spices laced throughout the dishes. He and Cassandra chatted easily about everything, trading stories of their families, school memories, and the strangeness of suddenly finding themselves at the Academy. It was possible, for the space of a meal at least, to forget about everything else—and the weight of what they still had to do.

They were enjoying themselves so much that it took a moment for Ashur to realize that something was off when their waitress came by with the check at the end of the meal. She lingered at the table, check still in her hand, and when Ashur looked up at her, there was fear in her eyes. He frowned and scanned the restaurant—no one else seemed to have noticed anything. Then he looked down at the bill and saw what was written there.

> THERE ARE MEN WAITING
> FOR YOU IN THE BACK.

Ashur's eyes met Cassandra's.

"Ready?"

"Do we have a choice at this point?" she said with a small, brave smile.

He dropped a few bills on the check and thanked the waitress quietly. Then he and Cassandra stood and followed her back into the kitchen. Loud, jangly music filled the space, along with the friendly chaos of cooks at work and the heat of the ovens and burners. She led them down a hallway and then out the door to a back alley. Two men in black suits Ashur had never seen before were waiting there, in front of a dark sedan with its windows blacked out.

"It's all right," he said to the waitress, who took a last look at the men and then nodded before heading back inside. He heard the door lock behind her.

One of the men, without saying anything, opened the door to the sedan. Cassandra and Ashur piled in, the air conditioning prickling their skin as they sat back against the rich leather. The two men got into the front, and then one of them handed back a pair of black bandanas.

"Please," he said quietly, almost politely. Cassandra looked to Ashur to see what to do, and he nodded and tied the bandana tightly around his eyes. After a few moments, the car began to move. For a time Ashur tried to follow the turns, building in his mind a map of the car's path. But the driver seemed determined to throw him off, looping back and forth in a nonsense pattern around the city. He wondered if the Academy was following them or if Sargon had decided it would be too risky to tip off Namirha. By the time the car came to a stop, he had no idea where they were.

He heard the car door open, and then felt one of the men's hands pulling him out of the car and into a standing position. There was the sound of a metal door opening, and then everything beyond the blindfold was black and still. The air was cool in here, wherever he was, stagnant and dank. Then the blindfold was removed, and Ashur squinted to see anything in the darkness.

"I wasn't expecting you to bring a friend," came Namirha's voice from the darkness.

"She helped me," Ashur said, trying to determine the direction of the voice, "after Boris nearly got me killed with his plan to get me back into the Academy. I would have drowned without her."

"A regrettable miscalculation," Namirha said. "And one that he will be punished for, appropriately."

Ashur felt a shiver run up his spine. Namirha talked about Boris the way another man might talk about a troublesome dog, but with none of the affection for a pet.

"I knew how she felt about the Academy," Ashur said. "She had told me herself. The narrowness of their thinking. The insistence that theirs is the only right way to see the world. I needed her help to complete my mission."

"Is that true?" Namirha asked. Ashur heard Cassandra clear her throat next to him. None of this was a lie, exactly—Ashur had heard Cassandra say many similar things, at the times she bucked against the Academy's curriculum. He wondered, though, if Namirha would believe them.

"I wasn't sure, at first," Cassandra said. "But the more Ashur explained to me, the more I found to agree with. People deserve to know the truth. The world has lived in the Academy's shadow for too long."

Silence then for a few moments. Ashur stood still, trying hard to slow the beating of his heart, waiting for his eyes to adjust to the darkness of the space.

"What do we think?" Namirha said. And then, all of a sudden, the room was flooded with light.

Ashur held a hand up to his eyes against the unexpected brightness. He saw they were standing in the middle of a vast warehouse, the distant walls and ceiling shrouded in darkness. Namirha was seated at the middle of a long horseshoe of a table, Boris sitting on one side. The other chairs were filled with figures who looked eerily familiar to Ashur.

"She doesn't seem to be lying," said a man wearing traditional Chinese robes. "Though the truth can be a powerful weapon, when wielded for its own purposes."

"Do you trust her, Sun Tzu?" Namirha said.

The Chinese man let out a quick, barking laugh. "I don't trust anyone. But the question is, can you use her?"

"I'd use her, all right," said a large man in an olive-green uniform at the other end of the table. The assembled avatars chuckled nastily among themselves.

"Take that back!" Ashur said, nostrils flaring as he took a step toward the hologram. The large man grinned nastily at him.

"Please," Namirha said, holding up a hand. He snapped his fingers, and the large man blinked out of existence. The other avatars seemed unbothered by this and continued to murmur among themselves. Ashur wondered if they perceived themselves as alive while they were here, or understood on some deeper level what they were. He had seen what the holograms were capable of in a classroom setting—how quickly they could take in new information and use their wisdom and intellect to quickly cut to the heart of the matter. Chained together like this, how powerful they must be—a hyperintelligent tool to be applied to whatever end Namirha directed them.

"I apologize, Cassandra," Namirha said. "Some of my advisers need reminding, at times, of the proper mode of conduct. More suited to the battlefield than the boardroom, I'm afraid, but their perspectives are invaluable nevertheless."

"How do you know my name?" Cassandra asked.

Namirha chuckled. "This will all be much easier if you assume I know everything about you," he said.

Ashur felt his muscles stiffen, taut with anticipation. Did Namirha suspect what they were really doing there? Either because he didn't believe Ashur, or because his paranoia extended to everyone? The assembled holograms meant that the Vault component Boris had stolen must be somewhere close by. The question was how close...and whether Namirha would let them anywhere near it. Sargon had told him that was the key: getting as close as they could. It was the only way the plan could work.

Namirha turned to Ashur and fixed him with an intent gaze. "Do you have what I asked for?"

Ashur felt for the vial in his pocket. He took it out and held it up to the light. A smile spread across Namirha's lips.

"Once I give this to you," Ashur said, "what happens then?"

"I've assembled my council," Namirha said, sweeping a hand at the figures seated around the table. "We've drawn up our battle plans. And now, armed with the knowledge of all the Academy members, past and present, we'll be ready to put those plans into motion."

Battle plans? Ashur thought. He looked over at Boris, sitting several chairs down from Namirha. His former friend looked so different from how Ashur had seen him earlier—none of his sneering arrogance or superiority. If he didn't know better, Ashur would have said Boris looked terrified. There was something pleading in his eyes. Ashur cocked his head to the side, and Boris gave a quick shake of his head and then looked down at his hands on the table.

"I've waited years for this moment," Namirha said. "Long, difficult years in the shadows. Observing my enemy. Biding my time. There is a particular sweetness that comes from a victory so long delayed. From vengeance, after all this time."

His voice was still calm, but there was something different about Namirha now. Something ugly and dark that the man had managed to keep at bay until now, and either because he was too excited or else no longer cared how he was perceived, it had come to the fore. Ashur looked again around the table— nearly everyone assembled that he recognized had some military background. Famous generals and tacticians; rebel fighters and criminal masterminds; men, almost all of them, skilled in the art and science of violence. This wasn't the group that Ashur would have expected if the ultimate goal of Namirha's plan was simply to reveal the truth about the Academy. He had no doubt that the man was genuine in his desire to see the Academy crumble, but surely there was more to it than what the man was saying aloud.

"Assuming, that is, that what you've brought me is genuine."

Ashur stared at the man. He and Sargon had debated this exact point—why risk letting the Director's DNA fall into the hands of a man as powerful and dangerous as Namirha? But Ashur had been insistent. Namirha would know if he showed up with anything other than what he had promised him.

"Let me prove it to you," Ashur said, tilting the vial slightly so that it caught the light. Namirha nodded and stood from the table.

"Very well. Boris!"

Boris fiddled with something on his matte-black Cube, and the rest of the figures seated around the table blinked suddenly out of existence. The massive space seemed eerily empty without them. Boris led the three who remained toward a small door in the far wall, their footsteps echoing as they made their way.

The first thing Ashur noticed once they were through the door was the warmth. Compared with the cool of the warehouse, the cramped little corridor was sweltering. A low electrical hum issued from all around them, and the walls were encased in thick material. They continued walking, the humming sound growing louder as they made their way deeper into the labyrinth of Namirha's design.

"It's been thirty years since I last saw the List," Namirha said as they walked. "He had it with him in Tehran. A different, more primitive form then—an ancient method for storing data, though effective in its own way. He kept it from me, deliberately. Iran was about to fall. I think often about how different these years might have been if I had been able to convince him otherwise."

Sargon never would have betrayed the Academy, Ashur thought to himself. *And he knew enough not to trust you.*

They came at last to a door made of thick metal that looked impenetrable. Namirha placed his palm on a scanner by the side and then looked back over his shoulder.

"There's no stopping once we go through this door," he said. "Do you understand?"

Ashur and Cassandra looked at one another. Ashur felt the metal of his father's gun against the small of his back.

"Yes," he said. Namirha smiled.

"Before we begin, a gift," Namirha said. "Something promised to you long ago. I didn't want you to think we forgot, Ashur."

The door swung open. In contrast to the high-tech array he had expected, the room was instead small and homey, with a rug laid across the poured-concrete floor and a small living room suite. In the corner was an easy chair. A man was sitting in the chair, smoking a pipe, his eyes closed as he listened to music only he could hear. But Ashur could hear it, too, if he let himself remember.

"Dad?" he said.

Odishoo opened his eyes and gave Ashur a familiar smile as he rose from the chair.

"Hello, my son," he said. "I've missed you so much."

Ashur tried to tell himself that this was not really his father. That if he ran across the room and threw his arms around this man, they would pass harmlessly through his image. That the figure standing before him now was not even a ghost but a trick of the light, a simulation born of data and machine learning and little bits of genetic code that had once animated flesh and bone. But it was impossible. Here, after so many years, was his father, finally returned to him. And so Ashur went to him, standing as close as he could without physically touching the hologram.

"I've missed you too," he whispered, his father laughing as he wiped holographic tears from his eyes.

"Look how much you've grown," Odishoo said. "A proper man now, no doubt about it."

"I wish you could have been here earlier," Ashur said. "Everything has gotten so complicated."

Odishoo laughed and shook his head. "Life is full of complications. I'm sure you did whatever you thought was best."

Ashur turned back to look at Namirha. The man nodded.

"It was Boris's idea. The boy can be sentimental."

Boris was looking at the ground, shuffling back and forth. Ashur couldn't quite tell whether he was being manipulated or being given exactly what he wanted. Maybe both. He wished that he could ask them all to leave so he could stay in this place with his father, or this specter, or whatever it was. But, of course, that was impossible.

"Come with us, Odishoo," Namirha said, opening another door that led back to the warehouse, "and see your son achieve his potential. The way you always knew he could."

THE ACADEMY

Hearing Namirha address his father, Ashur felt something inside him growing hot with fury. Namirha had claimed it was the Academy that killed Odishoo. Sargon had told him that it was Namirha. But now Ashur felt in his bones the truth of things. If it weren't for Namirha and his vendetta against the Academy—against Sargon and anyone associated with him—then Odishoo would still be alive. Actually alive, somewhere on this planet, and not just a virtual recreation. Who knew how Ashur's life might have turned out? Maybe he would be graduating from high school now, getting ready to go to college, excited for the next chapter of life, Odishoo cheering him on as he crossed the auditorium stage in a ridiculous cap and gown. Maybe he never would have heard of the Academy and all its complications. He could sense all that Namirha had taken from him, and all he wanted still to take. It took every ounce of restraint within his body not to take the gun from where he kept it tucked into his waistband and end this all now. But he didn't know how much Namirha had already set into motion. And until he did, he had to stick to the plan.

They were in a large windowless room now, the space filled with an impressive array of machinery, humming and beeping in a discordant cacophony. Boris began to fiddle with one of the machines, looking back over his shoulder every once in a while. Ashur snuck a glance at Cassandra—she caught his eye and gave him a subtle nod. They were getting closer now to the beating heart of the beast. That was the only way this all would work.

"The sample, please," Namirha said. There was hunger in his eyes now, the look of a predator before it brings down its prey. Ashur took a deep breath and handed over the small vial with the strands of his grandfather's hair inside.

Namirha carried the vial with great care, as though there were a bomb inside and not a few silvery filaments. Odishoo was walking around the room, marveling at all the machinery—his father had always been a curious man, interested in how things worked. It made Ashur's heart heavy, knowing that once he did what he needed to do, he might never see his father—this version, or any other—again. He wondered if that was part of why Namirha had allowed Boris to build the avatar in the first place.

Boris uncapped the vial and removed the strands of hair with a small set of tweezers. For just a moment he held the sample aloft, and in that hesitation, Ashur thought he saw again something like fear in the young man. But then he sighed, put the hairs on a little petri dish, and fed it into the machine before him.

For a few nervy moments, the only sounds in the room came from the machines. Ashur tried to control his breathing. Sargon had told him that Namirha would keep the core piece of Vault technology shielded—offline, air-gapped, and impossible to reach. The man was smart, and paranoid, and knew that the Academy would be doing everything it could to stop him. Giving Namirha the sample was the only way to ensure that they had a chance. But there were no guarantees.

"How will you do it?" Ashur said. "Once you have the List."

Namirha smiled and for a few seconds said nothing. He seemed to be debating the merits of letting Ashur in on his plans. Then finally, unable to resist, he chuckled slightly and relented.

"The information will be broadcast in real time," Namirha said. "Anyone on the planet with access to any form of media will know about it. Governments will try to stop the spread, but they will fail. They will try to discredit the information as fake—the ploy of some foreign adversary. But the truth will be self-evident. People are smart. They know what's real. And they'll know the truth once they see it.

"The release of the True List will represent the greatest single event in the history of human civilization. Greater than the fall of Rome, or the Archduke Franz Ferdinand's assassination. A true reshuffling of the global order."

"Franz Ferdinand's killing led to the First World War," Ashur said. At this mention, Boris looked up meaningfully from his work. There it was again—something pleading in his eyes. The look of a boy who'd realized what a mistake he'd made. Namirha nodded.

"Yes. Destabilizing events are rarely peaceful. People become scared. They want to protect themselves. And they begin seeing threats all around them. And the only way to deal with those threats is to snuff them out before they have a chance to strike. I expect such a pattern to repeat itself again."

"You're talking about World War Three," Cassandra said, unable to contain herself.

"I'm speaking about chaos," Namirha said. "Necessary, vital chaos. I'll leave it to the history books to decide what to call it after the fact."

"There won't *be* any history books if there's a nuclear holocaust!" Cassandra said.

Namirha sighed and turned to Ashur.

"Your friend has no vision. She seems as brainwashed as any of the other Academy stooges. Tell me again, why would you bring her here?"

"Because she saved me," Ashur said. "And because she isn't afraid to say when something doesn't make sense to her."

"And you, Ashur Yonan?" Namirha said. "Is what I'm saying making sense to you?"

Ashur was silent for a few moments. Namirha sounded crazy to him. He had already lied once—why not again? But even the thought of the lies tasted terribly bitter in his mouth. He tried to find some way to say yes without really meaning it—some way to reassure Namirha as his suspicions mounted. But before he had a chance, a sound issued from the corner of the room where Boris was working.

"Oh my God," Boris said. "It's real."

Namirha took a moment to absorb the news, and then he began to laugh.

"I must admit, there were moments of doubt," he said, his body shaking with laughter. "When you brought the girl. Those strange looks between the two of you. I thought you might be foolish enough to try and deceive me. I underestimated you, Ashur Yonan. You've done well."

"Of course he has," Odishoo said now, coming over from the bit of machinery he was inspecting and smiling vacantly. "Ashur always does well. Isn't that right, son?"

Ashur felt his back stiffen. It hadn't been as obvious when he'd interacted with famous figures from the past—there was always something uncanny about meeting celebrities, no matter how long they'd been dead. But he *knew* Odishoo. Even after all these years, he was so attuned to the sound of his father's voice, the way he regarded him, and how he moved through space. This projection before him was a decent facsimile. But it was not his father. Odishoo was gone—and was never coming back. There would, maybe, be some peace that came with this realization, in time. But now it filled Ashur with white-hot anger.

He turned to Namirha.

"How is it you were able to make the hologram of my father?"

Namirha frowned. "What do you mean?"

"I never gave Boris his DNA," Ashur said. "Without that, it's impossible to create the avatar. So how did you do it?"

"You ask me this now?" Namirha said. "When we are on the precipice of such great things?"

"Answer me!" Ashur said, his voice filling the space all around them.

Namirha shook his head and clucked his tongue sadly. "We could have done great things together. I believe that. But you Yonans are all the same."

"*You killed him!*" Ashur shouted, trembling with rage now. "You tried to get the True List using his DNA. You made it look like an accident."

"A worthy experiment," Namirha said, a vicious smile on his face. "To see if his DNA would work. Sadly, it didn't. But I have no regrets."

"You took my father from me!"

"And yet you gave me exactly what I wanted," Namirha said. "You proud, brave, noble fool. Just like all the others. And now your value to me is what, exactly?"

The room became very tense—no one moving, the sound of the machines deafening. Ashur could see the bulge beneath Namirha's suit jacket where a gun was holstered. His father's pistol was still pressed against his back. Slowly, Cassandra began to inch over toward where Boris was standing by the machines. Proximity, Sargon had told him, was important. Getting as close as they could get was their only chance.

"Stop that," Namirha said, taking out the gun and aiming it at Cassandra. "No more movement from you."

"I'll shoot!" Ashur said, his own gun in his hand now and aimed at Namirha. The man seemed entirely unconcerned.

"No, you won't," Namirha said. "You'd kill me, fine. But I'd kill the girl. And you'd never be able to live with yourself."

The man looked over at Boris. "Take whatever it is she has on her. We're finished with these two."

But Boris just stood in the corner, looking around at everything that was happening. Ashur kept his gun trained on Namirha but allowed his eyes to briefly travel over to where his former friend stood. For just a moment, their gazes met.

"He's crazy, Ashur!" Boris finally said. "The Academy is just the beginning. He wants to take over the world! You have to stop him!"

Namirha sighed, shook his head, and in one quick motion turned and shot Boris.

"No!" Ashur yelled as Boris crumpled to the ground.

Ashur squeezed off two quick rounds, but Namirha was already moving, ducking and weaving his way around the machinery. Cassandra scrambled over to Boris, cradling the young man's head in her lap.

"What is all of this?" Odishoo cried from the corner, his hands in his hair. "What madness!"

Ashur forced himself to ignore the avatar of his father. He took cover behind a large server stack, his gun trained on the corner of the room where he had seen Namirha disappear.

"You're too late to stop me, Ashur!" Namirha shouted from somewhere. "You gave me what I need. I have it now. If you give up, I might let you live."

"You're a liar!" Ashur yelled back.

"You're getting smarter," Namirha said. "Too bad it's too late for all of that."

Slowly, as quietly as he could, Ashur made his way to where Cassandra held Boris on the floor. His former friend had been shot once in the shoulder and once in the chest. His shirt was slick with blood. There was a small smile on his face as he saw Ashur.

"Hey, Ash," he said.

"Boris," Ashur said.

"Sorry about all of this."

Ashur shook his head. "We're going to get you out of here."

"That's okay, man. I'm pretty tired."

Another shot echoed from across the room, and Ashur could feel the brute velocity of the bullet as it whizzed by overhead. He fired off another round and helped Cassandra drag Boris behind another bank of blinking machinery.

"Is it really too late to stop him?" Cassandra said. Tears were streaming down her cheeks.

Boris laughed a little, small droplets of blood now coming from his mouth. "Unless one of you geniuses thought to bring the world's biggest Blink with you," he said.

Ashur and Cassandra looked at one another. He thought back to their first day down in the Vault, Cicero explaining the emergency override to disable to holograms and the simulations. Everything had been so new and strange then. How quickly that had changed.

Boris seemed as though he understood, despite whatever fog was descending over him. He smiled slightly.

"You freakin' heroes. Go clean up my mess." He pointed an unsteady finger across the room, to where a pulsating green light was flashing. "Get as close to that thing as you can. And try not to die."

"We'll be back for you, Boris!" Cassandra said. Another shot echoed, and the machine next to them began to hiss. Smoke started to creep out in a long tendril.

"Yeah, yeah," Boris said. "Just go."

Ashur and Cassandra looked at one another.

"Stay low," Ashur said. "Run as fast as you can. On three, okay?"

She nodded. Ashur counted down.

"One. Two. THREE!"

They sprinted across the room, Ashur firing two shots in the vague direction of Namirha. He kept his body between Cassandra and the far wall. Bullets whizzed all around them now as the room filled with the cacophony of gunfire, smoke, and the acrid smell of burning electrical equipment. He tried to pretend he was back on the Traitorball court with Jahi, the two of them pushing their way into the paint for another easy score.

A sudden, sharp pain ripped through Ashur's shoulder. He let out a low grunt as his body spun around from the impact of the bullet. Cassandra cried out and stopped moving, but Ashur gritted his teeth.

"Keep going!" he yelled at her as shots continued to ring out.

Ashur lunged to the side to stay out of the path of the oncoming bullets. His right shoulder was in a bad way, so he grabbed the gun in his left hand and knelt for a bit of stability. He fired once more, wildly, and tried to remember how many shots he'd taken. Namirha would be keeping count, no question. Still some bullets left.

Cassandra kept moving, the shots ignoring Ashur now and focused entirely on her. She was alone, undefended, and the bullets were getting closer. Ashur cursed himself for going down when wounded, for not having any way to defend her. She yelled as a round exploded a bit of equipment in front of her, and ducked behind a stack for safety.

He saw it then, the ventilation shaft running along the top of the wall. It looked sturdy enough, but it was tethered to the ceiling by a little band of metal. Ashur squeezed off another round. It went wide. He tried again—closer, but still nothing. How many rounds did he have left?

"Give up, children," Namirha's voice came, eerily calm. "You will not leave here alive. Why not go peacefully, knowing you leave the world better in your wake?"

"You monster!" Cassandra yelled.

Namirha laughed. "You imbecile," he spat back.

Ashur gritted his teeth, steadied his aim, and fired again. The bullet hit the metal band, and for a moment the ventilation shaft merely groaned, the sound of metal shearing. Slowly at first, and then all at once, it collapsed. Ashur heard a scream from the other side of the room.

"Go!" he shouted.

Cassandra did not hesitate. She sprinted to the spot where Boris had aimed them, dropped to her knees, and skidded across the final yards of the floor. The Cube that Sargon had given them, the Blink pre-loaded, was already in her hands. As she slammed her fist down on it, there was a brief moment where Ashur thought something had gone wrong.

And then, in a single groaning instant, the world plunged into darkness.

CHAPTER NINETEEN

Ashur stayed low in the now pitch-black room, creeping toward where he'd seen Cassandra. The pain in his shoulder was kaleidoscopic now, searing and red-hot. He heard her whisper his name and went to her, his gun drawn, waiting for the muzzle flash of Namirha's gun that he was sure was coming.

They had done their job. The Vault technology that Boris had stolen from the Academy was destroyed—the Blink device had made sure of that. Ashur would do what he could to keep them alive, but if they didn't make it out, it still would have been worth it. Cassandra and he had known the risk when they went after Namirha. He stayed very still, listening for the sound of footsteps.

What came instead was a roar, distant at first but growing in intensity. The sound of something very large colliding with something very solid. Suddenly, the far wall of the warehouse exploded, light from outside streaming into the pitch-black space. An armored vehicle now occupied the large hole in the wall, and men in black tactical gear began to pour out of it, the flashlights on their automatic weapons sweeping over the surfaces of the room.

Voices were shouting now, the confusion and chaos of a dangerous scene before things solidify. Ashur could feel the warmth of Cassandra's body as she huddled against him. Someone was coming toward them now, moving swiftly among the flashing lights. Sargon dropped to a knee and held Ashur's head in his hands.

"You did it," he said. "You did it, Ashur."

The exit wound was clean—the bullet had passed through the meat of Ashur's shoulder without hitting anything critical. Outside the warehouse the medical workers tended to his wound, Cassandra on one side and Sargon on the other. Ashur watched as they took a stretcher from the rubble, a small body covered with a bloody sheet. He tried not to think of his father, all those years ago, being wheeled into the ER after the accident. He forced himself to watch until they loaded the stretcher into an ambulance and drove off.

"Boris died trying to help us," he said. "He saw finally what Namirha meant to do. I don't know what Namirha told him, how he tricked him. But I don't think we could have done any of this without him."

"It takes a real man to see the error of his ways and work to fix what he's done," Sargon said.

"How did you find us?" Cassandra asked. Sargon allowed himself a very small smile.

"That Blink of yours knocked out power to most of downtown Dallas," he said. "Once we identified the epicenter, we knew where you were. We were ready. And we were lucky to be so close."

"What about Namirha?" Ashur said, grimacing as the EMT pressed against his wound.

"There's a reason I gave him that name," Sargon said. "We're searching for him now. But I don't expect to find him."

"He still has your DNA," Ashur said. "The key he needs for the True List."

"But you destroyed the technology he needs to build the avatar," Sargon said. "His prized advisory council is destroyed. The danger is still real. It's only a matter of time before he tries again, now armed with more than he had before. But we've bought ourselves some time. For the moment, we're safe."

The three of them were quiet for a moment amidst the noise and the activity all around them. There were sirens and flashing lights as far as the eye could see, the rapid forces of the Academy replaced now by SWAT teams and emergency medical personnel. Ashur wondered how the news would report on the activity—a gas leak, or a meth lab gone wrong, or some other horrible, normal thing that people would tut about and then forget altogether. There was so much in the world that people did not understand, things that were kept hidden from them. Of all the things Namirha had said, this was what echoed still to Ashur. He wasn't sure he believed in keeping so much secret. But if the choice was between secrecy and a madman destroying the world, then he felt secure in the decision he had made.

"The Academy owes you both a great debt of gratitude," Sargon said finally. "I owe you even more, personally. I know it must be difficult to think about anything else, after what's happened today. But would you consider coming back to the Academy, to graduate with the other apprentices?"

Ashur looked over at Cassandra. She was still wearing the clothing from their date night, her skirt now a mess and her cheeks stained with mascara. She had been so brave, so good—he doubted he could have found a way to destroy the stolen

Vault technology without her. But it was clear that the events of the day were weighing on her.

She caught his eye and reached out to squeeze his good hand. There was so much comfort in the feeling of her skin against his, safety in the strength of her grasp. She nodded, and Ashur turned to Sargon.

"Okay. We'll come back."

On graduation night, Ashur came back from the gym to find a new tuxedo waiting in his room. Next to it was a pin emblazoned with a lion, a pair of wings outstretched behind it. It perfectly matched the tattoo on his forearm, and the one on his father's arm before him. In the weeks since everything that had happened with Namirha, Ashur had found himself returning over and over to the memory of his father's hologram. He knew that if that avatar had lifted up the sleeve of its shirt, he would have seen that same lion staring back at him. But he didn't find himself wishing for any more time with the simulation. It made him long for the real man who was gone—and cling more tightly to the memories of his real father that still remained.

On the top floor of the tallest building under the Academy's dome, a jazz band was playing softly. The views from the floor-to-ceiling windows extended far beyond the dome and out to the skyline of downtown Dallas. The room was tastefully decorated with banners of purple and silver, and the marble dance floor was crowded with elegantly dressed couples—men in tuxedoes, women in designer dresses and jewels.

As he made his way through the room, he caught sight of Cassandra. She looked beautiful in a deep blue dress with a long slit running up the side of her right leg. She saw him and smiled, beckoning him over. Beside her in a wheelchair sat Jahi, most of his body encased in a cast but a big smile on his face. He'd come out of his coma the week before; he had a long road in front of him, but no sign of brain damage.

"They let you out of the hospital!" Ashur said, coming forward and grasping his friend's outstretched hand. Jahi grinned and shook his head.

"The Director had to call in a special favor. Apparently some people really wanted me here."

He and Jahi had been speaking daily since he'd regained consciousness; Ashur had told him everything about Namirha and Boris and all that had happened since he'd been struck by the car while trying to save them. Ashur marveled once again at Jahi's faith—he had such a strong connection with God, and if anything, it had only intensified with the accident and all the physical struggles that came with it. That, Ashur thought, was true faith—still believing when things got hard after a lifetime of being on top.

The three of them talked animatedly as the rest of their classmates milled around them. Cicero came by, and the three of them shared in a spirited toast with their instructor.

"I will miss this cohort," Cicero said. "And all the trouble you gave me."

"I'm sure the next batch will be just as tough," Cassandra said. They all laughed—it was hard to imagine that, with the way everything had gone.

Brodi was in a rehab facility, getting the help she needed. She had written them all long, sarcastic letters, cracking jokes and making fun of them, but mostly expressing, in her own particular way, how grateful she was that they had saved her and gotten her on a different path. But it was impossible not to feel the absence of Boris. Ashur still had such conflicted feelings about his former friend. In many ways, Boris had been responsible for everything bad that had happened while Ashur was at the Academy. But the man had also seen the error of his ways before it was too late and sacrificed himself to stop Namirha from realizing his plan. Was he a hero, or a villain? Ashur had decided he was neither—just someone who had been confused, made some bad mistakes, and then tried to fix them. He was a person, no more, and no less.

More people were spilling out of the elevator now, older men and women dressed up in their best clothing. Each graduating apprentice had been allowed two invitations for that night's ceremony—they'd been asked to choose the people most important to them, who had helped get them to this point in their lives. Ashur had reached out to Kiki for the first time since coming to the Academy, filling her in on some of the details of his life without giving away too much. He hadn't been sure how she would respond—would she be grateful for his silence since California, that he was giving her space for her new life in college, or angry that he had cut off all communication? But in true Kiki fashion, she had known exactly what he needed to hear.

I always knew you'd make something great of yourself, she wrote back after telling him a little bit about her pre-freshman orientation program and all the courses she was excited to take once the semester started. *I was just waiting for you to realize it, too. Now it seems like you have. And I couldn't be happier for you* .

But as much as he had wanted to invite her, he found it hard to imagine Kiki and Cassandra in the same room together. What if they hated each other—or, worse, got along and traded stories and little jokes about him? He was glad Kiki was doing well, glad to have a friend he could reach out to when he needed someone from his past life. But tonight's event wouldn't have been the right place for her.

Ashur saw a look come across Cassandra's face—she was staring at something just over his shoulder. He turned around and saw a man in an expensive suit, hair neatly combed and a big smile on his face as he made his way across the room. He looked like a local politician, the sort of man who sponsored the Fourth of July parade and Little League teams.

"I can't believe he actually came," Cassandra said.

"Your dad?" Ashur asked. Cassandra nodded. "You, ah, want backup?"

Cassandra looked at him, smiled, and leaned forward to give him a quick kiss. "Maybe later? This one I think I need to do on my own."

Ashur nodded and squeezed Cassandra's hand before she went off, waving at her father. Ashur and Jahi exchanged a quick look before Jahi broke out in a laugh.

"I can't believe it took you two this long," Jahi said. "I thought it'd be, like, a thing from the first class."

"We were at each other's throats," Ashur said.

"Have you never watched a rom-com? That's how these things work, man!"

Someone was calling out his name now, and Jahi smiled and waved at a handsome Black couple standing by the sushi station. Ashur had been introduced to Jahi's parents earlier, at the hospital, and had told them how brave their son had been, and how grateful he was to them for raising such a wonderful person.

THE ACADEMY

"You want to come hang? Plenty of sushi still left from the looks of it," Jahi said. Ashur shook his head and touched Jahi lightly on the back.

"Thanks, but go ahead. I'll catch up with you guys later."

Jahi wheeled himself over to his parents, leaving Ashur alone in the cavernous room, surrounded by people. He closed his eyes and thought again about Odishoo. How would his father feel, seeing him graduate from the Academy? Would he be proud of him, for achieving what he had not? Scared for what the future might hold? Or would he simply want his son to be happy, whatever form that ended up taking?

"Ashur?"

He opened his eyes and turned around. Rose was dressed in a beaded black gown, her hair done up, her makeup perfect. Ashur tried to remember if he had ever seen his mother so nicely put together. Looking at her, Ashur felt for the first time like he was catching a glimpse of the beautiful young woman his father had fallen in love with, all those years ago in Iran.

He hadn't invited her. Hadn't known quite how to ask, or where things stood between them. It had gotten so ugly at the end, and he didn't want her showing up only to ruin everything. But seeing her here in front of him now, he was glad that she had come.

"Hi, Mom," he said.

She gave a small, trembling smile that lasted only a moment before her lips returned to a flat line. But it had been there, however briefly. It had been a long time since Ashur had seen her smile.

"You've done well for yourself, I see."

No thanks to you, was the bitter thought that came immediately to Ashur. But he choked back those words. He could

369

feel so many things now, standing before her: anger and guilt, love and sorrow, everything in conflict. He wanted to demand answers for why she'd treated him so poorly, why she'd driven his father away, why she'd been such a terrible mother.

It's time to let those things go, Ashur, said a voice in his head. It was his father's voice—his *real* father's voice, not some uncanny holographic simulation designed to manipulate him. The same voice he had turned to for guidance so many times. *You're not a child anymore. You're a man now. Be the man I know you are.*

With his good arm, Ashur reached out and hugged his mother. Surprise flashed across her face.

"Ashur…" she began.

"It's okay, Mom," he said. "It's all okay. I forgive you, for all of it."

As he pulled back from Rose, he heard his father's voice in his head once again. *There's more to say…*came the voice, and he could almost see his father's smile.

"And…" Ashur said. He looked down, feeling all the resentment he'd built up toward his mother, all his memories of their difficult life together. He took a deep breath. "And I'm sorry for what I put you through. It couldn't have been easy, raising me on your own. I know it wasn't. I'm sorry for a lot of things."

Ashur could feel something hard within him begin to crumble, and then a lightness, as though a weight he didn't know was there had been lifted.

Tears were running freely down his mother's cheeks now, but she didn't break into sobs. She lifted her hand to touch Ashur's face. He noticed she wasn't wearing any rings on her fingers.

THE ACADEMY

"Your father would be so proud of you," she said. "Doing something good with your life. Making something of yourself. You look just like him tonight, you know."

Ashur's heart squeezed in his chest.

"I love you, Mom," he said.

This time when she smiled, it held.

"I love you, too."

They hugged again, and then a voice came over the loud-speakers, asking people to take their seats. Ashur led his mother over to one of the chairs assembled before a stage, and they sat next to one another, his mother's eyes still damp but a big smile across her face.

Ashur watched as Sargon made his way to the speaker's podium. He searched his mother for any shock of recognition, but she seemed stoic as she watched the man before her.

She knew all along, Ashur thought to himself. He wondered if she had ever thought that he would end up here, at the Academy. If she had worried about it. If she had fought to keep him from it. But maybe it was better this way—now that she could see the good it had done him after it seemed like nothing else was working.

Sargon stood before the apprentices and their families, looking out onto the crowd. Mixed in among the graduates were several Academy alumni that Ashur recognized—politicians, business leaders, famous entertainers, and several men and women whose work Ashur could only guess at. Now he was going to join their ranks.

"We are all put here on Earth as an audition," Sargon said at last. "To see whether we have what it takes to make an impact on the world. If you have the desire, and the drive, to make a difference, combined with the knowledge of your true purpose, there is no limit to what you can achieve. I believe that all of you apprentices assembled here today have that kind of potential, to be a force for good in the world.

"By being here, you have placed yourself among the best and brightest of your peers. You should be proud. But know that your path to success does not end here. We are endowing you with great responsibility, a responsibility that will only grow as you go out into the world and continue to learn about who you are and what you stand for. There is much hard work ahead of you yet, but I believe you all have greatness in you.

"I want to take a moment today to talk with you all about power. The more success you achieve, the more powerful you will become. Power is crucial to becoming a truly influential leader—it's what allows you to have impact. But it can work against you, too. Especially if you crave it for its own sake and acquire too much too quickly. So I want to leave you with a few words of advice—some of which you may have heard already from your brilliant cadre of instructors, and some of which might be new for you to consider.

"Gather a team around you who is not afraid to tell you the truth. Find friends and mentors who believe in your goals and will help you achieve them." A pained look crossed his face. "And remember, no matter how good you are at reading people, at some point in your life, you will be betrayed by someone you trust. Learn from that experience, as I have; be a wary judge of character. But do not let yourself be consumed by paranoia. Believe that people are capable of goodness, as I know all of you here today are.

"A few more thoughts before I let you return to the cel- ebration. Keep in mind that sometimes the most powerful person isn't the face you see everywhere; sometimes it's the voice behind the face, the one you don't see at first. Embrace your uniqueness, the things that make you *you*. But manage your reputation carefully, so that it becomes an asset, not a liability. Cultivate a sense of humor. And above all, respect—but do not fear—death.

"Pace yourself. Let yourself be mentored. Make sound choices. And respect the power that I suspect all of you will someday wield. If you do these things, you will make yourself, your family, your country, and this Academy incredibly proud. You will make me proud. I am so excited for what life holds for each of you and promise to be here—along with the full resources of the Academy—to help you in any way we can."

Sargon turned and looked right at Ashur.

"You are our future. And the future of our world. Now, go celebrate all you have already achieved!"

Applause erupted. The whole room rose to their feet as one. For just a moment, Ashur and Sargon looked at each other, the older man smiling down warmly at his grandson. And then he was the Director again, ready to smile and shake hands with the scores of parents and important guests that had come to hear how special and important their children were.

Ashur turned to his mother, found Rose's hand, and gave it a little squeeze.

"Come on," he said. "Let's go find something to eat."

Later in the night, Ashur was sitting at a table with Jahi and Cassandra, their families gathered around, all talking pleasantly among one another. It all felt so *normal*, Ashur thought, like a

PATRICK BET-DAVID

real graduation ceremony. It was hard to picture himself back in
California, back at Bob's Big Boy, trying to figure out where life
was going to take him next.

The Director came by the table, offering a round of hand-
shakes as he introduced himself to the parents. When he came
to Rose, he paused slightly, before she came onto her feet and
gave him a quick peck on each cheek.

"Director," she whispered before sitting back down. There
was a coolness there—and probably always would be, Ashur
thought. But he was grateful to his mother for making an effort,
for his sake. She hadn't had a drink all night, despite the generous open bar. Maybe things really were changing for Rose.

"May I borrow Ashur for a minute?" Sargon said. The rest
of the table nodded, and Sargon and Ashur wandered off to an
empty corner of the elaborate ballroom.

When they were out of sight of the crowd, Sargon placed a
hand on Ashur's shoulder and smiled.

"I can't be accused of playing favorites," he said. "Even if no
one else is my grandson."

Ashur laughed. "I understand."

"I just want you to know how proud of you I am. And how
grateful that I have a chance to know you. I made a mistake
when I cut myself out of your life. I thought I was protecting
you. But now it seems as though I needed your protection."

The two men embraced one another, and Ashur wished
again that his father could be there. Who knows how things
would have been between Odishoo and Sargon after all this
time? But if Rose could forgive him, then why not believe the
same could be true for his father?

A man in a dark suit walked swiftly up to the Director.
Ashur stepped back.

"What is it?" the Director said.

"Just got word from the CIA regional office in MENA," the man said. "There's been a break-in in Egypt."

"Cairo?" the Director said. The man shook his head.

"Alexandria."

"Damn," the Director said. "I thought we'd have more time."

"What is it?" Ashur asked.

The Director turned to him. "Cleopatra. She's there. Well, her *remains* are there. As are the clay tablets that she took from the Royal Library of King Ashurbanipal. You understand?"

Ashur thought for a moment, then it finally dawned on him. "I don't suppose those tablets reveal anything about how my Cube manipulates gravity and quantum energy?"

"Indeed, they do," the Director said. Namirha was back. He had the Director's DNA. Now he needed a Vault and Cube of his own. And he would stop at nothing to get them.

"This is my calling," Ashur said. The Director and the new-comer both looked at him, a bit perplexed. Ashur continued. "This is my purpose: protecting the world from people like Namirha. I'm going to be the man my father hoped I would be. I'm going to bring his killer to justice. And then I'm going to work to make sure the world is safe. That's how I'll make my mark on history."

A wide smile spread across Sargon's face.

"Spoken like a true Assyrian warrior," he said. "Come on. We have work to do."

ACKNOWLEDGMENTS

This is a love letter to all the individuals who inspired me to write this book—both those I mention here by name and countless others. This book wouldn't have happened if it wasn't for the many chaotic times in my life where I learned about war, pain, betrayal, love, compassion, positive paranoia, and how to study body language, and strengthened the gift of intuition to determine whether someone had good intentions or not.

There are at least fifty characters in the book that have come and gone in different phases of my life. This wasn't an easy book for me to write. I'm grateful for the many mentors who have long passed away that left behind their minds to study.

When I was younger, I was gullible enough to think that everyone had good intentions. Later I flipped to the complete opposite side, not trusting anyone. Now, the goal is to aspire to be a complete leader, where I can have a healthy balance of both trust and paranoia, able to decipher each unique situation I am put into.

I've waited years to publish this book. Many close friends and family members have read the book over the years; a few asked me why I would publish this book, due to some of the content and stories in it. Close loved ones wondered if it was a good idea for a business man to take years to write a fiction book. Consultants even told me that it could potentially hurt the reputation of my brand—which, quite frankly, has never been a reason I've used to decide whether or not to pursue a project.

There's a big difference between writing a business book versus a fiction book. In a business book, you simply share strategies of what's worked for you, as well what mistakes you've made, to save the reader both time and money. Writing a fiction book like *The Academy* is extremely sensitive—many of the events in the book have actually happened in my personal life.

I first started working on this book back in 2010. That's when the idea for this book was conceived. I was in the most chaotic phase of my adult life: I was building a startup, traveling nearly six months out of the year, while at the same time building a family. Things were moving very fast. I worked on this book either during late nights when the family was asleep or while on the road. Eventually I had to get away for a few days at a time at different properties like Palm Desert and other locations just to have a clear mind to write this book.

I started sharing the idea with a handful of people close to me and everyone kept asking: How do you plan on writing this while building a business? Each time I would try to push myself to not think about this book, it kept drawing me back in. I had so many moments where I would meet random strangers and, by the time I was done speaking to them, it was as if someone sent them to nudge me back to working on the book.

A day after I finally decided the name of the main character was going to be Ashur, I met a family who named their son Ashur, with the same exact spelling—yet they weren't Assyrian. On the same day, I met another man named Ashur who also wasn't Assyrian. The person who helped most with this book,

Mario Aguilar, was present at both of those moments. We both looked at each other stunned about the timing of this.

This was a constant battle, with me trying to get the idea of *The Academy* out of my head, to not have to pursue this project. Who in their right mind with zero qualifications to write a fiction book would be inspired to write it?

But no matter how much I fought it, Ashur kept resurfacing. Eventually I was convinced the world was filled with many Ashurs who needed to read this book. I'm convinced the future of the world is in the hands of existing leaders who will be inspired to do what's right. To avoid the temptation of doing evil. To aspire to be noble, even though at times being noble could cost you opportunities. This isn't easy to do, but it's a must for a few in order for the next generation to have hope that "good" exists; that being noble is an attractive trait that we all need more examples of. At the same time, it's important to be reminded that none of us walk on water and we need redemption and grace at certain seasons of our lives.

This book is a byproduct of someone who lived in war-torn Iran, and watched a once beautiful country, where the wealthy of the world would travel for vacation, turn into a place that has caused a ton of chaos in the world. I feel an immense privilege to live in a country where I have the freedom to express these ideas through a book like this one. Years ago, during a TV interview, someone mentioned to me that while I may have been born in Iran, I was in many ways made in America—I still believe that to be true, and am thankful for it.

I feel like I have to acknowledge not only those who helped with this book but also those who were with me in different seasons of my life.

Let me first start off by thanking God for introducing my father, Gabreal Bet-David, and my mother, Diana Boghosian, to each other, because without them, this story would never be told.

My wife, Jennifer Bet-David, who never questioned my internal fight of writing this book and encouraged me to do what was on my heart.

Another big reason for writing this is to be able to give a different perspective to my four children—Patrick Jr., Dylan, Senna, and Brooklynn—so they're ready for the real world. My oldest son, Patrick Gabreal Bet-David Jr., played a very big role in the final stages of the book. He read the book and gave great feedback and was involved in us choosing the cover of the book.

I'd like to acknowledge Mario Aguilar, who has always been there to help with this book. He was encouraging and curious to the point where he himself as a Guatemalan born in America became very interested in the history of Iran and the Assyrian community. So interested that he even got a tattoo that pays homage to this book. Mario, this book wouldn't have happened without you.

I'd like to thank Tom Ellsworth, who introduced me to James Scott Bell to help with the structure of writing a fiction book, as well as Joel Gottler, who encouraged me to be very hard on the purpose of the book to be engaging for the reader.

There were many people at the beginning stages who contributed a ton, such as Chris Perez, Annie Freshwater, Eric Caballero, and Lexi Wiley. Chris Perez introduced me to Dr. James Coyle from Chapman University, the director of global education, who read the book and gave very good feedback on the history side of the book.

A big part of history revolves around the late Shah of Iran, Mohammed Reza Pahlavi. I have researched him many times over the years, but after years of talks and meeting with his son, Crown Prince Reza Pahlavi agreed to do a three-hour podcast to discuss the history of Iran, then as well as now. It was a very big part of finalizing certain stories in the book.

One of the main characters of the book—the former director of Savak—was key to making this book complete. Something very strange happened in the final year before publishing this book. I felt I needed to have a former Savak member read this book to feel confident about publishing it. One day I get a random call from someone who is involved in Iranian politics (and has asked me not to mention his name), who told me that the former Deputy Director of Savak would like to meet with me. This led to multiple Zooms where we spoke about the history of Savak, after which he graciously agreed to read the book. After a few days, I got word that he wanted to have a follow-up meeting with me sooner than later. When we spoke, he asked me if the character Dobiel was about him and how did I get access to certain information about the history of Savak. This led to him traveling to me, where we had a full day of meetings on the history of Savak and Iran. This book wouldn't be the same without that final meeting with him, Mr. Parviz Sabeti. I asked him if he was comfortable with me acknowledging him in the book and he gave me permission to disclose his name. I'm thankful for this meeting.

When I finally made a decision that I was going to go through with this book, my agents Jan Miller and Austin Miller introduced me to Spencer Gaffney, who was the perfect guy to help bring this book home. It wouldn't have happened without him.

And of course, we have to thank Anthony Ziccardi, our publisher, who took the risk on publishing this book. It's important for the publisher to support the message that's in this book, and I'm thankful for his and his team's support.

ABOUT THE AUTHOR

Patrick Bet-David is a serial entrepreneur and #1 *Wall Street Journal* bestseller of *Your Next Five Moves*. He is the founder of Valuetainment network and the host of *The PBD Podcast*, which collectively garners more than three billion views worldwide across all platforms. He fled war-torn Iran with his family at the age of ten and moved to California after two years at a refugee camp in Germany. With few options after barely graduating high school, Bet-David served in the US Army's 101st Airborne. Bet-David's unique life experience was the inspiration for *The Academy*. Bet-David lives in South Florida with his wife, four children, and two Shih Tzus.